STARLIGHT

A silver-screen romance in wartime Edinburgh

Though content in her job, Jess dreams of a more exciting life. So when she is hired to work in the box office at the Princes Street cinema, she is thrilled. Jess is star-struck, not just by the silver screen, but also by handsome projectionist, Ben Daniel. But it is Ben's assistant, Rusty MacVail, whom she marries. As the Second World War looms, her beloved cinema is threatened, Ben comes back into her life, and Jess will need all her courage to face what lies ahead.

A Selection of Recent Titles by Anne Douglas

The Girl From Wish Lane
A Song in the Air
The Kilt Maker

STARLIGHT

Anne Douglas

Severn House Large Print
London & New York

This first large print edition published 2011
in Great Britain and the USA by
SEVERN HOUSE PUBLISHERS LTD of
9-15 High Street, Sutton, Surrey, SM1 1DF.
First world regular print edition published 2010 by
Severn House Publishers Ltd., London and New York.

British Library Cataloguing in Publication Data

Douglas, Anne, 1930-
  Starlight.
  1. Motion picture theatres--Employees--Scotland--
  Edinburgh--Fiction. 2. World War, 1939-1945--Social
  aspects--Fiction. 3. Edinburgh (Scotland)--Social
  conditions--20th century--Fiction. 4. Love stories.
  5. Large type books.
  I. Title
  823.9'14-dc22

ISBN-13: 978-0-7278-7992-9

Severn House Publishers support The Forest Stewardship Council
[FSC], the leading international forest certification organisation. All
our titles that are printed on Greenpeace-approved FSC-certified paper
carry the FSC logo.

MIX
Paper from
responsible sources
FSC
www.fsc.org   FSC® C018575

Printed and bound in Great Britain by the
MPG Books Group, Bodmin, Cornwall.

Part One

One

The evening before the interview, rain began to fall. Only summer rain, of course, for this was August. But miserable, all the same.

Jessica Raeburn, looking down at Leith's Great Junction Street from the window of the flat that was her home, felt her spirits fall, along with the drops sliding down the pane. Supposing it was like this tomorrow? She'd have to go to the Princes Street Picture House wearing a mackintosh over Marguerite's two-piece. So much for cutting a dash when she arrived!

'Think it'll fair up?' she asked, turning to face her mother and sister, who were playing two-handed whist at the scrubbed wooden table in the flat's living room. Beautiful women, both, they kept their blue eyes fixed on their cards, while to Jess, they looked as they usually did, like those classical figures you saw in the museums and such in Edinburgh. See their elegant noses and fine brows, their mouths like perfect bows!

'Who can say?' Marguerite asked absently, her mind on her next trick. Her fair hair was newly brushed, her face lightly powdered, and she was wearing a crisp blue cotton dress into which she'd changed after coming home from the

7

teashop where she worked. Even if only playing cards with her mother, she was always very particular about her appearance.

What young man had she put off that evening? Jess was wondering, knowing that there were always admirers hanging about after Marguerite, very few ever getting very far. Too choosy, folk said, yet she wasn't getting any younger. Twenty-nine that year! Imagine! But studying her sister's beauty, Jess ran a finger along her own turned-up nose and sighed.

Of course, she knew she was attractive in her own way. Like her long dead father, and he'd been a good-looking man, her mother always said – before the enemy gas of the Great War killed him off three years after the Armistice. How nice it would have been, Jess sometimes thought, if he'd lived. Then there'd have been four in the family, instead of three.

Soft dark hair and gold-flecked green eyes, tall, slim and straight – yes, at twenty-three, she was attractive, as plenty of young men had told her, for she had her admirers, too, even if at present there was no one special. Just as well, as all she wanted to think about, on that wet summer evening in 1938, was her interview at the picture house tomorrow morning. If only it could be fine, so that she needn't wear her old blue mackintosh over Marguerite's smart grey two-piece!

Better not ask to borrow her sister's good raincoat as well, though; it had been difficult enough to get her to lend her two-piece in the first place. Should really have saved up for something smart herself, Jess reflected, especially as she might have got it cost price at Dobson's. Too late now. Unless, of course, she didn't get the job at the Princes Street Picture House – but she wasn't going to think of that.

Suddenly, the game was over. Marguerite threw up her hands and gave her mother an exasperated smile.

'That's it, then – thirteen tricks each. Nobody's won.'

'I can keep all my matches?' Addie Raeburn asked, closing the lid on the box of spent matches, which were all she and her girls ever played for. 'Och, I really thought I was going to go down.'

Though in her late forties, Addie could have been ten years younger, which always surprised Jess, who knew how much sorrow her mother had seen, and how hard she'd had to work. Before the war, Frank Raeburn had been an insurance agent and hadn't done too badly, but after his death, there'd only been a widow's pension of ten shillings a week. Addie'd had to take a job cooking in a restaurant and move from their Edinburgh flat to a smaller place in Leith where rents were cheaper.

This very flat they were in now, which was over a greengrocer's; the only place Jess really knew, as she'd been only seven when they'd moved. But her mother had progressed since those early days, and now cooked luncheons for a ladies' club in Edinburgh.

Very well, too, for that first restaurant's chef had taught her to make excellent soups and

9

sauces, casseroles and delicious things in pastry, little cakes and meringues and all sorts of good things. Her daughters knew, for she often brought leftovers home in a basket, always saying they should make the most of them for she couldn't afford such cooking on her own budget. True, money was tight, but they considered themselves pretty lucky, eh? Compared with most in Leith.

Leaving Marguerite to gather up the cards, Addie now rose and said she'd make a cup of tea. As she moved into the tiny scullery where there was a gas cooker to boil the kettle, she said over her shoulder, 'Shame about this rain, eh? We might all have gone for a nice walk to the Links.'

'No' me!' Jess cried. 'I'd to wash my hair and get my things together.'

'All this fuss for that interview at the Princes,' Marguerite said scornfully. 'It's only for a job in the box office, after all!'

'I want it,' Jess said firmly.

'But you've got a good job in the cash desk at Dobson's,' her mother called from the scullery.

'I want this one, I'm really keen.' Jess shook her head, wondering how to make her interest plain. 'It's no' just because I like going to the pictures...'

'Though you do,' put in Marguerite.

'Yes, but it's the Princes I like, too. It's my favourite cinema, always has been. I think it's beautiful and it's where I want to work.'

'Even if they're paying five shillings a week

10

less than Dobson's? I think you're crazy.' Marguerite was taking cups down from the dresser. 'But you suit yourself what you do. All I want to say is, that if you spill anything on my best suit...'

'I know, I know!' Jess laughed. 'I needn't come home, eh? I'd better run away to sea – which will be handy, seeing it's just up the road!'

Two

It was true enough that the sea was just up the road, though Marguerite and her mother always declared that it could hardly be seen for all the ships and sailing craft, docks, buoys, piers and various constructions that made up the Port of Leith. There was the Shore, yes, but that was just the harbour, and as Addie said, 'hardly a beach, eh? Hardly golden sands, like at Portobello?'

Jess, however, didn't care about golden sands. From being a small girl, she'd been thrilled by the activity and bustle of the new place where they'd come to live, and couldn't understand why her folks didn't feel the same. As for not seeing the sea, why there it was! Beyond all the ships and vessels and constructions of the port, miles and miles of exciting water that could make you think of all the places you might go and the people you might meet. Like the cinema,

11

really.

Which was why Jess had set her heart on moving to the Princes Street Picture House. All right, she had a good job with Dobson's Department Store on the North Bridge in Edinburgh, got on with everyone, did her work well. But instinctively she felt there was nothing there to excite her, to stimulate her, to make her feel there was a world beyond her own. The box office job might be no better than Marguerite had said, but it might bring her nearer, mightn't it, to something different? Because the Princes itself was so different, and any job there would have to be different, anyway, from working on the cash desk at Dobson's. She was right, Jess was certain, to try for it. Of course, she might not get it. She still wasn't allowing herself to think of that.

In spite of all that was on her mind for tomorrow, she was able to relax a little when she sat with her mother and Marguerite, having a cup of tea and a spice biscuit. The atmosphere of the living room – in fact, of the whole flat – was always pleasant, partly because Addie had the touch of a homemaker and even on her limited means had made it comfortable and even stylish, and partly because there were none of the pressures of tenement life.

They might not have the spacious rooms of some of the Old Town houses, but on the other hand, had nobody shouting down the stair, or drunks coming in late, kicking doors as they went by, or arguments over whose turn it was to hang washing on the green. Here, in the evenings, there was no one at all to bother them, and if during the day there was all the bustle of a busy greengrocer's below, that didn't matter, the Raeburns being out all day.

Besides, they got on well with Derry Beattie, who had taken over the shop from his elderly father. John Beattie had been their landlord when they'd first moved in, after he and his family had moved out to a nice solid house near the Links, Leith's fine and historic open space of park and sports field. In those days, the flat had been very basic, with just a living room and two tiny bedrooms, one for Addie, one for the girls, but over the years there'd been improvements. A little bathroom. A scullery with a gas cooker. A separate entrance and stair.

All Derry's idea, and sometimes Jess couldn't help thinking guiltily it was because he was attracted to her mother. Shouldn't think that, of course, for Derry had a wife, Moyra, who was a sweet character, and it might not even be true. It was just that whenever Addie went down to buy a few apples or a cabbage and Jess was with her, she'd see Derry hurrying to serve her, fixing his eyes on her and smiling, then knocking a penny or two off the prices.

But that was all there was in it, Jess was sure. Those lingering looks, those smiles. Probably her mother didn't even notice, and wouldn't have encouraged Derry, anyway, even if he'd been single. Her thoughts were with Frank, so long in his grave.

Och, I've probably got it all wrong, Jess would tell herself. And they did need a bathroom, didn't they? And very nice it was.

Addie, still at the table, was now unfolding the evening paper and perching a pair of reading glasses on her fine nose.

'Still no sign of this slump ending,' she sighed. 'Still so many poor laddies out of work, eh? When will things start looking up?'

'They say only a war will do it,' Marguerite murmured. 'There's talk of it.'

'Another war?' Addie's eyes were horror-struck. 'No, no, that couldn't happen.'

'It's in all the papers, Ma. That fellow in Germany's just dying to cause trouble.'

'If I see anything about war, I never read it. It's just impossible! Impossible it could happen all over again.' Addie took off her glasses and folded the newspaper, her lips trembling. 'When I think of what your dad went through – are they saying that'd all be for nothing?'

'No, no, Ma, nobody's saying that!' Jess ran to put her arm round her mother's shoulders. 'The government will never let it get that far. They'll never let Hitler cause another war.'

'The government?' Addie smiled wryly. 'You think they can do something? Haven't done much for the men on the dole.'

'All this war stuff, it's just talk, Ma,' Marguerite said soothingly. 'I'm sorry I mentioned it.'

'Aye, well, let's leave it, eh?' Addie stood up. 'It's getting late, I think I'll away to bed. You, too, Jess. You've your big day tomorrow.'

And lying in her small bed next to Marguerite in

14

the old brass double that had once been their parents', all thoughts of war had faded from Jess's mind. In the half-light of the summer night, she could just make out the smart two-piece hanging on the cupboard door, and her best white blouse on the back of her chair. Everything else was also ready where she'd placed it earlier; her bag and high-heeled shoes by her bed, her hat on a peg on the back of the door. Now all she needed next day was good weather.

'Marguerite,' she whispered urgently.

'What?' her sister asked crossly.

'Can you tell if it's still raining? I think it's stopped.'

'You're waking me up to ask about the rain? Honestly, Jess!'

'Sorry. I'll try to go to sleep now. Oh, but I've just thought – with so many out of work, d'you think there'll be a lot in for the box office job?'

'Oh, yes, they'll be queuing from one end of Princes Street to the other!' Marguerite cried, then laughed. 'No, I don't think there'll be all that many. No' everybody's cup of tea. You're going to get it anyway.'

'Think so?'

'Sure to. Now let's say goodnight, eh?'

'Goodnight, Marguerite. And thanks. Specially for your two-piece.'

'Don't mention it,' said Marguerite, and almost immediately fell asleep, to be followed, amazingly, by Jess, who didn't even dream. Or at least, if she did, couldn't remember, when briliant August sunshine woke her up the following morning.

Three

'Queuing from one end of Princes Street to the other'?

Remembering Marguerite's joke as she arrived at the picture house at ten o'clock precisely, Jess gave a sigh of relief that it hadn't turned out to be true. After all, it might have been, with so many out of work and looking for jobs. But there was no one outside the Princes at all.

For a moment, she stood in the sunshine, for which she was giving heartfelt thanks, gazing at the cinema at the east end of Princes Street. Sandwiched in between shops, the white-walled building with its handsome glass entrance was not one of the largest cinemas in the city, but so attractive in its styling, inside and out, it was certainly one of the most popular. At least, with those who didn't mind paying a wee bit more to get in.

And that, of course, had always been Jess, who was now adjusting the jacket of Marguerite's two-piece and straightening its calf-length slim skirt. Not too over-dressed, was she? After her sister's scornful words, she'd begun to worry that she might be and had decided against wearing her best hat, the one she'd bought at Dobson's for a friend's wedding.

16

Better not look as though she was going to another wedding, eh? Or a garden party at Holyrood? Marguerite had been right, really. She was a working girl, applying for a working girl's post, even if she did hope it might lead to all sorts of things. Her plain white hat would add just the right touch, and giving it a final tweak over her dark hair, Jess took a deep breath and entered the elegant vestibule of the Princes, just as the clock was striking ten.

There were seven other young women already waiting, and as their eyes ran over Jess, sizing up another rival, hers ran over them. What a relief! No one looked too different from her. She needn't worry about being over-dressed, just smile, try to relax. What a hope, with her insides churning! But she did smile, and so did her rivals, as she asked cheerfully, 'No' late am I?'

'Och, no, it's just on ten,' someone answered. 'And we've just got here.'

'Seen anybody yet?'

'Aye, a lady came out of the foyer there, but just told us to wait, she'd be back in a minute.'

'Here she is now,' said a tall redhead, as a plump young woman in a blue dress and matching scarf appeared with a paper in her hand. She had a mass of lightly bleached blonde hair and round blue eyes, and as she gave them all a beaming smile, Jess remembered her.

'Good morning, ladies, and welcome to the Princes Street Picture House. I'm Sally Dollar, in charge of the box office, which is in the foyer behind me – perhaps some of you've seen me

17

before, on visits here?'

Oh, yes, Jess thought, she'd seen her before, when she'd bought her ticket, and had always thought how pleasant she looked in her little glass office.

'But you'll be interviewed by Mr Hawthorne, the manager,' Miss Dollar was continuing. 'In alphabetical order, so you'll know where you stand. Now, is everyone here?'

Checking them off on her list, Miss Dollar told them that she'd first be giving them a quick tour of the cinema, and then there'd be a cup of tea or coffee in the Princes Cafe and Tea Room if they wanted it.

'If we want it?' the girl next to Jess murmured. 'I'm dying for a cup already!'

But Jess was more interested in the tour, and as Miss Dollar called out, 'This way, ladies!' was the first to follow.

From the vestibule they moved into the foyer, familiar to Jess, of course, from her many past visits. Here was the box office itself, focus of interest for the girls, of course, though it was no more than a small glass-walled office with a couple of seats, and a counter with ledgers and files and the machine that dispensed the tickets. When everyone had had a brief look, Miss Dollar drew their attention to the foyer's marble flooring, decorative pillars, and the fine plasterwork of the ceiling cornices, all features in fact of the classical style of the whole cinema.

'And all costing a packet, as you might expect, when the Princes was built in 1912,' she added. 'But money seemed no object then. Later on,

18

when the talkies came in and the old piano for the silent films went, they bought a grand cinema organ – and how much that set 'em back, I couldn't tell you.' She gave a chuckle. 'But maybe you ladies will be more interested in the photos of the stars? They're all here, you know, round the walls.'

And so they were, as the girls exclaimed. Clark Gable, Henry Fonda, Charles Boyer, Greta Garbo, Marlene Dietrich – oh, all of 'em. Weren't they terrific?

'Charles Boyer's on this week, in *Algiers*,' one of the girls murmured. 'Och, he's so gorgeous, eh? That French accent!'

'Want to see the picture, then?' another girl asked.

'You bet! And *Jezebel* – that's coming soon.' The first girl sighed. 'With Henry Fonda. He's gorgeous, too. So stern!'

'Sorry to interrupt, but we'll have to move on,' Miss Dollar said cheerfully. 'This way to the auditorium. No Charles Boyer on at the moment. It's always like a church at this time of day – nobody around but the cleaners.'

They saw everything, from the cleaners at work in the hushed auditorium with its great Wurlitzer organ, to the staffroom and offices and the projection room behind the circle, described by Miss Dollar as the hub of the whole place.

'All very technical up here, as you can see, but everybody at the Princes has to have an idea of how things work. We all have to muck in, you might say, from time to time. One big happy family!'

At the looks on their faces, she gave another chuckle.

'But no need to worry. You'll no' be having to show the films. Sorry our projectionist is out just for the minute, or he could've said a few words. As a matter of fact, he'll be interviewing himself today – needs an assistant.'

'Did you say we were to be seen in alphabetical order?' Jess asked, as they all trooped along to the cafe that was as elegant and gracious as everywhere else at the Princes, though closed until matinee time to the public.

'I did,' Miss Dollar replied. 'What's your name, dear?'

'Jessica Raeburn.'

'Oh, what a shame, you're last but one to go in! There's only someone called Tricia Wright after you. Never mind, Mr Hawthorne will no' take long.'

'That's a relief,' Jess answered, gratefully accepting a cup of tea and a chocolate biscuit from a young woman who'd opened up the tea counter specially for them. 'And thanks very much, Miss Dollar, for showing us round.'

'Why, thank you for that, Miss Raeburn. No' many bother to say anything.'

Hope she didn't think I was trying to butter her up, Jess thought as Miss Dollar hurried away. For she really had enjoyed the tour, and did think the cinema beautiful.

'Miss Armitage!' Miss Dollar suddenly cried, after consulting her list. 'Will you come this way, please?'

'Oh, no!' the tall redhead whispered, putting down her coffee cup. 'That's me, then!'

How soon for me? Jess wondered, moving nearer to Miss Wright, who'd have to share the longest wait with her. But, in what seemed no time at all, she saw Miss Dollar's eyes on her and heard her cheerful voice, 'Miss Raeburn, please!'

'Good luck!' Tricia Wright generously called after her.

'Thanks,' Jess answered, her heart thumping, as she once again followed Miss Dollar.

Four

'Miss Raeburn, Mr Hawthorne,' Miss Dollar announced, throwing open the door of a small office that had not been shown before. 'Go along, dear,' she whispered to Jess, 'take that chair in front of the desk. Then I'll sit next to Mr Hawthorne.'

'Morning, Miss Raeburn,' the manager said, smiling, as he stubbed out a cigarette and rose to shake Jess's hand. 'I'm afraid you've had a bit of a wait.'

'That's all right,' she murmured, obeying Miss Dollar's instruction to take the chair in front of the manager's desk, letting her eyes, with a great show of confidence, meet his.

From the worry lines on his brow and the

21

beginnings of a double chin, she guessed him to be in his forties. His fairish hair was also receding from that worried brow, but his smile was one that met his brown eyes and it seemed to Jess that he'd be good-natured. But who could say? Looks were deceptive, folk always said.

'Well, now, I have your details to hand,' he began, glancing down at her application form open on his desk. 'And I see you've been four years with Dobson's in Cash and Accounts?'

'That's correct, Mr Hawthorne.'

'So – good experience in cash handling.' He moved his finger down the page. 'And before that you were with Marling's the stationer's. That'd be mainly counter work?'

'To begin with,' Jess replied. 'I'd always done well with figures at school and would have stayed on, only we needed the money, so I took the job at Marling's. When they asked me to help out with the cash one time, I liked it and did some evening classes. Then I moved to Dobson's.'

'Where they think very highly of you.' Mr Hawthorne looked down again at her references. 'But – about this particular post – there's more to it than people think.' His eyes went to Miss Dollar who nodded agreement. 'It's not just a question of selling admission tickets. We have to spend a lot of time here making things balance. I do, Miss Dollar does. Cash has to correspond to sales.' Little lines creased his eyes as he laughed. 'Story of my life, Miss Raeburn! So, there's checks and records to be kept, dealing with enquiries, and occasionally there's assisting

22

me, or others.'

'I did tell everyone that we all mucked in,' Miss Dollar murmured. 'One big happy family.'

'And that's right. This is a small cinema, you see, Miss Raeburn, and we have to be ready to do anything that comes up. That's why I wanted everyone shown round the cinema before the interview, so that they could see the set-up.'

'It was interesting, looking round,' Jess told him.

'Yes, well, the other thing is that as box office assistant, you'll often be working on your own. In the evenings, too. You'd be happy with that, Miss Raeburn?'

'Quite happy, Mr Hawthorne.'

He hesitated, shuffling papers round his desk.

'I'm still not sure, though, if you don't mind me saying so, why you want to make the move from Dobson's. We'd be paying you less, you know, and the hours are not easy.'

'Oh, I know,' she said quickly.

'And you wouldn't be doing the same sort of thing as you're used to. So ... what made you apply, then? Just the chance to see the films?'

'No, no, it wasn't the films – though I do like to go to the pictures.' Jess was already blushing. 'It was the cinema.'

'The cinema?'

'This cinema. The Princes. I love it. It's just so beautiful. So ... different.'

'Different from what?'

'I mean, from what you usually see. Everything that's ordinary.' She gave a nervous smile. 'Sorry, I'm no' explaining very well. I just know

23

I love it.'

There was a silence, as Mr Hawthorne and Miss Dollar stared at her and her blush, deepening, rose to her brow in a painful tide. Och, what a fool, eh? To go blethering on like that in an interview! She was lowering her eyes, looking down at her hands, when Mr Hawthorne finally spoke.

'Miss Raeburn,' he said quietly, 'so do I.'

After another silence, he rose, thanked her for her application and asked her if she'd mind waiting in the cafe for a little while. He might want to speak to her again. The interview was over.

'I do feel a fool,' she heard herself saying on the way back to the cafe, but Miss Dollar smiled and patted her shoulder.

'You've no need to feel that, dear. You did well.'

'I thought I'd be going straight home now.'

'Like the others, you mean?'

'The others have gone home?' Jess's eyes widened. But it was true, of course, no one had returned to the tearoom.

'We'll be letting them know. You, too. Now ... I have to find Miss Wright, eh? Poor lassie – the last to go in, eh?'

Five

When Tricia Wright, pale and nervous, had left
the cafe with Miss Dollar, Jess found herself
alone with the girl behind the counter – one
Pamela Gregg, according to her name tag – who
kindly asked if she'd like another cup of coffee.

'Oh, I would!' Jess answered quickly. 'I feel
I've just done a ten mile walk or something.'

'That bad, eh?' Pam Gregg, who was fair with
a broad freckled face, laughed. 'You're still here
though, eh?'

'They're going to be letting us know.'

'That right? Well, I'd no' be surprised if you
got news today. Like milk with your coffee? The
sugar's just there.'

As Jess moved away, walking slowly so as not
to spill any coffee on Marguerite's two-piece,
Pam called that she'd better be getting on with
setting the tables, they'd be opening for light
lunches in half an hour.

'And I'd better no' be too late,' Jess called
back. 'I've to go back to work this afternoon.'

'Better wait to see what happens, though.'

'I'll do that, all right!'

The door opened and a young waitress came
in, tying on a decorative apron, followed by a
tall young man with high, thin shoulders and

long legs, who stood for a moment or two, looking around.

'Any chance of a coffee?' he asked, his voice sounding English.

'We're no' really open yet,' the waitress told him, staring at him dubiously. 'You're no' here for the box office job, eh?'

'Box office?' He grinned. 'Good Lord, no. I'm here for interview with Mr Daniel. I'm a projectionist.'

'Give him a coffee, Nancy!' a plump, middle-aged woman called, appearing from the back of the cafe. 'I expect Ben'll be down in a minute.'

'I'll get it, Mrs Baxter,' Pam said. 'Black or white, sir?'

'Thanks, I appreciate this – black, please.'

The young man, taking his coffee, looked round the tables and, having spotted Jess, approached her with a friendly smile. 'Mind if I join you? I take it you're a candidate too?'

As he sat down without waiting for permission, she looked at him coolly. He had a mop of waving reddish brown hair and unusual grey eyes, almost three-cornered in shape and fringed with thick dark lashes. Probably, she supposed, he would be considered handsome by most. A charmer, anyway. But not her type.

'No' for the projectionist's job,' she answered, after a pause, at which he laughed.

'I didn't think so. Must be for the box office, then. Look, shall we introduce ourselves? I'm Russell MacVail, always known as Rusty.'

'Jessica Raeburn, always known as Jess.'

They shook hands and Jess relaxed a little,

allowing herself a smile.

'What time's your interview?' he asked, quick to smile back.

'I've already had it.'

'And you're still here? That's hopeful.'

'They're going to let us know,' she said uneasily. Why were folk so confident for her? She didn't dare to feel confident for herself. 'But aren't there any other people here for the projectionist's job?'

'That's what I've been wondering.' He took out a packet of cigarettes and offered it to her.

'Thanks, I don't smoke.'

'Mind if I do?'

When she shook her head, he lit a cigarette and grinned. 'Hey, maybe I'm the only candidate?' Then the grin faded and he shook his head. 'Unlikely the way things are. I had no luck finding anything round Woking.'

'You were given the sack?' Jess asked with sympathy. 'Oh, that's terrible. So, now you're applying up here?'

'My dad's old home, Edinburgh.' Rusty glanced at his watch and stood up, stubbing out his cigarette on his coffee saucer. 'Look, I've got to go. Have to report to the projection room in ten minutes. Think we might meet again?'

'I couldn't say. Depends on you.'

'If I'm lucky, you mean.' His unusual eyes were resting on her face. 'Keep your fingers crossed for me, then.'

She held up her hand, showing two fingers firmly crossed, and they both laughed until Rusty strode away, curly head held high, and

27

Jess, seeing Miss Dollar approaching, didn't feel like laughing any more.

'Miss Raeburn!' Miss Dollar called. 'There you are, then. Could you come up to the office, please? Mr Hawthorne would like another word.'

'Miss Raeburn, come in, come in! Please, take a seat.'

Mr Hawthorne was jovial, his worried brow relaxed, his eyes bright on Jess's face.

'Thank you for waiting – sorry it was so long.'

As though she wouldn't have waited! Glancing quickly at Miss Dollar, who was remaining at the door, sending out encouraging signals with another wide smile, Jess again took the chair facing the manager, her heart beating fast. What was this word he wanted, then? From his welcome, his whole manner, she couldn't help hoping it would spell 'Job'.

But it could be anything, couldn't it?

It was 'Job'.

With a ritual shuffle of his papers and a pleasant grin, Mr Hawthorne came out with it. The magic word.

'If you want the job, Miss Raeburn, it's yours.'

All applicants had been carefully considered, of course, but there was no question, he told her, that she was the best person for it. Both he and Miss Dollar hoped she'd be very happy at the Princes. And could she start next week?

Stunned, she was for a moment tongue-tied.

'I never thought I'd hear today,' she said at

last.

'We'll be notifying the others, but there was no point in keeping you waiting. So, what do you say, Miss Raeburn? Do you want to work with us here?'

'Oh, yes, I do, Mr Hawthorne, I do! I'm ... well, I'm thrilled.' Her eyes brightening, as it began to sink in that she'd been successful, she said again in a whisper, 'Thrilled!'

'And could you start next week, then? Thing is, Miss Dollar's lost her assistant to the Borders – had to move with her family – so you see we want someone fairly sharpish. You need only give a week's notice to Dobson's, I think, if you're paid weekly?'

'Yes, only a week is necessary.' Jess's head was buzzing. Only a week, and she'd be away from the work she knew and the people she knew. After four long years.

Didn't seem possible. It was what she wanted, of course, and it was true that she was thrilled at her move, but now that it was all happening, she found she couldn't quite take it in. How would it all work out? She was doing the right thing, she knew she was. But ... next week?

'All a bit sudden?' Mr Hawthorne asked sympathetically. 'And a big decision? But what you want, isn't it?'

'It is,' she declared, straightening her shoulders, trying to appear positive. 'I'd need the full week's notice, though.'

'Make it Monday week, then. How about that?'

'That'd be grand.'

They stood up, shaking hands, and Miss Dollar came forward and shook hands too and said she was really looking forward to working with Jess, who must call her Sally.

'And may we call you Jessica?' Mr Hawthorne asked.

'Oh, Jess, please.'

'We want you to feel at home here, you know, and as I say, be happy.'

'I'm sure I will be.'

'I've no doubt of it. Now, if you go with Sally, she'll take you to meet my secretary, Miss Harrison. She'll go through all the formalities with you. Then maybe you'd like a bit of lunch with us, in our cafe?'

'Oh, I'd have liked that – thank you very much – but I have to go back to work. I only got the morning off for the interview.'

'Another time, then. Goodbye for now, Jess. See you on Monday week.'

'On Monday week.'

Even after going through all the formalities the manager had mentioned with his rather angular, middle-aged secretary, Jess still felt dazed at the speed with which she'd changed her life. But when Edie Harrison wished her good luck with a kindly smile, she rallied with a smile of her own, thinking how everyone she'd met so far had been friendly and helpful, and how that made her feel again that she'd done the right thing.

'You'll take to this job like a duck takes to water,' Sally told her, perhaps reading her mind, as they returned to the foyer. 'That's what George and I felt, anyway.'

'George?'

'Mr Hawthorne. I call him that – we both worked at a cinema in Portobello together before we came here. He was assistant manager, I was an usherette. I know Daisy, his wife, as well, but och, what a worrier! Spends all her time telling him to take it easy. As though he ever would!'

'Wish I hadn't got to dash away,' Jess murmured, as they reached the box office. 'I could've had another good look round.'

'Plenty of time for that Monday week, eh?' Sally glanced at her watch. 'And we'll be opening up soon for the matinee performance. Hey, is that somebody you know?'

Jess, swinging round, saw Rusty MacVail coming towards them, his eyes lighting up, his hand raised in a wave.

'Hoped I might see you!' he cried. 'How'd you get on?'

'Miss Dollar, this is Mr MacVail, a projectionist,' Jess answered. 'Mr MacVail, meet Miss Dollar – my new boss.'

'You got the job? That's wonderful. Congratulations! Miss Dollar, it's good to meet you. Hope I'll be lucky enough to meet you again.'

'You don't know how you got on?' Jess asked sympathetically.

He shook his head ruefully. 'Been asked to wait.'

'At least they didn't say they'd let you know.'

'No, but there are plenty of other guys around. Just have to hope for the best. Can I get you ladies a coffee or anything?'

When Jess explained that she had to go back to work, he sighed and said he wished he could have walked her on her way, but after polite farewells left for the cafe, Sally staring after him.

'What a nice laddie, eh?' she whispered. 'Let's hope Ben Daniel gives him the job. Goodbye, then, Jess, I'll see you Monday week. As you know, we don't usually work mornings, as we've to do late shifts, but if you come in about ten, I can go through things with you before we open. That all right?'

'Oh, yes, fine. Thanks for everything, Miss Dollar ... I mean, Sally.' As she hurried to the door, Jess looked back and smiled. 'See you Monday week!'

By the time she'd announced her news at Dobson's, put in her notice and received congratulations mixed with groans from the manager and her colleagues, she was climbing over the moon again, all her little symptoms of shock melting away. It had been a good place to work, Dobson's, and she'd been grateful for the experience of being there, but it was right that she should be moving on now. To somewhere special.

The Princes Street Picture House, here I come! she thought, looking forward with pleasure to telling of her success to her family when they all met at home in the evening.

'Knew you'd get it,' Marguerite remarked. 'Is

my suit all right?'

'Perfect. Never spilled a thing.'

'Still canna make you out, Jess,' her mother said thoughtfully. 'Know what I think? You're just star-struck. Just want to be near those picture folk, eh? Won't be in the starlight in the box office, though.'

'Oh, yes I will!' cried Jess.

Six

Monday week. Well, it came at last, though her last week at Dobson's had seemed a long week to Jess. And then, at the end, there'd been all the embarrassment of the leave-taking and the leaving present – a writing case – to exclaim over, as well as the promises to meet up, the jokes about free tickets at the Princes, the dashed away tears, as she walked out of Dobson's for the last time.

'All good things come to an end,' Addie said later. 'What you have to do, is make sure you've got something just as good to go to.'

'Exactly,' Jess retorted. 'Something like the Princes Street Picture House.'

'At five bob less a week,' Marguerite reminded. 'Still, I think I do agree that it'd be a lovely place to work. A cut above most cinemas round here.'

'There you are, Ma!' Jess cried triumphantly. 'Marguerite agrees with me.'

'Just as long as you don't expect me to lend you my suit again to go to work. Once was quite enough.'

'No need to worry, I'll be wearing my own clothes now,' Jess said loftily. 'I know what'll look right.'

And on Monday week, Jess spent no time agonizing over what to wear, but appeared at the Princes on that first morning looking coolly attractive in a pale green blouse and patterned skirt. The day was hot and dry, and Sally Dollar, when she greeted Jess in the vestibule, was already feeling the heat, dabbing at her brow with cologne and saying she must go on a diet, she was far too plump for weather like this.

'Awful weather, anyway, eh?'

'Awful?'

'For going to the pictures, Jess! Folk don't want to be inside when it's nice!'

'But it's *Jezebel* this week – with Bette Davis and Henry Fonda.'

'Aye, might attract a few in for them, but we've no' got the air conditioning, you see.' Sally shook her bleached head. 'But we'll just see how things go. I'll let you off at five today, anyway, seeing as it's your first day and you'll be tired.'

'Tired? I'm sure I won't be.'

'Well, there's a lot to take in all at once. There's no need for you to stay – as I say, I shouldn't think it'll be busy. Probably won't even need Fred to control the queues, as there won't be any queues.'

'Fred?'

'Fred Boyle, our man-of-all-work, dear. I'll introduce you. Does handyman jobs around the place by day, doubles as commissionaire for opening time.'

'When he controls the queues?' Jess laughed a little. 'Do they need controlling?'

Sally shrugged. 'Depends who's in 'em. This being what you might call a superior cinema, we don't often get the roughs, but sometimes folk start complaining if they can't get in when they want to, and then there's trouble.'

'Think I'll be glad we have Fred, then.'

'Aye, it's amazing how people will take notice of a man when they'll just ignore a woman. Gets me, that does.'

'Men are stronger, that's all.'

'Women should still have some authority. But we'd best get on, Jess. I'll show you how to do the tickets first. Oops, here comes Mr Hawthorne – looks like he's off somewhere.'

The manager, wearing a dark suit that looked too heavy for the day, was carrying his hat and a briefcase and obviously feeling the heat as much as Sally.

'Morning, ladies,' he said, puffing a little. 'I'm just off to Glasgow – got a meeting with the owners. Thought I'd just wish you well, Jess. You'll be in good hands with Sally here.'

As Jess murmured her thanks, Sally said she'd be fine and walked with Mr Hawthorne to the entrance doors.

'Don't you go running for your train,' she told

35

him. 'There'll be plenty of others, remember.'

'I guess you've been talking to my wife,' he muttered, putting on his hat. 'But in this business, you don't keep the owners waiting. 'Bye, then. I won't be back till late.'

'The Princes will still be here.'

'Who are the owners?' Jess asked, when the manager had hurried on his way and Sally had returned to the box office.

'A Glasgow firm – John Syme's – owns half a dozen cinemas at least. But George needn't worry about upsetting 'em. They know this one's the best.'

'Never thought about cinemas having owners before,' Jess said with interest.

'Thought they just "growed"?' Sally smiled, dabbing again at her brow. 'No, obviously, owners are very important people, but Syme's will never let the Princes go under. It's too grand for that.'

With Sally a good teacher and Jess an apt pupil, the work of going through the box office routines moved swiftly by.

'You're quick to learn,' Sally observed, 'and I can see you're used to balancing cash and all that sort of thing. No' like poor Norma, who was here before you. Oh dear, she was a lovely girl, but got into such muddles sometimes. I was always having to sort her out! But I'll no' have any worries leaving you on your own.'

'What next, then?' Jess asked, pleased that she was doing well. So far, at least. Hadn't sold a ticket yet, though.

'Well, you've got the ticket prices sorted out, and where all the different sections are? Front stalls, ninepence, back stalls, a shilling. Back circle, one and six, front circle, half a crown, children half price except for matinees. Three-pence reduction for adults at the matinees for the front stalls, sixpence off the rest.'

'Oh, I know all about the reductions!' Jess said with a laugh. 'Paid 'em often enough. Never sat in the circle, though.'

'Take a peep at *Jezebel* up there this afternoon, then,' Sally told her. 'Go on, have a treat for your first day, eh? Now, I think we've just got time to nip along to the projection room to meet Ben Daniel. Oh, yes, and that nice young guy we saw the other day. Ben's showing him the ropes, so we'll no' stay long.'

'Rusty MacVail got the job? Oh, that's nice.'

'Aye, much the best candidate, Ben said. From England, you know, but I think his dad's Scottish. Come on, let's get along before we have a bit of lunch. The usherettes will be here by one.'

The projection room, separated from the auditorium by a specially built wall, appeared cramped to Jess with the projector taking up most of the space. Rather stuffy, too, in spite of the ventilation that had been put in to replace the windows that were not allowed.

'Natural light – very damaging to the film,' Sally had explained on their way. 'Always plenty of problems with the projection department, eh? Fire risks and all. That's why they have to be separated from the circle.'

37

'Fire risks?' Jess repeated, her eyes widening.

'No need to worry. Everybody's very careful. It's just that there's a lot of flammable material around, and it can get pretty hot in the box, as they call it.'

No wonder the two projectionists were in shirtsleeves, Jess thought, as she and Sally entered their 'box'. And then she smiled, because one was Rusty.

'Jess!' he cried, leaping forward to shake her hand. 'I was wondering when I'd get to see you!'

'I was so pleased to hear you'd got the job,' she murmured, aware as she let Rusty's hand go that the black-haired man next to him was looking like a thunder cloud.

'Oh, for God's sake, Sally, what's up?' he snapped. 'I'm in the middle of showing my new chap around.'

'Temper, temper, Ben,' Sally replied easily. 'We're no' staying. But I'm showing my new assistant round as well, and I thought she should meet you.'

'Oh.' His gaze went to Jess and seemed very slightly to soften, but so dark were his eyes – brown, almost black – it wasn't easy to tell. When he spoke, though, his voice seemed to have lost his irritation. 'And this is?'

'Jess Raeburn,' Sally told him. 'She's Norma's replacement at the box office. Jess, meet Ben Daniel, head projectionist.'

Tall – almost as tall as Rusty, but slim, rather than thin – Ben Daniel reminded Jess of someone she couldn't exactly place. The long face with the high cheekbones and distinctly marked dark brows, the deep-set eyes – yes, they were familiar. And the stern look – who had a look like that? Hadn't someone said, 'He's gorgeous, too – so stern!'

Of course – Henry Fonda!

As she and Ben Daniel formally shook hands, Jess found herself blushing. Oh, what a piece of nonsense, eh? Thinking Rusty's boss was like a film star. She was relieved when Sally said they must be on their way, they'd to have a quick sandwich before the girls arrived and it was matinee time.

'Seeing your first customers, eh?' Ben Daniel asked Jess with a smile. 'Or patrons, as our Mr H likes us to call 'em.'

'Patrons!' Sally echoed, shepherding Jess away. But Rusty was at the door.

'Good luck, Jess – shall we meet later?'

'She's got a lot on today,' Sally said firmly. 'Thanks, Ben! Jess, come on, then.'

'Goodbye, Rusty!' Jess called. 'Goodbye, Mr Daniel.'

'Call me Ben!' he cried after her. 'I'll show you round when we can fix it up.'

In the small staffroom where there were lockers and pegs and a washroom, Sally put on the kettle and opened up a packed lunch.

'I meant to tell you to bring a sandwich,' she told Jess, setting out cups. 'But I've brought enough for two, anyway. Can't afford to eat at the cafe every day, eh? Of course, when you start at one o'clock, you can have something at home,

39

anyway.'

'Feel bad, taking your lunch, Sally.'

'No, I told you, there's enough here for both of us. I should be cutting down anyway! What'll you have – cheese and chutney or ham?'

'So glad Rusty got the job,' Jess remarked, choosing cheese and chutney. 'Wonder how he'll get on with Mr Daniel, though?'

'Now, he told you to call him Ben!' Sally made tea and poured it out. 'Och, he's no' so bad. A bit tetchy at times, but then he's got a lot of responsibility. If things go wrong in the projection room, that's it – no picture!'

'What's his wife like, then? Another Mrs Hawthorne, forever worrying?'

'He's no' married. Escaped so far, anyway, and he was thirty last birthday. Plenty of girls after him, of course. Some think he looks like Tyrone Power.'

'Tyrone Power?' Jess frowned, as she considered a mental picture of another handsome, dark-haired actor. 'I suppose he has a look of him. Maybe seems more serious.'

'That's what draws the girls,' Sally said lightly, then, as Jess raised her eyebrows, vehemently shook her head.

'Hey, don't look at me! I'm no' chasing after Ben Daniel. I've got my own laddie and he's all I want. You'll meet my Arnold soon enough – he's always dropping in. Works in an office up the Mound.' Sally passed Jess an apple. 'How about you, then? Anyone special?'

'No one at all.'

'Think you've got an admirer here, though.'

'Who?'

'Why, Rusty, of course! Talk about sheep's eyes!'

'Sally, we've only just met.'

'Needn't take long, to know what you feel.'

'Well, I don't feel anything.' Jess crunched her apple. 'I've enough on my plate, learning a new job.'

'The way you're going, that won't take long. Listen, I think that's the girls coming in now.'

'The usherettes?'

'That's right. Renie MacLeish and Edna Angus are on this afternoon. Then Faith Pringle's swopping with Edna this evening. It's a complicated timetable – comes of having to work such late nights. But we all get our time off – never worry about that!'

Jess replied that she wasn't just then worrying about time off – only seeing the customers.

'Never saw any at Dobson's, you know. Only their bills of sale and accounts.'

'Heavens, it'll no' take you five minutes to get used to seeing the – ahem – patrons!' Sally told her. 'Best part of the job, I say. Meeting people. I never think of 'em as just money in the till. Except, if they weren't, we'd be out of a job. But here come the girls!'

Seven

'Hello everybody!' came the voices of the usherettes, who swept in to the staffroom, seeming
immediately to form a crowd, though there were
only two of them. But they were an exuberant
pair, one dark – that was Renie – one fair – that
was Edna – both rather pink in the face from
hurrying from the tram stop and falling over
tourists.

'Och, you canna move for 'em!' Renie cried,
opening her locker and taking out her uniform.
'At least they've got a nice day, eh? Sally, is this
your new assistant, then? How d'you do, pet?
I'm Renie MacLeish, this here's Edna Angus,
and number three – Faith Pringle – she's no' on
till this evening.'

'Welcome to the Prince's Palace,' Edna put in.
'Hope you'll be very happy. We are, Renie, eh?'

'Aye, though I could've done without coming
in to work on a day like this. I mean, you canna
see the sun in a cinema!'

Cheerfully stepping out of their cotton dresses,
the girls put on their blue uniforms and matching
hats, elbowed each other out of the way to make
up their lips at the one little mirror, and then said
they were ready.

'Opening time!' sang Edna. 'Where's Fred,

then?'

'Come on, Jess,' Sally said, putting their cups in the washroom sink. 'Into battle!'

'I'm ready,' Jess muttered, feeling for all the world as though she really were going 'over the top'. Have some sense, she told herself. All she was going to do was sell admission tickets to some strangers. Nothing to worry about. Why, on such a lovely day, probably nobody'd come to the matinee, anyway.

'Got a nice crowd out there,' Fred Boyle, the lanky, grey-haired man-of-all-work remarked, as Sally and Jess took their places in the box office. 'This your new assistant, Sally?'

'I'm Jess Raeburn,' Jess told him, shaking his large hard hand. 'Glad to meet you, Mr Boyle.'

'Fred's the name. Anything you want, just ask me. I've got stores, you ken. Want me to let this lot in, Sally?'

'Yes, please, it's time. Now, Jess, here they come. Our patrons!'

Pushing back her hair, swallowing hard, Jess stationed herself, ready to face the couple at the head of the small queue that was advancing.

'Two one and sixes, please,' the man said, laying down coins.

'Back circle?' Jess asked. 'Matinee price is only a shilling.'

'That so? Our lucky day, then.' The middle-aged man exchanging smiles with the woman with him, took back two sixpences. 'Thanks for telling us.'

'That's quite all right, sir.' Handing him his

43

tickets, Jess gave a pleasant smile and darted a quick glance at Sally, standing near by. OK? she telegraphed, and OK, Sally returned. Whatever was I worrying about? Jess wondered, and facing back to her queue, cried out, 'Next please!'

Everything continued to go so smoothly, and Sally was soon knocking Jess's arm and telling her to run up to the circle to see something of the big picture.

'Why not? You've been doing very well. No problems at all.'

'Except for the woman who wanted an extra reduction for her little boy, because it was the matinee.' Jess smiled. 'But you sorted her out, in the nicest possible way.'

'Aye, I'm always at my sweetest when I don't do what folks want. I mean, what's she expect? He's already half price. And what's he doing at a film like *Jezebel*, anyway? Should be taking him to *Mickey Mouse*, eh? Off you go, then, Jess.'

Entering the circle, hallowed place of the most expensive seats, Jess felt a child's anxiety at being somewhere she shouldn't. Oh, but she'd a right to be there now, a perfect right to one of the perks of the job, even if, just at that moment, she was on work time. Still, Sally had given her permission, as a treat, and she was a member of the cinema staff. That was the thing to remember.

Peering through the darkness, aware of the great screen ahead and the voices of the soundtrack in her ears, Jess was wondering just where to sit when a figure with a torch glided up and whispered, 'Hello, Jess. Sneaking a wee look at

44

Bette Davis, then?'

'Oh, Edna!' Jess had jumped a little and now was trying to look about her. 'Sally said I could pop up for a few minutes. It's OK, isn't it? I mean, there's no' many here.'

'Never get many up here for the matinee, hen. Evening's the time – that's when we get the courting couples, fellas showing off, buying the best seats.' Edna shone a torch along an empty row. 'Where'd you like to go? Front, or back?'

'Oh, back, I think. Then I can slip out easily.'

'Here, then. I'll sit with you for a minute. Then I'll have to do the ices. My turn.'

When they'd settled themselves into seats on the back row of the circle, Edna kindly whispered bits of the plot of the film to Jess, who'd really rather have managed without. Even though she'd missed the beginning, she got the message that Bette Davis, the so-called 'Jezebel' of the title, was one for flouting convention, especially when she turned up to a ball wearing a red dress when every other young girl was in white.

'What a shame the picture's no' in colour, eh?' Edna was hissing in her ear. 'That dress looks black!'

'Even worse than red,' Jess answered. 'No wonder Henry Fonda's glowering!'

Yes, and looking more like Ben Daniel than ever, she privately thought, and could even picture him running the projector behind her, as Rusty might be running it in real life.

'But this looks like a good film,' she commented to Edna. 'Think I'll have to see it right

45

through some time.'

'Be warned, then,' Edna replied. 'If you work in a cinema, you never get to see any picture all the way through. Sad, but true. Now, I'd better scoot.'

'Me, too. But I really enjoyed that. Being in the circle.'

'Pop up any time, then. Listen, would you like an ice cream? On the house?'

'Thanks, but I'd better get back to Sally. Nice to talk to you, Edna.'

'And you, Jess. No' been so bad, has it?'

'What?'

'Your first day.'

'No' bad at all!' cried Jess.

And by five o'clock that first day was over, and Jess, slinging a cardigan round her shoulders, was telling Sally it was true, she'd really enjoyed it.

'Though I'll have to admit, you were right,' she added. 'I do feel a bit tired. Seems strange. I don't usually feel tired.'

'It's just the strain, dear, of taking everything in on your first day. Everybody feels it.' Sally gave her a little push towards the door. 'But you're no' going to find any trouble with this job. Just hope it has enough for you.'

'Enough? I should say so! It's a Princes job, isn't it? That's enough for me.'

'Off you go, then, Jess, and I'll see you tomorrow. One o'clock, eh?'

'One o'clock it is.'

'And look out for your admirer.' Sally gave one of her chuckles. 'He's been let off early and all, and he's out there, waiting.'

'Rusty is?' Jess didn't know whether to feel flattered or exasperated. All she wanted really was to get home.

Outside the cinema, when his tall figure came leaping up to her, she sighed. 'Oh, Rusty, you've no' been waiting for me, have you?'

'Too right, I have.' His eyes were dancing. 'I thought we'd go for something to eat – celebrate getting our jobs.'

'Ah, I'm sorry. It would've been nice, but I have to get home. My mother and sister will be wanting to know how I got on. And to tell you the truth, I feel dead tired. Can we make it some other time?'

His eyes had stopped dancing, his smile had faded.

'Sure, if it's what you want. Where's home, then? Maybe I could walk with you for a bit?'

'I'm taking the train. I live in Leith.'

'So, let's go to the station.'

The evening was still warm – even sticky; there was the feel of thunder in the air. Luckily, they hadn't far to walk, the cinema being at the east end of Princes Street, convenient for the station.

'Here's my train already in,' Jess told Rusty when they reached the platform. 'It'll only take me a few minutes to get home. I prefer it to the tram.'

He wasn't listening, had fixed her with his grey eyes. 'Look, Jess, I'm sorry. I shouldn't be harassing you this way, following you around,

47

that sort of thing. Just, we seemed to hit it off so well – I thought...' He stopped and gave a sudden grin. 'Let's say, I'll behave myself in future, OK?'

'Rusty, you haven't been harassing me. What a thing to say!' Jess was watching the guard with his green flag at the ready. 'Think I'll have to go now, but it's all right, I'm no' annoyed or anything. I'll see you tomorrow.'

'We could still have a meal, eh? Just as a couple of colleagues?'

'That'd be grand.' Hastily opening a door, she boarded the little train. 'Goodbye, then, Rusty.'

'Goodbye, Jess.'

Anybody'd think I was going a long way off, she thought with a smile, as she waved and he waved back. Poor Rusty – he did seem disappointed, whereas she felt on the crest of a wave. Soon, she'd be telling her mother and Marguerite about her first day, and making them see that she'd done the right thing. And finding out as well if Ma had brought back anything interesting to eat.

But when she eventually squeezed into a seat in the crowded train, it was not her mother's face that came into her mind, or Marguerite's, or even the disappointed Rusty's. It was Henry Fonda's, as she'd seen it in *Jezebel*. Or was it Ben Daniel's, in the projection room? The images seemed to mix and flow and just for a second, her eyelids drooped and closed.

'Terminus!' cried a voice near at hand. 'All change! Everybody change!'

And Jess left the train for home.

48

Eight

'Like a duck takes to water' had been Sally's forecast for Jess's success in her new job, and though she didn't care to think of herself as a duck, Jess knew that she was in fact swimming very well.

Everything seemed to be just as she'd hoped it would be, and that was unusual in itself. So often, anything you looked forward to turned out to be a disappointment, and so many had thought her move to the Princes to be a backward step, Jess had always had to remember that they might be right. But it hadn't turned out that way at all.

In the handsome surroundings of the cinema, she felt all the magic she'd longed for, and if that might seem hard to understand by those who saw her job as merely routine, well, she couldn't really explain it. But as she had told her mother, even just working in the box office, she felt herself in the light of the stars at the Princes.

Something that people would surely understand, anyway, was that she felt not only wonderfully on top of her job, but also the warm glow that came from being liked. Everyone at the cinema seemed pleased she'd come to work there. Even Mrs Baxter, who ran the cafe, and her waitresses; even Fred, the handyman, and Trevor Duffy, the middle-aged man who played the cinema organ. It was almost as though she'd found another family.

Not that Rusty would want her to feel that, she knew, for being like a brother to her would not appeal. As for Ben Daniel – he always seemed as friendly as everyone else. If there were more to his feelings, she didn't know. Had her hopes, though. Hopes so secret, she didn't even put them into words. Just knew they were there.

Certainly, he hadn't been long in calling her to the projection room. Appearing at the box office one afternoon and fixing her with his brooding gaze, he'd asked if she'd mind coming in early some time, before the matinee, so that he could give her his crash course. Nothing to worry about. She wouldn't be asked to do anything, it was just that, as she knew, Mr Hawthorne liked everyone to have some idea of how the cinema worked.

'Oh, yes, I'll look forward to it,' she'd told him, at which he'd given a faint smile.

Two days later, she presented herself in the projection room, where Ben, in his shirtsleeves, welcomed her.

'No Rusty?' she asked.

'He'll be in later. We often work alone.' Ben set a chair for her. 'Now, how much do you know about this side of things? Ever thought how the film you watch comes to be there, on the screen?'

'I've never thought much about it at all.'

'No reason why you should, as a picture-goer. But now you're working in a cinema, you might find it interesting.'

'Oh, I will,' she said earnestly. 'I want to know as much as possible about the way things work here.'

For a moment, he studied her. 'I believe you do. Folk often talk like that in here, and half the time, they're just being polite. But you mean it, don't you?' He laughed shortly. 'Are you going places, Jess?'

'Going places?'

'Well, there's a ladder in cinemas, you know – same as everywhere else. If you want to go up it.'

She turned pink. 'How would I be going up ladders? I've just started in the box office.'

'Have to start somewhere.'

He laughed again, then pulled forward a metal box and opened it.

'Let's get on, eh? This is a box of film reels and is the way the reels are delivered. So, first job is to check them off and then load into the projector – in the right order. Want to see where they go?'

For some time, he showed her the various parts of the projector – the spools, shutters, channels, apertures, light source and controls – while explaining how to run the film smoothly through and check that the sound was working properly.

'Pretty technical,' he told her, 'and no one's expecting you to take it all in, but at least you'll have some idea of how your favourite film gets up there on to the screen.' He grinned. 'All an optical trick, you know. Just an illusion.'

'I don't believe it!'

'Yes, it's true. Motion pictures are only still pictures presented in a certain way. It's your eye that does the work, really.'

'Now you're spoiling everything for me,' she told him, not altogether in fun, but he shook his head.

'Come on, it's no different from knowing that the stars aren't really there on the screen. No Charles Boyer, no Clark Gable, no Greta Garbo.'

And no Henry Fonda, who's right here, she thought, looking away, in case he read her mind. But he was already showing her how he spliced the film when it broke down – the thing the audience most hated, as she would know.

'Och, yes! I can remember going with Ma to the silent films and they were always breaking down. Then there'd be catcalls and whistling and I don't know what.'

'You might like to learn how to join a film yourself sometime. Never know when it'd be useful.' Ben glanced at a large clock on the wall. 'Better leave it for now, but you can always ask Rusty to show you. OK?'

'Sure, I'll ask Rusty.' She smiled, as she moved with Ben to the door. 'Thank you very much for the crash course, then. I really appreciated it.'

'My pleasure.' His dark brown eyes seemed to be resting on her face just a little longer than was necessary. Or was that her imagination? He was

52

opening the door for her, anyway, and they were standing close, exchanging those looks, when Ben stepped back and cried, 'Why, here's the man himself. Hello, Rusty! I've just been giving Jess the tour of the projector.'

'Ah, why wasn't I here?' Rusty asked.

'Maybe you could give her a lesson in splicing the film sometime?

'Any time. Any time!'

As Jess made her thanks again and left with one swift backward glance at Ben, Rusty followed.

'We never did have that meal,' he told her. 'Haven't forgotten, have you?'

'No, but it's difficult when we both work evenings.'

'We do have evenings off. Let's fix something up.'

'Let's,' Jess agreed, and offered to find a time they could meet by studying the timetable.

Nine

It was some weeks later, at the end of September, that Addie, who'd been reading her evening paper, suddenly flung it down and cried, 'Now, did I no' tell you girls that the government would see we were all right? And it's true. See, it says here, there's going to be no war!'

'It was me said the government wouldn't let a war happen,' Jess said quickly. 'Don't you remember?'

'Did you? I thought I said it. Anyway, here it is, in the paper!'

'Where?' asked Marguerite. 'Where does it say it won't happen?'

'Here, on the front page. The Prime Minister's come back from this meeting with Hitler and he says Germany doesn't want war with anybody.' Addie adjusted her reading glasses to look at her paper again. 'See, there's going to be "Peace in our Time"!' She gave a triumphant smile. 'Just like I said, there'll be no war. We can all thank God for Mr Chamberlain.'

'We'd better listen to the wireless at nine o'clock,' Jess said, studying the picture of Neville Chamberlain, the Prime Minister, with his smiling face and his piece of paper from

Munich that seemed to bring the promise of peace. 'What a relief, eh?'

'But is anybody celebrating?' Marguerite asked.

'I think folk just want to get on with their lives and be grateful,' her mother answered. 'I know that's what I want.'

But Jess said nothing. She was feeling guilty over another celebration that hadn't happened yet. The meal with Rusty, to celebrate both of them getting their jobs – she still hadn't fixed it up and his looks were getting more and more reproachful. He was a sweet fellow, she didn't want to let him down, and if it meant tying a string round her finger to remind herself, she'd get round to it. Early in October, she finally did.

'About time, too,' Rusty muttered, when she told him. 'I was beginning to wonder if you really wanted to come out with me at all. If it's so difficult for an evening, why couldn't we have met on a Sunday?'

'Because there's nowhere open on a Sunday – you know that. And it's no' true that I don't want to see you.'

'We could've gone for a walk and had tea somewhere. There are places to have tea.'

'I thought you'd prefer a proper meal. Honestly, Rusty, you are being rather unfair!'

At the sight of Jess's aggrieved expression, Rusty had immediately apologized and said of course he'd be willing to go out whenever she found it convenient, take whatever she was offering.

55

'I'm just the humble slave,' he'd told her. 'Yours to command.'

At which they'd both laughed and promised not to fall out before they'd even had their first meal together.

'Nice you're going out again,' Addie remarked, when Jess told her at breakfast about her supper date that evening. 'You've done nothing but work since you started at that picture house.'

'Who's the fellow?' Marguerite asked, spooning up porridge. 'Anyone nice?'

'His name's Rusty MacVail. He's the assistant projectionist – came up from England, started the same time as me.'

'H'm.' Marguerite's lovely eyes were slightly glazed. 'Thought you might have had some rich guy chatting you up at the box office.'

'Rich guys don't usually come to the cinema on their own,' Jess said coldly. 'And no one's chatted me up so far.'

'I should hope not,' her mother cried, rattling some more coal into the kitchen range. 'I worry about you, meeting all those people at the box office. And then you've to come home late.'

'No' that late. We close up before the end of the picture. Rusty has to stay on, of course, or he said he'd walk me to the station. Not that he needs to.'

'Sounds keen.' Marguerite commented. 'Don't rush into anything, though.'

'Take a leaf out of your book, eh?' Jess asked, smiling. 'No need to worry. Rusty's sweet, but no' the one for me.'

56

'Better let him know, then,' Addie advised. 'Can cause a lot of trouble, if you just let things go on.'

'I think he knows already.' Jess rose to clear away the breakfast things. 'Anyway, I won't be in for tea, Ma. We're going out straight from work.'

'Make sure you pick somewhere smart for the meal,' Marguerite advised, pausing at the kitchen mirror to smooth her hair. 'And don't offer to go Dutch. Men don't like it.'

'Marguerite, I have been out with a man before!' Jess cried irritably. 'I know you're the expert, but I can sort out my own evening, thanks very much!'

'Your sister's only trying to be helpful,' Addie said, taking a turn at the mirror to put on her hat. 'And it's true, you've no' been out for a while. Will you tidy up, then, as you've the morning free?'

'Don't I always?' Jess sighed, thinking she'd much rather be at work than tidying up. Of course, that day she'd only be doing the afternoon shift, anyway, after which she and Rusty would be making for the cheap cafe she'd chosen for them and she would be offering to pay her share.

As though she'd be willing to take any notice of her sister's advice! 'Pick somewhere smart – don't offer to go Dutch...'

Why, the last thing Jess wanted was Rusty paying out for an expensive restaurant! And as for not going Dutch, Marguerite simply didn't understand that she and Rusty were just good friends. For what man Marguerite knew, would ever have settled for that?

As the time came for Jess and Rusty to leave for their evening out, Sally seemed delighted for them, as though all credit were due to her for spotting Rusty's interest. Why were some women so keen on that sort of matchmaking? Jess wondered. After all, it would never occur to her to talk of Sally's Arnold Adams as though they were about to get engaged at any moment, even though that might be the case. A large, cheerful man of thirty or so, he certainly popped in to see Sally often enough, sitting on a stool at the back of the box office, smoking a cigarette and waiting for a lull in customers so that he and Sally could have a giggle together.

'Wish we could both have finished early,' Jess told Sally, buttoning up her coat, while Rusty stood champing at the bit, longing to get away. 'Hate to leave you working.'

'What nonsense!' Sally cried. 'It's time you had a nice evening out. You enjoy yourself with Rusty, and don't worry about me. Anyway, Arnold will be round later on. We're going for a drink after I close up.'

'Jess, can we go?' Rusty groaned. 'I'm starving.'

'Just coming.'

Outside the cinema, the October wind hit them, buffeting them across Princes Street, as they held on to their hats and their scarves whirled. Facing them was the Mound – the artificial hill

58

created when the old Nor' Loch was excavated for the New Town – while on the skyline to their right, beyond the silhouette of the Assembly Hall, the great block of the Castle looked down. All very famous, and if they'd been tourists, they might have stopped to admire the splendour. All they wanted, however, was to get in somewhere out of the cold.

'Shall we take a tram?' Rusty asked as they began to climb the Mound.

'Och, no, we're only going to the High Street. No distance at all.'

'Says you, because you're fitter than I am. This hill's pretty steep.'

'You're too much stuck in your projection box, that's the trouble with you.'

'I love it,' he said seriously. 'Just like you love your box office.'

'We're two contented people, then.'

'Hey, I didn't exactly say I was contented.' Rusty took Jess's arm in his. 'Listen, I wish you'd have let me take you to that good restaurant I told you about.'

'What, The Vinery? It's far too expensive.'

'Ben recommended it.'

'Ben?' As they reached the top of the Mound and began to turn for the High Street, Jess kept her eyes down. 'So? He's got more money than we have.'

'I'm not worrying about the money, Jess. I wanted to make this evening something special.'

She turned her gaze back to his face. 'Look, we said we'd just go out as colleagues, eh? So, I'm going to pay my way, no arguments allowed, and the place we've chosen will suit me fine.'

'Oh, God, you're not suggesting we go Dutch? That'd spoil everything!'

Jess gave a long sigh. Don't say it, she groaned inwardly, don't say Rusty's the sort of chap Marguerite knows, who takes offence if a girl tries to pay? There were plenty who didn't mind at all, as Jess knew from experience, but seemingly Rusty felt he'd be letting himself down in some mysterious way if he let her go halves on the bill.

'Colleagues often go Dutch,' she told him quietly. 'Why shouldn't I share with you?'

'Like I said, I wanted to make this evening special. Special for you.' His tone was light, but his look was serious. 'It's already special for me, anyway, because you agreed to come.'

'OK, let's say this time it's special,' she said, her heart softening a little. 'But if there's another time, we'll think again.'

'You mean, there will be another time? Jess, that'd be terrific!'

'Come on – you said you were starving. Let's get to the cafe!' she cried. 'I'm hungry too.'

Ten

In the High Street cafe Jess had selected for them, they ordered steak and chips with grilled tomatoes, and fruit tart to follow.

'Of course, they're no' licensed here, so there's no drink,' Jess told Rusty, 'but they do good meals and that's what matters.'

'I take it you know this place well?' Rusty asked.

'No, I've just come with friends now and again.'

'The friends being male or female?'

Jess leaned forward. 'Listen, if I promise I won't ask about your friends, will you promise no' to ask about mine?'

'Done!' he answered with a grin. 'But I can tell you this, there's nobody in my life at the moment.'

Studying him, she wondered why. There was no doubt that that was a handsome face across the table from her, and a pleasant one. She could imagine girls being attracted easily enough, especially by those unusual eyes, that smiling mouth. Yet, it seemed there was no one special, pining away for him, back in England?

'You'll know me again,' he said suddenly, his voice very soft, and she gave a start of embarrassment.

'Sorry, I was just wondering ... why there was no one in your life at present.'

He grinned. 'Does that not count as asking about my friends?'

'Sorry.' She flushed a little. 'Never mind, then.'

'No, it's OK. I don't mind talking about it. Let's say, I just never found Miss Right.' He leaned forward. 'But now I can ask – how about you?'

'Oh, me.' Lowering her eyes, Jess worked away on her steak. 'Let's say I'm no' looking for anyone.'

Thank goodness, Rusty needn't know, she told herself, that if she wasn't looking for anyone, it was because she'd already found him. And secretly hoped that he'd found her, even if so far he'd made no move to tell her.

'Really love that job of yours, don't you?' Rusty asked cheerfully.

'We did say, we liked our work.'

In an effort to distract his attention from herself, Jess asked with an apologetic smile, 'Listen, don't think I'm nosey – though of course I am – but I wish you'd tell me how your folks came to live in England. I mean, if your father's a Scot?'

'I don't think you're nosey, Jess. It's good you're interested in me, because I'm interested in you.'

'But we're talking about you.'

'OK. Thing is, it's not so strange, you know, for Scots to end up in England – they're usually looking for jobs. Anyway, before the war, my dad trained as an electrician, but there wasn't much call for his type of work then and he wasn't doing well. Somebody said he might have more luck down south, so, he upped sticks and went down to Woking.' Rusty grinned. 'Found work, met my mother, fell in love, got married.' He raised his hands. 'That's how a Scot came to live in England.'

'Sounds romantic. When did you come along, then?'

'1914, just before my dad had to join up. He was lucky, he came back.' Rusty paused. 'Only died two years ago, in fact, just after my mum.'

'Ah, Rusty, I'm sorry!' Jess reached over to touch his hand. 'I didn't know you were on your own.'

'It was a bit of a blow, I'll admit, the two of 'em going. I got the house, of course, made a bit of money from the sale, put it into savings. But ... what's a house, Jess? What's money? When you've lost your folks?'

She pressed his hand more firmly, her eyes full of sympathy.

'I know, Rusty, I know what it must have been like for you.'

'Didn't help that I lost my job when the cinema where I worked shut up shop. I think I told you that, didn't I? And I couldn't find anything else locally? Finally, saw an advert for this job in Edinburgh where my dad used to live, and thought I'd go for it – make a fresh start.' Rusty's eyes rested on Jess's face. 'So, there you are. That's my story. Your turn now.'

* * *

63

After some show of unwillingness, Jess finally told of her own short life – her father's early death, her mother's struggle, how she and her sister had still had a reasonably happy life in Leith – and Rusty listened closely. When she'd finished, he nodded, and for a moment pressed her hand.

'Sounds to me like you're a pretty brave family, Jess.'

'We've been luckier than some.'

'Well, you and your folks made the best of things and that's to admire. One piece of luck for you, I think, was having a sister. I've always been sorry I was an only child.'

'Oh, yes, I've got a sister,' she agreed. 'Did we say we were having the fruit tart?'

They were silent until their puddings were brought, when Rusty said gently, 'Am I speaking out of turn, or don't you get on with your sister?'

'She's called Marguerite and very beautiful. So's my mother.'

'Of course they're beautiful – they'll be like you.'

'No, I'm no' fishing for compliments. I'm OK. They're more than that.' Jess glanced swiftly at Rusty. 'And I love them both – I do honestly. But ... well, the thing is ... Marguerite, being older than me, was always more of a companion to Ma, and a help to her, you see. So, they're close ... and I'm ... no' quite so close. Don't think I'm complaining. I mean, they love me, too.'

'I understand, Jess. I can see how it's been.'

They were both silent, concentrating on their fruit tart, until Rusty put his spoon down, pushed back the lock of hair on his brow and made a sign to the waitress.

'As we can't have a drink, Jess, let's at least have coffee and get cheerful, eh?'

'Rusty, I think anyone could be cheerful when you're around,' Jess said sincerely.

When they had settled the bill, which they did quite amicably with Jess paying her share, they had to face the cold again, and it seemed natural that they should walk arm in arm up the High Street.

The heart of the city, Jess told Rusty, for he knew little of its history. Apart from the castle, everything that was old and colourful could be experienced here, and the setts on the road, that the tourists called cobbles, had seen so many feet over the centuries – what tales could they have told?

'Sometime, you'll have to give me a guided tour,' Rusty commented. 'But what shall we do now?'

'Well, it's getting late – think I'd better get back home.'

'Late? Why, the night is young!' His face had fallen, making her feel guilty, which annoyed her. 'We could at least go for a drink, seeing as we couldn't have one with the meal.'

'You mean, to a pub? Are you joking? My mother would shoot me. You know what pubs are like here – no' for women.'

'Sally and Arnold were going to a pub.'

'Well, Sally can probably do what she likes. Ma keeps tabs on me.'

Rusty sighed deeply. 'All right, I'll take you home, then. Don't say I can't come on the train with you, because I'm coming, whatever you say.'

'I'll say, thanks very much,' Jess retorted, repenting of her irritation and laughing. 'It'll be nice to have company.'

Eleven

On the train, he sat close and told her he didn't know Leith at all. His father had lived in the Old Town and that's where his own lodgings were, but Leith was a complete unknown. Still, Jess, as a Leither, would be able to tell him all about it.

'I'm no' a Leither!' she cried. 'I'm an Edinburgh girl. Ma only took the flat where we are now because it was cheaper than where we were. But I love Leith, anyway. Some folk disapprove – say it's all sailors and fallen women – but I say it's exciting and a fine place to live.'

'Another place for you to show me, then. At this rate, I'll soon be an expert on this part of the world.'

'You are half Scottish. It's your world, anyway.'

'I've got two worlds, that's my trouble.'

'You miss England?'

He nodded. 'And my folks. But, it's strange, I do feel an affinity with Scotland. Maybe if I can get to be head projectionist some time, I think I'll settle.'

Jess's eyes widened. 'Head projectionist? Why, that'd mean Ben would have to leave!'

'Wouldn't be the end of the world, would it?'

At the coolness of Rusty's tone, Jess said quickly, 'No, but he's very good, isn't he?'

'And handsome?'

Jess stood up, clutching her bag. 'Train's stopping. We're there.'

'Didn't take long.'

'Won't take long to get to where I live, either. It was nice of you to bring me home, but you needn't have done, you know.'

'Who's talking about need? I wanted to take you home.'

On the short walk to the flat, they didn't attempt to link arms, and it seemed to Jess that Rusty had lost his usual good humour. Had she given herself away? Shown too clearly her dismay at the thought of Ben's leaving? No, she'd recovered very quickly – he couldn't have noticed anything. Still, when they reached her door at the side of Derry Beattie's shop, she stole a quick glance at Rusty and saw that for the first time his face was turned away from her. He was certainly upset.

'This is it,' she said cheerfully. 'This is where I live.'

He stopped in his tracks, staring around at the traffic hurtling along Great Junction Street and the people hurrying by.

'Where?' he asked. 'Where d'you mean?'

'Here, over this greengrocer's. We've got the flat upstairs.'

'Oh, I see.' He looked up at the lighted, curtained windows, and suddenly seemed to relax. 'Over a fruit shop – that's nice.'

'Used to love to look at the apples and oranges,' she told him. 'Used to love to smell all the different fruits and vegetables. Still do, in fact.'

He was looking at her now, smiling down, as she was rapidly trying to decide whether or not she should ask him in. No, she didn't think so. This was only the first time they'd been out, and if she were to bring him up to see her mother and Marguerite, they'd be sure to think he was more than she'd said he was. It was true, it was still not late and she felt bad ending his evening for him, but what could she do?

On a sudden impulse, she reached up and kissed his cheek.

'There you are, Rusty – a colleague's kiss. Goodnight, and thank you for a lovely evening.'

'A colleague's kiss?' he repeated, and took her in his arms. 'Well, here's another.'

Not true, thought Jess, as his mouth met hers in a long, sweet and deliberate kiss. Oh, not true at all! Pulling herself away, she felt a touch of unexpected excitement coursing through her, and was annoyed with him again, that he should have been able to make her feel like that.

'I thought you said you were going to behave yourself in future,' she said coldly. 'We're supposed to be just a couple of colleagues.'

'I was hoping you didn't want just that.' He was winding his scarf around his neck, keeping his eyes on her face. 'I'm sorry, Jess, I couldn't help myself.'

'Yes, well, all right, but I've got to go in now.' The effect of his kiss having now faded, Jess was feeling more in command and admitting to herself that she had been a bit unreasonable. Fellows did like the goodnight kiss, she knew that – it was just that she hadn't expected Rusty to kiss her in that way.

'See you in the morning,' she told him. 'Now, you'd better hurry for your train. Get out of the cold.'

'We'll go out again, won't we?' he asked quickly. 'I haven't been struck off your list?'

'What list?' She laughed. 'OK, we'll go out again. If we can fix it up.'

But when he was walking slowly away and she looked up at what she knew to be the living room window, she thought she could just see a curtain being replaced and a figure move behind it. Marguerite taking a look at Rusty. Letting herself into the stair, Jess ran up to the flat. Talk about being nosey!

'Well, what did you think of him?' she asked at once, as her mother and sister looked up from another card game.

'Who?' Addie asked.

'Rusty, of course. I saw you peeping, Marguerite!'

'Heard your voices, couldn't resist it,' Marguerite answered blandly. 'Seemed a lovely guy, from what I could tell.'

'Yes, he's very nice. Tall and handsome.'

'Tall and handsome and very nice,' Addie repeated with a smile. 'But still no' for you?'

'No' for me,' Jess agreed.

Twelve

As autumn slowly turned to winter, things at the Princes were going well. Perhaps because people were easier in their minds after the Munich agreement and felt more like going out, ticket sales were up, which meant the staff, too, were relaxed, and even optimistic about the future.

Trevor, the organist, outdid himself, playing his popular tunes, while the cafe was always full, and the usherettes couldn't keep up with the demand for ice cream, which Jess had to keep on ordering. As for Mr Hawthorne himself, he was in a perpetually good mood, much given to praising everybody, particularly Jess, who was fast becoming, as Sally described it, his 'blue-eyed girl'.

'Honestly, I think if he could promote you somehow or other, he would,' she told Jess, who only looked at her with widening eyes.

'Promote me? Whatever are you talking about, Sally? I'm no' looking to do your job, when you're the best there is!'

70

'Hey, listen to us!' Sally cried, with one of her chuckles. 'Are we the mutual admiration society, or what? But I don't mean he wants to put you in my job – I just think he'd like to make you his assistant. Get you to help with the budgeting and cash handling and all his chores, because he's got no help, you ken.'

'How about Edie?'

'She's fine for what she does – secretarial and that – but she's got no head for figures. She'd run a mile from a budget!'

'He could do with an assistant, then,' Jess said slowly, her mind fixed on new and dizzying prospects. 'But there's no such post, is there?'

'Afraid not.' Sally tapped Jess's arm. 'But you could always try for something at one of the big cinemas, after you've been here a bit. I tell you, you're a natural for running things, and George would give you a good reference.'

'Try for another cinema?' Jess cried, scandalized. 'Sally, I'd never leave the Princes! This is where I want to be.'

'Ah, that's nice, dear. But you're ambitious, eh? Got to go where the work is.'

'Somebody leaving?' asked a voice that could always send Jess's heart fluttering, and she couldn't help blushing slightly as Ben Daniel looked in at the box office, a smile in his dark brown eyes, a cigarette at his lip sending smoke over his fine dark head. 'Not you, Sally, is it?'

'No, no, Ben, I'm staying put. I'm just telling Jess here that she should maybe think of trying for a better job sometime. No need to stay in the box office.'

71

'It's a piece of nonsense!' Jess cried. 'I haven't been here five minutes!'

Ben's eyes moved to her and he nodded. 'But you've got potential,' he said quietly. 'Didn't I say you'd be going places? Climbing the ladder?'

'I like it here.'

'Ah, now, would that be because of a certain young man not a million miles away?'

Oh, no! Jess froze. Oh, no, he'd seen her with Rusty! The very thing she hadn't wanted to happen!

No wonder he hadn't made a move to be more than friendly towards her, then. Like Sally and others, he thought Rusty was her young man, which he was not and never would be. Why, she'd only agreed to meet him now and again because she felt sorry for him, all alone in a strange city. And they'd only walked in the parks, or by the Water of Leith on Sunday afternoons which were free to them in a way the evenings usually weren't. There was nothing between them – nothing! But she could tell from the smile on Ben's face, which was a replica of the smile on Sally's, that she'd be wasting her breath saying so.

All the same, she had to speak.

'If you mean Rusty, we are just good friends,' she managed to bring out coolly, though the deepening flush on her cheeks did nothing to change the smiles on the watchers' faces.

'We believe you!' Sally cried happily. 'Thousands wouldn't. Ben, shouldn't you be in your box? We're going to be opening any minute.'

'On my way. Just had to snatch a smoke.' He grinned. 'Good film this week by the way – comedy with Katharine Hepburn and Cary Grant.'

'Oh, I know, and I love those screwball films!' Sally glanced at Jess. 'You should do your famous nipping up to the circle, dear, and give yourself a treat.'

'I have to check the ice cream,' Jess answered and, without looking again at Ben, left the box office.

'She doesn't like you to say Rusty's her young man,' Sally whispered. 'Don't ask me why.'

'I never said he was,' Ben replied. 'Got an ashtray round here? I'd better dash.'

On her way back to the box office, her face blank, her thoughts whirling, Jess heard her name called and swung round to see Pam Gregg approaching from the cafe.

'Hello, there, Jess! Mrs Baxter's got me doing the rounds for Nancy.' Pam shook a small box and grinned. 'Like to contribute to her leaving present?'

'Nancy's leaving?' Jess was remembering the young waitress, Nancy Scott. 'Oh, yes, she's getting married, eh? Come back to the box office, Pam, I'll have to get my bag.'

'Is Sally there?'

'Yes, just for the afternoon.'

'Good, I'll catch her, too.'

A waitress's post going at the cinema cafe? For a moment or two, Jess wondered if Marguerite might be interested. No, it wasn't likely. She'd

73

have to work evenings, which would not appeal – hours at the teashop were much shorter. Still, she would mention it, Jess decided, just in case, and scrabbling in her bag for something to give Pam, managed to avoid Sally's still knowing gaze.

'When's the interview?' she asked Pam, who said she wasn't sure.

'But it'll be some time in December. Nancy's wedding's at the end of the month.' Pam shook her head. 'We're going to miss her so much, you ken. Just hope we can get someone we all like.'

'You girls and Joan Baxter can get on with anyone,' Sally said comfortingly. 'And Joan'll pick the right lassie, never fear.'

Who wouldn't be Marguerite, Jess thought, as Fred arrived to open the doors. Because she wouldn't want the job, anyway.

When Rusty came loping in to see her in his break that evening, Jess wasted no time in buttonholing him.

'Rusty, did you tell Ben we were going out sometimes?'

'Ben? No!' Rusty's grey eyes sparkled with irritation. 'Why should I? What the hell has it got to do with him?'

'Nothing, only he seems to know.'

'No secret, is it?'

Jess, turning to attend to a customer, made no reply. 'So, it is a secret?' Rusty pressed, when she was free. 'Look, why are you so upset? Has Ben said something?'

'He made some silly remark.'

'He's not usually silly.'

'He was teasing – the way people do.'

'And you minded?'

'It's just that I don't want him – I mean anyone – to get the wrong idea.'

For a long moment, Rusty stood looking down at her, his eyes so strangely cold, his mouth a straight hard line.

'Sorry going for a few walks with me has got you so worried,' he said curtly. 'Now, I have to get back.'

'Rusty!' she called after him, but he was already moving swiftly across the foyer, as an irate man began tapping coins on the glass wall of the box office.

'Two front stalls, miss, WHEN you're ready!'

'I'm sorry, sir.'

'Shouldn't be rowing with your fella when you're at work, you know.'

'Two front stalls,' Jess said icily as she handed him his tickets. 'And your change. Thank you, sir.'

'Thank YOU!' he cried, glancing with satisfaction at the woman by his side.

Good job Mr H. hadn't seen that little exchange, Jess thought grimly. Couldn't see him wanting to promote her after something like that. Hadn't been her day, had it? But, for sure, it wasn't the customers' fault. Big smile, Jess, she told herself, and was rewarded by surprised smiles from the next couple buying tickets.

At home, her bad day over, Jess remembered to mention the cinema cafe job to Marguerite,

75

being quick to add that she'd probably not be interested, seeing as there'd be evening work.

'Who says I won't be interested?' Marguerite asked. 'I was just saying to Ma the other day that I could do with a change.'

'That's right,' Addie put in. 'And you can get stale, doing the same job, day in, day out.'

'Maybe I'll apply, then.' Marguerite turned thoughtful blue eyes on Jess. 'When's the interview?'

'Probably early December. I could ask Mrs Baxter, the lady who runs the cafe. She's a widow – very nice, very capable.'

'So, could you find out how much they're paying and what the hours are, as well? I'm thinking I might well try for it.'

'I'm no' sure it'll be your cup of tea,' Jess said uneasily. She was beginning to wonder if she really wanted her sister working so close. 'I think the wages are the same as you're getting now, but then there'll be the longer hours. Everybody's very free and easy, as well.'

'You're saying I'm no' free and easy? I can fit in anywhere, if I want to.' Marguerite gave a little laugh. 'And this might be my chance to meet some rich Edinburgh chap, eh? Never see one in The Galleon Tea Rooms, I can tell you!'

'Well, if you do go for interview, don't wear your pale grey two-piece, will you? The one you let me borrow?'

'Have you forgotten? It's winter. I'll be wearing my navy-blue woollen suit with a coat on top.' Marguerite smiled. 'Who'd remember that grey two-piece, anyway?'

Thirteen

Christmas loomed and after Jess had organized the decorations for the cinema – tinsel, holly and paper streamers – she asked Sally if they weren't going to have a staff party? Dobson's had always had a do in the back room, with food and drink and a two-piece band for dancing.

'Can't run to that,' Sally told her. 'And it's no' easy, getting everybody together, with the evening working and that. What George likes to do is just have us all up to his office for a drink at lunchtime on Christmas Eve, when there's no matinee.'

'And we all bring something to eat?'

'No, no, dear, Daisy Hawthorne brings sandwiches and a Christmas cake. She's very good about that.'

'I'll look forward to it, then.'

'Aye, and you'll be looking forward to having your sister here after Hogmanay, eh?' Sally shook her head. 'What a lovely girl! Joan Baxter said she couldn't resist giving her Nancy's job, even though she's a wee bit old.'

'Yes, it'll be nice,' Jess agreed. 'Having Marguerite working in the cafe.'

Nice. Well, she hoped so. As soon as Marguerite had said she'd try for the job, Jess had

77

known she'd get it. Who'd turn her down? It must have been plain from the moment she slipped off her coat and strolled into the interview in her navy blue suit, that she was going to add something special to the cinema cafe, and Mrs Baxter would have been bowled over, as people always were.

Whether or not Marguerite would get on with Pam and the other waitresses remained to be seen. Jess had her suspicions that some of her sister's colleagues at the Galleon had been rather resentful of her manner, as well as envious of her looks, but maybe things would be different at the Princes. Just as long as she, Jess, didn't get involved. After all, she wasn't responsible for her sister.

It was some time since she and Rusty had met outside work. After his show of hostility, he had recovered enough to be friendly when he saw her, but had not asked her to walk with him again – a sign, she guessed, that he'd been deeply hurt by her aim to keep their meetings secret. Although she was still anxious not to let Ben see them together, she felt bad about hurting Rusty, and wished there was something she could do to make it up to him. With Christmas fast approaching, it came to her.

'Rusty, could I have a word?' she asked, when she saw him in his break one afternoon, smoking a cigarette in the foyer.

'Any time,' he answered politely.

'I was wondering ... if you're no' doing anything for Christmas dinner, would you like to have it with us? Ma and my sister and me?'

A flush rose to his cheekbones and his eyes grew wintry.

'This you feeling sorry for me, Jess? Thanks, but I think I'll have to say no.'

'You've got other plans?' she asked, her own cheeks colouring at his tone.

'No, but I'll be OK. Don't worry about me.'

'Oh, come on, Rusty! If you're no' doing anything else, you could come to us? We'd all be happy if you did.'

'I've never even met your mother, or your sister.'

'Well, you'll be meeting Marguerite soon. She's coming to work at the cafe.' Jess put her hand on his thin arm. 'Please, Rusty, it's Christmas, eh? Don't be mad at me.'

'You're so keen to have me say I'll come,' he said with a short laugh. 'Just as long as I don't tell Ben about it, eh?'

Her face now crimson, Jess turned away.

'It's all right,' she said, her voice shaking. 'You needn't come. I'm sorry I asked you.'

As she walked rapidly back to the box office, he made no move to stop her, only drew hard on his cigarette, then stubbed it out, and left the foyer.

'Oh dear, got a cold?' a young man asked, seeing Jess's eyes filling with tears as she gave him his ticket for *The Adventures of Robin Hood*, the Christmas attraction. He laughed. 'Or is it a case of "Smoke gets in your Eyes"?'

'I don't smoke,' Jess retorted. 'That'll be one shilling, please.'

79

*   *   *

Christmas Eve found the staff of the Princes gathering in Mr Hawthorne's office, their eyes lighting up at the sight of bottles and glasses and a large, iced cake, flanked by plates of sandwiches and mince pies.

'Come in, come in!' the manager cried genially, cigarette in hand. 'Bit of a squash, but you won't mind that. Daisy, my dear, pass the sandwiches, while I do the drinks.'

Daisy Hawthorne, thin as a stick, with a lined little face and pale hair dressed in pin curls, fluttered around as people took plates.

'I've made cheese and tomato, egg and tomato, ham and mustard ... oh dear, what else?'

'They're all lovely, dear,' Sally told her, as Edie Harrison, the secretary nodded approvingly. 'But don't I always say you shouldn't go to so much trouble?'

'Come on, girls, what can I pass you?' Ben Daniel was politely asking the usherettes, and nodding to Jess. 'How about you, Jess? Ham and chutney?'

Jess, who'd been carefully avoiding eye contact with Rusty standing nearby, turned with alacrity to help herself from the plate Ben was holding. How smart he was looking! So often seen in shirtsleeves, he'd obviously taken special trouble for the drinks and put on a dark jacket and tie. Seemed more than ever a second Henry Fonda.

Rusty, too, had made an effort to dress smartly, but the way Jess felt at the moment, that was of no interest. Yet, when plump and cheerful Mrs

80

Baxter came to him with a piled up plate, Jess felt absurdly relieved. She didn't really want him to be alone and out of things, and after Mrs Baxter told him to take two of her sandwiches, and three would be better, Jess was glad he did. And that he smiled.

'Eat up, laddie, eat up! Put some weight on. My word, if you stand sideways, nobody can see you!' Mrs Baxter laughed heartily. 'No' like me, eh?'

'Fred, what are you having?' Mr Hawthorne cried. 'I bet you're ready for a top-up, eh?'

'Wouldnae say no, Mr Hawthorne, thanks,' Fred said, allowing his glass to be refilled and swiping another sandwich from Mrs B's plate as she moved on. 'Och, it's nice to think o' having tomorrow off, eh? No' everybody does, you ken. Some folks work Christmas and take Hogmanay.' He grinned. 'Me, I like both!'

'Rusty's looking rather glum these days,' Ben said in a low voice to Jess. 'What have you been doing to him?'

'I told you there was nothing between us,' she answered promptly, glad of this chance to make things clear again. 'You didn't believe me, but it's true.'

'No wonder the poor devil's so sad, then. Listen, are you ready for a mince pie? Or are you waiting for the cake?'

'Oh, the cake, I think.' Jess's heart was singing, as they moved to watch Daisy nervously wielding the knife on her handiwork. 'Are you all set for Christmas, Ben? Going away or anything?'

'Just spending it with my dad. How about you?'

'Having a quiet time, with my mother and my sister.'

'This the one who's coming to work in the cafe? That'll be nice for you. Excuse me, if I just pass these pies around for Mrs H.'

'Last Christmas, Nancy was here,' Pam murmured, as Jess moved to speak to her. 'Funny to think of her on her honeymoon, eh? And now your sister's got her job.'

'Marguerite's looking forward to coming,' Jess said quickly. 'I'm sure she'll fit in.'

'Aye, but she's that good looking, eh? We were thinking she might've been married by now. Bet she's had her chances.'

'Not found the right one yet.'

As Renie MacLeish came up, carrying a large slice of Christmas cake, Jess turned to her with some relief. Hearing Pam speak of Marguerite had only reinforced her own worries about her sister's move to the cinema cafe. But she must just put it out of her mind, she told herself, it wasn't her problem. And laughed readily, when Pam said if Renie had tried really hard she might have found a bigger piece of cake, eh? And clapped, when Renie retorted that having seen the number of mince pies Pam had put away, she couldn't afford to point the finger.

'So, why is there no mistletoe around this year, I want to know?' Renie went on to ask, taking a bite of her cake. 'I was that looking forward to catching Ben Daniel, you ken, but I canna just go up without an excuse, eh?'

Catching Ben Daniel? Jess's heart gave a leap. She'd never thought of such a thing for herself, but if other girls were going around kissing – why not?

'Why not?' asked Pam, seeming to echo her thought. 'It's Christmas, after all. I was thinking of catching Rusty – if that'd be OK with you, Jess?'

'Why shouldn't it be?' Jess asked, suddenly having to remember him, the effect of her words somewhat spoiled by Rusty suddenly appearing at her side and asking if she could spare a moment? Ignoring the smiles of Pam and Renie, Jess, her face expressionless, shrugged and followed him to a corner of the room.

'What is it, then?' she asked sharply. 'Something else I've done to upset you?'

'Jess, I'm sorry. I don't know what's got into me lately – and at Christmas, as well. Can you forgive me?'

At the look of contrition in his eyes, she had relented already and put her hand on his arm. 'Rusty, I'm the one should be asking that. I made you feel bad, and I'm sorry.'

'You asked me to your home, and I didn't even thank you.' He lowered his voice. 'I suppose, it's too late, is it? To do that now?'

'Would you still like to come?'

'Is the offer still open? Your mother won't mind?'

'Sure, the offer's still open. And Ma will be pleased to see you. So will Marguerite.'

A smile lit his face.

'I'll come, then, and be glad to – thanks, Jess.

83

Thanks very much.'

At the sound of someone tapping a spoon for attention, they turned to see Ben standing by the manager and his wife and preparing to make a speech. Just a few words of thanks, for the Christmas drinks and excellent food, and would Mr and Mrs Hawthorne accept the wine and chocolates the staff would like to give them?

'You bet!' cried George, as Daisy blushed and lowered her eyes, and the round of applause brought the little staff party to a close.

'And I never got to kiss Ben Daniel,' Renie sighed, as she helped to gather up plates. 'Next year I bring my own mistletoe, eh?'

Me, too, thought Jess. But will I have to wait so long?

'If we're all here next year,' tall, blonde Faith Pringle murmured. 'They say there still might be a war, you know.'

'No, no, we've got peace in our time,' Edna Angus told her. 'Is that no' right, Mr Hawthorne?'

'Sure it is, Edna!' he answered robustly. 'We'll all hang on to that. Merry Christmas, everybody! Just the evening performance to go now, then you get your day off.'

'See you tomorrow?' Rusty whispered to Jess, and she smiled and nodded, determined not to spoil her good intentions of giving him a pleasant Christmas by wishing Ben might have been there too.

Fourteen

The Raeburns didn't have turkey for Christmas dinner – too big, too dear – but Addie roasted a splendid piece of pork with the sort of crackling Rusty sighed over with such pleasure, the women at the table couldn't help laughing.

Afterwards, there was a rich plum pudding – the same, Addie told them, as she'd made for her ladies at the club. 'Though of course they had to have it early,' she added. 'Seeing as we close down for the Christmas holidays.'

'So, what do the ladies do then?' Rusty asked.

'Och, we've very few who stay and they move out somewhere. The others have all got homes – just like to get out of 'em, the way their husbands do, at the New Club and such.' Addie laughed. 'And why not, eh? They come in, read the papers, have a chat and a nice meal – puts the time in for 'em. They've no jobs, of course.'

'I'd die of boredom without a job,' Jess declared. 'I'm glad I wouldn't have to give up work if ever I got married, like teachers and civil servants have to do. I think that's so unfair.'

'The best thing for me about getting married would be giving up work,' Marguerite said with a smile. 'Reading the papers, having a chat and a nice meal – what could be better?'

'What a shame you've to start work at the cafe next week, then,' Jess commented. 'Might get a nice meal, but you'll be too busy to read the papers.'

'Might meet my husband, eh?'

'Might indeed,' Rusty remarked, resting his gaze on Marguerite's lovely face, at which Jess leaped up and said they should clear away and go out for a walk while it was still light.

'Well, no' to the Shore,' Addie protested. 'I like the Links.'

'All right, as you did all the cooking, Ma, we'll do what you want and go to the Links,' Jess told her. 'Rusty, I'll give you another history lesson. Plenty of history about the Links.'

Although the wide spaces of the Links were now mainly devoted to parkland where folk could stroll or play football or cricket, long ago, as Jess described to Rusty, they'd been the scenes of many different activities. Fighting the English for one. Inventing golf for another, for in the eighteenth century, a company of Edinburgh golfers had there played the first competition golf in the world. Aye, and worked out the rules of the game even before the famous Royal and Ancient club in St Andrews. Now had Rusty known that?

'No,' he answered, smiling, as Addie and Marguerite walked ahead, well wrapped up against the wind and the chill. 'I don't know one thing about any of this. How come, if you're not a Leither, you know so much?'

'I like to find out about places, and Leith is my place now.' She took his arm in hers. 'Listen,

I'm so glad you came today, Rusty. And Ma was thrilled having another one to cook for.'

'It's been one of my best Christmases,' he said seriously. 'I can't tell you how grateful I am. Your mother made me so welcome – your sister, too.'

He hesitated, his eyes still on the two women walking ahead. 'Jess, mind if I tell you something?'

'Depends what it is.'

'It's a compliment. To you.'

'With those two around?'

'Specially with them. They're just as you said – lovely looking women. But, Jess, so are you. Lovely, and different.'

'Different, aye, that's true.'

'No, hear me out. You keep comparing yourself with your mother and sister, but you've got something else – a real warmth, a real interest in everything. You're the sort of person folk want to be with.'

'Oh, come on...'

'No, I mean it. And look, I'm not saying your mother's not sympathetic or warm-hearted. I can see she's really kind and friendly – look how she welcomed me today – but you have this gift of relating to people and places, which I think is ... well, more important than ... anything.'

'You were going to say looks, weren't you?'

'No! Why won't you believe me? You're just as nice looking as your folks.'

'Just different.'

As Jess's laughter floated away on the wind, Rusty groaned and shook his head.

'Ah, you're hopeless, Jess! You don't listen to a word I say.'

'Let's call the others and go back now. I could do with a cup of tea and a piece of Ma's Christmas cake.'

When evening came and Rusty had thanked Addie again for his truly grand day and she'd thanked him for the flowers he'd brought, Jess went with him to the station. There was such a pleasant affinity between them by then, she was truly glad she'd invited him to her home and was quite sorry to see him go. Also surprised, perhaps, that he didn't ask if they might meet again outside work, but in a way relieved. Best not to get too involved again.

After his train came in and they'd kissed briefly on the platform, she waved him away and walked slowly back to the flat, her thoughts turning to Ben. What sort of a Christmas Day had he had, she wondered, and began to feel a deliciously warm anticipation of seeing him again, when they opened up the cinema for Boxing Day.

Fifteen

Two days after Hogmanay, Marguerite began her new job at the cinema cafe.

'I'll pop in to see you before the matinee,' Jess told her, as her sister prepared to leave the flat that morning. 'Just to see how you're getting on.'

'Thanks, but there's no need for that. I have done some waiting on before, you know.'

'Oh, sure, but first days are difficult, eh? And I could show you round and introduce you to folk.'

'Honestly, Jess, anyone'd think you were in charge!'

'That's Jess for you,' Addie put in, nodding sagely as she buttoned up her heavy winter coat. 'She'll end up running something or other, mark my words. Marguerite, good luck, pet. Not that you need it, eh? You're another that knows what she's doing. Why've I got such clever daughters?'

'Because you're clever yourself, Ma,' Jess responded. 'Look out for me, Marguerite – and take care on the black ice.'

'Oh, stop your fussing!' her sister cried, laughing, though a little irritated. 'It's no great thing, is it? Starting work at the Princes.'

'It was for me,' said Jess.

Clearly, Marguerite was different from her, for when Jess entered the cafe later, no one could have seemed more composed than her sister on her first day, as she moved tranquilly around, setting out cutlery and glasses for the lunch tables. And, of course, looking delightful, in a slim-fitting black dress with a little band of muslin pinned to her shining hair and a matching frilly apron that might have come straight from a musical comedy.

It was no wonder, Jess thought, sighing, that the brows of the watching waitresses – Pam, Ruthie and Kate – were somewhat furrowed, while Mrs Baxter's was so beautifully clear, no doubt because she was already regarding Marguerite as an asset she'd been lucky enough to catch. In fact, she said as much to Jess as she gave her a coffee at the counter.

'Come to see your sister, dear? Heavens, she's a find, eh? The Galleon's loss is our gain, and no mistake.'

'I don't see why she's so wonderful,' Pam murmured. 'No offence, Jess, but what can she do that the rest of us can't?'

'I suppose she is very experienced,' Ruthie, bright-eyed and dark-haired, remarked. 'I mean, there she is, setting the tables and we're no' even helping.'

'Should be experienced,' Kate, a very young redhead, said tartly. 'Why, she's years older than us!'

'Ssh, now,' Mrs Baxter said sharply. 'Jess doesn't want to hear you discussing her sister

90

like that. And it's time you others were helping her, anyway!'

'It's all right, Mrs Baxter,' Pam retorted. 'She's finished.'

'Why, Jess, there you are,' Marguerite said with a smile, as she came swaying up to the counter. 'Come to check up on me?'

'That'd hardly be my job,' Jess returned swiftly. 'Mrs Baxter here's the one for that.'

'I've already said that she's doing very well,' Mrs Baxter said firmly. 'We've had a very good training session here this morning and Marguerite's picked it all up in a flash, no trouble at all. Now we're ready for the lunches, but I'll just go and check in the kitchen with Maisie.'

'All right if I show Marguerite round the cinema?' Jess asked. 'Introduce her to people?'

'Oh, yes, there'll be time for that before we open. Girls, Jess is going to show Marguerite around. You carry on, all right?'

'All right, Mrs Baxter,' the waitresses chorused, as the manageress left them, while Marguerite looked at Jess.

'Will I be OK in my apron? Looks a bit silly, eh? We'd nothing like it at the Galleon.'

'You'll be fine,' Jess was beginning, when the swing door of the cafe opened, and her colour changed. It was Ben who was coming through, smiling at her in his usual way and waving a hand to the waitresses who were waving back.

'Look who's here!' called Pam. 'Want a coffee, Ben?'

'Feeling frail then, Ben, after Hogmanay?'

91

Ruthie asked cheekily.

'Better have it black, eh?' Kate suggested.

He laughed. 'No coffee. At least, not yet. I'm treating myself to lunch today, so don't forget the discount.'

He was still laughing as his eyes moved from Jess to Marguerite, who'd been standing quietly to one side, listening to the badinage, but then his laughter died.

'Ben, this is my sister,' Jess said quickly. 'Taking over from Nancy, you remember? Marguerite, this is Ben Daniel, the head projectionist.'

'Rusty's boss?' Marguerite asked, putting out her hand, which, after a moment's hesitation, Ben took and held.

'You've met Rusty, then?' he asked, clearing his throat.

'Jess asked him over for Christmas.'

'Very nice.'

'He'd nowhere to go,' Jess put in, her eyes glued to her sister's hand still clasped in Ben's.

And then she half closed her eyes as Ben finally let Marguerite's hand go, and the question came into her mind that was to echo and keep on echoing: What have I done?

What had she done? She'd told her sister about the vacancy at the cafe. She'd opened a door she hadn't even thought about, and Marguerite had gone through and met Ben. Or he'd met her, for it was plain to see that interest was flowing from him in a great rushing tide, while Marguerite was as composed as before, standing, watching, as still and beautiful as an expensive flower.

A silence had fallen on the cafe, with the

waitresses watching too, and seeing all too well what was happening, even if Marguerite seemed quite unaware. But then she'd had a lot of practice in acting out this part, thought Jess, who knew that she must put on an act herself, must at all costs conceal the anxiety that was rising within her.

'Ben, I was just going to show my sister round the cinema,' she said huskily. 'Will you excuse us?'

'Round the cinema?' he repeated, gradually regaining his own composure, though his deeply set dark eyes never left Marguerite's face. 'Why I could do that, Jess. Be glad to, in fact. Your sister might like to see the projection room.'

'But you're going to have lunch, aren't you? You'll no' have time to show her round.'

'I'm not worried about lunch.' He smiled briefly. 'I've eaten too much over Hogmanay, anyway.'

'Please don't trouble yourself, Mr Daniel, Jess will show me round,' Marguerite said quietly.

He hesitated, finally standing aside to let her pass with Jess. 'OK, fine. We'll leave it like that. But it was nice to meet you, Miss Raeburn. Do hope you'll be very happy here.'

'Thank you.' She turned to smile. 'And my name's Marguerite.'

'Marguerite,' he repeated softly. 'Please call me Ben.'

'Wait here a second, will you, Jess?' Marguerite murmured, as she and Jess progressed through the foyer. 'I think I will take off this apron – the

93

cap as well, if you can call it a cap.'

'What did you think of Rusty's boss, then?' Jess couldn't resist asking, as her eyes went unseeingly over the portraits of the stars lining the walls.

'Very nice chap. Charming, in fact.'

'Some folk think he's good looking.'

'Oh, he is. Tall, dark and handsome, I'd say. Reminds me of somebody.' Marguerite put her apron and cap over her arm and smoothed her hair. 'Some actor, I think.'

'Which actor?'

'Laurence Olivier? Could be him. When's his new film coming, Jess? *Wuthering Heights* – I'd really like to see that.'

'No' before the spring.'

Jess, marvelling at her own ability to appear just as usual before her sister, opened the door to the little staffroom where two of the usherettes were having a cup of tea before opening time. 'Girls, this is my sister, come to work at the cafe. Marguerite, meet Renie and Faith.'

So far, so good. But, as the young women exchanged smiles and chatted, Jess's mind was wandering. Maybe she'd got it wrong. Seen something that wasn't there? Ben had certainly been struck by her sister's looks, but then so many men were and it didn't always mean that they'd fallen in love, did it? Surely, it was too soon to believe that Ben had fallen for Marguerite, just like that?

All right, it happened. Love at first sight. 'Needn't take long, to know what you feel,' Sally had once remarked, and it might be that

94

what Ben was feeling was written all over his face. Or maybe not. Why should Jess make herself miserable when she didn't really know the truth of the matter?

Her spirits rising, she took her sister's arm and said they'd better continue their little tour; she'd to prepare for the matinee and Marguerite had to return to the Princes cafe, to serve lunches for the first time.

'Lovely to meet you!' cried Renie, as they went on their way.

'And you!' Marguerite called, and Jess glancing at her, couldn't help envying her ease of manner, her peace of mind. For though Jess had managed for a little while to look on the bright side, now the tide of anxiety was rising again and as she continued to show her sister around, she couldn't forget the look on Ben's face when she'd first introduced Marguerite.

After Trevor Duffy, Fred Boyle and Edie Harrison had all met the new waitress, and there'd been smiles and chat and admiring stares, even Mr Hawthorne came out of his office to shake Marguerite's hand and wish her all the best in her new job.

'Grand to have another Miss Raeburn at the Princes,' he told her. 'Don't know if you know it, but your sister's a treasure.'

'Oh, I know it, Mr Hawthorne,' Marguerite said with a smile. 'I'll just have to do what I can to live up to her.'

'We'd better go,' Jess said uncomfortably. 'Time's getting on.'

'Now, when have you ever been late for any-thing?' the manager asked cheerfully. 'But we'll let you go. All the best again, Marguerite – hope we may call you that?'

'Please do,' she said, with a serene smile, while to the watching Jess, it seemed incredible that her sister seemed to be paying as much attention to Mr Hawthorne as to Ben Daniel. Was she really not interested in him, then? Perhaps that in itself might be hopeful? That Ben, whatever his feelings, might get nowhere?

Oh, but what good would that do Jess? As she opened up the box office and prepared to greet the first picture-goers of the afternoon, she saw, clear-sightedly enough, that it would do her no good at all. Why would he turn to her, because her sister had turned him down? Love wasn't something you could just shunt around from one person to another, was it?

If it were, though? If by any chance Ben's love, unwanted by Marguerite, did come her way – would she take it?

Oh, yes, sighed Jess, giving a man his tickets for *The Adventures of Robin Hood*, which had been retained for another week by popular de-mand. But then she turned for comfort to her earlier hope, that Ben might not be as attracted to her sister as she feared.

And that got her through the rest of the day, and even most of the night.

Sixteen

For the next few days, Jess watched like a hawk to see if Ben hung around the cafe, or if Marguerite went up to the projection room. Nothing happened. Ben was not seen around the cafe, Marguerite paid no visits to the projection room. As far as Jess could tell, the two of them had not met since they'd shaken hands on Marguerite's first day at the Princes.

What a relief! But, of course, Jess couldn't relax her vigilance. At any time, things could change. Sometimes, she wondered if it might help to discuss the matter with Rusty, but the idea had no sooner come into her mind than she dismissed it. Of course she couldn't discuss Ben with Rusty! He'd be far too hurt. Even when she did ask casually if Ben had given Marguerite his little talk on film projection, it had been enough for Rusty to raise his eyebrows and wonder why she was interested.

'Oh, no reason,' she'd answered swiftly. 'Only he does like to do that talk for new staff.'

'Not waitresses,' Rusty had declared. 'They'd hardly need to know the workings of the cinema. But wouldn't Marguerite have mentioned it, anyway?'

'Maybe not,' Jess replied, wondering – why

97

wouldn't she? Unless it had meant something.

Though seeming her usual keen and efficient self to most people, Jess wasn't altogether surprised when sharp-eyed Sally asked her once when they were on duty together if everything was all right.

'How d'you mean?' Jess asked, playing for time.

'Well, you know what I mean, dear. You've been so ... well, what shall I say? Jumpy, eh? Looking around a lot, not settling.'

'Jumpy? I wouldn't say that. I'm fine. Why would I be jumpy?'

'You tell me. No' something to do with your sister, is it?'

'Marguerite? No. I don't really see much of her, seeing as she works in the cafe. Anyway, there's nothing wrong. I don't know what you're on about.'

'She seems to be doing very well in her new job,' Sally said cheerfully. 'A great attraction, I'd say. Puts the others in the shade, eh?'

'The others are pretty enough themselves.'

'Oh, sure they are. No' the ones the men are after, though.'

'What men?'

'The ones that come in the cafe, of course. And then there's our dear Ben.'

Jess sat very still, concentrating every part of her being on not showing the effect of Sally's words.

'Ben?' she repeated casually. 'What's he been up to?

'Didn't waste much time, apparently, making a play for your sister. Pam says he walks her to the station every night, soon as they close. Has done from the start.' Sally's gaze was bright on Jess's averted face. 'Did Marguerite never say?'

'Don't suppose she thought it was important.'

'I'm no' so sure. Pam thinks she likes him. Seemingly, she's quick enough to give fellows the message, if she doesn't.'

'That's true,' Jess agreed. 'But fancy her – liking Ben.'

'Fancy,' Sally murmured. She gave a little sigh. 'Well, if you're OK, Jess, that's good. That's a relief. I did wonder if you might be maybe worrying about the war.'

'The war? I thought there wasn't going to be one.'

'Some folk are beginning to think that bit of paper Mr Chamberlain had doesn't mean a thing.'

'How can they know that?'

'Arnold says nobody should trust Herr Hitler. He's planning world domination. Everybody under the jackboot, Arnold says.'

'We'll just have to hope he's wrong, then.'

'He's never wrong,' Sally declared.

Late that night, when Jess and Marguerite were preparing for bed, Jess resolved to speak. She had watched closely when her sister had arrived home from work. Had seen a delicate flush on her cheeks and a sparkle in her eyes, for which something more than the January cold might have been responsible. Had known the time had

99

come to face the truth, whatever it was, for until it was known, she, Jess, couldn't learn to live with it. Live with it? Oh, God, how easy that was to say!

'Marguerite, know what Sally told me today?' she asked, after she'd seen her sister climb into bed, clinging with shudders to her hot water bottle.

'All I know is that it's freezing in here,' Marguerite returned. 'Oh, these sheets are icy!'

'It is January, eh? We'll probably have snow by morning.' Jess was trying to hug her own hot water bottle that was stone and kept slipping from her grasp. 'Well, listen – Sally said Pam had told her that Ben Daniel was taking you to the station every time you worked late. I never knew that.'

'What of it?' Marguerite had now pulled the bed clothes to her chin.

'I'm just interested, that's all. Seemingly, he's keen.'

'Just says it's on his way.'

'He's going out of his way. He lives in Canon-mills.'

'All right, so he wants to take me to the station. Can we go to sleep now? I'm tired, Jess. I've had a long day.'

'I just want to say, if you start going out with him, I hope you don't ... hurt him. It'd be a shame. He's nice, we all like him.'

'Hurt him?' Marguerite sat up, staring at Jess through the darkness. 'Who says I'm going to hurt him? I like him, too. As a matter of fact, he's asked me to go out on Sunday and I've said

I will.' She lay down again with a thump. 'And I've no plans to break his heart, if that's what you're on about. Goodnight, Jess.'

'Goodnight, Marguerite.'

While her sister soon began to breathe regularly in sleep, Jess lay wide awake, feeling as chilled inside as the air around her bed. It seemed to her that she would never be warm again. Never have the hope again for a future that had been her comfort. Ben had been a dream, she saw that now; no more real than his shadow on the silver screen. He would never be hers, never come alive for her. Only for Marguerite.

How was she to accept that? As the long hours crawled by, it didn't seem possible. Only slowly did it come to her that whatever she'd lost, she still had work. She still had the Princes. All right, she worked in the box office, but she wouldn't always work there. There was a ladder, wasn't there? And she would climb it. Maybe then, she could forget Ben.

Having seen this small light at the end of her tunnel, she felt better. Even slept for a little while. But when she rose the next morning, there were tears in her eyes. Tears she must never let anyone see. Least of all, Marguerite.

Seventeen

It didn't take long for those at the Princes to spot that Ben Daniel and Marguerite Raeburn, the new waitress, were in love. Wasn't difficult, was it? Seeing as they weren't trying to keep it a secret. Seeing as they were always meeting up, in spite of having separate jobs. Always looking at each other, smiling fond smiles, touching hands. Always walking off, arm in arm, into the night – well, to the station – at the end of work, and no doubt kissing on the platform. Would it all end in tears? Or wedding bells? Some looked at Jess for an answer, but how would she know? Anyway, she never said anything.

'Ah, they're so sweet,' Sally would sigh. 'So lovely to see folk so happy!'

Though the girls at the cafe sighed over losing the fancy-free Ben, most at the Princes agreed with her, just as long as it all worked out, which as the weeks went by, seemed likely.

From only walking to the station together, the happy pair began to go out whenever they could arrange the same evening off, sometimes going for a meal, sometimes to the theatre, sometimes even to other cinemas, where they could sit entwined on the back row and be sure no one they knew was watching. Then came the time when

Ben took Marguerite to meet his widowed father, followed by Marguerite's taking Ben to meet Addie. And heavens, everyone said, this was looking serious! Looked like there would be wedding bells after all!

'Think it's serious?' Addie asked Jess.

'Seems like it.' Jess was clearing the table, concentrating on stacking dishes ready for carrying to the scullery.

'I must say, I'm surprised, then.'

'Surprised? Why?'

Addie laughed. 'Didn't Marguerite always say she was looking for a rich Edinburgh man?'

'Ben's wages aren't bad.'

'He's no' rich, though.'

'He's handsome.'

'A bit on the serious side, I thought.'

'Nothing wrong with that.' Jess, wishing her mother wouldn't study her face with such interest, carried away her dishes. 'Anyway, Marguerite has to settle down sometime.'

'Aye, I'd like to see her settled. And how about you and that nice Rusty, Jess?'

'We're still good friends.'

'What a shame,' sighed Addie.

Still just good friends was what they were, though, even if they had taken lately to walking together before the cinema opened for the matinee. Usually, the April weather wasn't warm enough for them to eat sandwiches in Princes Street Gardens or the kirkyard of Greyfriars Church – favourite haunts of the city workers. They'd therefore take shelter from the wind in a little cafe they knew, order something on toast and share the bill. No more arguments over going Dutch, and everything so pleasant and restful, Jess was beginning to find her spirits quite soothed by such sorties as these with Rusty.

Which was why her heart sank when, over one of their little lunches, he too began to talk of Ben and Marguerite.

'Think it's serious?' he asked, echoing her mother. 'Between those two?'

'Why is everyone so interested?' Jess cried, as soon as the waitress had served her poached eggs and departed. 'And why ask me?'

Rusty stared. 'Come on, you know why people are interested. All the world loves a lover, they say, don't they? And the world's pretty nosey about how things are going to turn out.'

'Yes, but why should I be expected to know?'

'Well, Marguerite is your sister. She might have said.'

'She's never said. Even Ma doesn't know what her plans are.'

'I'm sure she and Ben could make a go of it,' Rusty remarked, beginning to eat his sausage and mash. 'I mean, I've never seen anyone so in love as Ben. He's a changed man.'

A changed man. Changed by her sister. At the shadow that crossed Jess's face, Rusty hastily put down his knife and fork and touched her hand.

'I'm sorry,' he said quietly. 'There I go, being as insensitive as usual.'

'I don't know what you're talking about!' she

cried. 'Why should I mind what you say about Ben?'

Rusty was silent for a moment, his eyes on her face so sympathetic, she couldn't bear to look at them.

'If I've spoken out of turn, I'll say sorry again,' he said at last. 'You know the last thing I want is to upset you.'

Another silence fell, with Rusty still gazing at Jess, and Jess sitting with head bent. Suddenly, she pushed away her plate and looked up.

'Rusty, I don't know what to say. I've been a fool, eh? Might as well admit it. Never had any hope, anyway.' She took out a hankie and wiped her eyes, though she hadn't actually cried. 'Does ... does everybody know, d'you think?'

'No, Jess, they don't, I promise you. I only know because ... well, I care for you.' Rusty smiled and held her hand again. 'Means my antennae are pretty sensitive, I suppose. Look, let's not say any more.'

'All right, but it's been good – to talk about it, I mean.'

'Any time, you can come to me.'

'I know, but I'm trying to put it all aside, you see. I'd say, forget it ever happened, except it never did.' She gave a tentative smile. 'Ben and me – it was all in my head. A dream. It never existed.'

'Dreams can be real enough. They keep a lot of people going.'

'Well, I want to manage without,' Jess declared. 'I mean it. Look, we'd better get the bill. Time's going by.'

'You will weather this, you know,' Rusty told her seriously. 'Maybe you've already begun.'

But Jess made no reply.

Walking back to Princes Street, not arm in arm, but close, they were pleasantly at ease. In fact, when Jess glanced up at Rusty's handsome face, it seemed to her that he had become again that carefree fellow she'd met in the cafe on their interview day. For the first time, she felt a pang of guilt as she realized how far he'd moved from his old self since then, and that she was probably to blame. Still, if he had for a time changed from those early days, he appeared to be changing back again, and that must be due to her, too.

As they strolled along beside the west gardens of Princes Street, she glanced again at the tall, rangy figure at her side and decided she wouldn't say anything to spoil things. If Rusty seemed relaxed and happy, it must be because the two of them had suddenly become so much closer, so much more like true friends. Maybe it would be enough for him? At least, for now? It was what she wanted, anyway. Yes, very much indeed.

'Hang on,' Rusty said, suddenly drawing to a halt. 'What are those fellows up to, then?'

'What fellows?'

'The ones by the Mound there, looking at the gardens.'

Her gaze followed his, to where a group of men were standing at the entrance to the gardens, studying the ground.

'I expect they're just gardeners. Might be time

to plant out the floral clock, or something.'

For a moment, Rusty thought about the famous Edinburgh showpiece, a round flowerbed laid out like a clock at the corner of the Mound. Then he shook his head.

'Those men don't look like gardeners, they're wearing suits. My guess is they're not thinking about any clock.'

'What, then?'

'Air-raid shelters.'

'Air-raid shelters? In Princes Street Gardens? Rusty, what ever are you talking about? Who's going to need air-raid shelters? There isn't going to be a war. Mr Chamberlain promised.'

Rusty took her arm again. 'Come on, let's cross over. We're going to be late.'

'No, I want to know what you meant. Who said there'd be air-raid shelters here?'

'I saw it in the paper. Said it was on the cards. Just a precaution.'

As lunchtime crowds jostled past them, Jess kept her eyes fixed on Rusty's slightly averted face.

'A precaution? They wouldn't go to so much trouble.'

'Jess, nobody knows exactly what's going to happen. But Hitler's occupied Czechoslovakia, and he's already in Austria. If he takes Poland, that'll be it. We're committed to giving our support. We'd have to declare war.'

'I know that, but they said Hitler had no plans for invading Poland, so, we'd be all right. That's what they said, Rusty.'

'It was Hitler who said he'd no plans to invade

anywhere. Next thing we hear, he's threatening to bomb Prague if they don't capitulate.'

Her face suddenly pale, Jess turned to cross the street.

'Well, let's go back, let's go to work.' She shrugged. 'What else can we do?'

'It may never happen,' Rusty said quietly, when they'd entered the foyer of the cinema. 'There's all kind of talk going on – you don't know what to believe.'

'Yes, we'll just have to wait and see.' Jess put her hand on his arm. 'Listen, it was nice, being with you today, you know. I ... felt the better for it.'

'Did you?' He was stooping to look into her face, thin shoulders bent, his hands on hers. 'Could we meet again, then?'

'Yes, I'd like to.'

'You wouldn't consider ... another Sunday afternoon? No strings, I promise.'

She hesitated, her eyes on the foyer clock.

Why not? Why not go back to what they'd had? No strings, he'd said. So, why not?

'A Sunday afternoon ... would be very nice. Thanks, Rusty.'

'Oh, Jess,' he murmured, his grey eyes alight. 'Thank YOU.'

Eighteen

Air-raid shelters in Princes Street Gardens? It had seemed a joke, until, suddenly, on a perfect summer's day, men were digging and there they were. Shelters for the bombs that everyone now was expecting to fall on the city. One minute, it seemed, folk had been happy to think there'd be peace in their time; the next, they'd accepted – there must be preparations for war.

'Aye, they say there are millions of gas masks coming our way,' Sally told Jess, her voice hushed with concern, but her face flushed with excitement. 'Is it no' terrible, to think we might need 'em?'

'It is,' Jess muttered, thinking of her father. She looked around the cafe, where she and Sally had decided to treat themselves to a light lunch. At the counter, she could see Marguerite serving someone with coffee, looking so beautifully serene, it was hard to believe she must be as worried as everyone else. 'In fact, I can hardly believe it.'

'Oh, there's more. We're all supposed to be practising doing blackouts of our houses. I ask you, when it never even gets dark at this time of year! And then did you no' hear about the plans to evacuate all the kiddies away from the cities? And for calling up the young men – and women, too?' Sally shook her head in mock despair. 'All this because they say that awful Hitler will invade Poland.'

'He hasn't done it yet,' Jess remarked, finishing her egg salad and trying to sound hopeful.

'Oh, he will, though. And then the balloon will go up. We'll be at war.' Sally's eyes were sparkling. 'You know what I'm going to do?'

'Get married?'

'No! I'm going to join up. My Arnold as well. Marriage can go on the back burner.' Sally gave a little smile. 'We're no' needing a honeymoon, if you take my meaning.'

'Why, Sally – I'd no idea!' Jess, blushing, looked away from Sally's cheerful blue eyes. 'I mean, I never thought...'

'Why should you, then? I'll admit, it's unusual, but no' so risky as it used to be. I mean, women don't necessarily have to land in the family way these days, you ken.'

'So I've heard,' Jess said, still blushing.

'Aye, well you remember it, dear, when the time comes. But for us, no' getting married was all because of Arnold's mother, really. She's a widow, and so difficult, you wouldn't believe! Always said she couldn't face him leaving her, and up to now, he's just given in. But if war's declared, she'll have to accept he's got to go and that'll make it easier for us, you see, when we do eventually get married.'

'I still don't see why you want to join up.'

'Excitement, dear! Have a bit of a change. You

110

might feel the same. After all, we'll probably be called up, anyway.'

'Leave the Princes? Folk will still want the cinemas, Sally.'

'Aye, but they'll have to find older people to run 'em.' Sally waved to Pam who was passing. 'Bring us a couple of coffees, sweetheart! We need cheering up, we're talking about the war.'

'Fatal,' cried Pam. 'I'm just putting it out of my mind.'

Turning back to Jess, Sally looked at her slyly.

'Talking of marriage, how about you and Rusty, then? You seem so happy together these days. I know you say you're just good friends...'

'So we are. We go out walking, have tea or a meal, enjoy each other's company – that's it.'

'For him as well, dear? Are you sure?'

'Here comes our coffee,' was Jess's measured reply.

Sally, stirring sugar into her coffee, let her eyes wander towards Marguerite, now carrying a tray of lunches towards a table in the window.

'Well, don't tell me your sister's got no plans to marry,' she said softly. 'I mean, she and Ben – they're crazy about each other, eh? When folk feel the way they do, something has to happen, you know. Have to move one way or another, that's the way things go.'

'I've no idea what Marguerite's plans are,' Jess declared stiffly. 'She never says.'

Nineteen

At home that evening, when she and her mother were tidying up after their supper, it seemed to Jess that Addie was looking unusually weary. It might have been that she was just tired after hard work in a hot kitchen, but more likely that she was depressed by the prospect of another world conflict. After all, she'd lived through the war that was supposed to end wars.

All this talk of gas masks, for instance. How could a woman who'd seen her husband slowly dying from the effects of wartime gas, tolerate the thought of yet more wartime gas killing off people at home? More gas, more bombs, more deaths...

Oh, poor Ma, Jess thought, hurriedly bringing Addie tea. 'Might never happen, you know,' she said comfortingly. 'This war, I mean.'

'It'll happen,' Addie sighed. 'And it'll be over Poland. I was just talking to Derry when I came in there. He said the same. It'll be Poland that does it. Hitler's mad keen to take it.'

'We don't really know how things will go.'

'No, but it's obvious the government thinks it does. Why all these gas masks, if they're no' sure? Why air-raid shelters? Poor Derry was that depressed. Moyra's ill again, and then there's all

112

the worry about the shop. No oranges, you ken.'

'Oranges?'

'Well, he'll have to manage on what we can grow, eh? And when did we grow oranges?'

The evening was so fine, they felt they should have been out, getting fresh air on the Shore, or walking to Addie's favourite Links, but lost in thought, neither of them made a move.

Jess was remembering her conversation with Sally, before she'd gone off on her free afternoon to buy some blackout material.

'To block out the sun?' she'd cried, leaving Jess to open up the box office. How like Sally to be excited by the prospect of war, of joining up, seeing something new! And not wanting to marry her Arnold yet, because she'd already, as she put it, had her honeymoon with him. Ah, but she was full of surprises, wasn't she?

Would I do something like that? Jess asked herself, but came up with no answer. She honestly didn't know, the situation had never arisen. Not with Rusty, certainly, though they did kiss from time to time, and sometimes she saw a look in his eyes as they rested on her that made her remember it had been her idea to be just good friends.

As for Ben – her mouth tightened. She'd never had the chance, had she? Never would have. Not with this sister coming in now, with a strange smile on her face and her left hand held out for them to see.

'Why, Marguerite, what is it?' Addie asked, as Jess sat without moving, her eyes riveted on her sister's hand. 'What have you got there?'

'A ring,' Marguerite answered softly. 'I know you've been wondering, so now's the time to say ... Ben and me – we're engaged.'

As her mother immediately ran to hug Marguerite and exclaim over her news, Jess sat without speaking. There it was then, the absolute end to her dream. Something she'd been expecting, and in a way, was relieved to have to face at last. Ben was to marry her sister, become a part of the family – even her own brother-in-law. Well, she must accept it. Hadn't she already told Rusty, she'd resolved to put her special feelings for Ben out of her mind? She must move on, that was the next thing. Move on, yes, but where?

'Jess, Jess, come and look at this ring!' her mother was crying, her face wreathed in smiles. 'Oh, I'm that pleased for you, Marguerite! Ben's a grand lad, and I know you'll be very happy. But what a sly boots you are, then! Why'd you never drop a hint or two? Why'd you no' bring him here tonight?'

'Drop a hint or two?' Marguerite laughed. 'Why, you didn't need any hints, Ma. You knew Ben and I were going to get wed some time or other. And I did want to bring him tonight, but I thought it was too late, you mightn't be up, or something. I've asked him to come on Sunday, with his dad, when we can all have a little celebration together – if that's all right with you?'

'Of course it's all right,' Addie replied. 'I'll get a really good joint, before we all have to go on rations, eh!'

'It's a beautiful ring,' Jess remarked, finally rising from her chair and taking her sister's hand. 'See how the stones shine!'

'It was Ben's mother's,' Marguerite told her, looking down at the ring's entwined diamonds and circle of pearls. 'His dad was a watchmaker, you know. Worked for a George Street jeweller's. When he married Ben's ma, they let him have the ring at reduced price, and before she died, she said it was to come to Ben.'

'For when he got engaged,' Addie murmured. 'I must say, I've never seen a prettier ring. Perfect for you, Marguerite.'

'Perfect,' Jess agreed, flinging her arms round her sister and kissing her cheek. 'Congratulations, Marguerite! I hope you'll be very happy.'

She felt the better for having been able to make her congratulations. Could even chat now with her sister, while their mother bustled about, making tea and cutting into a sultana cake. Could ask her about her plans, and why she and Ben had suddenly decided to announce their engagement.

'It's the way things are going with the war,' Marguerite answered quietly. 'Looks like Hitler is going to sign some agreement with Russia, and Ben says that'll mean he'll be sure to attack Poland. Won't have to fight on two fronts, you see. So, we want to get wed before we have to join up.'

'Why, you won't have to join up!' her mother cried, pouring the tea. 'Surely, if you're married, you'll be let off?'

115

'I want to join up, Ma. If Ben's away, fighting, the last thing I'd want is to be sitting at home, knitting socks for the troops, or doing waitress work.' Marguerite sipped her tea, thoughtfully. 'Maybe I'll try for the women's air force. Ben's keen to join the RAF.'

'I suppose it'd be exciting, in a way,' Jess said slowly. 'Something different. But I'm thinking of the Princes. Who'll keep it going?'

'Who cares, if there's going to be a war?'

'Folk have to have some entertainment,' Addie stated firmly. 'Keeps their minds off their troubles.'

'Exactly,' Jess murmured. 'But I'm still hoping that the war will never happen.'

'Talk about an ostrich!' Marguerite rose, stretching her lovely arms and yawning. 'It's no' like you, Jess, to shut your eyes to facts.'

Except where Ben's concerned, Jess thought. Facts then had become confused with dreams, until Marguerite had blown the dreams away.

'When's the wedding going to be?' Jess asked, after a pause.

'As soon as possible. We want to be married before we have to go to war.'

'Go to war,' Addie echoed, as slow tears coursed down her cheeks. 'Oh, Marguerite!'

'Have some more tea, Ma,' Jess said quickly, and both sisters put their arms around their mother and stayed with her until she leaped up, dashing away her tears, to add hot water to the teapot.

'Aye, we'll all have more tea, eh? And then think about Marguerite's celebration.'

Twenty

On August twenty-third, after Nazi Germany and Russia had officially signed their non-aggression pact, a strange calm descended on the British people. While everything in their lives seemed to remain just as usual, it was as though they were actually in limbo, held, waiting, in fine summer weather. For what? Hitler to invade Poland? Bombs to fall? Troops to invade? The balloon to go up, anyway, as Sally had put it.

'Don't you feel as though you're waiting for the other shoe to drop?' Rusty asked Jess, on the last day of August.

'Other shoe?'

'You know, it's what folks say, when they're listening out for something that has to happen.'

'Well, I say, we just carry on until it does.'

'Shall we go out on Sunday?'

'Of course. Why not?'

He shrugged, looking away, as they stood together in the foyer. 'Shoe might have dropped by then.'

'We'll face it together, then.'

His face lightened. 'It's nice to hear you say that.'

'Well, we are friends.'

'Friends. Yes, we're friends.'

'Listen, Rusty, why don't you come over for your dinner on Sunday? We can walk on the Shore in the afternoon.'

'I can't always be sponging on your mother,' he protested. 'It's not long since she asked me to the engagement celebration – when Ben came over with his dad.'

'They won't be there this week, just came over for the celebration.'

'It'll be the wedding next, I suppose?'

'That's going to be very quiet. Just at the register office.' Jess began to walk towards the box office. 'See you on Sunday, Rusty.'

But on Friday, September first, Hitler invaded Poland, and by Sunday September third, Great Britain and Germany were at war.

The Prime Minister's announcement came at eleven fifteen a.m. Addie, Jess and Rusty listened to it together, sitting round the wireless in the Leith flat, as bright sunshine streamed through the windows, and the smell of beef slowly beginning to roast in the oven made that Sunday morning feel like any other. But, oh, God, how it was different!

As Mr Chamberlain's measured tones filled the room, Addie put her handkerchief to her eyes.

'I have to tell you now that no such undertaking has been received...'

Of course not. As though Hitler was going to withdraw his troops from Poland just because he'd been asked to!

'...and that consequently this country is at war with Germany. Now may God bless you all ... I am certain that the right will prevail.'

'Switch it off, Jess,' Addie muttered. 'Just switch it off, eh?'

'So much for peace in our time,' Jess murmured, doing as her mother ordered.

'Poor old Chamberlain,' Rusty said, shaking his head. 'He'll have to resign, I expect.'

'I hope he does!' Addie cried. 'He believed what he wanted to believe. What good's that?' She dabbed again at her eyes. 'Oh, I wish Marguerite was with us, eh? But she's at Ben's, making dinner for him and his dad.'

'She'll probably look in this afternoon,' Jess said soothingly. 'Shall I just do some potatoes, then?'

'Here, I can peel a few spuds for you,' Rusty offered, trying to appear cheerful, when an extraordinary wailing sound suddenly echoed round the room and held them, still as statues, staring at one another.

'My God, what's that?' Addie cried. 'It's never an air-raid siren already, is it?'

'I'm afraid it is.' Rusty, at last finding the power to move, put his arm round Jess, who was standing with a small vegetable knife still in her hand. 'It's the Alert.'

'What'll we do?' Jess asked. 'Go down the stair?'

They were still debating what to do when, only a few minutes later, another sound rose around them, this time a long low melancholy note, rather than a succession of rising and falling

119

wails.

'The All Clear!' Rusty cried. 'Thank God for that! Must have been a mistake, eh? A false alarm.'

'A mistake?' Jess, breaking away from his arm was staring round the sun-filled room. 'How? How could it have been a mistake?'

'I've no idea, but it's over now, anyway.' He tried to smile. 'Come on, let me have the knife, Jess, and I'll do the peeling.'

'Thanks.' She managed an answering smile. 'Ma, how about giving us some of that bottle of sherry Ben brought the other Sunday? We could do with it.'

'Sherry?' Addie repeated vaguely. 'Oh, yes. Get the little glasses down, then.' She put her hand to her brow. 'I'm no' one for the drink, but you're right, we could all do with something now. Rusty, will you pour it?'

'You bet! And thanks very much. What a morning, eh?'

'I want to get out this afternoon,' Jess said. 'See if the world's still standing.' She raised her glass. 'Here's to peace.'

'That's too far away,' Addie murmured sombrely. 'I'll say, here's to us. May we all survive.'

'Here's to us,' they echoed, and drank.

'Now, let's get on with the dinner,' Jess cried, straightening her shoulders. 'And then we can go out for our walk, Rusty. Everything has to go on just as usual, war or no war.'

'What a hope,' he replied.

Twenty-One

'I don't want to go to the Shore,' Rusty declared, when they were out of the flat, the washing up done, the living room tidied, and Addie taking a rare rest in her little bedroom.

'Why not?' Jess asked, surprised at the firmness of his tone. 'You know I like it.'

'Yes, but there are too many people about on the Shore. Let's go to the Links instead.'

'All right, if it's what you want.'

'It is.' He took her arm. 'It is what I want.'

The afternoon was warm and pleasant, seeming, by contrast, to make the bad news of the day worse. But people were out, strolling just as usual in the golden weather, some talking in low voices, some only looking ahead with baffled eyes. What's happening? they might have been asking. Who is going to take this away from us? What do we have to do?

In the wide spaces of the Links, however, it was possible, as Rusty had hoped, to get away from the crowds, once they'd left the main promenaders behind and moved towards the shrubs and trees, where there were seats and a few children playing ball.

'Let's sit down,' Rusty said, pointing to a seat that was isolated in the distance. 'Over there, where we can be on our own.'

'What's all this worry about people?' Jess asked, sitting down on the rough bench that had been warmed by the sun.

'I want to talk,' he said seriously. 'And I want you to listen.'

'Don't I always listen?'

He smiled briefly, as he sat near her on the bench and took her hand. 'You know very well, I'm the one that listens.'

Shielding her eyes from the sunlight, she studied him, slightly raising her eyebrows. 'I've never seen you like this before, Rusty. Is it because of what's happened?'

'Partly. I expect we've all been changed by what we heard this morning.' He smoothed her fingers in his. 'But I was going to talk to you, anyway.'

'Talk, then,' she said lightly.

'All right. I want to tell you that I'm going to join the air force.'

'The air force?'

Unprepared, she felt an instant pain, as though winded by a blow. So this was the beginning, was it? The big shake-up of their lives? The kaleidoscope of war sending them on the move, never to be the same again?

'Rusty, I ... I don't know what to say.'

'Try goodbye.' His grey eyes were steady on her face.

'I don't want to ... say goodbye.' It came to her as a continued shock that that was true. She couldn't imagine saying goodbye to Rusty. Why, he'd always been there, in her life, from the time they'd started work at the Princes together. How would she manage without him?

'I'll miss you,' she said, bending her head. 'We're such good friends.'

'No,' Rusty said shortly. 'No, we're not friends. At least, I'm not. I've never been just your friend, Jess. Don't pretend you thought that.'

'I thought you were happy about it,' she whispered, after a pause. 'Being my friend.'

'Happy?' He laughed. 'You've no idea, have you? What it's been like for me? I used to think I'd like to get out of lodgings – have my own place – a flat, or a bedsitter. But then I'd have had to invite you, and I knew I couldn't do it. Imagine having to sit around, watching you make tea, talking about being my friend – when all I wanted was to tell you I loved you.' He loosed her hand from his and turned away his face. 'To ask you to marry me. And, all right – make love. Why not? I'm just a man, Jess, a human being, for God's sake. Not made of stone.'

For a long time, she was silent, her face bright red, her eyes cast down. Then she stretched out her hand and gently caressed his cheek as he sat like the stone he'd said he was not, until he very gradually relaxed and with a long shuddering sigh held her close.

'Oh, Jess,' he said with a sigh, 'Jess.'

'Rusty, I'm sorry,' she murmured, her face against his. 'You were wrong. I did know how you felt. But I just kept telling myself you were happy, because ... well, I liked what we had. It

123

was all right for me, I thought it was all right for you, but I was just selfish, eh? And never seeing straight.' As tears came to her eyes, she brushed them away. 'Now, I'm being punished.'

'Punished?'

'I'm going to lose you. You're going away and we don't know what'll happen. And I feel so bad!'

'There's no need to feel guilty, Jess. You never let me think I was the one for you.'

'Maybe you should've been,' she said quietly.

For some time, he looked at her without speaking. Finally, in a low voice, he said, 'There was Ben.'

'Don't think about Ben. He never existed.'

'Oh, yes, you said that before. I wasn't sure what you meant.'

'I meant, he never existed for me, as a real person. What there was, I'd dreamed up.' She touched his hand. 'Had to learn that the hard way.'

'And you have learned it?'

'Well, I've let him go.'

Rusty sat back, pushing his hair from his brow, his eyes on Jess never moving.

'So, where does that leave me? Am I in your mind now?'

'Of course you are, Rusty!'

He held her hands again. 'What I mean is, have I any hope? Please don't look so far away. You know I love you, you know I can't just be friends any more.' He was beginning to crush her hands in his and his, she could feel, were trembling. 'Jess, do you think you could ever marry me?'

As her eyes searched his face, the words sank in. Of course, he'd already told her that that was what he wanted all the time they'd been seeing each other, pretending to be friends. All he'd wanted, he'd said. To tell her he loved her, to make love to her, to ask her to marry him. All the time, that was what he'd been thinking. And now, she had to think of it, too.

Why not, then? Why not think of it? He had become very dear to her, very special. And he was no dream, no figure stepped down from the starlight. He loved her and his love was real. They could make a life together, if they were spared to do so, and it would be a good life. Her gaze on him grew tender, her lips parted, as he waited, scarcely breathing, until he cried –

'Jess? Please say something!'

'Rusty, I'm saying yes. Yes, I will marry you. Whenever you like.'

They moved into each other's arms, clinging and kissing, so dizzy with their own emotion that their surroundings seemed dizzy, too, spinning them into new worlds ...

Until suddenly Rusty drew back, his face so set and pale, Jess cried out in alarm.

'What is it? What is it?'

'I can't let you do this, Jess. It wouldn't be fair. You're just being kind...'

'I am not being kind!'

'Because I'm going away. That's it, isn't it? You want to do something for me, because I'm joining up. I can't let you do it. Not something like this. It's too important. It affects our whole lives.'

'Will you listen to me?' She shook him by the arms. 'I'm marrying you because I want to marry you, and that's the only reason. It has nothing to do with your going away. Can't you see that?'

'No.' He shook his head, his expression still sombre.

'No, Jess, you need more time. You need time to be sure.'

For a long moment, she looked into his unhappy eyes.

'Rusty, we have no time, have we? That's what the war's done. Taken away time. Please don't worry about me any more. I know what I'm doing.'

'Oh, Jess.' He drew her into his arms again. 'Didn't I once say I'd take whatever you were offering? I know I'm not really the one for you yet, but I might be, and if you really want to do this...'

'I do.' She laughed. 'There, don't I sound as if I'm being married already?'

Then he laughed with her, and they kissed again with sweet, quieter kisses, until Rusty murmured against Jess's face, 'Don't look now, but we have an audience.'

When she swung round, she saw three small children staring at them with large, interested eyes, and stretching out her hands, she whispered, 'Oh, Rusty, have you any pennies to spare?'

Up came a young woman, however, who

hurried the children away, at the same time casting back disapproving looks at the young people on the bench.

'There's a time and place for everything!' she cried. 'And it's no' always the Links!'

'I wouldn't say that!' Rusty retorted, smiling, as he gave his hand to Jess, and rose with her from the bench.

'Shall we go back?'

'Yes, let's tell Ma.'

'Let's,' he agreed, burying deep down any lingering doubts, while Jess, he guessed, was doing the same. 'Let's tell your Ma.'

Twenty-Two

One by one, most of the staff of the Princes had drifted away, leaving George Hawthorne wild with worry until he found replacements. It wasn't just that Ben and Rusty had departed for the services – you had to expect young men to go to war – but the girls had gone as well, and that never used to happen in the old days.

As he complained to Jess – women at war! What a piece of nonsense!

'Well, I suppose Sally and Marguerite have gone to war, but the others are making munitions.'

'Called up, anyway,' he groaned. 'Even the waitresses. So there's you and me and poor Joan

Baxter having to train all these older folk, and as she was saying, why'd your sister have to go? She's married, eh? And they're not taking married women.'

'Marguerite wanted to go, seeing as Ben had to join up.'

'And very fetching she looks in that WAAF's uniform, eh?' The manager sighed and ran his hand over his damp brow. 'Thank God you got married too, Jess, and didn't fancy leaving us. You do so much for me these days, I don't know what I'd do without you, to be honest. I mean, I've still got Edie and Fred – they're too old to be called up – but you're the one with the energy, the one who knows what's what.'

'I love everything I do,' she told him honestly. 'It's no trouble to me.'

Training new usherettes and the woman who was now her assistant in the box office ... helping Mr Hawthorne to master the new regulations that kept pouring in by every post ... keeping track of ice cream and all the other supplies that looked like being threatened as shortages began to bite ... even giving moral support and sometimes advice to the two retired fellows who'd taken over as projectionists ...

Yes, Jess supposed she did do a lot, but it was true that she was happy doing it, and it helped to take her mind off her constant anxieties for Rusty. Though he was still only training, as he'd told her in his letters from RAF Kenlin, she couldn't of course help thinking of what was to come. It was the same sort of anxiety Marguerite would be feeling for Ben, but she was herself

128

away on basic training, worrying their mother, who had her own problems. It seemed doubtful now that the ladies' club would be able to keep going in wartime.

'Worry, worry, worry,' Addie groaned, when she came to visit Jess in the small flat in Newington that she and Rusty had taken on their return from honeymoon. 'Seems that's all there is to our lives these days.'

Not quite all, Jess thought, hugging the memory of that rushed little honeymoon near Berwick, as though it were some sort of talisman. What a revelation those few days with Rusty had been! She'd had no idea sex could be so magical, yet, thinking back, that first exciting kiss he'd given her outside her mother's flat should have provided some hint.

There'd been signs even then, that there could be an affinity between them – she'd even been cross that he could stir her as he did – but then all that had been forgotten, as she'd insisted they just be friends. Until they'd leaped into shared delight in a creaking old bed in a guesthouse overlooking the Tweed, and scarcely surfaced until it was time to leave. Time to return to the world of work and war and the tearing wrench of separation.

No doubt it had been the same for Marguerite and Ben, who'd been married only a week before Jess and Rusty, and had spent an equally short honeymoon down in London. They'd had to part, just as Jess and Rusty had had to part, but it didn't make it any easier to think of their anguish. Like most things that were hard in life, you went through them alone.

Still, Jess had her job and was able to throw herself into it and be glad she was helping to keep the Princes afloat. It was very important at a time like this, as everyone agreed, that the people should have something to make them forget their troubles, and cinemas in this regard were absolutely crucial.

'Yes, Jess, you'll see, we'll be busier than ever,' Mr Hawthorne told her. 'Which is why it's good that we're all pulling together, keeping things going. We're needed, that's the thing.'

'As long as you don't do too much yourself,' Jess told him seriously. 'Last thing Sally said to me before she went away, was to make sure you didn't overdo things.'

'Fusspot!' he cried. 'Just like my wife.'

'No, Mr Hawthorne, you really must take care. You say you couldn't do without me, but the Princes needs you, you know.'

'All right, all right, Jess. I'll wrap myself in cotton wool. Now, to business – you haven't forgotten we've got *Gone With the Wind* coming week after next? We'll need to sort out the publicity material for the foyer. Big cut-outs of Clark Gable and Vivien Leigh, and posters of Tara and Atlanta burning et cetera.'

'No, I haven't forgotten, Mr Hawthorne.'

'You must call me George, Jess. Like I say, we're all pulling together now.' He rubbed his hands and smiled. 'My word, the tills would be rattling soon, if we had any, eh? As they say, it's a dark cloud that has no silver lining.'

How can he be so cheerful? Jess wondered, as

130

she turned away to check on the promotion material for the foyer. And though *Gone With the Wind* might make them a lot of money, wasn't that the story of a war that destroyed a whole way of life? Oh, no, she'd better not think along those lines. The Allies were going to win this war to keep their way of life, or maybe even achieve something better. That was the way to look at things. Look on the bright side, as they were always being told.

'Jess, shall I open up now?' little Flo Culloch called, coming out of the box office. She was the married woman of fifty who was now Jess's assistant, very conscientious, very nervous, very pleased to have a job.

Jess glanced at her watch. 'Oh, yes, matinee time. Open up, Flo. I'm just going to find a nice big cut out of Clark Gable for the foyer.'

'Clark Gable?' Flo breathed. 'My hero! Apart from my man, of course. You know what I mean?'

'Oh, yes, I know what you mean,' said Jess, turning aside, as Fred arrived, whistling, to let the patrons in.

Part Two

Twenty-Three

Sometimes, just to gain a breather from her constant stream of duties in that first year of war, Jess would slip into the auditorium when a film was showing and take a staff seat at the back, or even stand. Exchange smiles with the plump, middle-aged usherettes by the light of the screen. Run her eye over the patrons, whose own eyes would be riveted on the huge faces above them, as they smoked their way through packets of cigarettes, and munched whatever they'd been able to find to eat.

So good to see so many, Jess would think, for no matter what was showing, afternoon or evening, the cinema would be full, and just as George Hawthorne had prophesied, if they'd had any actual tills, they would have been ringing with the sound of money. And very welcome the money was, anyway, for the increased revenue had sweetened the cinema owners into funding the new post of assistant manager, once talked about by Sally. Which, of course, 'surprise, surprise', George had said, must go to Jess. So – no more box office for her!

Except that, the way things were, she still filled in when required, for Flo's assistant, Netta Wylie, was only part-time, just as she sometimes had to take a torch and do an usherette's job, or splice the snapped film for old Ron Clerk or Hughie Atkinson in the projection box, their fingers not being as deft as they'd once been.

Oh, but she didn't mind! It was what they'd always done at the Princes, and along with her new responsibilities for George, it gave her an extra feeling of pride in her work. True, she wasn't in the services and felt guilty about that, but she was at least helping to provide something that was necessary in wartime, and that was a boost to morale. Here, in the cinema, service people and civilians alike could forget the anxieties of their real world, and feel – even if for a little while – at peace. Why, she even felt that way herself; which was why she liked to make her brief visits to the auditorium and leave her own cares at the door.

One April afternoon in 1940, she'd slid in to see again the spell-binding opening of Alfred Hitchcock's *Rebecca*.

Ah, there it was! The long overgrown drive, 'twisting and turning as it had always done', towards the beautiful house, and the quiet little heroine's voice, echoing over the fascinated audience – 'Last night I dreamt I went to Manderley again...' Oh, how it drew you! Oh, was there ever such an opening to a picture!

Jess, sighing from her standpoint at the back of the stalls, had forgotten, just for the moment, all the work piled up in her share of Edie's office, but not of course dear Rusty, away with RAF Kenlin, beyond Inverness, training to be an air navigator. He might not always be at the front of her mind, but he was always in her mind somewhere, though he'd told her often enough not to worry. It would be some time before he was qualified to go on what he called 'ops'. And maybe they'd never happen for him, if this 'phoney' war there'd been so far would continue.

After all, there'd been no invasion, no German air raids. Maybe there'd be no Allied raids, either, and Rusty would be safe? They both knew they were clutching at straws. Hitler was just biding his time, the Luftwaffe, the German air force, just waiting for the word to attack.

For a few more minutes, Jess watched the film, then made her way into the foyer, blinking in the light, as Sadie Munn, one of the temporary usherettes, joined her.

'Is it no' a lovely picture, then?' she whispered. 'That poor lassie – you canna help feeling sorry for her, eh? So scared of everything!'

'At least she got to live in Manderley,' Jess answered with a smile.

'Aye, but it burned down!'

'All got our problems, Sadie.'

'You can say that again. But here comes Flo – Jess, is she looking for you?'

'Jess!' Flo was calling, hurrying from the box office. 'Jess, your sister's here!'

'Marguerite?' Jess cried. 'Why, I never knew she was coming on leave!'

It seemed that Marguerite, who was stationed at RAF Drem, an air station some miles south-west of North Berwick, had come over on a weekend pass. She'd be going back on Sunday evening.

'Thought, if you were free, Jess, we could go to Ma's together. She's back from the factory at five, isn't she?'

'You've been to your place?' Jess asked, hugging her sister and marvelling at her beauty and elegance, even in her WAAF's uniform. 'How's Ben's dad?'

Since their marriage, Marguerite and Ben had moved in with Ben's father in Canonmills, which seemed to suit them and him very well, for he was intensely proud of his new daughter-in-law, who was always very sweet to him.

'Yes, I've been home,' Marguerite answered now, 'and Dad's no' too bad. Missing us, of course, but managing. That's all anybody can do these days, I suppose. How are things with you?'

'Fine, fine, and it's so grand to see you, you know. Yes, let's go to Ma's together. I can get off in about half an hour, if you want to have a cup of tea first.'

'In the cafe?' Marguerite shrugged. 'I've just looked in – seems like a shadow of what it was.'

'You're right there. They close early and only serve tea and sandwiches. And have you seen the sandwiches? Poor Joan Baxter's tearing her hair. It's getting more and more difficult to get supplies these days. Even our ice cream is no more. But I can give you a cup of tea in my office. We've got our own kettle now.'

'My word, you're the grand one, eh?' Marguerite commented. 'Got your own office, and it's no' the box office!'

138

'Come on, you know I share it with Edie. But she's no' in today – got to get her teeth fixed.'

'We can have a nice chat, then – except I shouldn't be keeping you from your work.'

'Don't worry – I'll catch up later. It isn't every day I see my sister over from RAF Drem!'

In the little office she shared with Edie Harrison, Jess made tea and produced some rather old Marie biscuits.

'All I've got,' she said apologetically. 'Couldn't be plainer, eh?'

'After what we get at Drem, anything's an improvement!'

'But you're enjoying being with the RAF?'

'Jess, I love it.' As she sipped her tea and crunched her biscuit, Marguerite's eyes sparkled and her cheeks turned pink, making her seem, Jess thought, like a film star suddenly appearing in technicolour. 'Oh, it sounds awful, I know, but when I think of all those long, boring years I spent serving tables, I'm almost grateful for the war.'

'Grateful?' Jess repeated, staring. 'I bet Ben doesn't agree.'

'Well, obviously, I'd rather be with Ben. In fact, I miss him all the time. You know we write every day?' Marguerite smiled. 'Yes, there's me, who never put pen to paper, writing a letter every single day! But being where I am, with the girls and the chaps – oh, it's just so different, Jess. So exciting. I'll bet a lot of folk are finding that life's changed for them, now the war's come.'

'I expect you're right.'

'Well, look at you, Jess. You wouldn't be doing more interesting work, if it wasn't for the war, would you?'

'I'd still rather have Rusty home, even if I was in the box office.'

'Oh, yes, well, as I say, so would I rather be with Ben. I'd hoped we might meet this weekend, but he couldn't get the leave, so there he is, stuck down in the Borders and no' feeling too happy.' Marguerite set down her cup, her colour fading a little. 'Seems he's had a disappointment.'

'Oh?' Jess was gathering up the cups. 'What's that, then?'

'Well, you know he's on this training course? He'd thought he'd be picked for aircrew, but seemingly his night vision's no' quite good enough. He's going to have to settle for being some sort of ground technician.'

'Marguerite, what a shame! Oh, I can imagine he minds about that. Though, I mean, the ground chaps do good work too.'

'But aircrew are the glory boys,' Marguerite said glumly. 'Like your Rusty, eh?'

'He's training to be a navigator, won't be flying planes.'

'Ben will still be envious.' Marguerite glanced at her watch. 'Jess, shall we go?'

'Aye, let's see if Ma's back from the factory.' Jess gave a wry grin. 'She's making camouflage nets, you know – bores her to tears!'

140

Twenty-Four

Addie was delighted to find her girls waiting for her when she came home from the factory, especially Marguerite who, of course, only came back from the airfield at rare intervals.

'Oh, it's so grand to see you!' she cried, throwing her arms round her elder daughter. 'I do miss you, eh? And you too, Jess...'

'No need to say you miss me, Ma,' Jess said with good humour. 'I know you don't see Marguerite as often as you see me.'

'Still, things are different now, with both of you gone.' Addie sighed deeply. 'But there it is – bairns grow up. You'd have left, anyway, war or no war, and if there's nobody to play cards with, well, that's how it's got to be.' Dabbing at her eyes, she began to set out cups. 'How's Mr Daniel, then, Marguerite? Poor man, he's in the same boat as me, eh? All on his own.'

'He's OK, Ma, but don't worry about tea,' Marguerite told her. 'We had a cup in Jess's office, and I'll have to cook for Ben's dad when I get back.'

'What a piece of nonsense! Of course you'll have to have your tea here. Jess and me'll want something anyway.' Addie shook her head despondently. 'Ah, if only I was still at the club, eh? Could always rustle up a nice meal then, but there's no' much good food around the camouflage nets, eh? Och, I canna tell you how tired I get of pulling that netting around and sticking leaves in, or whatever else they want us to do!'

'Let's set the table and see what we can find,' Jess said, taking a tablecloth from a drawer. 'There's always the fish and chip shop, anyway.'

'Are you joking?' her mother asked. 'There's queues a mile long there these days, and then you're lucky if they've any decent fish. Tell you what, though, Alf Rowe the fishmonger's still open. He might have a bit of finnan haddie, eh? That'll no' take long to cook. Jess, here's my purse – see what you can find, eh?'

'I'll take my jacket off,' Marguerite said at once. 'Don't want it smelling of fish.'

Jess was in luck. Alf Rowe did have some smoked haddock and Addie was soon able to produce an acceptable meal, of fish poached in milk, potatoes recklessly mashed with the butter ration, and fresh vegetables, courtesy of Derry downstairs.

'Aye, he's keeping going somehow, poor Derry,' Addie murmured. 'He can get the vegetables, but fruit – forget it! I mean, when'll we see a Canadian apple again?'

'How's Moyra?' Jess asked. 'Has the doctor decided what's wrong?'

'Did I no' tell you?' Addie's lovely eyes were bleak. 'It's the TB. No' in the lungs, but inside, seemingly. Aye, that's why they thought it was something else to start with. Anyway, she's in the Jubilee Hospital and Derry's in such a state. Oh, he's a broken man. What he'll do, if she goes, I canna say.'

'I'm very sorry to hear that,' Jess said, her eyes fixed on her mother. 'Moyra's such a lovely person.'

'Awful thing to get,' Marguerite murmured with a shudder. 'I think I'd rather be blown up than have something like that.'

'Marguerite, what a thing to say!' Addie had turned pale. 'Listen, you've no' heard if there are raids likely, eh?'

'No, never heard.' Marguerite stood up to collect their plates. 'But they will be coming, Ma, we'll just have to brace ourselves.'

'Maybe no' here,' Jess said quickly. 'I mean, we've no shipyards or anything.'

'We've the docks,' Addie said quietly. 'Right here in Leith. But how can you be so sure that Hitler will want to bomb us? He's done nothing so far.'

Marguerite, exchanging looks with Jess, shrugged.

'Well, I suppose I could be wrong.'

'Of course you could,' Jess agreed. 'Don't worry, Ma, none of us is going to be blown up. And listen, I think we should go and visit Moyra, eh? If we're allowed?'

'Oh, no, no!' Marguerite cried. 'Better not. TB's infectious!'

'I'm sure you don't get it from visiting. Anyway, you needn't go, you'll be at Drem.'

'That's right.' Marguerite's brow had cleared. 'But you take care, eh? See what the doctors say,

143

before you go to a TB hospital. Look, Ma, if you don't mind, I'll have to go back home now, but it's Saturday tomorrow, so we can meet then. Let's have a coffee at Logie's, say ten o'clock? My treat.'

'Wish I could join you,' Jess said, 'but I work Saturday mornings now.'

'Well, we'll all have Sunday dinner here,' Addie declared grandly. 'You bring Mr Daniel, Marguerite, and I'll sweetheart the butcher into getting me a joint.'

And I'll bet she'll do just that, Jess thought, as fond farewells were made and Marguerite departed. Sometimes it could be a distinct advantage to have a good-looking mother. Why, just think of all the fruit poor Derry used to let her have at reduced prices! Now he had someone else to think about and that was his own dear wife. Was he a broken man, as Addie had said? Probably, but might not, of course, stay that way. Would Marguerite and Jess have a stepfather one day? Perhaps not. Addie still went regularly to put flowers on her husband's grave.

'When are you seeing your Rusty then?' Addie asked Jess later, when Jess, too, was preparing to go home. 'Can he get one of these weekend passes?'

'He's got a week's leave in May,' Jess answered, smiling. 'I'm counting the days.'

'That's nice.' As she had no one to play cards with, Addie was laying out a game of Patience. 'You've made a good choice of man there, Jess. You'll never have any trouble with Rusty, I'm sure of that.'

'He's good natured, all right.'

'He is. No' like Ben.'

'Why, Ben's nice enough, Ma.'

'But moody. Very handsome, but sees the dark side. Now Marguerite's never been one for putting up with anything, I think you'd say?'

'I'd say,' Jess agreed, laughing.

'It's just the way she is. Likes everything smooth and easy, and if Ben ever tries to make things hard – well, it'd be better if he didn't, eh?'

'I wouldn't worry, Ma, they're so much in love, they'd never hurt each other.'

Addie, placing a red queen on a black king, smiled. Whether over her cards, or for some other reason, Jess couldn't be sure.

Twenty-Five

Bliss arrived with Rusty, home on leave, and relief that he was all right. Looking very well, in fact, if a little strange, with the obligatory short haircut, but lean and tanned and with a new confidence in his manner. He was having a grand time, he told her, there was absolutely no need for her to worry about him, unless she wanted to worry about his failing the course, which was all that worried him. But then all the guys worried about that. Nobody wanted to give up the chance of being aircrew.

'But when you're on these ops,' she murmured, after they'd made wonderful love on his first day back. 'It'll be different, then.'

'You know the slogan,' he told her, pulling her close. 'It may never happen. Might never be in action.'

'You want to be, though.'

'Sure, I do. It's what I'm training for. But why think of it now? We've got better ways to spend my leave.'

Lying against him, kissing his lips, Jess agreed that thoughts of anything weren't at that moment necessary.

Luckily, for that week of Rusty's leave, Jess had managed to persuade George to let her take holiday. Though when she'd first proposed it, he'd only lit another cigarette and groaned.

'You want to go on holiday, Jess? For God's sake, why?'

'Well, I haven't had any time off since last November. And Rusty's coming back on leave.'

'Oh, well, then, I suppose I can't say no.' George took out a handkerchief and wiped his face, which, now she came to study it, seemed to Jess to be too pale and too damp. 'Don't take more than a week, though, will you?'

'I won't, that's all Rusty's got.' Jess hesitated. 'Are you all right, George? You look a bit under the weather.'

'I'm fine. It's just this warm weather – never suits me, you know.'

'It's not all that warm. Nice, but still chilly.'

'Think so?' He began to sort in his desk

146

drawer. 'Maybe I should take my tablets. Keep forgetting, that's my trouble.'

'You're on tablets?' Jess tried to see the label on the bottle, but he was holding it away. 'I didn't know. What are they for?'

'Oh, this and that. Would you be a dear and get me a glass of water, Jess?'

When he'd taken his pill with the water she fetched, he grinned and told her not to look at him as though she were Sally. 'Or my Daisy, come to that. Fusspots, the lot of you, eh? You take your holiday, then, Jess, and give my best to Rusty.'

'Why, he'll be sure to look in to see you.'

Again, George grinned. 'Better not. I might give you both jobs if I see you here!'

Even so, they did look in at the Princes and George seemed much better, shaking Rusty's hand, and saying he was coping, they'd no need to worry, should just have a good time. Which, obviously, they were, he'd added, his eyes travelling over their happy faces – he'd never seen them looking so well.

'Poor old George,' Rusty remarked, as they'd left. 'Always seems to carry the world on his shoulders. It's not that difficult, running a cinema, is it?'

'Why, I'd say there was plenty to it,' Jess replied, a little nettled. 'More than you might think.'

'Well, you'd know, seeing as you're probably doing most of the work for George these days. I'm glad you're out of the box office, anyway.'

'I didn't mind the box office!'

147

'Ah, but you were always set to go places – according to Ben. Which reminds me, how's he doing? He doesn't keep in touch.'

'I only hear from Marguerite occasionally,' Jess said carefully. 'Latest news is that he didn't make aircrew. His eyesight's not quite good enough.'

'Oh, no.' Rusty whistled. 'If I know Ben, that'll upset him.'

'Yes, he's disappointed. But he can do well as ground crew, can't he? There must be plenty of important jobs there.'

'Of course there are. He'll be OK.'

But though he said no more, Jess could tell that Rusty was thanking his lucky stars he'd been selected to fly as navigator. The fact that he'd probably be safer not flying wouldn't matter to him, as it would matter to Jess. As Marguerite had put it, aircrew were the glory boys – and who wouldn't want a chance for glory? Of course, he might fail the course; apparently, it was particularly hard. But slipping her hand in his, Jess knew she didn't want him to be safe that way. To fail – that would be too much for him to face.

The lovely days went racing by, filled with visits to Addie and Ben's father ... bus trips to the countryside ... peeps over barbed wire at the Forth, or the sea at North Berwick ... meals out when they could find cafes that had something to spare ... or just long strolls round Edinburgh, arms entwined, at peace, in a world of war.

Only one tiny cloud disturbed Jess's horizon,

and even then she wasn't sure it was really there. Perhaps it was just her imagination that Rusty seemed to want to visit pubs more than he used to, that he felt the need for a drink in a way that was new?

On his first evening back, he'd suggested going round to their 'local' after supper.

'What local?' Jess asked. 'I don't even know which it is.'

'Well, whichever's nearest, if that's easiest.'

'But we don't usually go to pubs, do we? You know what I think – they're more for men than women.'

Rusty took her hand. 'OK, let's go to one of the hotel bars. Much more suitable.'

'Why do we need to go for a drink at all, though?'

'We don't. It's just ... you know ... convivial.'

She studied him for a moment. 'That's what you do with the chaps at Kenlin, is it?'

He grinned ruefully. 'You've caught me out. Suppose it is.'

'You've got me now, Rusty, you don't need to be convivial with other people.'

'You're right!' he cried and swept her up into his arms. 'Come on, let's just the two of us be convivial together, then.'

The following evening, though, he again suggested that they might as well try the nearest hotel, but this time for a meal. Why not? There'd be something to eat, even if it wasn't anything special, and would save Jess having to cook.

And first, we'll have a drink, Jess thought,

which of course happened.

'You must admit, this is pleasant,' Rusty said, sitting back with a whisky he said he'd been lucky to find, while Jess sipped at a sherry. 'I mean, makes you feel better, doesn't it?'

'Taking in some alcohol?' Jess asked.

'No, the whole thing ... the atmosphere ... being able to relax. That's part of going to a pub, you know. It's not just the drink.'

'I've nothing against drinking, Rusty. In moderation. You can't afford to depend on it.'

'Well, of course, that goes without saying.'

'Some of the people here, in the tenements and such, they drink to forget their troubles. Only brings more troubles.'

Rusty moved restively and drained his glass. 'You're not exactly telling me something I don't already know. So, now I've had my drink in moderation, can we go and eat?'

'I'm sorry,' Jess said earnestly. 'Didn't mean to lecture.'

He smiled and took her arm. 'I know, sweetheart, and I understand. But if you think I'm going to turn into an alcoholic on the strength of one drink, you're worrying about nothing.'

'Why, I never said I thought any such thing!' she cried, but as they moved into the restaurant and studied the sparse menus, she couldn't help wondering how many drinks Rusty had when he was enjoying the atmosphere of the pubs around Kenlin.

On the following two days, he made a point of not suggesting they go anywhere for a drink, and she began to feel guilty that she'd even thought he might need one. Probably it was true, she'd been worrying about nothing. And they were so happy together, why would he need anything more?

Next day, however, they went walking out of town, stopping off at a little inn in Swanston, where, of course, it was only natural that they'd have to have a drink or two before and with their meal. All the time Rusty was drinking, his gaze on Jess was so clear, so direct, she told him not to worry, she wasn't being critical. She felt herself that this was true, and that her imagination had been overworking. After all, when they'd gone out together before the war, there'd never been the slightest hint of his drinking to excess. If he'd learned to enjoy going out with his friends on the course, who could blame him? Everyone knew that servicemen – even trainees – would need to relax.

'I'm glad you understand,' Rusty said softly, as though he'd been reading her mind, and his hand covered hers on the table. 'Believe me, you've no need to worry.'

'Except about you coming back in one piece from those "ops" you talk about.'

'I'm still only on the course, remember?'

'I wish the course could last for ever.'

'Hell, it feels like it's doing just that!' he said laughing.

But however long Rusty's course might seem to be, his leave was only too short, and before they could even brace themselves, the last farewells were upon them. Hugs, kisses, tears –

151

everywhere along the station platform, couples were, like Jess and Rusty, making final desperate embraces, eyes on the clock, on the guard's flag, until it was all over. Those leaving had boarded the train; those staying were waiting, to watch and wave, as the flag went down and the train began to move.

'Be back soon!' Rusty cried above the shriek of the engine's whistle. 'And, remember, I'm only on the course!'

Jess, trying to smile, felt her eyes prick with tears, but she waved and waved until the train had disappeared, then, with the others around her, finally turned and left the platform.

What to do now? Go back to the empty flat? No, might as well look in at the Princes, just across the road. See what was on her desk. Probably a pile of things for her attention. Her eyes still smarting, she walked slowly from the station, then fast across the road, and back to work.

Twenty-Six

Although Addie and Jess had tried more than once to see Derry's wife, Moyra, in hospital, they'd had no luck. She was not well enough, they were told, to receive visits, except from her husband.

'Oh, Derry, this is sad news,' Addie had said to him. 'Can they do nothing for her, then?'

'They're trying an operation,' he told her, his face taking on its crumbling look that followed any talk of his wife. 'Maybe, after that, she'll pick up.'

'She will, Derry, she will!'

'Aye. Well, we'll have to wait and see.'

It was on a day in late June that Jess and her mother finally got permission to visit Moyra for a short time. The operation had not been described as a success, but had made things easier for her and it seemed she was feeling a little better. Just the two of them would go, in the afternoon, it was decided, as Derry always made his visits in the evening after the shop had closed. And there would be no need to take anything, he told them, as flowers weren't permitted and Moyra's diet was strictly controlled.

'Oh dear, I'm no' looking forward to this,'

153

Addie murmured to Jess, as they arrived at the Jubilee, an old hospital on the north side of the city, set in large grounds. 'I'm no' one for sick visiting.'

'Nor me, but we do want to see Moyra. What must it be like for her, stuck in bed all day? Derry says the patients aren't allowed to do anything.'

'Cure sounds as bad as the disease, eh?'

If only it was a cure, Jess thought, approaching the nurse at reception for details of Moyra's ward.

Her bed was one of only four in a small, bare room overlooking the gardens. Everything – floor, walls, paintwork – smelled of disinfectant. Beds were made with what seemed to be military precision, the covers starkly white, the bedside lockers empty of all but glass water jugs and tumblers. There were no curtains, no photographs and no flowers, but there were, at least, the four patients to provide a reminder of humanity, still, quiet figures though they were. But Moyra, nearest to the window, was managing to smile.

'Addie?' she whispered. 'And Jess? Oh, it's good to see you!'

'Please don't stay long,' a nurse said, placing two chairs, one at either side of Moyra's bed. 'No more than half an hour. Mrs Beattie has to rest.'

Oh, yes, Moyra had to rest, Addie and Jess silently agreed, for the way she looked, lying in her white bed, any movement would have been too much for her. Yet her cheeks were flushed,

154

and her large shadowed eyes showed brightness, as she lifted her hands to take theirs.

'Moyra, pet, how are you?' Addie asked, as Jess sat, glancing briefly at the other patients in the ward. They had no visitors themselves and were showing little interest in Moyra's. But how must she and her mother seem to them, anyway? Two beings from another world? A world the patients had once known, but might never inhabit again?

No, no, Moyra, at least, was said to be feeling better. She would come back to the world. She must.

'They never say,' Moyra was answering Addie now. 'We never ask.'

'But how do you feel?'

'I'm ... I'm no' too bad. But tell me about you folks, eh? Tell me what you're doing – tell me about Marguerite ... and everybody.'

For a short time, they talked of that outside world. Of Jess's husband up in Kenlin, and Marguerite's husband in the Borders. Of Marguerite herself and how she was enjoying being in the WAAFs. Of Addie and her camouflage work, and of Jess and her cinema work. Of the films that were being shown – *The Wizard of Oz* and *Goodbye Mr Chips*, war films and musicals. Laurel and Hardy, the Crazy Gang.

'People will watch anything to keep their minds off their worries,' Jess said, smiling, and Moyra smiled too, and said, 'I bet.'

But she was growing tired, her features drooping, her flush not fading but deepening, until Addie knocked Jess's arm and nodded her head

155

towards the door.

'We'd better go,' she whispered to Moyra. 'We'll come again, though – very soon.'

But Moyra, with surprising strength, suddenly caught at Addie's hand and held it.

'Addie, will you promise me something?'

'Anything, pet. Just ask.'

'Will you ... look after my Derry?'

'Look after him?' Addie repeated, glancing in a puzzled way at Jess, who was sitting without moving. 'You mean, do some cooking for him, Moyra? I do already. I often take him a bit of stew or something I've made...'

'No, no, I don't mean cooking. Just, after I'm gone, will you see he's all right? Take care of him, because he's no good on his own.'

'Moyra, what are you talking about? You're going to get better. You'll be looking after Derry yourself.' Addie's face was as flushed as Moyra's own, her eyes as bright. 'Now, don't let's hear any more talk about going. That's an absolute piece of nonsense!'

'Just promise me,' Moyra said, still clinging to Addie's hand. 'Set my mind at rest.'

'She will,' Jess leaned over to say quietly. 'She'll do what you want, Moyra.'

'That's good,' Moyra whispered, letting Addie's hand fall. 'That makes me feel better. Thank you, Addie. Thank you.'

While Addie was still staring in astonishment, the nurse returned.

'Time for your nap, Mrs Beattie,' she said briskly. 'Goodbye, ladies, thanks for not over-staying your time.'

156

And as Moyra obediently closed her eyes, Jess and her mother quietly slipped away.

'Well, what do you make of that?' Addie cried, when they were away from the ward. 'Why on earth should Moyra ask me to look after Derry? I'm just a customer!'

'You're a friend, Ma,' Jess told her. 'Moyra knows that.'

And it was true, she was thinking, Moyra knew. Perhaps more than Addie herself. A wife's eyes could be sharp.

'All right, I suppose you could say I was a friend. Doesn't mean I'd have to look after him!' Addie pulled out a hankie and wiped her eyes. 'Oh, that poor lassie, then, thinking she's going to die! She's getting better, eh? She said she felt better.'

'Ma, why don't we have a cup of tea? I saw a notice – there's a canteen here that visitors can use.'

'No, no, Jess, I don't fancy anything here. Let's go to that nice wee cafe near Stockbridge library. Then I'll just go home.'

'And I'll go back to the Princes. I've a few things to do.'

They didn't talk much over the tea, each feeling too depressed, and parted soon afterwards to go their separate ways, with Jess promising to see her mother again soon.

'Aye, I'd be glad if you would,' Addie said in a low voice. 'I could do with company.'

'Just don't go worrying about Derry, Ma.'

'It was you who made a promise for me, Jess. Now, what am I supposed to do?'

'Just carry on as usual.'

'And if Moyra dies?'

'She's going to get better, you said.'

'As though I'd know!' Addie cried, hurriedly walking away towards a bus stop, while Jess turned her steps towards the town, so deep in thought she didn't see Ben Daniel approaching until he called her name.

Twenty-Seven

It took her a moment or two to recognize the tall man in air force uniform standing in her path and putting out his hand.

'Jess, don't you know me?' he asked, as she stood blinking in the sunlight. 'Don't tell me I've changed already. It's Ben. Ben Daniel.'

'Ben!' She was blushing with embarrassment. 'Of course I know you! It's just the sun – your face was in shadow.'

'Oh, God, now I'm only a shadow? Oh, but it's grand to see you, Jess. Haven't set eyes on you since I joined up.'

'It's lovely to see you too, Ben. But what are you doing here? Are you on leave?'

'Had a couple of days owing – came over to see Dad. He's got his chest trouble again, but don't worry, he's not too bad. I've got him a couple of library books and I'll do a bit of shopping for him later.'

'Don't you want to do the shopping now?'

'No, I want to take you for a cup of tea and have a good old chat.'

'Oh, Ben, I'm sorry, I've just had some tea with Ma. I'm going back to the Princes now.'

'OK, I'll walk back with you.' He smiled as they fell into step together. 'It's such a hot day, you'll be ready for another drink at the Princes cafe, won't you? Marguerite tells me its pretty terrible these days but I expect they can still do a lemonade?'

'A lemonade would be grand,' Jess said, trying not to find anything remarkable in Ben walking beside her, trying not to be pleased, even, that he should want to spend time with her. All she'd once felt for him was dead and buried, that was for sure, but then he was her brother-in-law. Maybe it was right she should be glad to see him.

Over the lemonade in the crowded cinema cafe, she covertly studied him in a way she had not been able to do for some time. The long, handsome face was unchanged, except perhaps that there were tiny lines beside the sensitive mouth; lines she hadn't noticed before and thought might be the result of his recent disappointment.

Should she mention that? Say she was sorry that something wrong had been found with his eyes? Those fine brown eyes, so nearly black, resting on her now? No, it would be a mistake. Ben was a proud man. He'd hate to be reminded that he had any defect, especially as it had prevented his being aircrew.

'I know what you're thinking,' he said quietly. 'I expect Marguerite told you about my eyes, didn't she? Now you're wondering why they look just the same and I'm not carrying a white stick?'

'Ben, no! How can you talk like that?'

'Sorry, I'm just rather bitter, that's all. It's not as if I can't see perfectly well, you know. They turned me down just over night vision – but I swear it was OK anyway.' He finished his lemonade and banged the glass down. 'So, unlike Rusty, I'm not going to be allowed to do what I want to do.'

'It's a shame, Ben. A real shame.'

'Yes, well, let's say no more about it. How is Rusty, anyway? Living it up in Kenlin?'

'He's doing well. Or at least, he was when he came over in May. I haven't seen him since then.'

'And I haven't seen Marguerite.' When Jess shook her head over his case, Ben took out a cigarette and lit it. 'We're like Box and Cox, aren't we? When one gets leave, the other doesn't. What it is, then, to have a wife who's in the air force too?'

Jess was silent, not sure what he wanted her to say. That Marguerite should have stayed at home, waiting for him? She had a right to join the forces if she wanted to.

'I worry about her, you know,' Ben was saying, keeping his voice down, though only Joan Baxter would have remembered him at the cafe, and she was not in evidence. 'Can't help it.'

'Marguerite's in danger?' Jess cried.

'No, no, when I say I worry about her, I'm really worrying for myself.' He drew on his cigarette. 'Come, on, Jess, you know how Marguerite attracts people. Attracts men. So, who's at Drem?' Hs dark eyes burned. 'Men, Jess. Marguerite is surrounded by men. Don't you think I should be worried?'

'No! That's ridiculous! Why, you're newly-weds, like Rusty and me. Marguerite would never get interested in someone else. She loves you!'

'Oh, I know. I know she does. But I'm not at Drem and other men are. That's the problem. Propinquity. That's the thing.'

'Isn't it the same for you, then? How many WAAFs do you see every day?' Jess sat back in her chair, her brows drawn together, her gaze on Ben cold. 'Don't you think Marguerite could be worried about you? Only, she trusts you.'

For some moments he stared at his cigarette, then stubbed it out.

'I suppose I deserved that. Suppose, if I'm worrying about her, I'm not trusting her.' Suddenly, he reached for Jess's hand and pressed it. 'Thanks, Jess.'

'I haven't done anything.' She slowly removed her hand from his.

'Yes. Yes, you have.' Ben looked at his watch and stood up, Jess with him. 'Glad I met you today. And not just for what you said. I'd better get back to Stockbridge now, for Dad's shopping. Hope there's something left.'

'I hope your Dad's all right,' Jess said a little stiffly. 'Give him my best. It was nice seeing you, Ben. Take care, then.'

'Wish we could have met again, but I haven't got long. Oh, but listen, I forgot to congratulate you on your new job. Assistant manager, eh? I knew you'd do well.'

She thanked him, relaxing a little, and asked if he wasn't planning to go up and speak to the stand-in projectionist. Maybe give him some tips?

'No, I'd better not interfere. And the funny thing is, I've no interest in my old job at present. It's as though all I've got has to go into my war effort, even if I can't do my best job, because the powers that be won't let me.' As his mouth twisted a little, she saw again the lines around it, and was saddened.

'You'll do your best work, Ben,' she said gently. 'Because you always do.'

'And you, Jess, always say the right thing, don't you?'

Giving her a swift, brotherly kiss, he paid for the lemonade and left her, marching from the cafe as though on parade, while Jess still stood by their table. And then Joan Baxter did appear and came bustling up.

'Was that Ben I saw just then? Now, why didn't he come in and have a word? And has he paid the bill? Should have been on the house. Can't have our staff forking out now, can we?'

'You've never let me off,' Jess remarked.

'Why, you're not serving in the forces, are you, dear? When you come in with your Rusty,

162

I'll let you off too.'

Come in with Rusty. How Jess wished she could. With Rusty, she'd be safe.

Twenty-Eight

The year moved into July and high midsummer, yet still there was no sign of the 'phoney war' turning real. What was Hitler up to? There was no doubt that he would attack Great Britain some time. Of all the countries on his list for invasion, it would probably be the one he most wanted to conquer. Soon, then, invasion would come. And there were those who rather wished it would, so that they would know what they had to face. Jess, though, just wished with all her heart that they could keep going as they were. No bombings, no invasion, no deaths. She knew it wasn't possible.

One thing that cheered her up was the arrival of Sally on leave, looking wonderfully well in her ATS uniform, though, as she blithely admitted, she hadn't lost a bit of weight!

'Och, no, I'm struggling with my skirt band every day, but so what? I'm enjoying myself, and so is Arnold, judging from the letters he writes. Just wish he could've got leave with me, but no luck this time. Got two stripes already, though, would you believe?'

'Why is everyone having such a good time in

the services?' Jess asked, as they had coffee in the cafe. 'Rusty, Marguerite – now you. I thought folk would be pining for home.'

'Thing is, as my mother used to say, the weight's not on yet. Now, what she meant by that was, the real test is still to come.' Sally shrugged. 'And that's true, eh? We're all just training. We've no' done any fighting yet.'

At the look on Jess's face, she quickly touched her hand. 'Ah, don't worry, dear. Rusty'll be fine. He'll come through, sure he will. But I noticed, just then, you didn't mention Ben. What's up with him? Isn't he enjoying his RAF days?'

'Didn't make aircrew. Something wrong with his eyes for night flying. He's upset.'

'I bet, knowing Ben!' Sally, having ordered second coffees for them both, grandly threw a saccharine tablet into hers. 'Just a sop to the diet, eh? Well, there's no' much sugar anyway.' Her face grew serious. 'Tell you who's no' looking so well to me, Jess, and that's George. Oh, my, his face is either like a pasty or a beetroot, eh? And he's that out of breath! Can you no' get him to slow down, then?'

'You know what George is like, Sally. He just calls me a fusspot and goes his own way. Does take his tablets, though.'

'Well, that's something.' As she studied Jess, Sally brightened. 'Ah, but it's grand to see you, Jess – doing so well and all! I bet you're really keeping everything going, eh?'

'George does that, Sally. I do what I can to help.'

164

'And that'll be plenty. But marriage is suiting you as well, eh? Even though you've been separated already. What a start for you both – and Marguerite and Ben too. That Hitler has a lot to answer for, and no mistake.'

'Think something will happen soon, Sally?'

'Arnold says any time, but more likely the autumn. Hitler will have made all his preparations by then.'

'Autumn,' Jess repeated. 'That gives us a bit more breathing space, then.'

It was some days later that Mr Hawthorne called Jess into his office. Panting a little, he sat at his desk studying his desk diary, and motioned to her to take a seat.

'Got a little visit planned for us, Jess.' Smoke from a cigarette he'd rested in an ashtray wreathed his face as he grinned. 'Not anywhere you won't know.'

'A visit? Where?'

'Leith.' He took up his cigarette, gave it a last puff and stubbed it out. 'I did say you'd know it. But do you know the Clarion cinema?'

'The Clarion? Off Commercial Street?' Jess frowned. 'It's closed, isn't it?'

'It is, but our owners have asked me to take a look at it. With business booming, they're thinking they might take it on. Want to come with me to see what it's like?'

Her expression a little cagey, Jess hesitated.

'The problem would be to find staff for it, George. You weren't thinking of asking me to transfer?'

'You? Good God, no!' George's eyes were round with horror. 'You know I can't do without you here. No, John Syme'd have to scratch round to find folk, and it might not work out anyway, but I said I'd tell them what I thought. There'd be money in it for the owners, if they could get it going.'

'There would. These days, people can't get enough of the pictures.'

'Want to come, then?'

'Yes, I'd like to.' Jess smiled. 'As long as you don't want me to leave the Princes.'

George, rising, shook his head.

'Never worry about that, Jess, it's out of the question.' He picked up his desk diary again. 'So, let me see – what day shall we go? How about ... the afternoon of July the eighteenth?'

'That'd be fine.'

'Right.' He laughed. 'Think they can manage here for a couple of hours without us?'

'Of course they can.'

Jess, already looking forward to her outing – the first with George that she could recall – made her way to the door, while he, sitting down heavily at his desk, was already lighting another cigarette.

As planned, in the late afternoon of July eighteenth, they left the Princes together and boarded a tram for Commercial Street, there being no sign of the taxi George would have preferred. High above them, in the clouds, a lone plane circled, but they had no idea it was there.

Twenty-Nine

'Did you ever go to the Clarion?' George asked Jess, as they approached Leith.

'Of course! I went to all the cinemas. I remember seeing *Snow White* there before the war.'

'What was it like, then, as a cinema?'

She shrugged. 'All right, I suppose. Pretty run of the mill.'

'John Syme told me the owners had lost money on some other enterprise and just sold everything they'd got. Only nobody bought the Clarion at the time.'

'I think myself it'll need too much doing to it. And where will they get the men to work on it, anyway?'

'You're probably right, the idea will come to nothing.' George's smile seemed relieved. 'At least we'll have had a nice trip out. But isn't this our stop?'

They had left the tram and were walking towards the turning for the cinema when, beneath their feet – it seemed crazy – the ground rocked. At the same time, some distance away, an almighty noise hit their ears like a blow.

A noise, Jess called it, but it wasn't like any noise she'd ever heard before. Not like the

167

warning siren, which she was certain she hadn't heard. Not like a gun firing, or a rocket soaring. Not like anything except itself, a heavy, ominous thud. A crump that filled her full of dread, and sent people screaming everywhere.

'Oh, my God!' cried George, grasping Jess's hand. 'What was that?'

'I'll tell you!' cried a man in air force uniform running by. 'It's a bomb! We're being bombed!'

'Bombed?' Jess gasped. Her heart missed a beat, as she thought of her mother in Great Junction Street. But then relief flooded through her, as she remembered that Addie would be at the camouflage factory in Edinburgh, she'd be safe. Thank God, she'd be safe. And Derry in his shop? Please God, he'd be safe too.

'But we had no warning,' Jess cried to the young airman. 'We never heard a siren.'

'I saw the plane,' he told her. 'It was a Jerry. All on his own. A Jerry. I recognized the sound. Better get to a shelter. He won't have finished yet.'

Glancing hurriedly at George, Jess saw that his face was putty-white and shining and he was beginning to breathe fast.

'An air-raid shelter,' he said thickly. 'We have to find an air-raid shelter.'

But even as he spoke, another, nearer, heavier thud sounded and again the pavement seemed to rock around them as people cried and screamed and a man, shaking from head to foot, was calling that a great crater had appeared just up the road.

'Oh, my God, a bloody great crater,' he kept

shouting. 'Can you no' see it? A bloody great crater, big as the moon! Oh, save us, oh Lord! Spare us, oh Lord, for we are repentant sinners! Oh, Lord, save us!'

'Quick,' Jess cried to George, 'let's get away, find a shelter!' But to her horror, she saw that his eyes were now closed and that his breath was coming in great gasps, their wrenching sound more frightening than even the thud of the bombs that had fallen.

He was having a heart attack. George was having a heart attack. What could she do? He was having a heart attack, here in the street, and he was going to die. Unless she could do something, unless somebody could do something.

Frantically, she unloosened his tie and his shirt collar, and then, as his legs gave way, laid him on the pavement, her cardigan under his head, and called aloud for help.

But who would hear in all the terrible confusion? It was like a nightmare, the sort you long to leave by waking, until a solidly built woman in a nurse's uniform came running towards them, shouting that she could help, she could help, where was the patient?

She took one look at George, and turned to Jess.

'Has he a nitrite capsule?' she asked. 'Quick, quick, tell me!'

'I don't know, I don't think so,' Jess stammered. 'He's got tablets...'

'Too late for tablets. Look, dear, what we've got to do is get this fellow to hospital, or he's going to die. There'll be ambulances on their way – flag 'em down ... tell 'em it's an emergency ... and, please God, they'll come for him!'

'Couldn't I phone the hospital myself? I can find a phone...'

'The lines will be jammed, you'll never get through.' The nurse's eyes were on George's face, her fingers on his pulse. 'Run, then, run!'

Where? Jess cried to herself, as the feeling of nightmare returned. Where can I run?

A small knot of people had gathered around George and one of them – a middle-aged man – shouted now, 'Quick, there's a policeman! He'll help – come on, lassie, I'll go with you!'

'A man dying?' echoed the policeman. 'Well, there's already folk dead here – that first bomb fell on a tenement.'

Folk already dead ... Jess swayed on her feet. War in all its horror held her in its grasp. Folk already dead, and George would join them. There was nothing she could do.

'There's an ambulance!' cried the middle-aged man beside her, pointing to a vehicle with sounding siren coming rattling down Commercial Street. 'And another behind. Can we no' get the poor guy to hospital, officer?'

'I'll see what I can do,' the policeman said.

Thirty

The news at the Royal Infirmary was long in coming, but it was good. George, saved initially by the ambulance crew, was going to pull through. He was now 'stable' and 'as comfortable as could be expected', his trembling wife was told, and she could see him, but only for a minute or two. No need to try to tell him, but he was a very lucky man.

'Oh, thank you, thank you,' Daisy quavered, as a young doctor guided her away. 'Oh, I can never thank you enough, never!'

But at the door of the small waiting room where she and her sister, Jess, Addie and Edie had spent long hours in suspense, she did not forget to turn and look back to Jess. 'And thank you, too, Jess, for all you did for poor George. I'll never forget it.'

'Aye, it was a mercy you were there, eh?' Alison Wright, Daisy's sister, murmured. She was as thin and nervy as Daisy herself, and though had come to offer support, spent most of the time in the waiting room shivering and crying, and fetching more tea.

'Oh dear, oh dear, what would have happened if you'd not got him into that ambulance, then? I hear it was the oxygen that saved him.'

'And what would have happened if they'd both been a bit nearer the bombs!' Addie cried, clutching Jess's hand. 'When Jess rang me at work and told me she'd been in Leith, I couldn't take it in. I couldn't believe she was safe. I kept asking her over and over again if she was all right, and the money for the phone kept running out and she'd to keep putting coppers in. Oh, it was a nightmare, so it was – a nightmare!'

'It was,' Jess said tiredly. 'That's all it was. A nightmare.'

'Seven people, they say, killed in the tenement,' Edie wailed. 'Would you credit it? Out of the blue! No siren, no warning, just in their homes, and then gone. And poor Mr Hawthorne nearly gone, too. Oh, when you said he was here in the Royal, Jess, I was in such a state! I thought all I should do was get here, to be with Daisy, and I just told Fred and Flo to look after things and up I came.'

'Well, I'm sure my sister was very grateful,' Alison said graciously. 'But of course I came with her myself. She's very highly strung, is Daisy. I knew she'd never manage alone.'

'It's good she's got you,' Addie told her, rising and taking Jess's arm. 'But if you don't mind, I must get my girl home now. She's still suffering from shock, she needs complete rest.'

'I'm all right, Ma,' Jess said at once. 'I want to wait for Daisy. See how George is.'

'Here she is,' Alison cried. 'Oh dear, looks like she's crying. How is he, pet, quick, how is he?'

'He's all right,' Daisy answered in strangled tones, as she pressed a hankie to her eyes. 'They

172

keep saying he's going to be all right.' She began to sob in earnest. 'But he doesn't look all right. So pale and so still, just lying there, not talking. Not saying a word!'

'Of course he'll not look all right yet,' her sister said soothingly, putting her arm around her. 'But you have to go by what the doctors say, you know. If they say he's all right, well, that'll be true, won't it? Now, why don't we try to find a taxi – you can sometimes catch one outside the hospital – and come back tomorrow? Did they say you could see him tomorrow?'

Still sobbing, Daisy nodded, and after a quick glance at the watching faces, Alison led her away.

'I'd better go, too,' Edie murmured. 'If I run, I can get the last tram home. Jess, shall I see you tomorrow?'

'No, no,' Addie said firmly. 'After what she's been through, she's going to need some time off.'

But Jess shook her head. 'No time off, Ma. I have to look after things, for George's sake. Edie, I'll see you as usual.'

'Oh, Jess,' Addie sighed, as Edie hurried away. 'At least you'll come back home with me, eh? No' go to your empty flat?'

'I've got a better idea, Ma. My place is nearer. Why don't you come home with me instead? We needn't go back to Leith tonight.'

Addie's weary face brightened. 'Are you sure, pet? Oh, I think I'd like that. Let's go then.'

'And if there are any taxis outside the hospital, should we take one? Just for once?'

173

'Just for once,' Addie agreed.

It was only when she was in the taxi, on her way home, that Jess remembered she hadn't rung the owners to tell them of George's illness. Tomorrow, she would have to ring Mr Syme in Glasgow, and see what he wanted to do.

Thirty-One

Next day, at the Princes, the atmosphere was subdued, as after a death. And, of course, even if Mr Hawthorne had actually survived, there were deaths to mourn. Seven in the tenement. And maybe more to come. No one felt safe. How could they, if a lone raider was able to appear in the sky without warning and rain down bombs on civilian targets? They'd been expecting air raids when the phoney war finally ended, but somehow had always thought they'd focus on the things the Germans feared, not poor folk in tenements. But that was war for you, and now they knew just what they were facing.

Jess, feeling as vulnerable as everyone else, knew that others at the Princes were looking to her to hold the place together. In fact, there was no one else. She was not only assistant manager, she was the only one with an overall view of everyone's work; the only one, apart from Edie and Fred, to have worked at the cinema before the experienced people were taken away by the war. And, while Fred could manage the jobs he knew and Edie could type the letters and do her filing, for anything more, it was no good asking.

One problem was that everyone was so obviously on edge. Even when Jess was able to call them all together and tell them that Mr Hawthorne was improving, there were still tears flowing and nerves showing; so much so, she began to wonder in the end if things would ever return to normal.

Routine was a wonderful support, though, and gradually, as the shock of what had happened began to wear off, everyone slipped back into doing what they always did with their usual efficiency, and Jess could heave a sigh of relief. And to thank heaven she'd booked *Spring Parade*, starring the young singer Deanna Durbin, for this particular week. Just the thing for escaping the world and settling everyone's nerves.

Even mine, Jess had thought, until, crossing the foyer some hours later, she saw John Syme coming through the doors towards her, when she began to tremble. Inside, anyway. Outwardly, she appeared quite composed as she went forward to shake his hand.

'Mr Syme – I'm very glad to see you.'

'Terrible news about George, Mrs MacVail, not to mention what happened in Leith. Hard on you, too, as you were there.'

'I'm all right, thanks. Everyone's pretty upset here, but the news is good. I rang the hospital about Mr Hawthorne this morning.'

'So did I. Soon as I get the OK, I'll go to see him.'

'Mrs Hawthorne's going to let me know when visiting's allowed. Would you like to come to my office, Mr Syme?'

'Better make it George's. As you share with Miss Harrison, I believe, and we have things to discuss.'

John Syme was in his late forties, a distinguished looking businessman, with dark hair just beginning to show grey at the temples, and a nose that was on the sharp side. Jess had met him two or three times, the last being when he'd interviewed her after George had selected her as his assistant manager. He'd made no objection to her appointment, though she knew he'd wondered about her credentials, and she'd considered herself lucky over that. How lucky was she going to be when he brought in some outsider to tell her what to do in George's absence, though?

As she showed him into George's office, her thoughts were not on her own position, however, for her gaze had gone straight to George's desk with all his things just as he'd left them, and she couldn't help her eyes filling up with tears.

'It's all right, Jess,' Mr Syme said kindly, setting down his briefcase. 'Mind if I call you Jess? He's going to be back, you know. No question.'

'I know. I'm sorry. It just hit me for a moment.'

'Of course. It would. Now, shall we sit down?'

'Would you like to take the desk, then?'

'If you prefer.'

When he had taken George's chair behind the desk, Jess seated herself in what she always thought of as the interview chair; it was where she'd been placed by Sally on the day she'd been appointed to the box office job so long ago. Perhaps it wasn't so long ago, only seemed so. And now she was waiting, as assistant manager, to hear Mr Syme's ideas on finding a new and temporary manager to be her boss in the absence of George. Who would it be? Where would such a person be found? Don't worry, she told herself, someone would be found, all right. Someone would want to work here, just as she did.

Looking up, she found Mr Syme's narrow grey eyes fixed on her face.

'Difficult for you, all of this,' he observed. 'I know you've always got on well with George.'

'Yes. He's always been very helpful to me.'

'Thinks very highly of you, too.'

To that, she made no reply, and after a moment, Mr Syme took out his cigarette case, studied its contents, and closed it.

'Trying to give them up,' he said with a brief smile. 'Especially since the only ones I can buy are those I don't like. You don't smoke, Jess?'

'No, I've never started.'

'Sensible girl. But then you are – very sensible.' He leaned forward a little. 'Would it surprise you to know that I've already thought of you as a replacement for George? Temporary, of course?'

At first she was speechless, staring at him with wide, gold-flecked eyes.

'Me?' she said at last. 'To replace George?'

'My suggestion. Unfortunately, one of my company, when I telephoned him this morning after you'd told me about George, was of the opinion that you were too young.'

The sound of her spirits plummeting must surely have echoed round the room, she thought wildly, and almost felt like smiling at the idea she could ever have been considered to run the Princes Street Picture House. But that was wrong. She didn't feel like smiling.

'I see,' she murmured. 'Well, I suppose I am. Young.'

'But not too young. Others on the board agreed with me. In fact, we think you'd do a good job. Temporarily, of course.'

'But one man didn't agree.'

Mr Syme sat back. 'I've persuaded him.'

'Persuaded?'

'I explained that of all the people we might find, you're the only one who really knows the Princes, and that you've been working lately as assistant manager with George himself, so you'd be au fait with all that he has to do. I also explained that George has always thought you very competent, with good ideas of your own, and – this is pretty important – that you'd be the one he'd like to look after things while he's away.'

Shrugging a little, Mr Syme gave another of his brief smiles. 'That's what I call persuasion, Jess.'

'And he accepted me?' she asked huskily. 'Without an interview?'

'These are difficult times. We need somebody to take charge immediately to run things as smoothly as possible for the time while George is away. We've decided you're that person. Are you interested?'

Interested? Again, she could have smiled.

'Mr Syme, I don't think interested is the right word.'

'You mean, you'll take the post?'

'I'll take the post. If you're sure you want me.'

'It's been decided. As a temporary measure only, but of course, you understand that. Now, there'll be formalities to see to, salary to discuss, a contract to be drawn up, and so on – I'd like you to come through to Glasgow one day next week, so that we can finalize matters.' He took a diary from his briefcase. 'Would Wednesday suit?'

When he took his leave at the cinema doors, he shook her hand and wished her all the best in her new post.

'One thing you won't have to worry about – after what's happened, we're not pressing ahead with any idea of renovating the old Clarion. I expect you'll be glad about that.'

She was. Didn't even like to think of the ill-fated expedition to Leith to look at it. Would never again want to hear even its name.

'But George will be pleased, you know, that you're holding the fort for him.' John Syme was continuing. 'Let's hope we can visit him soon.'

'Oh, yes, Mr Syme! And that he won't be away too long.'

He gave her a long considering look. 'Whatever happens, this will be good experience for you. Remember that, Jess.'

'I will, Mr Syme.'

'Call me John,' he said pleasantly, and left her.

Stunned, was how she felt. Stunned at her new position which she could never have imagined could be hers so soon. Yet not elated. Stunned, apprehensive, perhaps, but not elated, not happy. Because the post had only come to her because of what had happened to George. How could she be happy about it?

As she returned to George's office, though, she did begin to feel a little better about stepping into his shoes. It wasn't as if he were not coming back. She could take the view that she was going to do her best to keep the cinema going for him, and take pleasure in that. It would be what he would want, and it was after all pretty nice to know that the owners – except for one – had confidence in her.

By the time she'd thought all these things, she knew she was ready to sit at George's desk and tackle the paperwork already there, though taking his chair still gave her a strange feeling. Everything looked ... sort of different, didn't it? To be in charge. Heavens, that was different, too.

Whatever would the staff say? And her mother? And Rusty? She smiled a little. And Ben? He was the one who'd told her she was going places, climbing ladders. And here she was, in a new place, all right: George Hawthorne's.

After a few moments, she rose and returned to her old office, where Edie was tidying up for the end of the day.

'Edie,' she said, 'Can I interrupt you for a moment? I've something to tell you.'

Thirty-Two

Of course, as soon as he heard what had happened in Leith, Rusty managed to get himself a weekend pass to come back to Jess.

'I never thought you'd do it,' she gasped, when they'd released themselves from the first long embrace in George's office that she'd finally come to think of as hers. 'I mean, you've so much on – your course and the tests coming up and everything – I didn't even dare to hope you might come.'

'After what you've been through?' Rusty shuddered. 'I asked for compassionate leave and the CO agreed without a word – and why not? I mean, when I think of you in Leith and how close you were to those bombs, I'm not joking about needing compassionate leave. And then there's poor old George to think about, as well. How is he, by the way?'

'Recovering, but slowly. He's allowed visitors now, so shall we go to the Royal together?'

'Sure. I'd like to. First, though, we're going home, aren't we?'

'Oh, yes, we're going home!' She laughed. 'I'm giving myself a bit of time off. You realize that I can?'

Rusty looked round the office that he'd always known as Mr Hawthorne's and nodded.

'Sorry, hadn't thought about it – I was just too mad keen to see you. But you've done very well, Jess, you certainly have.'

'I'm only acting manager until George comes back, of course. Probably because I just happened to have experience of the Princes.'

'And with so many guys in the forces, there wouldn't be much choice, I suppose.'

'Guys?' Jess's eyes were suddenly glittering. 'You're saying, that if there'd been a man around, I wouldn't have got the job?'

'No, no, of course not.' Rusty's expression was already penitent. 'It's just that ... well ... fellows like John Syme and his board – they'd probably think of finding a man first. That's all I meant, honest! You know I think you could do any job you fancied.'

He drew her again into his arms, but it was only when he'd pleaded with her not to be 'mad at him', he really hadn't meant to upset her, that she finally relaxed enough to return his kisses.

'Think how lucky we've been,' he whispered. 'Think what might have happened.'

And remembering the seven who'd died in the tenement, she shed a few tears, before telling Edie that she'd be leaving early, Rusty was with her.

'And I'm sure you're right to give yourself some time off, Jess!' Edie cried. 'You should be at home resting anyway – not working yourself to a frazzle!' Turning her gaze on Rusty, she told him how pleased she was to see him and how well he was looking in his uniform.

'And aren't you proud of Jess here, then? We are, you know. We're all as pleased as Punch that Mr Syme appointed her.'

'Only temporary,' Jess said hurriedly. 'I'm hoping George will soon be back with us. Be sure to tell Fred to be careful about locking up, Edie, won't you? And to check the blackout before he goes?'

'Jess, he always does, so stop worrying. Enjoy your time off for once!'

But, in the tram going home, Rusty, looking at Jess with her brows bent and an abstracted look in her eyes, knew that she was never going to stop worrying about the Princes if she had to leave it for a while. Unless, of course, he could persuade her to put it out of her mind – while they made love.

The love-making was so deeply satisfying, it was a terrible wrench to get up, get dressed, find something to eat and make their way to the Royal. But Rusty had meant it when he'd said he wanted to see George, and Jess was always keen to see how he was.

'To be honest, he doesn't look so well to me,' she told Rusty before they entered George's ward. 'They say he's made a good recovery, but he seems so down, you know. As though he's too far down to come up.'

'He's bound to be in low spirits for a while,

183

Jess. Think about it. One minute he's fine, the next facing death, and even when he's better, he's still in hospital and someone else is doing his job.'

'He's glad I'm doing it. He's said so.'

'Of course he's glad. He'd rather you than anybody else. But it doesn't mean he wouldn't rather be back at the Princes himself.'

'He will be, very soon. I'm sure of it.'

But when they saw him, sitting in a dressing gown by his bed, George didn't look as though he'd be returning to work any time soon. Everything about him seemed to have narrowed. His face, his shoulders, his once broad chest. Even his hands had changed; become the hands of a sick man, pale and delicate, showing every bone.

But it was the bombs that were causing the trouble, he told Jess, when she and Rusty had taken chairs near him and he'd made a gallant attempt to greet them. 'I'd be all right, if it wasn't for them.'

'The bombs?' Jess repeated. 'How do you mean, George?'

'I still hear them. I hear them sounding. And the noise is terrible. Well, you remember it, don't you?'

'It was terrible,' she agreed. 'But I don't hear it now.'

'You don't?' George shook his head. 'Wish I didn't. But it's the same with the pavement. I mean, the floor. They make me get up, you know, I have to exercise. Walk up and down the ward, and oh, my God, soon as I set off, I feel the whole thing rocking underfoot, just like it did in Leith. I have to stop and lean on some-body's bed, but people are very kind, they don't complain. Then the nurse usually comes and takes me back.'

Jess and Rusty looked at each other.

'What does the doctor think?' Jess asked, putting the magazines she'd brought on George's locker. 'Have you told him about all this?'

'Oh, yes. He says not to worry, it'll all go. It's just the result of ... now what was it? German word.' George's brow furrowed. 'Trauma. That was it. Would be a Jerry word, wouldn't it?'

'It's good, though, that there's nothing to worry about,' Rusty said, trying to sound cheer-ful. 'Maybe they'll let you go home soon.'

'And Daisy will be looking forward to that,' Jess added, but George's expression did not lighten.

'She is, but I've told her, I'm not going home until I stop hearing the bombs. It wouldn't be fair on her. Too much of a worry.'

'But George, you will stop hearing them. The doctor says so.'

He shrugged. 'We'll have to see if he's right.'

'He is right, George. He knows what he's talking about. And when it happens, you'll be better and able to come back to work!'

He gave her a long sad look.

'I don't know about that, Jess. I don't know about that at all.'

'Looks to me as though you might have George's job for longer than you think,' Rusty said, break-ing a silence as they made their way home. 'He

185

isn't going to be coming back for quite some time, is he?'

'You're thinking of how he is now,' Jess replied. 'But the doctor says there's nothing to worry about. When he gets over his ... what they call it ... trauma, he'll be back to his old self.'

'Hope so.' At the turning into their street, Rusty paused. 'Think I can find any cigarettes round here? I'm dying for a smoke.'

'I thought folk in the services had plenty of cigarettes?'

'I've still run out. How about that corner shop? They might take pity on me.'

'Might have some Woodbines,' Jess said doubtfully. 'I only buy the paper there, I don't know about the cigarettes.'

'I'll try, anyway. You go on, then. Put the kettle on!'

Back at the flat, Jess, with heavy heart, thought about George, then put on the kettle and moved to the bedroom to fling herself for a moment on the bed. How warm it had become! Warm and humid. She could scarcely breathe.

From her pleasant rest, head against the pillows, her eyes fell on Rusty's canvas bag on the chair where he'd left it. Better unpack it, she supposed. And there was the kettle singing, too. She'd have to get up.

Considering how little he must have brought for such a brief visit, Rusty's bag seemed strangely heavy. What on earth had he put in it? Feeling guilty for no reason at all, as she was going to unpack it anyway, she undid the

186

buckles and looked inside. Wrapped in Rusty's clean shirt and underpants was a bottle of whisky.

Thirty-Three

'Got some!' Rusty called, coming into the flat smiling, a packet of Players cigarettes in his hand. 'Soon as he saw my uniform, the guy produced these for me. Saved my life.'

'Saved your life?' Jess, facing him in their small living room, held out the bottle of whisky. 'And what would this do, Rusty?'

His smile faded. 'Just got that before I left, Jess.'

'Got it from where? Whisky's hard to find.'

'Exactly. Someone I know tipped me off about a source. Had to bring it with me, but you need not worry, I'm not intending to drink it all at once.'

He flung himself into a chair and, tearing open the packet of cigarettes, took out his lighter and lit one, his eyes on Jess defiant.

'Wish you'd stop looking at me as though I were some sort of criminal.'

Jess put the bottle down and took a chair herself.

'Why do you need it?' she asked in a low voice. 'Why drink it at all?'

'Why not? It's a ... help, that's all.'

187

'A help? You need help, Rusty?'

'Look, I don't want to talk about this. Can we leave it.'

'How much does a bottle of whisky cost these days? At black market prices?' Jess, fighting tears, sprang up and began to walk about the room. 'Oh, Rusty, you must be spending all your pay!' But as she turned to look at him again, she caught her breath. 'Or are you using the savings? The money from the house your folks left you?'

'No, I am not using the money they left me!' he cried. 'I've never touched it, never would, without you. Because that bottle's just a one-off! You think I drink whisky when I go out with my mates? I drink beer and the cheapest they've got. And when have I not sent money home to you? I know it's a pittance, but I've never missed, have I?'

'I know you send me money and you know I add it to the savings. For our future, Rusty. For when the war's over and we can think of a house and a family, maybe. That's what matters, isn't it? Our future?'

'I've said I haven't touched our savings. Why don't you trust me?'

'Because I don't believe you only drink beer. You've just said, the whisky's a help. How do you know that, if this bottle's a one-off? You must have drunk it before. And I saw you drinking whisky at the pub, if you remember.'

'All right, I like whisky, I admit it.' Rusty drew on his cigarette and stubbed it out. 'I save up for it and buy it when I can, which is not that often. So, can we leave this now? I don't want to talk

188

about it any more.'

'All right.' She studied him. The handsome face averted from her, the long thin hands turning his cigarette case, over and over, the unusual eyes cast down. It was plain that he was not going to talk to her at that time; she would do better to wait.

'I'll make the tea, then. Like anything else to eat? Haven't got much, but there's cheese, and Ma gave me a few tomatoes. Derry let her have some.'

'Thanks, I'm not hungry. How's Derry's wife, then?'

'Still in hospital. The outlook's not good.'

'I'm sorry.'

After they'd had their tea, they went to bed, but not to make love, or to sleep. The summer night was sultry, their bodies lying close, sticky and hot, and there were times when Jess longed to get up, stand at the window and search for cool air. But, of course, the window was shrouded in black out curtains, there was no cool air, and she didn't actually want to move. This was her chance to make Rusty talk to her. To tell her why he needed help – and from that bottle, still on the table in the living room.

When he groaned with the heat and rolled away from her, she put her arms around him and brought him back, leaning close and pressing her lips to his chest.

'Rusty,' she whispered. 'Talk to me. Tell me what's wrong. I know there's something. Don't try to hide it.'

For a long time, he only held her, sighing against her, sometimes kissing her, then letting her go.

'Oh, Jess,' he murmured. 'Jess – I feel so bad. Hollow. Like the straw man.'

'Tell me,' she urged. 'Just tell me. Because, what happens to you, happens to me. So, I have to know – what's wrong.'

'Oh, God, Jess...' He again held her tight against him, then let her go. 'It's the flying.'

'The flying?' She was mystified. 'But you're no' a pilot, Rusty. Is it the navigating, then? Is it too difficult, or something?'

'I can do the navigating. That's fine. No trouble at all. It's just being what I wanted to be. Aircrew. One of the glory boys. I was selected. Accepted. I couldn't believe it. I mean, there was poor Ben, feeling the same as me, and turned down, and I was selected. I passed all the aptitude tests. I seemed a natural. I was so proud.'

'You were right to be. You did well.'

'Yes, but it's all changed, Jess. And I daren't let anybody know. I couldn't face it – admitting...'

He was silent for a moment, then turned aside to lie staring into the darkness.

'Admitting...?' she prompted gently.

'That I'm afraid.'

After a while, they clung together again, still without speaking, until Jess asked quietly, 'Afraid of flying, Rusty? I don't understand. Why should you be afraid when you weren't before?'

'It sounds strange, I know, because in the early days it's true I was OK. We had a lot of training flights, as you can imagine, and I was just like everyone else, enjoyed them all. Couldn't wait to qualify and get posted to real ops.' Rusty laughed shortly. 'Imagine that?' He laughed again.

'Go on,' Jess urged him. 'Rusty, go on.'

'Well, what happened was that one day we were on one of our routine training flights and something went wrong. We began to lose altitude, and the pilot couldn't seem to correct, to get us up again. All happened in seconds, though seemed like years, and I could see the ground coming nearer and nearer, the fields and hedges growing bigger, and I thought, This is it, we're not going to pull out, we're not going to survive. I thought of you, Jess, and my folks, I kept thinking, I'm going to meet my folks ... and then I just ... closed my eyes. Next thing I knew, we were up again, zooming up into the heavens, and the pilot was laughing. So was I, laughing.'

Still staring unseeingly into the darkness, Rusty seemed not to notice when Jess held on to his hands, trying to live through what he was telling her, as he was living through it yet again.

'We were fine, you see,' he was murmuring, 'we were safe. Came down without trouble, shook the pilot's hand. It was all over. Just one of those things. Everyone walked away.'

Thank God she hadn't known about this at the time, Jess was thinking. Thank God they'd all survived. But Rusty was no longer thinking of giving thanks.

'From that day onwards, I've never wanted to fly again,' he told her, his voice so low she could hardly catch it. 'Every time I get in the plane, I see the earth coming to meet me, I see the fields and hedges, just like before, I feel the plane falling. At the same time, I'm doing my job. Plotting the course, concentrating with all I've got. But all I'm feeling, Jess, is fear. And that's the way it will always be. I know that now.'

'No, no, it needn't be like that, Rusty! You could get help!'

'I've got help, remember? Didn't you find it in my bag?'

'Whisky's no help. No help at all. What happens when they find out? What happens if you can't do your work?'

'My work? I don't drink on duty, Jess! I'm not completely mad. No, I drink when I'm free, in my own room in my billet, and I get by. Don't go on about it, there's no point.'

'I thought you said once that the pleasure of drinking was being sociable – convivial was the word, wasn't it? But now you drink on your own.'

'That's the way it's got to be. I wish to God it could be different, but it's not possible.'

'Well, you know what I think, then?' She had left the bed and was tying on her cotton wrapper. 'I think you must go to the CO and tell him you can't fly any more. You must ask for ground duties. It's the only thing to do!'

'It's the last thing I'll do!' he cried, flinging back the sheet that had been their only covering.

'You have no idea how I'd be thought of if I asked for ground duties, if I told the CO I was scared of going up. Can you not see how that would make me seem?'

'It must often have happened before. People get stressed...'

'Before they've even been in combat? I'd never tell the CO how I feel. Don't ask me. Just don't ask me.'

'Let's go in the kitchen,' she said, after a long pause. 'Make some tea. And you could have another cigarette.'

'Thank God for that.'

It was better in the kitchen in the artificial light, the two of them sitting at the table, wearing their old dressing gowns, both drinking tea and Rusty smoking. Marginally better, anyway.

'I've been thinking,' Jess said, shaking the teapot and pouring herself more tea. 'What happened to you on that flight, Rusty, was a bit like what happened to George. Trauma, the doctor called it, and George hasn't got over it yet. But he will, that's the point. And so will you.'

She looked at him hopefully, but he only smoked in silence.

'Don't you think so?' she pressed.

'No,' he answered at last. 'It's different for me.'

'Why? Why is it different?'

'Because George isn't going to be among bombs again – at least, I hope not. He's got the chance to get over what happened to him. But there's no chance for me, it's always there.'

'Always there?'

'It's my job.' He stretched out his hand and took hers. 'Ah, you see, I shouldn't have told you. I've given you my burden.'

'Just a share. And I want it, anyway. Didn't I tell you, what happens to you, happens to me?'

'Does that mean,' he asked carefully, 'that you do care for me now? I mean ... really care?'

'Why, you know I do! We're married!'

Yes, they were married, and she did truly care for him, and for the rest of the short weekend said no more about the whisky. But when Rusty returned to Kenlin, Jess couldn't find the bottle. She knew he had taken it with him.

Thirty-Four

Though no one had really expected Moyra Beattie to make a full recovery, her death when it came in August still had the power to shock. As Addie said, with the sadness of experience, that was because death was always a shock, however folk might think themselves prepared for it.

'Look at me with your dad,' she murmured to Jess and Marguerite before the funeral. 'I knew what lay ahead, but when it happened – that was different, eh? And it'll have been the same for poor Derry. His sister's had to make all the arrangements. No good asking him, she said.'

'Poor Derry,' Jess echoed. She glanced at the clock. 'Well, we'd best away to the kirk. I expect there'll be a good turn out, eh? With all Derry's customers?'

'I daresay.' Addie was putting on a large black hat and studying herself in the mirror. 'Women and all. Was a time when women didn't go to funerals, you ken. In fact, a lot still don't, though I suppose it's an old-fashioned idea.'

'Why ever shouldn't they have gone?' Marguerite asked, adjusting a black armband on her uniform sleeve. 'Seems ridiculous to me.'

'Just the custom. Are you ready, then, girls?'

Though they told her they were ready to leave, it was Addie herself who seemed now to be hesitating at the door.

'Think I should say that I might not be going back to the house afterwards. The sister's laying on refreshments, but I'm no' keen.'

Jess and Marguerite exchanged looks.

'What's up, Ma?' Jess asked quietly. 'Why don't you want to go back to Derry's house?'

'Well – you know why.'

'I do not. You tell me why.'

'It's because of what Moyra said that time. About wanting me to take care of Derry when she'd gone.' A flush had risen to Addie's cheek. 'I'd feel that embarrassed.'

'What's all this?' Marguerite asked. 'Have I missed something?'

'It's just that when we sent to see Moyra in hospital, she asked Ma to look after Derry when she was gone,' Jess told her quickly. 'She didn't

195

mean anything – it was just she was ill and worried.

'Aye, well, now she is gone, and I keep thinking of what she said,' Addie muttered. 'I'm no' anxious to look Derry in the face.'

'You look him in the face every time you buy a pound of carrots, or he gives you tomatoes!' Jess cried.

'Aye, but after his wife's funeral, and in her house, it'd no' be the same.' Addie set her mouth firmly. 'I'll let you girls go without me. I'll say I've to get back to work, which is true.'

Marguerite put her arm in her mother's and walked her through the door.

'Come on, Ma, it'll look funny if you don't go to the house. You're Derry's neighbour. People will wonder about it, and you'd never want that.'

'That's true.' Jess closed the door behind them. 'We'll stick with you, Ma. You needn't talk to Derry on his own.'

'All right, then,' Addie sighed. 'But I just wish poor Moyra'd never said what she did.'

Making their way to the local kirk, as Addie walked ahead with other neighbours, Marguerite told Jess how well it had worked out for her to attend Moyra's funeral.

'Never thought I'd get the leave, you see. But when Ben said he'd be coming home before his posting, I twisted the CO's arm. I mean, it's the first time we've ever managed to be on leave together, eh?'

'How long's he got?'

'A week, like me.' Marguerite's smile vanish-

196

ed. 'Then he's away to the south of England. You heard he'd passed out well on his course?'

'Never thought he wouldn't. Why England, though?'

Marguerite stared. 'Why, you know what's happening, don't you? The Luftwaffe's attacking our planes and air stations all along the south coast. Have been since July. The phoney war's over.'

'I've been trying to put it out of my mind,' Jess said in a low voice.

'Because of Rusty? He'll be finishing soon, eh? And then where for him?'

'No idea.' Jess began to quicken her pace. 'Let's catch up with the others. Don't want to be late.'

As so often, the funeral service was an ordeal, with friends and customers remembering Moyra when she was young and fit, and thinking of her now, cut down by cruel illness while still not old, and having to leave her poor husband to mourn. But no bairns, of course, which had always been their tragedy. Och, what a miserable world it was then, and with news of what the German planes were doing, not likely to get any better!

Leaving at the end of the service, Addie managed to shake Derry's hand without raising her eyes to his ravaged face, and afterwards, going back to the house on the Links, which had been his father's, stayed close to her girls, while the cold ham and sandwiches were passed around and the tea poured.

'You see, it was all right, Ma,' Jess told her.

'Derry's got so many people to see, you won't have to talk to him at all.'

'You're making something out of nothing, is what I think,' Marguerite declared. 'Just keep on as usual and forget what Moyra said. All she meant was make him a bit of stew now and again, or a pudding or something. What else?'

Addie shrugged and said perhaps it was true she'd read things into Moyra's words that weren't there. What a relief, eh? Now, why didn't they offer to help Win, Derry's sister from Perth, who had so much to do? It was too late now to go back to work, anyway.

'Think I'll have to get back, though,' Jess said, looking at her watch. 'I've things to check. Marguerite, I'll see you soon, eh?'

'Course you will. Ben and me want you to come round with Ma for your tea one evening. Dad would like that, and Ben would, too.'

'Thanks, I'll look forward to it.' Jess took a last sandwich and thought, OK, that was a white lie, but what of it? She was always just a little uneasy, being with Ben, but she could hardly say no to meeting her brother-in-law again, and he would soon be leaving for the dangerous area of the south. Not aircrew, though, was he? Not like Rusty.

Back at the Princes, she was surprised and pleased to find someone waiting for her in Edie's office. It was George.

Thirty-Five

'George, how grand to see you!' she cried, while Edie smiled from her desk. 'Oh, but you're looking well!'

He didn't, in fact, look particularly well, being still very pale with a collar that was too big for his neck, and still the air of an invalid that made him seem strange. Yet, when Jess showed him into his old office, he seemed to be trying to be cheerful, walking well with his stick and taking the visitor's chair without any sign of emotion.

'Here you are then,' Jess said, a little awkwardly. 'Back in your old office. You should be behind the desk, you know.'

'No, no.' He shook his head. 'That's your desk now.'

'I'm only filling in for you, George, and you're on the mend. You'll soon be back with us.'

Again, he shook his head. 'Fact is, Jess, I'm not coming back.'

She took her own seat behind the desk and, fiddling with a pen, stared into his serious eyes.

'I don't understand – why don't you want to come back? This is your job, it's what you want to do.'

'Did want to do. Now ... I don't feel up to it.'

'You still ... hear the bombs?' she asked delicately.

'No, the doctor was right, they've gone. And the rocking floor. But that doesn't mean I'm the same as I was. I know now that I'll never be the same. I have to take too much care. I have to worry all the time what I can do.'

'Have the doctors told you that?'

He shrugged. 'They don't understand how I feel. Every heart case is different, that's the point.'

'So, you'll no' be working at all?'

'Oh, I'll still have to work, though maybe only part-time. I've Daisy to think about, you see, though she'd keep me at home, if she could.'

'What are you going to do, then?'

'It's all fixed. Daisy's brother has a small business making parts for various engines. He needs an admin assistant to keep an eye on the paper-work side of things, and he's offered me the job. It'll be less stressful than here, and I can do my own hours.' George leaned his bony hands on his stick and gazed appealingly at Jess. 'It's sad, I know, to say goodbye to the Princes. Don't think I don't feel it.'

'I'd never think that, George.'

'But it's time for me to hand over the baton. I'm just glad it's to you.'

Jess continued to roll her pen between her fingers.

'Can't be certain it will be to me, though. No' for a permanent job. I was always told I was just temporary.'

'You'll be permanent. I've already spoken to

200

John Syme and he said straight away, there'd be no question of asking you to stand down.' George rose slowly to his feet. 'He'll be getting in touch, so don't worry about it. Where on earth would they find anybody better than you, anyway?'

'I just can't imagine this place without you, George, that's the thing.'

'You know what they say – everybody can be done without. Now, what about a cup of coffee in the cafe? And then a complimentary cinema ticket for me, if you can spare one? You're showing a Spencer Tracy film I wouldn't mind seeing.'

'*North-West Passage*?' Jess nodded. 'George, you know you can have all the complimentary tickets you want.'

'Because I might actually get to watch a film or two nowadays, you mean? I'll bet you don't.'

'Remember Edna Angus? One of the usherettes? She said to me once that if you worked in a cinema, you never got to see a film right through. So, you're right, George. These days I hardly get to see one at all.'

They laughed together, but after they'd had their cup of coffee and Jess had shown George into the circle for his Spencer Tracy film, she had to return quickly to her own office to try to come to terms with George's news.

Of course, she could have been on top of the world, she told herself. Wasn't she now to be permanent manager of her beloved Princes, as soon as she received confirmation from John Syme? That should have been something to celebrate, surely?

If it had come at some other time, yes, she would have celebrated. Now, though, she had to think not only of George, sitting in the circle instead of at this very desk, but of the war that was now taking a new toll, with the bombing in the south, and of all who'd be involved. Maybe her own Rusty, who'd be finishing his course soon? Maybe Ben, who'd be in the danger zone, even if not flying. All the people who'd be at risk if Hitler started bombing cities, as he'd said he'd do.

Oh, what was the point of a job like hers, then? She'd always thought so much of it. Stocking the silver screen. Keeping the projectors turning. Taking people's minds off their troubles, transporting them to Never-Never Land, where, let's face it, she'd spent some time herself. Was any of it worth doing? Shouldn't she just go out and join up, as Sally had done, and Marguerite?

No. She straightened her shoulders. That wasn't the way to look at things. The Princes did do a good job. She did a good job, too. People did need what she and the silver screen could provide, for life was dark enough for most of them without taking that away. She'd keep on. She'd have to, for her life too would have been dark without her work.

Setting herself the target of tidying her desk, which usually made her feel better, she jumped as though shot when her telephone rang.

'Princes Street Picture House,' she intoned. 'How can I help you?'

'Jess, is that you?' she heard a man's voice say,

and before he'd given his name had recognized it. 'This is John Syme speaking. Can you spare a minute?'

'Certainly, John,' she replied. 'Only too happy.'

Thirty-Six

'Well, well, Jess, that's something, isn't it?'

Ben, acting the perfect host for Marguerite's family visiting his father's house, was smiling, though keeping his eyebrows raised. 'Manager of the Princes, at your age! Amazing.'

'I told you in one of my letters that she'd been made manager,' Marguerite said sharply. 'No need to look so surprised.'

'That was temporary, though. This is permanent. Makes a difference.'

'It does,' Addie chimed in. 'I think she's done very well.'

'And so do I,' Mr Daniel agreed, with a smile for Jess. 'You've obviously impressed those bosses, eh?'

'Not all of 'em,' Jess felt constrained to admit. 'It was Mr Syme who wanted me to get the job. I suppose there wasn't a lot of choice.'

'Now, don't run yourself down,' Addie told her. 'They wouldn't have appointed you if you weren't right.' She stood up and looked across to Marguerite. 'Want me to give you a hand with that fish pie, pet?'

'Oh, yes, please, Ma,' Marguerite cried. 'I thought you'd never ask!'

When Jess was left alone with Ben and his father, she looked around the little front room, and politely remarked on its pleasantness. Privately, she was surprised that Marguerite had not so far left her mark on a room so carefully furnished by her late mother-in-law. But then she hadn't had much time to do anything before joining up, and also wouldn't want to upset Ben's father. No doubt he wanted to keep all the antimacassars embroidered by his wife, and her choice of framed lithographs, artificial flowers and enough ornaments to set up a shop. Yet, Jess had been sincere when she'd said the room was pleasant. There was an atmosphere of a couple's shared affection here which still lingered, though only one half of the couple remained; the sort of atmosphere Jess, in fact, rather envied.

'How are things with Rusty?' Ben asked, coming to sit next to her on the sofa, while his father nodded in his chair. 'Isn't he due to finish his course soon?'

'Yes, quite soon. He's been doing very well.'

Ben lit a cigarette. 'Met a chap from Kenlin the other day who knows him. Said he was a good guy.'

'So he is.'

'But this chap mentioned he hadn't seemed so fit lately. OK on the job, but a bit – you know – nervy off it.'

Jess looked away from Ben's intent gaze. 'I

don't know why he should've said that. Rusty's fine.'

'That's good, then. I'm glad to hear it.'

'I tell you, that fellow doesn't know what he's talking about!'

'Yes, all right, he got it wrong.' Ben hesitated a moment. 'But, if you should ever need any help, Jess, remember, you've got a brother now.'

'That's very kind of you, Ben, but why should I need help?'

He shrugged. 'I suppose everybody needs help, the way things are. We're so alone, aren't we? Now that France has fallen, who's left? Hitler's going to step up this bombing, you know. It'll be the cities next.'

'You weren't talking about the bombing just then, though, were you?'

'Well, you've had experience of it.'

She raised her eyes to his. 'Why don't you say straight out what's worrying you?'

Again, he hesitated.

'Seems, in fact, I've rather worried you. Didn't mean to. I'm sorry. All I wanted to say was that if ever you do need a friendly shoulder and I'm home, you can count on mine.'

'But you're being posted down south, aren't you?'

'That's right, but I'll get leave.'

'I hope you'll be all right,' she said quietly.

'As a matter of fact, I'm looking forward to it.' He gave a wry grin. 'I've got over not being air-crew, you know. Planes in the sky need work on the ground, and chaps like me can do it.'

'Of course you can!' she cried. 'I bet you'll be

205

rocketing up the promotion lists in no time!'

His expression softened. 'So I've been told. But, what's it matter? We all do what we can, don't we?' He stubbed out his cigarette and rose. 'I see Dad's waking up, and I'm starving – don't know about you? Shall we find out what Marguerite and your ma are doing in the kitchen?'

After the evening had passed very pleasantly and they'd all enjoyed Marguerite's meal – 'Ma's', really,' she'd said modestly, 'I only found the cod.' – Ben walked Addie and Jess to the tram stop where they kissed him goodbye. He was leaving the next day.

'Take care,' Addie said, putting her hand on his shoulder. 'Come back safely to Marguerite, eh?'

'You bet. And you two look after yourselves as well.' He glanced at Jess. 'Hope all goes well for Rusty,' he murmured. 'Drop me a line if you've time.'

'I will,' she promised, watching him walk away, waving, but as she waved too, her heart was heavy in her breast. He knows, she thought. He knows about Rusty. He didn't put it into words, but she could tell he knew, all the same. That was why he'd asked her to call on him if she needed help. But how could she do that? How could she talk about Rusty's problems with Ben?

'Here's mine!' Addie cried, as her tram came into sight. 'Jess, come round day after tomorrow, eh, to say goodbye to Marguerite? Poor lassie, she's to go back to Drem and she'll be all the time thinking of Ben, down there with all the jerry planes!'

'I'll be there,' Jess assured her, seeing her on to the tram, then standing back to wave goodbye.

'Yours next!' Addie cried from the platform.

'Hope so!' Jess called.

But as she stood at the stop, still waiting, her thoughts had returned to Rusty. What did the future hold for him? If his superiors discovered his drinking, would he be court-martialled? He'd sworn he never took risks at work and she believed him, because he'd never risk other lives as well as his own, but someone had said something to Ben and Ben had drawn his own conclusions. If only she could see Rusty – find out what was going on.

'You wanting this one, hen?' a woman asked in her ear, and giving a start of surprise, Jess saw her tram was beside her at the stop. Although folk said the trams made enough noise to wake the dead, she'd been so deep in her own thoughts, she hadn't heard her number and almost missed it.

'Oh, I do!' she cried, 'thanks!'

And jumping on to the platform, she was borne away to her lonely home.

Thirty-Seven

On a warm, thundery afternoon in August, Jess was in her office, working on a plan she had for children's Saturday morning cinema, still trying not to think of what was happening in the south where the Battle of Britain continued to rage.

Every day, the planes from the Luftwaffe came over, attacking airfields and radar stations, and every day, the planes of the British Fighter Command went up to do battle. How long could it go on? Until Hitler realised he wasn't going to win, and turned to something else. And everyone was pretty sure what that would be – bombing British cities. He was never going to forget the reprisal raids by the British over Berlin in return for an earlier, mistaken, attack on London. It would only be a matter of time before the raids came, and might invasion follow? In the meantime, the fights in the skies went on.

There was nothing the onlookers of the country could do except, as the order went, 'carry on' – with their own lives, their own work, which was why Jess was concentrating hard on her new project for the children.

It was not something the Princes had offered before, but Jess was keen to make her cinema more a part of the community, and with so many children now returned from the country districts where they'd been sent as evacuees, she was sure her idea would be welcome. After all, cinemas in other areas had been doing it for years – why not the Princes, the best in the city?

Mustn't appear to believe we're too grand, she thought, pencilling in the types of film that would appeal to her new audience. Mickey Mouse and the Disney cartoons, of course, and Popeye, and maybe some of the old *Our Gang* series. But then they'd need a few educational films as well – geographical stuff, maybe, and animal welfare. Maybe she should set up some meetings with the schools – see what they'd recommend.

'Hello, hello, anybody home?' came a voice at her door, and it was Sally's.

'Sally! How nice to see you!' Jess cried, jumping to her feet. 'I didn't know you were on leave.'

'Permanent leave,' Sally answered with a laugh, as they hugged each other. 'Oh, my word, Jess, aren't you the grand one! Manager of the Princes, no less! Didn't I always say you'd do well?'

Settling herself in the interview chair, Sally's round blue eyes rested appraisingly on Jess.

'But, oh, lassie, you've lost weight, eh? Is it worrying over Rusty, then? Has he got his posting yet?'

'No' yet, but I'm expecting him home any time for leave after the course. Then, he'll be away.' Jess tried to smile. 'Like Ben, you know. He's been posted to the south of England.'

'Poor Marguerite.' Sally shook her head. 'At least Arnold's still in Scotland. Och, what a time we're all having, eh? Poor George, as well. I was that upset when I heard about him, you know. Thank the Lord you were around to take over!'

'I'd never have got the job if it hadn't been for the circumstances, Sally. I'm no' going to pretend otherwise.'

'You'd have got it eventually, Jess. I always knew you weren't going to stay in the box office. But listen ... I've something to tell you.' Sally leaned forward and put out her left hand. 'See that, dear?'

Jess stared. 'A wedding ring, Sally? You're married? And you never said a word!'

'It was all very hush-hush. Special licence. Just the two of us and a couple of witnesses. But I'm here to tell you all about it now.'

'Why, though, Sally? Why'd you suddenly decide to get married, when you said you wouldn't?'

'Come on, now, you're the bright one, eh? Why do folk sometimes get married in a hurry?'

'You're no'...you're no' telling me you're...'

'I am, dear.' Sally gave one of her famous chuckles. 'I'm expecting. And after our two mothers, you're one of the first to know.'

'I can't believe it,' Jess was murmuring. 'I just can't take it in.'

'Haven't you noticed anything unusual about me, then? And I don't mean I'm showing, because at the moment I'm just my usual overweight self. But something's different.'

Hair's blonder, face is plumper – Jess, frowning, suddenly cried, 'Why, Sally, where's your uniform?'

'First prize to Mrs MacVail! And why I'm no' wearing my uniform is because I'm on that permanent leave I mentioned. I'm out, Jess, out of the army. For me – the war is over!'

At the dazed expression on Jess's face, Sally chuckled again.

'For obvious reasons, expectant mums are given the boot, and as I'm expecting, that's me out. It's a joke, eh? After all the advice I gave you, to go and fall for a baby myself?'

'Listen, I think I'll get us some tea.'

'And biscuits, if you've got any, dear!' Sally called. 'I'm starving.'

Over the tea and the ginger snaps Edie had produced, Sally explained how she'd been, as she put it, caught out.

'Aye, caught out, Jess. Caught in the trap. Thing was, Arnold and me'd had no leave together, and then we wangled a weekend pass and went to a hotel for a bit of a treat. We were that excited, we just clean forgot our you know what, and Arnold said, "What the hell, we'll be all right for once."'

'Talk about famous last words!' Sally cheerfully drank her tea. 'Next thing I knew, I was saying goodbye to the girls and on my way home, having to tell my mother and Arnold's and putting up with all the wailing and gnashing of teeth etcetera. Thank God I'd got my wedding ring!'

Sally pressed Jess's hand.

'Sorry you weren't there to see me married, dear, but I've come round soon as I could to tell you.'

'And I appreciate it. But when's the great day for the baby?'

'Oh, not till January. A nice long way off. Before that, Arnold and me are going to rent our own flat. There'll be no staying with my ma or Arnold's. My baby's going to have his own home. Or her own home, as the case may be.'

Sally rose and gave Jess a last tight hug.

'Now, I'd better go. But we'll meet again soon, eh? Have a coffee, or something, now that I'm a lady of leisure?'

'And if you ever get tired of being that, and the baby's got a minder, maybe you'll come back to the Princes?' Jess asked. 'Oh, it'd be so good to have somebody like you around here again!'

'Hey, I might take you up on that. Going to walk me out?'

On their way through the foyer, they passed the same pictures of the stars that Sally had pointed out to the candidates on the box office interview day. Which, to Jess, always seemed to belong to another age, when she'd been a much younger, quite different person.

'There they are!' Sally cried. 'All the stars, eh? Oh, my, I could tell you were star-struck all right, Jess. You were up there with them, weren't you? Eyes shining like it was Christmas. Remember how you used to like Henry Fonda?'

'When did I say I liked Henry Fonda?' Jess asked quickly.

'Well, was it Tyrone Power, then? Or Laurence Olivier? I'm sure it was one of those handsome heart-throbs.' Sally's cheerfulness failed her for a moment. 'All seems different now, eh?' Her lip trembled. 'World seems darker.'

'Don't say that!' Jess cried. 'Think of all you've got to look forward to. The baby and everything.'

'Aye, but it's the chaps we'll want home, eh? And Arnold's with the Black Watch – they're always in the thick of battle.'

'He'll come home, Sally,' Jess said urgently, wondering why people brought out such words without meaning. But of course she knew why. They were for comfort. For hope. You had to say something. 'Rusty, too,' she added.

'Well, you watch out when you meet Rusty again,' Sally cried, casting aside her sudden fit of the blues. 'Aye, you take care. Or there'll be two of us with the green ration books for expectant mothers!'

I'll take care, all right, Jess told herself. In the future, yes, she would want a baby, but not now, when she was so keen to make something of her job. As for Rusty's future – she couldn't bear even to contemplate that one day he might not have one at all.

'I'd just like to pop in to see the dear old place,' Sally was murmuring, bouncing into the box office, but of course she couldn't stay long for Flo was on her own and the queue waiting for tickets was winding into the street.

'Watch out, you'll have to lend a hand,' Jess said with a laugh, at which Flo, giving a

213

harassed smile, said she wished Sally could, and Sally herself promised, next time she was in, she would.

'Not to worry,' Jess told Sally. 'I'll help Flo for a while, seeing as Netta is not due in till five. We're still what you always said we were, you know – one big happy family!'

'Ah, that's good, Jess, that's good!' Sally cried, and hurried away, back to her waiting mother, calling as she went that she'd be in touch.

'Don't forget!' Jess cried, and telling Flo to go for a cup of tea, stepped back with ease into her old job, just for half an hour.

When she arrived home that evening, there was a letter on the doormat. Thank God, from Rusty.

He had done well. Passed out near the top of the list, which meant he was truly a navigator. He would be home at the weekend, for end-of-course leave, so get ready to celebrate. No mention of a posting, of course, for the censor would probably only have crossed it out, but while she was preparing to celebrate, she'd better prepare herself for Rusty's news of it.

Thirty-Eight

Somehow, Rusty seemed to know, even in the darkness, that Jess was smiling, and ran his finger round the outline of her mouth as they lay together on his first night home.

'What's the joke?' he whispered. 'Or is that smile for me?'

'All my smiles are for you.' For some time, she kissed him, then pulled away, still smiling. 'But I was thinking of Sally.'

'Sally? We've just made love, and you're thinking of Sally Dollar?'

'Ah, but she's isn't Sally Dollar now, she's Mrs Arnold Adams. She got married, and you'll never guess why. There's a baby on the way!'

'Help, earth-shattering news!' Rusty grinned, reaching out for his cigarettes on the bedside table. 'So, what's so funny?'

'I wasn't smiling about the baby. In fact, I think it's lovely – Sally's really thrilled, whatever she says. No, I'm just remembering all the advice she gave me and how she said she wouldn't be married for years. And then she falls for a baby herself!'

Rusty, smoking, for some time made no comment.

'That was the funny thing,' Jess said, trying to

see his expression. 'Don't you think so?'

'But now Sally's thrilled. How would you feel, Jess?'

'About having a baby? Well, I'd like one some time, but I don't feel ready yet. I've got my job.' Her fingers kneaded the edge of the sheet. 'And then – the time's no' right, is it?'

'I'm not so sure. Maybe it's exactly right for you to have a baby.' Rusty, feeling for the ashtray by the bed, put out his cigarette and took Jess in his arms. 'Mine, Jess.'

In spite of the warmth of the night, she shivered and drew away.

'I know what you're thinking,' she whispered. 'You're thinking a bairn would be something of you, aren't you? For me to have – if you...'

He put his hand over her lips. 'No words. Don't put those thoughts into words. I'm coming back.' He laughed. 'Haven't gone anywhere yet.'

'Where are you going, Rusty? You haven't told me.'

'An airfield in Kent. Mainly reconnaissance work.'

'That's a relief. I thought you'd be bombing.'

'Not yet. For me, anyway.'

'You will be going on raids, though?'

'Look, I don't know what I'll be doing exactly.'

She was silent, staring into the unknown, but knowing there was no point in questioning him further. After a while, he said quietly, 'You still don't want to, Jess? I mean, start a baby?'

'No, it wouldn't be right just now.'

216

'Because you know what it's like, to have no dad?'

'Hush, don't talk like that, Rusty!'

'Well, the other thing is, you've got your job.'

'And I've got my job. I'll no' deny it means a lot to me.' Holding him close, she kissed him passionately. 'But no' as much as you.'

'You want to go to sleep now?' he asked tenderly.

'Oh, I don't think so,' She flung her arms around him. 'Might be a bit of a waste.'

'My thoughts exactly,' Rusty said.

In the morning, bliss over, reality set in. As Jess prepared their frugal breakfast, she knew she was going to have to speak about things that mattered. For her own peace of mind. This was the time, before Rusty left her, to discuss what hung over her like a dark cloud, except when making love rolled it away. But they couldn't make love all the time.

'Sorry, the breakfast's no' up to much,' she told him, when Rusty came into the kitchen, smelling of soap from the bath she'd run for him, his short hair damp and on end. 'There's bacon, but no eggs. I used them for that cake you like.'

'Hey, bacon's a feast! It's what the pilots get.' He gave her a smacking kiss on the cheek and sat down. 'But you've got some, haven't you?'

'You know I'm no' fussy over bacon. Toast'll do me.'

Pouring tea, she looked away from his happy face, so that she should not be distracted. But maybe she should say nothing? Let things go. Share his happiness on this last weekend before his posting? No. Resolutely, she turned aside from that easy option. She had to speak. There was no other way.

'It was grand that you did so well on the course,' she said, carefully scraping a little butter on her toast. 'There were no problems, then?'

Already, his gaze was wary, as he looked at her over his teacup. 'I told you I'd no problems with the course, Jess.'

'But you do have problems, Rusty.'

He set down his cup, pushed away his plate.

'What are you trying to say, Jess? Just tell me.'

'Well ... I saw Ben before he went south. Marguerite asked Ma and me round.'

Rusty's lips tightened. 'And what's Ben got to do with anything?'

'He told me he'd met someone from your course.'

'Who?'

'He didn't give his name. But this chap, whoever he was, said he knew you and that you were a good guy...'

'Ha!' Rusty cried. 'So I am, then.'

'I said that, too, but, apparently, the chap thought you were...' Jess hesitated. 'A bit nervy. Maybe not so fit ... as you'd been. I'm wondering ... why he said that.'

'So am I. He has his cheek, discussing me with a complete stranger.'

'Ben is sort of your brother-in-law, Rusty.'

'But the other fellow didn't know Ben, did he? What the hell gave him the right to tell Ben anything at all about me, for God's sake?'

'Does he know about your drinking?' Jess cried. 'That's what's worrying me. If he knows, who else knows?'

'Nobody! Nobody knows, or I'd have been out on my ear by now. There's no need for you to worry. It's my secret, and yours – no one else's.'

Bravely, her gaze locked with his. 'I think Ben knows.'

Rusty pushed back his chair and stood up.

'He couldn't,' he said huskily. 'He's not even been up to the airfield. There's no way he could know.'

'Unless this fellow from the course knows. And told him.'

Watching him now, Jess was painfully wondering how she could ever have thought Rusty looked happy. And she had done it. She had wiped the bliss from his face as though with a wet towel. She had ruined his time with her, and it might be his last. Yet, as she ran to take him into her arms, she knew she couldn't have taken any other course. There'd been no other way, except to tell him, warn him.

'Rusty,' she gasped, 'I'm so sorry. I'm so sorry I've upset you. But I had to tell you – I had to try to make you see...'

'See what?' he asked dully. 'That I'm hurting you? I know that already.'

'Hurting yourself! How are you going to carry on, keeping your drinking a secret? You know it isn't possible. It will come to light and then ... well, I don't know what will happen ... but, oh, Rusty, could you no' try to give it up?'

219

He slowly ran his hand down her face, and looked away.

'I wish I could, Jess. I wish I could.'

They put the dishes into the sink and sat down together on the sofa in their living room, winding their arms around each other as though all was well, as though they were still the carefree lovers of the night. But to Jess, it was as though they'd both grown older, taken on the cares of a lifetime they could never shake off – except that they had to.

Dredging up strength she didn't know she had, she pulled herself free from Rusty's embrace and took only his hands.

'If you want to, you can,' she said softly. 'I know it will be hard...'

'Jess, you don't know anything,' he said wearily. 'It's not possible, just to stop like that. Especially not the way things are.' He pulled his hands from hers. 'What do I do? Join one of these associations? These gatherings where they try to help you? And then I say, excuse me, I'm just off to bomb Berlin, or something, and I'm too scared to get on the plane? Be reasonable, Jess, I can't do anything like that while we're at war.'

She stood up. 'Are you saying you won't even try?'

He rose to stand beside her. 'No, I'm not saying that. I know I'm at risk, I know I could be in deep trouble. But if I say I'll try, it doesn't mean I'll succeed.'

'No, but just to hear you say that, Rusty, just to

220

hear you say you will try, whatever it costs – that means so much to me.' Her voice trembled, her eyes stung with tears. 'So much – you've no idea...'

He held her close without speaking, and after a long moment, she drew away and, dabbing away her tears, managed a smile.

'So, shall we get ready and go to Ma's? The butcher's let her have a joint this week. She's going to do Yorkshire puddings.'

Sunday dinner with Addie? Roast beef and Yorkshire puddings? Just like old times. Roll away the war, then. Roll away the problems.

'Let's go,' Rusty said lightly. 'Shame I have to wear my uniform, but it's the rule.'

'I like you in your uniform,' Jess told him.

'I like you anyway,' he whispered, and for some time they clung together, while around the city the sun shone and war seemed far away.

Thirty-Nine

In early September, some days after Rusty had left for Kent, the Luftwaffe bombed London. The Battle of Britain was over. The 'Blitz' had begun.

'Of course, it's just what we knew Hitler would do,' John Syme remarked to Jess after one of her regular meetings with his board in Glasgow. 'He's lost the Battle of Britain, so now he's trying air raids. Won't make any difference, we'll never give in.'

'But the poor Londoners,' Jess murmured. 'They're bearing the brunt of it.'

'For now, yes, it's London's turn. Tomorrow – who knows?'

'They'll be targeting other cities?'

'Sure to. They'll move on to Liverpool, or Birmingham, places like that.' John shook his head. 'Or maybe here.'

'Edinburgh?' Jess's gaze sharpened. 'You really think that?'

'No. Not really. We haven't enough industry to make it worth their while. No, if it's anywhere in Scotland, it'll be Glasgow. The shipyards. The docks.'

'I suppose we shouldn't expect the south to take it all,' Jess said in a low voice. 'I feel terrible, anyway, thinking of so many folk in danger. So many lives already lost.'

'Pilots, civilians – that's modern war, I'm afraid.' John studied her thoughtfully. 'How are things for you, then, Jess? Your husband's away now? I won't ask where.'

'He's away. I can tell you it's in the south.'

'Hard for you.'

'Me and thousands of others.'

'Still. When it's you, it's you. At least, you've your work. Plenty to do. Packed audiences every night, from your audience figures, and not too much need to worry these days about sales targets. Budget seems to be working out well, too. We're pleased, Jess.'

'I'm glad.'

222

'And we liked your idea of the children's Saturday morning programmes. Let me know how that progresses.'

'I will. I've a couple of meetings lined up with the schools, now that the summer holidays are over.

'Summer holidays?' John laughed. 'What are those?'

Travelling back to Edinburgh on a crowded train, Jess pondered on John's casual mention of possible raids on Edinburgh. He'd soon substituted Glasgow, but who knew what was in Hitler's mind? And it only took one rogue raider, as she well knew, to cause horror and tragedy.

Think of those seven lives lost in the tenement. Think of poor George, who would never be quite the same again. She herself, though she had never suffered as George had suffered, could still remember the crump-crump of those bombs falling on Leith. Could still wake in the night sometimes, hearing them again.

Imagine what it would be like to be in the kind of raids the Londoners were enduring! Night after night, to hear the sirens, go to the shelter, wonder if you'd survive, and if you did, would your house still be standing when the raid was over? Nightmare!

But as the train drew in to Waverley and passengers began to disgorge, Jess knew she had her own nightmares to face that were quite separate from those wrought by bombs. One was hearing that Rusty wasn't coming back. That was the worst. Of course it was. Nothing would matter if that happened.

The other was that he had been found out. Found out, drinking. Somehow, in his new posting, the nightmare went, he had let his drinking affect his work, which was now the real thing, flying on real ops, having a real job, not training any more. So that anything he did wrong now would mean – oh, God, what would it mean? She didn't know. That was where her nightmare always ended. Where her mind closed down.

And closed down now, as she crossed the busy station and saw ahead of her a tall, dark-haired airman, limping badly and supporting himself with a stick. A tall, dark-haired airman she recognized and called to, through all the people jostling in her way.

'Ben! Ben! Wait!'

And Ben Daniel turned and stood resting on his stick until she reached him.

'Jess! What a bit of luck seeing you! Where did you come from, then?'

'Why, I might ask the same of you. But what's happened to you? Oh, God, you're injured?'

'Nothing to worry about. Just damaged my leg a bit. Listen, you wouldn't care to come for a cup of tea, would you? They'd nothing on the train and God knows when I'll find a taxi to get home.'

'Of course I'll come with you!' she cried, thinking if she was late back to her desk, what of it? The Princes would survive. 'Here, let me take your bag.'

'How embarrassing – a young lady carrying my bag! No, thanks, Jess, I can manage.'

But she took it anyway and carved a passage through the crowds to the station buffet.

'I'm told the rock cakes are just the same as ever,' she told Ben with a smile. 'If no' exactly pre-war.'

'Hey, I wouldn't care if they were pre-war. I'm starving.'

Forty

The bad news was that there were no rock cakes, the good news being that there were scones. Hard as rock, anyway, but still something to eat, and even came with a scrape of margarine.

'No jam?' asked Jess, who was getting the tea, while Ben, at a nearby table, took off his hat and gingerly stretched out his damaged leg.

'No jam,' the elderly assistant told her smartly. 'There's a war on, you ken.'

'I'd noticed,' Jess retorted, and carried away her tray.

'Here we are,' she told Ben, setting out their large thick cups of tea and the famous scones. 'This will keep you going.'

'You're an angel, Jess. Though I feel a terrible fraud, letting you do all the fetching and carrying.'

'Come on, you have a bad leg. How did you damage it, anyway?' Sipping her tea, she looked across at him, preparing to smile – and caught her breath. Across his brow, originally hidden by his cap, was a wide, livid scar, while running down his cheek was another, still showing signs of stitches. On his hand, holding his cup, was a mass of smaller cuts and faded bruises.

'Dear God, Ben, what happened?' she whispered. 'You have been injured, haven't you? And Marguerite's never said a word...'

'She didn't know until yesterday when I told her I was coming up.' Ben had lowered his dark, shadowed eyes from Jess's look of concern. 'I managed to get through on the phone to her at Drem, so now she's trying to get a few days' leave.' He began to eat his scone. 'It's not as bad as it looks, Jess, no need to look so alarmed. As they say, I was just in the wrong place at the wrong time.'

'What wrong place? Just tell me what happened.'

'OK, I was in our hut at the airfield when a daylight bomber let us have it. Missed the hut, but the blast blew me across the ground – well, dragged me, I suppose you might say. Lacerated my leg, damaged my face and my hands where I'd tried to save myself, and knocked me out. When I came round I was in hospital, bandaged to the eyeballs, suffering concussion.'

'Oh, Ben! And you never told Marguerite?'

'No, I didn't want to worry her. She's got enough on her plate, servicing the planes at Drem. What the hell – I wasn't seriously hurt. Why upset her? I didn't tell Dad, either, until yesterday.'

Ben put forward his empty cup. 'You couldn't

226

get me some more tea, could you, Jess? Look –
I've got some money somewhere...'

'Don't be silly, Ben, I think I can afford a few
coppers.'

When she brought more tea for them both, he
drank his thirstily and lit a cigarette.

'Thank God for a Woodbine, eh? But that's
enough about me. I'm OK. They've let me come
up here to recover a bit, but I'll be going back.
No real damage done.'

'No real damage?' She bent her head. 'I'm just
thanking God you survived. Were other people
involved? Were they all right.'

'Most of 'em,' he answered carefully. 'Let's
talk about you, though. How come you were
here at the station?'

'I'd just come from a meeting with the owners
in Glasgow. It's a regular thing. I have to make
my report on audience figures, budgets – things
like that.'

Ben's eyes glowed. 'Jess, I'm impressed. But
then you know that, don't you? And Rusty – he
must be proud of you. How is he, then? And
where is he, come to that?'

'He's at an airfield in Kent. Doing reconnaissance, he said. That's all I know.'

'Passed out well from his course, I take it?'

'Oh, yes, very well.'

'So, no problems?'

'No, no problems.'

Heaving a great sigh, Ben crushed out his
cigarette and, reaching across the table, took
Jess's hand.

'Jess, you remember what I said to you, don't

you? If you ever wanted a friendly shoulder and I was home, mine would be available? Well, I'm home, and I've still got a shoulder.'

'I think I said I didn't need any help.' She looked down at her hand in his, and slowly drew it away. 'But thanks, Ben. Thanks all the same.'

'Would it make things easier if I told you I knew what was wrong?'

Her eyes met his, then fell.

'I ... guessed you did. I don't know how.'

'MacPherson, the guy I met – he told me.'

'Oh, God. He did know, then? I was so afraid he might. I told Rusty, but he was so sure no one knew...'

'Several of the lads on the course knew. You can't be a solitary drinker in the RAF without somebody suspecting something. Why skive off to your billet all the time if you don't have to?' Ben groaned. 'He was damned lucky his CO never got to hear of it.'

'The lads on the course – they can't have said?'

'No, Josh MacPherson said they wouldn't shop him. As long as he didn't put anybody at risk. He was too nice, he said, they liked him. But now he's on ops, Jess, things are going to have to be different. You know that, don't you?'

'Yes, and so does he. He's promised to try to give up, he really has.' Jess's hands were shaking and she clasped them under the table, while her eyes beseeched Ben for the reassurance she knew he couldn't give. 'And I think he will. He knows the danger, no one better.'

'I wish to God I'd been able to talk to him,

228

Jess. I think that's why Josh told me what he did, because he hoped I'd be able to help. But sometimes I think Rusty doesn't trust me – I don't know why.'

'Of course he trusts you, Ben!'

He shrugged. 'Well, he was my colleague, and I like to think he's my friend. I don't want him to be hurt, or to hurt you, so, for both your sakes, he has to sort himself out. Why in God's name does he need to drink, anyway?'

'Because he's afraid of flying. It happened after he almost crashed on a training exercise. After that, he couldn't face going up without the thought of the drink to come.'

Ben's face was suddenly expressionless. 'Aircrew, and he couldn't take it? He should have given it up. He should have just told them straight out, he couldn't do it. Some of us never got the chance.'

They left the buffet, walking slowly at Ben's pace, and found the queue for the taxis – a great long crocodile of people stretching round the station.

'My God, I'd better try for the tram,' Ben muttered. 'I daresay I could do it.'

'You should take priority,' Jess cried.

'Because I'm a wounded soldier!' He laughed. 'Take a look – half the queue fits that description. I don't like to ask, Jess, but if you could manage the bag, I think I'd be all right.'

'Of course, I'll take the bag and see you to the tram.' Jess's eyes filled with sudden tears. 'Only too happy.'

'Hey, hey, I'm all right,' he said lightly. 'This
229

is just temporary.'

'And I said I was thanking God for that.'

In spite of his protestations, she escorted him all the way to his father's house, where she saw him in and his father cling to him with the same sort of quick tears as her own. And then Ben hugged her and kissed her cheek, asking her to come round soon with Addie, when Marguerite would be there.

'And has it been a help?' he whispered. 'To talk?'

'It has. It's lightened the burden.'

'The shoulder will always be there, Jess.'

'I know, Ben. And thanks.'

But that night, as she'd expected, the nightmare of Rusty's disgrace returned. Because Ben knew, and others knew. How long before someone knew down in Kent?

Forty-One

But no one ever knew, down in Kent. Perhaps, as time went by, someone would have discovered what was going on, but, for Rusty, time ran out. In March 1941, on a raid over Germany that was for bombing, not reconnaissance, his plane was shot down, and for Jess there came a nightmare that was real. The telegram.

Of course, all yellow envelopes arriving in

wartime brought nightmare, or fear of it. So much so, that people sometimes couldn't readily take in their content – which was what happened to Jess.

The telegram was delivered early, before she'd left for work, and she'd opened the door to the knock, expecting nothing more than ordinary post. But when she saw the telegraph boy and what he held in his hand, the world seemed to swing and she with it, so that she would have fallen had he not reached out to hold her steady.

'Want to sit down?' he asked kindly, used perhaps to her type of reaction, for he seemed to be looking for a chair.

'No, no – I'll just ... see what it says...'

But when she'd torn the envelope open and read the words pasted on little slips of paper within, she couldn't seem to take them in.

'Regret to inform you...'

Oh, God, he was dead. Rusty was dead. Killed. Shot down. Here, it said so. 'Regret to inform you...'

'He's dead!' she cried. 'My husband's dead!'

And let the telegram fall from her hand, as she leaned against the open door.

'Missus, he might no' be deed,' the boy said, reading the message, which he'd picked up from the ground. 'It says here, he's been reported missing. Did you no' see that, then?'

No, she hadn't seen it. She didn't then know what she'd seen. A message that wasn't there, for though Rusty's plane had come down over

231

enemy territory, it was not yet known what had happened to its occupants. All that could be said in the telegram was that LAC Russell MacVail was missing and that further information would be given when available.

Missing, then. That meant there was still hope. A hope so frail, it seemed to bend and fall as she reached out to take it, but was still not to be denied.

'Missing,' she whispered to the boy, who was now turning to go. 'Wait, I'll get my bag...'

'No, thanks, Missus, that's all right.' He touched his cap. 'Just hope you get good news, eh?'

Hope, there was the word again.

'You're a good boy,' she said softly. 'I'll always remember you.'

But already he was on his way, smiling in embarrassed fashion, as he swung himself on to his bike and pedalled fast away.

That morning, Jess did not go into work; she went to the phone box. The first call was to her mother at the camouflage factory, the second to Edie at the Princes cinema, the third to Marguerite at Drem, and the fourth to Sally, who was lucky enough to have a telephone in her flat.

Then she sat down in her living room, folded her hands and thought of nothing, as though she must be very, very careful and save herself from thinking the wrong things. Better not to think of anything, than have all the wrong thoughts come flooding in.

So it was, when Addie came hurrying round, she found her active, vibrant Jess just sitting on her sofa, staring into space. Jess reduced to a statue? Nothing could have brought home more clearly what that telegram had meant.

'Jess, Jess, he might be all right!' Addie cried. 'They say he's missing, he's no' dead. Folk go missing all the time, and they turn up.'

'How many do you know?' Jess asked.

'Och, never mind! Everyone knows it's true, what I say. But have you no' even made yourself some tea, you poor girl? Hot sweet tea is what you need. You're as white as a snowflake, you're suffering from shock. Come on, we'll get the kettle on, eh?'

Slowly, with her mother's help, Jess thawed. Began to feel again, to let the thoughts she so dreaded sweep in to her mind; to face the images she'd always known she'd have to face.

'Now, it's just as I say, Rusty's no' dead, just missing,' Addie kept telling her. 'What you have to do is hope. Cling on to hope. And don't give in, till – well, till you know what's happened. Here, pet, have some more tea.'

'No, I don't want any more tea.' Jess rose to her feet, feeling as stiff as though she'd run a mile. 'I think I'll go into work after all, Ma.'

'Never! You're too shocked, Jess. You'll never be able to concentrate.'

'I will. It'll be good for me, it'll help. If I stay here, I'll just think the worst.' Jess's voice thickened with tears. 'I'll keep seeing Rusty – as he might be – and if I go to work, I'll have to look at other things.'

'Well, if you're sure.' Addie was dubious. 'But tonight, come to me, eh? Don't sit here on your own.'

'All right, I will.' Jess was on her way to the bathroom to splash cold water over her face, comb her hair, try to seem as usual. 'Thanks, Ma.'

'I've got a nice bit of stew ready, and Derry will be bringing some vegetables. He's coming up for his tea.'

'Derry?' Jess paused. 'Is he feeling better, these days?'

'I'd no' say that. But I often give him a meal – it's easier than carrying stuff down.'

'Yes, I suppose it is. I'll come round then, after work.'

Oh, poor lassie, thought Addie, wiping her eyes and clearing away the teacups. Oh, poor Jess. Didn't help at all, did it, that so many folk were in the same boat?

Forty-Two

Everyone was so kind. All her staff – Edie and the usherettes, Flo and Netta, Trevor and Fred, Joan from the cafe, Ron and Hughie from the projection room – all came to hug her, murmur words of comfort, even share tears.

'Now should you have come in?' Trevor asked solicitously. 'We'd have managed, you know.'

'Aye, we'd have kept going,' Ron agreed. 'The film's OK – niver a break this time, you ken.'

'Thank heavens it's not a war film,' Joan Baxter whispered to Flo. *'Pride and Prejudice –* that'll not make things worse for poor Jess.'

'I wanted to come into work,' Jess told them, so grateful for their concern, yet suddenly longing to be alone in her office. And of course, they understood, and left her to deal with her loaded desk on her own, while Edie quietly slipped in coffee and went out again with her hankie to her eyes.

But then Marguerite arrived, and the sisters fell into each other's arms, tears flowing, and more coffee was served, as Marguerite smoked a cigarette and said she'd got a lift from Drem with the Wing Commander, who'd come in on business. Dear man, he was, too, and so sad to hear about Rusty – well, as everyone was at the airfield.

'But the Wing-Co sent a message, Jess,' Marguerite told her. 'He said no' to give up hope, even though it might be some time before you hear what happened to Rusty. Information comes very slowly from enemy forces, you see, and when a fellow is captured...'

'Captured,' Jess repeated faintly.

'Well, yes, that's what we're hoping for, isn't it? So, when somebody's captured, he gets taken to a temporary camp for formalities and such, has to give his name, rank and number, before he goes to a proper prisoner of war camp. So it all takes time, but if you don't hear anything for a while, it's good news, really.'

'I suppose Rusty could try to escape,' Jess murmured. 'I mean, before he was captured.'

'Very few get away. Imagine, trying to get through Germany! But, listen, I managed to phone Ben and he says just the same as the Wing-Co. Don't give up hope, Jess. There's every chance that Rusty's all right. Ben's going to try to ring you here himself.'

'It's good of him. And good of you to come, Marguerite. Means so much.'

'Good of me to come? What else would I do? I know you'd want to be with me, if anything happened to Ben. Well, of course, something did, but thank God he's recovered now. The scars have faded and his leg's OK. Not a hundred per cent, but it works – that's all that matters.'

Putting out her cigarette, Marguerite said she'd better go, she'd arranged to meet the Wing-Co in George Street for her lift back.

'Keep your spirits up, Jess, and remember, we're all with you.'

The sisters kissed and embraced again, then Marguerite went hurrying away, and the phone rang with Ben on the line, saying how devastated he was at the news, but repeating all the Wing-Co's advice.

'Anything I can do, Jess ... no, I mean it ... let me know. I'm thinking of you and Rusty all the time.'

'I know, Ben, and I'm grateful. Thanks for phoning – I do appreciate it.'

'And the minute you hear anything, you'll let me know?'

'I'll let you know.'

As soon as she'd put the phone down on a fond

farewell, it rang again and this time it was Sally. Her mother was going to look after baby Magnus, and was it all right if she came round?

'Just have to see you, Jess. Just for a wee while, all right?'

'That'll be fine, Sally. Come any time. Bring Magnus too, if you like.'

Magnus, Sally's pride and joy, had been born in January, was the image of Arnold and a deeply happy, placid baby; everyone at the Princes loved to see him.

'That's all right, dear, Ma's keen to take him. Oh, but you're being so brave, aren't you? Oh, I can tell. But let it go, if you want, then. No point bottling it up, is what I say.'

'You're probably right. But just now, it's a help to be here.'

'It would be, dear, it would be. See you soon, then.'

'See you soon.'

Oh, how kind everyone was! Jess, putting down the phone, laid her head down, too, on her desk, and let her thoughts wash over her. How kind. How they all wanted to help. But they knew and she knew that no one could help. This was for her alone.

Where was that hope, then? How long would she have to keep going, with only hope to sustain her? Time stretched away from her into infinity, for she couldn't imagine ever being free from this state of limbo in which she found herself. All she could do was keep going. Run the Princes. Do her best. And as Sally's knock came on her door, she gathered herself together as she would so often have to do, and went forward to greet her.

In the event, she didn't have to wait as long to escape from limbo as she had expected. Halfway through April the unbelievable news came that LAC Russell MacVail was alive. Alive and uninjured, and with the rest of the crew of his plane, now a prisoner of war in a Stalag Luft, a camp for captured aircrew run by the German air force.

Hope had triumphed. Prayers had been answered. For a while, Jess walked on air. Until reaction set in, and she began to wonder how Rusty would cope with losing his freedom for the rest of the war. Would he have enough to eat? Could she send food parcels? And, at the back of her mind, was the question she didn't even want to frame – how would he manage without alcohol?

'Why, it's the solution to his problem!' Ben cried, when they next met. 'Your worries are over!'

'I hope so,' Jess answered, thinking there it was – hope back in her life. And must remain, while she and Rusty separately lived through the long years ahead, until the war was over and they could be together again. Always providing, of course, that their side won.

Forty-Three

And their side did. But only after years of fighting. Long hard battles on several fronts across Europe, ending with Hitler's suicide in his Berlin bunker and the declaration of victory for the Allied forces in May 1945.

Victory! Instant happiness seemed assured. Certainly, there was rejoicing at first. Singing and dancing and flag-waving. But it wasn't possible to keep on dancing, and gradually, the questions began. Where was the end of rationing? Why was it taking so long to see all the troops back home again? And why had so few of the prisoners of war in Germany been repatriated so far?

Everything, it seemed, was going to take time. There were formalities, you see, for bringing an end to war. Paperwork. Demob suits to be made, for returning service personnel. Gratuities to be worked out. And getting prisoners of war repatriated from their camps – well, that wasn't so easy. Sometimes the Russians were involved. Had to tread carefully. But all in good time, everyone would be back home, and one day, the food situation might improve as well. People would just have to be patient. Oh, and perhaps remember that there was another part of the war not yet finished, and that was in the Far East. Spare a thought for the relatives of those involved in that!

'I do worry about the war in the Far East,' Jess told her mother. 'All the prisoners of the Japanese – the men still fighting. I know we've been lucky.'

'Aye, that's true,' Addie agreed. 'But it'd be nice if we could see your Rusty home, and Marguerite and Ben as well. At least I'm back at the ladies' club, eh? No more camouflage nets for me!'

'That's one bit of good news, all right. When's the grand re-opening?'

'July, and we're all working flat out to get it ready. Then I'll be back to my cooking again, though what I'll find to cook with is anybody's guess.'

'You're well known, Ma, for making something out of nothing.'

'Maybe, but it seems to me things are no better on the food front than when we were at war. And Derry says he's no idea when we'll get imported fruit again. How he's managed that shop of his, in all the shortages, is a miracle!'

'It is,' Jess said, hiding a smile at the mention of Derry's name. Nothing was ever put into words concerning the relationship that had developed between her mother and Derry Beattie, but both Jess and Marguerite knew that one was there. It might have been that they simply didn't want to take on the commitment of marriage, both having lost partners they'd dearly

240

loved. Or that they were just comfortable with what they had – shared lives that amounted to marriage in all but name. Whatever the truth of the situation, the sisters had never seen their mother so content, and that was all that mattered to them. If she didn't want to confide in them, so be it. Everyone was entitled to a secret or two.

'Aye, well, we'll just have to be patient, I suppose,' Addie sighed. 'Like they're always telling us. But one of these days, you'll see, they'll all come walking in. You'll have the girls back at the Princes, Marguerite in the cafe again, and Flight Lieutenant Ben in the projection box with dear Rusty. Then it'll all be like they've never been away.'

'Think so?' Jess asked. 'I wonder if they'll want to come back to things exactly as they were before?'

'Course they will! I'm glad I've got my job back, I can tell you. And maybe they'll find things aren't exactly the same anyway.'

'What's different?' Jess asked.

'Why, you're the manager, Jess, instead of Mr Hawthorne. I'd say that was different for a start!'

Of course she was right. Jess wondered why she hadn't thought of it.

'All come walking in,' Addie had prophesied, and it was true. One by one, the pre-war staff came back from their war work to the Princes, giving Jess the sad task of saying goodbye to their replacements.

241

'Och, don't worry about it!' Sadie Munn cried. 'We always knew we'd have to go when the war was over.' She laughed a little. 'And we're no' the only ones losing our jobs – look at Mr Churchill losing the election, and Labour getting in! Who'd have thought that?'

'They say the forces wanted a change after the war,' said Jess, who'd been as surprised as the rest of the country by the defeat of the prime minister. 'A new Britain to come back to, maybe.'

'Aye, well, it'll be a change for me to be at home again, and I'll no' mind. Nice for you to have your girls back as well, eh?'

Renie, Edna, Faith; Pam, Kate, Ruthie – all the familiar faces were around again, though there had been a few changes. Renie, Edna and Pam now had husbands, though Faith, who'd married a sailor, had already left him.

'Aye, it was one o' thae wartime romances, eh?' she told Jess with a laugh, on first returning. 'Didnae last five minutes, so here I am back at the dear old Princes and glad of it!'

'But haven't you done well, Jess?' Renie exclaimed. 'You could've knocked me down with a feather when I heard you were manager now!'

'So surprising?' Jess asked a little coolly.

'Jess was always going to do well.' Sally, now sharing work at the box office with Netta, was quick to spring to her defence. 'And Mr Hawthorne wanted her to take over from him, when he fell ill.'

'Oh, I'm no' saying you weren't the best one for it,' Renie said hastily. 'You being so good at figures and that. We always knew you'd end up running something.'

'So, when's your sister coming back?' Edna asked Jess. 'And handsome Ben?'

'Any time now, I should think,' Jess answered, adding in a lowered voice. 'And maybe Rusty, too.'

'I should hope so,' Sally said firmly, as the usherettes fell into sympathetic silence. 'That poor laddie should be home by now.'

Oh, so he should! But Ben and Marguerite came back first, both giving the slight impression that they weren't as ecstatic as they might have been about being once again in their old jobs.

Ben, fully recovered from his injuries, had ended the war as a Flight Lieutenant, and was obviously finding it a bit of a shock to be back in his projection box, especially with Ron Clerk, who got on his nerves and was no substitute for the absent Rusty. While for Marguerite, after the exciting days in the WAAF, being a waitress again had clearly lost its appeal. There was often a frown on her smooth brow, and a petulant droop to her lovely mouth, but she never spoke of what she was feeling, and Jess thought it better not to comment.

'Maybe the time's come for Marguerite to have a baby?' Addie hopefully suggested to Jess. 'Now that Ben's poor dad has passed away, they've got the house to themselves and all the space they want, eh? Some folk'd give their eye teeth to have a bairn in a nice place of their own like that.'

'I don't see Marguerite with a baby, some-how,' Jess remarked.

'Well, can I see you?' her mother asked.

'Maybe one day. Got other things to think of now.'

Other things to think of. Or a person. But as the weeks went by, Jess had almost given up hope. Something must have gone wrong. Maybe to do with the Russians, or something. Had Rusty's camp been moved to Siberia? Oh, what a piece of nonsense! Don't get carried away, Jess told herself. It's just red tape, it's just the paperwork. He'll come walking in, like Ma said. And then it'll be as though he'd never been away.

On a warm summer's day, she was in the foyer, putting up a publicity notice for *The Picture of Dorian Gray*, a coming attraction. She stood back and looked at the photographs of the star, a handsome, black-haired actor named Hurd Hatfield, who had, she thought, rather a look of Ben. Then she permitted herself to smile. It was a long time since she'd kept seeing likenesses to Ben in film stars. Heavens, what a child she'd been in those days! Ben looked like himself, that was all there was to it.

Suddenly, behind her, she heard a voice speak her name.

'Jess?' And then again, as at first she was too stunned to reply – 'Jess?'

Slowly, she turned her head. Was it possible? After all these years? Of not knowing, not see-ing, of sending off letters and parcels and only

244

occasionally receiving a few lines back – 'soup was thin, bread was black, good to have the socks'. Was it possible, the long wait was over and that this was ...

'Oh, Rusty!' she cried, bursting into tears, and putting out her arms to him. 'You're home!'

Forty-Four

He'd always been thin, but now he was just walking bones. As she took him in her arms, Jess could feel his shoulder blades like knives through his shirt, and the face looking into hers was so gaunt, so fleshless, it seemed a stranger's. Yet the eyes, so painfully large, were Rusty's eyes – she would have known them anywhere.

Still, she cried out at how thin he was. What had happened to him? Why hadn't he let her know he was coming?

'Meant to, Jess, but it's all been ... so difficult. It's all taken ... so much time.'

'And you've nothing with you, Rusty, no' even a jacket. Where's all your stuff?'

'At home. I went there first. Had no key, but Mrs Fox let me in.'

Mrs Fox. Their upstairs neighbour, who held a spare key. What a shock she must have had, seeing this strange, emaciated man on her doorstep!

'Thank God she was in – oh, poor Rusty!'

She stepped back, her eyes bright on his face, gazing so long he gave a faint smile.

'Did I not ask you once, Jess, if you'd know me again?'

'I know you, Rusty. I just can't believe you're here. Are you real?'

'I'm not sure. Things haven't seemed real to me for a long time.'

'I am, though?' She caught at his hands. 'Look at me, Rusty! I'm here, I'm real.'

They held each other again, kissing lightly, not passionately – oh, nothing about this home-coming, it seemed to Jess, was as she'd imagined it. Releasing herself from Rusty's thin arms, she looked anxiously round the foyer, which was still empty. There was still no one around to see them. But it would be opening time soon and everyone would be arriving.

Sally, whose turn it was for the box office, and Renie and Edna for the auditorium; Trevor for the cinema organ; Fred to open up; customers to see the film. Just at that moment, she didn't want to see any of them, only wanted to be alone with Rusty, to try, somehow, to make sense of this reunion she'd wanted for so long.

'Look, we'll be opening soon,' she told him. 'Folk will be arriving – we don't want to see them yet, do we?'

'I just want to go back home, Jess. If that's all right?'

'Of course it's all right! I'll phone for a taxi.'

'Haven't been too well, you see. Had a flare-up of an old problem in the transit camp here – not quite over it.' Rusty ran his hand over his brutally cropped hair. 'I'm sorry, I'm really sorry. None of this is how I'd planned it.'

So he was feeling the same? Jess had guessed it. And it was clear he'd been ill. More than ever, she longed to get him out of the cinema and home, and pulling forward a chair, asked him to wait while she told Edie she'd be out for the rest of the day and booked the taxi.

'I don't need a taxi, Jess. I came on the tram – I can go home on the tram.'

'No, no, we don't want to be taking the tram. But I'll just speak to Edie and then we can go to the rank, if you like. Will you just wait here?'

'Sure. I'm not going anywhere, except with you.'

When she had phoned Edie on the intercom from the box office and cut short her squeals of joy, Jess returned to Rusty.

'Quick, let's go – we've just got time, before everyone starts arriving.'

'You seem very worried about getting away, Jess.'

'I only want to be with you, that's why. At least for today. Tomorrow, they can all see you, if you feel like coming in.'

'I'll be OK after a good night's sleep.'

'In your own bed,' she said softly.

'Now, that won't seem real.'

They exchanged tentative smiles, then left the cinema, hurrying, as though on the run, as though they'd something to hide, scarcely seeing the people beginning to gather for the matinee, only feeling safe in the taxi they found waiting at the rank.

'You'll feel better at home,' Jess whispered. 'Everyone does.'

'Oh, I know.'

'Just hope I can find you something to eat.'

'Don't feel hungry.'

'I have some tinned soup. Isn't that disgraceful? Offering you tinned soup for your first meal home?' Jess tried to smile. 'What would Ma say?'

'I'm looking forward to seeing your ma again.'

'Oh, she'll be so glad to hear you're back! I might try to slip out to the phone box and ring her at work.'

'Do that,' Rusty murmured, and lying back, closed his eyes. 'Tell me when we're home.'

'I'll tell you,' Jess said and, leaning against his shoulder, took his hand.

Forty-Five

The soup was pea and ham, which, as Rusty said, was an improvement on the cabbage broth of the prison camp. But he didn't want the omelette Jess said she could make him, courtesy of Derry, who had let her have a few fresh eggs from one of his sources.

'Are you sure?' she pressed. 'You've lost so much weight, Rusty, you really need to eat to get your strength back.'

248

He shook his head. 'I have to go carefully, don't want to risk more problems. Wouldn't mind a glass of milk, though, if you could manage it.'

'Oh, yes, yes!' Relieved she could give him something he wanted, Jess raced off to the kitchen, returning with the milk which he slowly began to sip. For a while she watched, then came to kneel beside his chair.

'Tell me what's wrong,' she said quietly. 'Tell me what's causing the trouble.'

'Just a stomach thing. Relic of camp food, I guess. The doctor who checked us out said it'd gradually go.'

'You were pretty ill, weren't you? In the transit camp? That's why you didn't get in touch?'

'I'm better now.' He ran his fingers down her cheek. 'Now I'm home, with you.'

'You must have had a terrible time, all those years,' she said in a low voice. 'You never really said – in your letters.'

'Honestly, it wasn't too bad. Could have been a lot worse. Provided you didn't try to escape, and I never did, you weren't badly treated.' Rusty's gaze was soft, melting with concern. 'Look, I don't want you being upset, Jess. I survived – that's what matters.'

'Yes, you're right, it's all that matters.' She held him tight for a moment, protesting as he tried to pull her to his knee. 'No, Rusty, I'm too heavy. Look, I'll go back to my own chair.'

'For God's sake, I'm not as much of an invalid as all that!' he cried. 'If I can't even have you on my knee, I might as well give up.'

'No, just think about getting better. Stronger. Maybe we should see our local doctor – see if there's anything he can do.'

'All it needs is rest and time. Then I'll be as I used to be. All the guys are pretty much in the same boat.'

'If only you could have let me know how you were, though.' She sat facing him, twisting her hands in her lap. 'Or just that you were back. I'd no idea what was happening – no way of finding out. I even thought the Russians might have spirited you away.'

'The Russians?' He gave a rare smile. 'They weren't around us, though I did hear they hadn't done much to help guys to get out from other camps. We just had to wait till the powers that be decided we could go. Then there was more hanging about and the journey back to the UK. Spending time in the transit camp, where I was ill – getting checked up and demobbed, sent on our way. Even got a gratuity, you know – a present from a grateful government.'

'Well, they are grateful,' Jess said seriously. She kissed Rusty on the cheek. 'We all are – God knows we are.'

He was silent, before saying lightly, 'Don't suppose Marguerite was too pleased about her leaving present. I believe the women got less than the men.'

'Never!'

'Knew you'd be annoyed. But how is Marguerite? And Ben? And George and Sally?'

'I told you about Sally having the baby? She's back at the Princes, working part time. Wee

250

Magnus is so cute – four years old now, her mother takes him. And George is keeping going with his brother-in-law. Seems resigned to it. Often pops in to the circle to see a film.' Jess sighed. 'I think he still misses us, to be honest.'

'Poor old George. And Marguerite's back at the cafe?'

'Yes, and Ben's back in the projection box. Missing you, he says. Keeps complaining about old Ron, but I'm grateful to Ron and the others who came in while you folk were away. They did a good job, they kept us going.'

'Now you sound like the manager,' Rusty remarked. 'Which, of course, you are. Strange, that.'

'What's strange?'

'Why, that when I come back ... you'll be my boss.'

'Does that bother you?' she asked, after a pause.

'No, of course not. I'm proud of you, Jess.'

Was he? She stood up.

'Rusty, you look all in. I think you should try to get some sleep.'

'Shall I help you clear away?'

'Two soup bowls and a glass?' She laughed. 'I think I can manage, thanks. No, I'll just see if the geyser's working – you might like a bath.'

'Oh, God, yes. Most of us back from the camps take baths all the time. To remind us we can.'

Some time later, when Rusty was in their double bed, wearing a pair of ancient pyjamas Jess had found for him, she unpacked his bag and hung up his few clothes. All were new, for he'd had nothing but his old uniform to wear on his journey from the prison camp, and had been kitted out at the transit camp. There were some shirts and underclothes, a sweater and his demob suit, plus a hat she knew he would never wear, and some socks.

'Pretty good, eh?' he called from the bed. 'More presents from the government?'

'Well, at least you've something to wear.'

'Better not put any weight on, or that suit won't fit.'

'Never mind the suit, you're going to put on weight. Ma said on the phone, she's already thinking out meals for you.'

'Can't wait.' He laughed, then closed his eyes and lay back against his pillows. 'Are you coming to bed, Jess?'

'Just going to put your case away.'

The last time she'd unpacked a bag for Rusty, it had contained a bottle of whisky. There was no whisky now, and no mention of his earlier drinking had passed between them. Please God, there would be no need to speak of it ever again, Jess prayed, along with sending a thank you for Rusty's safe return. Was it a bit of a cheek, sending up prayers of gratitude, when she'd never been to the kirk for years? Never mind, it seemed right. When she was so grateful.

Grateful, and happy. Yet, when she slipped into bed and lay beside Rusty for the first time since that last leave long ago, she was filled again with feelings of unreality. Was he really here, in their bed, as she'd so often imagined him? Or was she still in dreamland, wishing him home, clinging only to hope?

Stretching out her hand, she very gently laid it on his chest, at which he stirred and sighed and she too sighed, for she knew now that this was no dream, he was here, he was with her, in their own bed.

'Are you all right?' she whispered.

'Never thought I'd be wearing pyjamas,' he muttered. 'On my first night home.'

Suddenly he turned and held her for a moment.

'Jess, I'm sorry. It'll be all right, I promise, but ... tonight ... I'm sorry.'

'Rusty, I understand. There's no need to say anything.'

'Feel so bad.'

'Look, you shouldn't. This will all sort itself out. And like you said – you survived. We both survived. That's what matters.'

'That's what matters.'

Soon, she could tell by his breathing that he was asleep, but there seemed no prospect of sleep for her. Time passed, while she lay awake, staring at the ceiling, until she got out of bed and moved to the window.

No blackout curtains now, of course, and the street outside was plainly visible, washed by the light of the moon. For a long time, she stood, watching the night birds in the trees opposite, and the movement of the leaves, thinking about the momentous day. How things had changed, in just a few hours! Rusty was home and everything in her life had taken on a new colour, a new meaning.

But how would it all work out? She'd thought his return would bring an end to anxiety, yet she seemed to have exchanged one set of worries for another, and somehow along the line had lost confidence. The truth was, she couldn't tell how things would work out. Whether they ever would. For, if Rusty was real enough, he was not yet the Rusty who had gone away.

'All the guys are pretty much in the same boat,' he had said, and she was sure that that was true. It was going to take time for him, and men like him, to come back to what they had been. Take up a life they'd left, while living with memories of a life no one at home could share.

She held the curtain, still looking out at the silent street. How much time, though? She must just be patient, let things take their course.

'Jess?'

There was his voice again, and turning, she found him beside her, bony arms outstretched.

'Jess, can't you sleep?'

'Bit overwrought. So much happening.'

'Poor girl. It's been too much, hasn't it? But true what I said, you know.' He put his arms around her. 'It will be all right.'

In the pale light surrounding their two figures at the window, she looked into his face.

'I know,' she said simply.

And as they went back to bed, arms entwined, she suddenly felt – perhaps it would be true.

Part Three

Part Three

Forty-Six

On a warm June Sunday in 1946, Addie Raeburn's family – Jess and Rusty, Ben and
Marguerite – had gathered for one of her famous
roast lunches. (How does she do it? Ben had
asked Marguerite – not in the black market, is
she? And then had laughed shortly, as she only
looked at him pityingly, for he'd learned long
ago not to be surprised at Marguerite's own
sweet-hearting of the butcher into letting her
have something over the ration.) Anyway, the
roast lamb was excellent, and so were the green
peas provided by Derry, also a guest. And that
was no surprise either, the way things were.

Addie, however, was not in a good mood, and
as soon as the meal had been cleared away and
the washing up done, had continued to grumble
about the latest bad news to hit the British
people.

'Would you credit it?' she cried, as Jess moved
around, serving cups of tea or the new instant
coffee she'd found. 'Bread rationing! Yes, it's
official. Bread's to be rationed from next month,
cakes, scones and flour as well. How am I going
to do my baking if I canna get enough flour?'

'You'll manage, Addie,' Derry told her proud-
ly. 'You always do.'

'Aye, but think about it. We've just been through a terrible war, and put up with every shortage going, but we never ever had our bread rationed. Now we're at peace, they tell us we can have nine ounces a day! Fifteen for a manual worker, nine for the rest of us – I mean, what's gone wrong?'

'They say there's a wheat shortage,' Ben remarked. 'But the rumours are that there's more to it than that.'

'Seemingly, it's all to do with negotiations with America and Canada,' Derry said. 'Other countries in the world are in a bad way and food has to be found, so we've shown willing by offering to save grain and ration bread.'

'Where'd you hear all this?' asked Jess, as though interested, but her eyes were only on Rusty who was taking no part in the discussion.

'Evening paper,' Derry answered. 'And I bet it's true. I mean, would the government make itself unpopular if they'd any choice?'

'Canna trust governments,' Addie said darkly. 'I heard that while we're going to have our bread rationed, some farmers abroad have been feeding too much grain to their animals. Now that's a piece of nonsense, eh?'

'All I know is that it's going to be a nuisance, having to worry about more stupid little bits of paper,' Marguerite declared. 'We've already got ration books and points and clothing coupons, and now we've got bread units as well. It's ridiculous.'

'Wonder how much nine ounces of bread actually is,' Ben murmured thoughtfully. 'How many slices, do you think?'

'What the hell does it matter how many slices it is?' Rusty shouted, suddenly clashing down his coffee cup and jumping to his feet. 'Who cares? When you remember what's happened in this world, haven't we got something better to think about than how many slices of bread we're going to eat, for God's sake?'

'Rusty!' Jess cried. 'There's no need to speak to Ben like that!'

'Not to worry,' Ben said coolly. 'We know Rusty's not himself.'

'I'd like to know why,' Marguerite put in, her blue eyes glacial. 'It's time he got over what happened in the war, like the rest of us are having to do.'

'We weren't all in prison camps,' Derry said sharply.

'That's right,' Jess chimed, glaring fiercely at her sister.

'Let's all calm down,' Addie said, gathering up cups. 'Let's no' spoil a nice day.'

'I'm going, anyway,' Rusty muttered. 'Sorry if I snapped, Ben.'

'I said not to worry.'

'And we're going, too.' Marguerite draped a pale blue cardigan around her elegant shoulders. 'Come on, Ben, we've work to do.'

'Work?' Addie repeated. 'On a Sunday?'

'I'm taking a couple of days off to paint our living room,' Ben said morosely. 'Marguerite wants us to clear out my mother's stuff today.'

'No need to make it sound as though I'm throwing it away!' Marguerite cried. 'It can all

259

go in boxes in the attic, if you want to keep it.'

'Of course I want to keep it!' Ben's dark eyes were smouldering. 'My mother's things – what do you think?'

'Don't be upset, Ben,' Addie said soothingly. 'It's natural for Marguerite to want to do the house her way. Every woman does.'

'I've been wanting to do it for ages,' Marguerite murmured, moving to the door. 'Only I knew Ben would make a fuss.'

'I am not making a fuss!' he cried. 'Just don't want to see my mother's stuff pushed out.'

'I tell you, it's going in the attic!'

'If you'll excuse me, I'm going for a walk.' Rusty, not looking at anyone, unhooked his jacket from the back of his chair. 'Many thanks, Ma, for a wonderful meal. Jess, are you coming?'

'You'll be back for a cup of tea?' Addie cried. 'Marguerite – I thought you'd stay on, too. I've a lovely Victoria sponge and there won't be many more of them, after this bread rationing sets in!'

'Sorry, Ma, got to get on. Ben, let's away. Lovely dinner, eh?'

'Grand,' Ben muttered. 'Thanks, Ma, Derry. Rusty, I'll see you.'

'Fine,' Rusty answered, clearly desperate to get himself out of the door. 'Come on, Jess.'

'We might look in for tea,' Jess told her mother. 'If you've managed to make a cake.' She let her eyes slide quickly over her sister and brother-in-law, then looked away. 'Goodbye, Ben ... goodbye, Marguerite.'

'Don't get mad at me, Jess,' Marguerite said swiftly. 'I only said what's true.'

'Why does the truth have to be so hurtful?' Jess asked, and hurried down the stairs.

Forty-Seven

He might at least have waited for her, Jess thought, following Rusty towards the Shore, but there was his still thin figure striding ahead through the Sunday crowds, not even looking back.

'Rusty, wait!' she called, and he did then stop until she'd reached him, but made no apology for leaving her, only pushed back his now thick, waving hair and kept his eyes looking straight ahead.

'What's got into you this afternoon?' she asked breathlessly, though even as she put the question, knew it was pointless. The way he'd been that afternoon was the way he was so often nowadays. Spiky, thorny, difficult. Quite different from the sweet-natured Rusty she used to know and had married. Sometimes, she reminded herself, it was only what she'd expected. When he'd first returned, it had been obvious that it would take some time for him, and men like him, to adjust to life back home. What she hadn't expected was that it would take so long.

'Got into me?' he repeated, turning his gaze on

her. 'Nothing's got into me. What I feel about folk at home nattering on about their little problems has always been with me.' He struck his chest with his hand. 'Here.'

'Are you talking about Ben?' Jess asked coldly. 'He was in the war, just like you. He was also blown up, like some of the folk at home you talk about. Me, for instance.'

Colour flared on Rusty's cheekbones.

'You know I didn't mean you,' he said quickly. 'And I shouldn't have lost my temper with Ben.' He took her arm. 'Come on, let's go to the Shore.'

'You usually prefer the Links.'

He shrugged. 'You like the Shore. I don't care where I go.'

With her husband in such a mood, maybe Jess didn't either, but it was true that she still liked strolling round the old harbour, looking out from the quay to the small boats that had replaced the graceful sailing ships of long ago. The docks were the key to Leith's prosperity now, though there was talk of post-war recession, with ship-building and other industries falling into decline, but on a pleasant Sunday afternoon, with people everywhere and one or two cafes open, it was possible to look on the bright side. Maybe even persuade Rusty to cheer up.

Having looked down at the famous Water of Leith that had its source here, but so often, as now, needed cleaning, they moved on past the old Custom House to find a bench where they could sit. While Rusty stretched out his long legs and took out his cigarettes, Jess cast covert

262

glances over him.

He had put on a little weight since his return; lost the skeletal appearance of those early days, with even his face appearing not quite so gaunt. Yet he was still painfully thin, still gave the impression that he was not yet over some serious illness. An illness, Jess had finally realised, that came from within, and was the more difficult to treat.

Drawing on his cigarette, he suddenly turned and caught her gaze.

'What are you thinking, Jess? I'm being unreasonable?'

'I suppose I do think that. Folk have a right to complain when things seem to be going backwards.'

'Maybe, but what they forget when they complain is that they have something a hell of a lot of people have lost.'

She stared at him, raising her eyebrows.

'I'm talking about their lives,' he said quietly. 'Think about it, Jess. All the people who aren't coming back. All the civilians dead in the raids. Do you know how many died in Japan when we dropped the atomic bombs?'

'If we hadn't dropped those bombs, there would have been hundreds killed anyway, Rusty. It would have taken years to bring the war in the Far East to an end. That's what I've read.'

'That may be true, and I've no sympathy with the Japanese army after the way they treated our prisoners, but the numbers of ordinary folk killed by the bombs were horrendous.' Rusty's fingers on his cigarette were trembling. 'Even

263

smaller numbers of deaths are terrible to think about. Londoners in the Blitz, the people of Coventry, Dresden, Clydebank, nearly every tenement destroyed.' He shook his head. 'When I think of how many souls I might have killed myself in bombers, I feel sick, Jess. As though I can't look at my face in the mirror any more.'

'Rusty – that's war. It had to be fought, we had to defeat evil. You mustn't blame yourself.'

His shadowed eyes turned to her again. 'You know what, Jess? I was glad to be captured. I was glad to be in that camp. Cabbage soup – what the hell – I wasn't sending down death any more.'

'And now it's over,' she said urgently. 'Now you can forget, and get on with your life, because that's what the fighting was for. To let people live their own lives, be free.'

'I'm not free,' he said in a low voice. 'I can't forget.' He stood up, grinding his cigarette end with his heel. 'Might as well be a prisoner still.'

They began to walk slowly back, each locked in thoughts so dark, the people passing by, the sunny afternoon, seemed to fade from their consciousness. But before they reached Great Junction Street, Jess took the courage to speak of something she rarely allowed to surface in her mind.

'Rusty, you know I asked you once – when you'd first come back – how you managed...'

As her voice faltered and died, he gave a wry smile and finished the question for her.

'How I managed, not drinking? Yes, I remember your asking me that. And I told you I survived. Had to.'

'So that was good, wasn't it? I mean, you used to say you wished you could give it up, and then you did.'

Her eyes on his face, she waited for him to agree. When he said nothing, something began to beat in her head like some low menacing drum.

'Rusty?' She waited again. 'Rusty, that's true, isn't it? You had to give it up, and that was good?'

'I want to be honest with you,' he said at last. 'Honesty's what you should have.'

The drum was so loud, she almost put her hands to her ears, but her voice was a whisper.

'What are you saying? You'd never think of starting again, would you? Never go back to drinking?'

At first, his eyes would not meet hers, and she cried to him, 'Look at me, look at me! Tell me you wouldn't, Rusty. Tell me you would never start drinking again!'

With an immense effort, he made himself look at her. As he had said, he owed it to her to be honest, to let her read the truth in his unhappy eyes. But when she couldn't seem to take it in and kept searching his face for comfort, he told her, putting out a hand she would not accept.

'Jess, I already have.'

'There you are, back again!' cried Addie, hurrying about with tea things. 'Nice walk? Plenty of people about, I expect? The others wouldn't stay

– had to get back to their sorting out. Derry – is that kettle boiling, then?'

'Just made the tea,' he called. 'Rusty, take a seat, you're looking all in.'

'A piece of my cake'll brighten him up.' Addie pulled forward chairs. 'Come on, Jess, you're a wee bit pale, too. I always say, too much sun's no' good for you.'

But her eyes on her daughter were sharp, and Jess knew she would soon be trying to find out what was wrong. But Jess would never tell her. Not about this. She would never tell anyone, not even Ben. Though it was possible he knew already.

Forty-Eight

As so often before, work was the salvation for Jess. And there was plenty of it. Always something on her desk that required an instant decision. Always letters to be written, accounts to be checked, liaisons with firms or schools to be arranged, new suppliers to be found. And nothing in the post-war world, as everyone was discovering, was easy.

Sometimes it helped to talk to George Hawthorne, who liked to look in to see her before taking his seat in the circle. Still working for his brother-in-law, he'd had no further trouble with his heart, yet never seemed confident that he would survive.

'Just have to take things easy,' he'd say. 'Just have to be careful. Only got one life, you know.'

And she would say, 'But might as well be busy, George.'

She knew he would never let himself be too busy again, and marvelled that he could be so content with his quiet existence, after the way he'd once let work drive him. Perhaps she'd be the same, if she'd had the same brush with death. She didn't know, didn't care to think about it. There was already too much in her mind to worry about, and most of it was not to do with work.

'So, what's nagging at you today?' George asked, one late summer afternoon, as he drank Edie's tea in Jess's office. 'Now don't tell me it's audience figures, for they're the best ever, eh?' He smiled. 'Nothing can beat the movies, Jess.'

'Oh, the figures are wonderful, no doubt about that. My problem is finding the films for people to see.'

'Hollywood on strike again?'

'Have been, but that's no' the only thing. The films aren't getting made because there's still so little studio space. You remember how it was in the war, George? How they were always requisitioning studios for something else? Same in America, as it was here?'

'Too right, I remember,' he said with feeling. 'We lost a lot of films that way.'

'Well, it's no' much better now, which means

267

I'm having to do more and more reruns.'

'And the patrons don't like too many reruns, of course.'

'And don't want war films any more, except for the really good ones like *The Way to the Stars*.' Jess twirled a pencil thoughtfully. 'Might try for that one again, maybe. But what folk really want are comedies and musicals. Anything with Danny Kaye or Betty Grable.'

'Ah, yes, Betty Grable's legs.' George sighed reminiscently. 'How much did she insure them for?'

'A lot,' Jess answered with a laugh, and as they continued their talk, felt the better for it, as she always did. In spite of his willingness to give it all up, George was the only one who knew what she had to do, and took some satisfaction in sharing her problems with her.

'How's Rusty?' he asked, leaning on his stick at the door, when he'd finally decided it was time to see his Hitchcock thriller. 'Settled in well now?'

'Oh, yes,' she answered brightly. 'He's fine.'

'Hard on these boys, having to take up their lives again. Well, not just the boys, of course. There's your sister, back in the cafe, eh? Saw her just now – gave me a lovely smile with my coffee.'

'Marguerite's all right,' Jess murmured, wondering just a little if she was, and gave George a smile herself as he left to make his way to the circle.

'Enjoy *Notorious*!' she cried, and he waved his stick.

'Ingrid Bergman and Cary Grant – what more could a fellow want?'

Alone again, Jess sat for a few moments, thinking, against her will, of Rusty.

'He's fine', she'd told George. If only... How could he be fine? How could he be well? When he'd set himself on a path he knew could only lead to disaster? And the irony of it was that he'd been cured. He'd had it in his power to be free of his addiction, and had chosen to throw his freedom away.

'It's not as bad as it sounds,' he'd told her that distressing day when they'd walked back from the Shore. 'It's only at lunchtimes that I take a drink, Jess, and that's what half the population of Edinburgh do, I bet you.'

'You can't afford to take a drink,' she'd told him bitterly. 'It's never going to be one, is it?'

'Look, I can take it or leave it. I'm not an alcoholic, I never was, and in the camp I had to learn to do without it, and I did. So where's the harm?'

'Where's the good?' she'd flared. 'Why drink at all if you don't need it?'

And at that, he'd looked away.

'I do need it,' he'd said quietly. 'Just to help me through.'

'Through what?'

'Well, this bad patch.'

'You've been home some time, Rusty. Why are you still ... so unhappy?' Tears had thickened her voice, as she'd stood aside from people passing. 'I do all I can...'

'Jess, it's nothing to do with you. It's just ... I dunno ... the world, I guess. It's what I've seen. I told you – I can't forget.'

'Maybe we could see somebody – to help?'

'They'll change the world?' He'd shrugged. 'No, there'd be no point. But Jess, I don't want you to think you don't help me. You do. And I love you.'

'If you'd really loved me,' she'd told him, her voice still breaking with tears, 'you wouldn't have taken that first drink again.'

Weeks had gone by, and their lives seemed to be ticking by as usual. They still made love, were still outwardly the same happy couple, but for Jess everything had changed. Every lunchtime, she thought of Rusty making for a pub or a bar. Every evening, when he was late back, she'd picture him drinking, and when he returned, would believe she could smell the alcohol on his breath, though to be fair, she could never be sure.

With hindsight, she now wished she'd arranged to have lunch with him every day, but with her heavy workload and outside commitments, they'd decided it would be too difficult. And perhaps wouldn't be a good idea, anyway, as husbands and wives didn't want to live in each other's pockets, especially when their jobs were so different. Too late to do anything about it now. Rusty had taken his first drink – and many more. There was nothing to be done.

It was some time later that there was a tap on her

door and at her call, Ben put his head round it.

'Ben – come on in,' she told him, working hard on a smile. 'What can I do for you?'

'I was sort of hoping I might do something for you.' Closing the door behind him, he came to her desk, but did not sit down. 'I know you're a very busy woman, but how about meeting for a sandwich somewhere – when you've time?'

'A sandwich? At lunchtime?'

'Why not? We haven't talked in a long time, have we?'

She studied his handsome face that had just the faintest reminder of a scar beneath his hairline, wondering what this was all about. When had it been usual for her and Ben to spend time talking? Go out for a sandwich together at lunchtime?

'Is Marguerite coming?' she asked, rising from her desk.

'No, she just likes to get something at the cafe.'

His very dark brown eyes resting on her face seemed just a little cagey, and it came to her as an inspiration that he wanted to talk to her about Rusty. Almost all the talks they'd ever had, had in fact been about him, and this one she felt certain would be no different. But what should she do? She had vowed to discuss Rusty's drinking with nobody, yet now it seemed to her that she wouldn't mind speaking of it to Ben. He'd known about the earlier situation and she knew she could trust him.

'It's isn't always easy for me to get away,' she said slowly. 'But I'd like to meet you, Ben.'

271

'Good.' He briefly touched her hand. 'You've been looking rather down lately, you know. I've been worried about you.'

'There's no need to worry about me.'

'Well, let's just say you'll take some time off with me, then. Maybe not have a sandwich. Maybe go somewhere nice for a decent meal. If we can find such a place in these godforsaken times.'

'I'd much prefer a sandwich,' she said firmly. 'When do you suggest we go?'

'Day after tomorrow. I'm due on at one, as you know, so we'll have to make an early start.'

'Suits me. I don't in any case want to be away too long.'

'I'll call in here for you, then.'

'That'll be fine. Thanks, Ben.'

They exchanged long serious looks, then Ben's features relaxed into a smile and he went out. How careful they'd been, Jess reflected, as she moved back to her desk, never to mention Rusty's name.

Forty-Nine

Two days later, Jess and Ben were facing each other over a small round table outside a West End cafe. The August day was hot and Ben, in cotton shirt and flannels, had taken off his tie, sighing with relief, as a waitress brought their spam and salad, the only thing on the menu, as it turned out.

'Put a tie on specially for you,' he told Jess, who was looking pleasantly cool in a pale-green dress. 'Never wear one in the box, as you know.'

'Since when have you dressed up for me?' she asked with a laugh, hoping to disguise the misgivings she was feeling at having lunch with him and not telling Rusty.

'Ah, well, I knew you'd be smart, and this is quite a decent cafe. Sorry there's only the same old spam. Not even a decent sandwich!'

'I don't mind spam and the salad's just the thing for today.'

When are we going to cut the small talk? Jess wondered, as she sipped her lemonade. When is he going to start talking about Rusty?

But the surprise came when he spoke, for it was not of Rusty, but Marguerite.

Taking up his knife and fork, keeping his eyes on his plate, he asked quietly if Jess remembered

273

his talking of Marguerite once before?

'When I said I was worried, do you remember?'

'Back in the war? When she was at Drem?'

'That's right. And you put me in my place. Said I wasn't trusting enough, and Marguerite had, after all, to trust me.'

Suddenly, Ben looked up and in those fine eyes she'd once so much admired, Jess read a real anxiety.

'What's wrong?' she asked quickly. 'Why are you bringing this up now, Ben?'

'Because I'm worried again.' He drank long and deeply of the lager he'd ordered. 'Not because she's surrounded by men the way she was at Drem, but because she seems ... as if she's changed. Changed towards me. Don't ask me to say how. I just think she doesn't feel the same.'

'Ben, I'm sure that's no' true...'

'Has she said anything to you?' he asked urgently. 'Please, tell me, Jess. If there's something wrong, I want to know. I want to face it. I can't ask her, I can't put it into words, because that might make it seem real.' He laughed lightly and brushed his brow with his hand. 'Maybe it is, though.'

'Marguerite's never said anything to me,' Jess told him earnestly. 'And I'm sure there's nothing to tell. Ma sees her all the time. She'd have known, she'd have spoken of it, and she hasn't.'

'You think I'm worrying about nothing?'

'I think it's just the post-war thing, Ben. Folk having to adjust and not knowing how. It's no' easy, coming back and starting the old life all

274

over again.'

'We never really had any life before wartime,' he said thoughtfully. 'But we were always so crazy about each other, I never imagined things would be different when the war was over. Fact is, we're not getting on. I suppose you've seen that?'

'Well...'

'Oh, I know, it's obvious. I try to be patient, but when I think how much Marguerite seems to have changed, I don't know how to cope. You can understand that, Jess?'

'Have you spoken to Marguerite herself about this? Asked her straight out, if there's anything wrong?'

'God, no!' He pushed aside his plate. 'She might tell me.'

For some time, they sat in silence, until the waitress took their plates and they ordered coffee.

'I hope you didn't mind me asking you out to bend your ear over my troubles?' Ben asked. 'Felt I had to talk to somebody.'

'You know I want to help if I can.'

'Well, you have helped. It always helps to talk to someone sympathetic.'

'Marguerite doesn't actually know we were meeting for lunch, then? You gave me the impression you'd asked her.'

'No, I couldn't, could I?' As the waitress set down their coffees and left, Ben lit a cigarette. 'Did you tell Rusty?'

Colour rose to Jess's brow and she pretended

275

to be busying herself stirring her coffee.

'No,' she answered at last. 'I didn't tell him.'

'Did you think I was going to talk to you about him?' Ben asked carefully, at which Jess's risen colour deepened.

'Were you?'

'I don't know. I'll confess, I was mainly thinking about Marguerite, but if you'd said anything – wanted to, I mean – I might have said that he's...'

'What?'

'A worry to me, too.'

'Oh, God!' she said softly, and stood up. 'Ben, can we go?'

'Sure. I'll get the bill. Mustn't be late, anyway. Shall we go back through the gardens?'

'Yes, I'd like to walk somewhere.'

On such a fine day, Princes Street Gardens were of course filled with people. City workers and mums with children; elderly people dozing on the benches; younger ones racing each other across the grass. All to Jess seemed so carefree, compared with herself and Ben, but who knew what worries they were concealing? Who would think that she herself had problems, or handsome Ben, strolling at her side, swinging his tie?

'Tell me why you're worried about Rusty,' she said at last. 'As though I didn't know.'

'Ah, Jess, I'm sorry.' Ben caught at her hand and let it go. 'I honestly thought, when he came back, that the camp had cured him of his problem.'

'It had, that's the sad thing. But, seemingly, he

doesn't want to stay cured.'

'You have to try to understand, he's in a low state of mind, and Edinburgh's full of pubs. Drink helped him before – so he believed – and I can see why he must have thought it'd help him again.'

'Never thought about me!' she cried. 'Never asked my help!'

'Probably hoped he could keep it a secret.'

'He told me when it was too late. Said he wanted to be honest.' Jess stared fiercely into Ben's face. 'How long have you known, anyway?'

'Probably from the beginning.' Ben hesitated. 'Sometimes, when we're both on, I can tell he's been drinking, though he conceals it pretty well.'

'He told me it was just at lunchtimes that he had a drink. Said it was nothing, he could take it or leave it alone.'

When Ben made no reply, Jess drew to a halt.

'You don't believe that, do you?'

'No. Do you?'

She gave a long, troubled sigh. 'No.'

'The truth is, Jess, I think he's drinking a lot more than we know. He's going to have to get help. Otherwise, he's going to damage himself and you.'

'Get help? You make it sound so easy. Get help how?'

'Well, there's the doctor. He might be able to help. Might be medication or something.'

'I don't see Rusty talking to a doctor somehow. He hates to talk to anyone about the

277

problem.'

'OK, there are these help groups. People who gather to support each other. We could find out if there's one here.'

'People who support each other? People who have given up drink?' Jess shook her head. 'If someone doesn't want to give up, those groups wouldn't work, would they?'

'Deep down, Rusty does want to give up, Jess. He only uses it as a prop.'

'If he'd really wanted to give it up, he'd never have gone back to it.'

She began to walk on, more swiftly, so that Ben had to hurry after her.

'Jess, wait! Let's talk this through...'

'There's no point, Ben.' She slowed down, glancing at her watch. 'Look, time's getting on, and you should be back by one.'

'Yes, ma'am,' he said smartly, giving her a mock salute, at which she bit her lip.

'Sorry, Ben...'

'Don't worry, only joking. But I also have a watch, you know.'

Only joking. Was he? She still wasn't sure how he really felt about her being in charge, or even how Rusty felt. Nothing had been said; it was just occasionally, as now, there were little slips that showed what might lie beneath their supposed acceptance.

'Come on.' He took her arm. 'Let's think about what to do. You can't deal with this yourself, you know. In fact, neither of us can deal with it. We need outside help and we should try to find it.'

'The group you mentioned?'

'Yes. We need to check if there's one here. God help us, there's so much alcohol swimming round Scotland, there must be somewhere folk can go if they want help.'

'And who's going to ask Rusty to go along, if we do find one of these groups?'

Ben's eyes were soft with sympathy. 'Dear Jess, that'll have to be you.'

They arrived back at the Princes with time to spare and stood for a moment outside Jess's office, each feeling a sudden awkwardness that they'd spent the lunch hour together without their partners' knowledge. Yet there had been, of course, nothing to feel guilty about. Unless they felt guilty about discussing those partners in the first place.

'Don't know that we got very far,' Ben murmured, dark eyes searching Jess's face. 'Yet it helped, didn't it? Our meeting?'

'It did,' she said warmly. 'But I want to say again that you needn't worry about Marguerite.'

'And if I can't say the same about Rusty, at least we have a plan of action. We'll be in touch, eh?'

'Oh, yes. And thanks, Ben. For the lunch and everything.'

'My pleasure. Now – to work. Remind me what I'm showing today. Not still *Notorious*?'

She laughed. 'No, it's *Spellbound* – as though you'd forgotten. Another of my reshowings.'

'And another Ingrid Bergman. Who'll complain?'

Fifty

Ben soon reported back that there was a support group in Edinburgh that Rusty might try, if he could be persuaded. He really seemed to have his younger colleague's welfare at heart, and Jess expressed her gratitude. But a great reluctance seemed to come over her whenever she thought of tackling Rusty on this so delicate a subject that was, nevertheless, cutting through their marriage like a sword with a sharp blade.

Already, she had begun to notice worrying changes in him that she knew she could not ignore, though they were not the changes she might have expected. He never behaved like a stage drunk, for instance, reeling in late at night, slurring his words and having to be put to bed. Nor did he ever offer her violence, or threaten her in any way. No, but what had happened was more frightening, for it was as though his whole personality had become blurred. He was himself, yet not himself. A mysterious double – what she'd heard the Germans called a doppelgänger – who still shared her bed, went through the motions of life and work, yet wasn't someone she knew at all. That was frightening, all right.

'You haven't spoken to him yet?' Ben asked her,

as the weeks went by and November was upon them, foggy and strangely warm. 'For God's sake, Jess, what are you waiting for? You know things can't go on like this!'

'I know, I know. It's just, getting through to him, I can't face it somehow.'

'Do you want me to do it?'

'No, no. I'll do it, I will.' She darted a quick glance at Ben. 'Is everything all right at work, Ben? He can cope on his own?'

'So far. I don't know how long for. Sometimes, I think I'll come in to find he's put the reels in the wrong order or something, but at the moment he's managing. Doesn't mean you shouldn't speak to him, though.'

'I'll speak to him, Ben, I promise. As soon as I find the right time.'

It came after another of her re-showings, one she realised, too late, she should never have chosen. The film was *The Way to the Stars*, one she'd mentioned to George as a favourite with the public, set in wartime. It would make a good fill-in, she'd thought, until she remembered that Rusty would have to take a turn showing it from the projection room. And as a film that followed the sometimes tragic fortunes of the men and women serving on a RAF airfield, it would be certain to bring back memories he didn't want.

How could she have been so crass? She, who knew so well that his control hung by a hair's breadth, that the slightest thing might push him further into his own private black hole?

Summoning up all her courage, she caught him

before the first matinee and told him she'd like a word.

'What about? You look worried.'

'It's just the film, Rusty. You realize it's *The Way to the Stars*?'

'What of it?'

'Well, it's set in an airfield, isn't it? It's all about the war. I thought ... it might ... bring things back.'

'Bring things back?' He smiled briefly. 'I don't need a film to do that.'

'I know, but I don't want you upset.'

Just for a moment, he seemed to lose his vagueness, to return to the man she knew, and she wished with all her heart she could just hold him, keep him, like that, as he used to be. When he put his hand on her arm and fixed her with a soft gaze, she could have burst into tears, but managed a smile instead.

'That's nice of you, Jess,' he was murmuring. 'To think of me.'

'I'm always thinking of you.'

He touched her face, then drew away.

'Don't worry about the film, Jess. I've seen it already.'

'When? You weren't here when we showed it.'

'Saw it in our demob centre, when I first came back.' He shrugged. 'Top brass idea of cheering us up, no doubt.'

'So you'll be all right with it?'

'Of course I'll be all right with it. You know I don't watch every film the whole way through, anyway.'

'That's a relief, then.' As he glanced at his

282

watch and said he had to go, it came to her that he seemed so much more his old self, she might just be able to talk to him that evening about getting the help he had to have.

'Rusty,' she cried, hurrying after him as he turned towards the projection room. 'Rusty, can you come home early tonight?'

'You're leaving early? You know I can't do that. Somebody has to stay till the end, and it's my turn to lock up.'

'I'll lock up with you, then we can both go straight home.'

Their eyes met and she knew he understood her. No finding a pub that was still open, she was saying. No drinking on his own in the cinema, which was something she was sure he did.

'What's the hurry to get me home?' he asked, and she could tell his brightness was fading and she was losing him, but she still pressed him to agree – they'd lock up and go home together.

'If it's what you want,' he said at last.

'It is what I want.'

'OK. See you tonight, then.'

'Yes, tonight. Thank you, Rusty.'

With a puzzled look, he left her, and she, returning to her office, fell on the work on her desk as though it were a lifeline. Which, of course, it was.

Fifty-One

Sitting next to Rusty in the tram going home, Jess tried to make small talk.

'So warm, isn't it?' she asked. 'I mean, for November. Yet they say there's a cold winter on the way.'

'Never know what the weather's going to do in this country,' he muttered.

'There's talk of a fuel crisis, too.'

'Are you trying to look on the bright side?'

She laughed, but he didn't, only lit a cigarette and stared ahead. Better not ask him about the film, she thought, as the task before her grew in magnitude. Maybe she'd postpone talking about the help group for another time? No, no, she wouldn't. It had hung over her head long enough. Tonight was the night. Now or never.

'I've got some ham we can have when we get in,' she told him. 'We won't need much, seeing as we had something earlier on.'

'A sandwich will do.'

'And tea, of course.'

'Oh, God yes. There's always tea.'

When they'd had their small supper and washed up, and Rusty said he'd turn in, he was ready for his bed.

'If you wouldn't mind, I'd just like to talk to

you first,' Jess told him.

'Here it comes. I knew there was something coming my way.' Rusty flung himself into his armchair. 'What have I done now?'

'It's more what I want you to do.'

At that, he sighed, and stretched out his legs.

'OK, tell me what it is and then we can get to bed.'

'Remember, during the war, you said there were groups you might have gone to for help...'

At the word 'help', she saw him stiffen in his chair and a shutter descend over his face, but he said nothing.

'Only, you couldn't go to them, of course, because of the war,' she struggled on. 'Well – what I wanted to say was that you could go to them now. And there's one here, in Edinburgh. I've got the address.'

He sat up straight, his grey eyes steely.

'You've been looking up this place without a word to me? Without even asking if I wanted to go?'

'Yes, I have, because I wanted to make sure it was there before I told you. Now we know it exists, we know you can get help. You could go there and try it. Or maybe see the doctor?'

'I am not going to see the doctor. I don't believe any doctor could give help, even if I needed it.'

'It's an addiction, Rusty. Some people call it an illness.'

'I'm not seeing the doctor, Jess. Don't ask me to.'

'All right. But you do need help, Rusty. You

know that's true.'

'I have never said I needed help.'

'Yes, you did. When we discussed it back in the war. You said then you wished you could stop. I remember your very words – "I wish I could, Jess, I wish I could."'

'That was in the war. I was in a very difficult situation. Things are different now.'

'How, different?'

'Well, the prison camp cured me, whether I wanted to be cured or not. So, my drinking now is not the same as before. As I've told you, I can take it or leave it alone.'

Silence fell, as Jess kept her eyes on Rusty's, never moving her gaze, until, finally, he looked away.

'You know that isn't true,' she said softly. 'Don't you? You know it isn't true, that you can walk away from drink?'

He sat without moving or speaking, his eyes fixed on the packet of cigarettes he had earlier taken from his pocket. But as he made to light one, Jess stayed his hand.

'Don't, Rusty, don't smoke just now. Think about what I'm saying. Admit what I say is right. You can't give up drinking.'

'Look, Jess, I don't know – I don't know what's right and what isn't...'

'You do, Rusty, you do! You know you can't give up drinking on your own, you know you need help.' She went to him and put her arms around him. 'Take the first step,' she whispered. 'And I'll take it with you. We'll get through this together, if you'll just face the truth.'

'I'm not sure I can,' he said quietly. 'Is that what you want me to say?'

'I want you to say you need help and you're willing to try to get it. That's all. That's the first step.' She leaned her face against his, her eyes filling with tears. 'I know it's not going to be easy, Rusty. I know what it'll be like for you. But it could help, you see, it could be worth it.'

For a long time, they sat together, their faces close, their hands clasped, until at last, Rusty said in a low voice, 'Jess, I'll do it. I'll try this group. See what they can do.'

'It's all I ask, Rusty. It's all anyone could ask.'

Because it was a lot to ask, wasn't it? Later, when they had slowly prepared for bed, and then lay sleepless, the question hammered in Jess's brain – was it too much?

Seemingly, it was, for when Rusty some days later swallowed his pride and went to his first meeting of 'Dependency Helpline', he did not stay. In fact, he came home so early, Jess, who had seen him to the hall but had not been allowed to wait, needed no telling what had happened.

'What went wrong?' she asked quietly. 'I know something did.'

'Jess, I couldn't stand it. The minute I went in, I felt wrong, as though I shouldn't be there.' Rusty sank on to a chair at the kitchen table. 'I looked around at the people, and they were standing up and giving their names and talking about their drinking, and I thought, 'My God, what am I doing here?' They said I was very welcome and I'd be given some sort of mentor

287

who'd help me through, and the first time would be the worst, but I knew all along it was a waste of time. I wouldn't be staying. I wouldn't be standing up, giving my name.'

His eyes met Jess's, then immediately fell.

'I'm sorry,' he muttered. 'Honestly, I am. I'd have liked it to work.'

'You didn't give it time to work,' she said after a pause.

'No, because I knew it wouldn't. I knew the set-up wasn't for me.' He stood up, running his hand through his hair, and glanced at the kitchen clock. 'Think I'll go out for a bit.'

'You've had something to eat?'

'I'm not hungry.' He moved to the door.

'Better take your coat, it's colder tonight.'

'Colder weather on the way, maybe?'

He took his coat from the peg in the hallway, and pulled on a tweed cap.

'I'm sorry,' he said again. 'But I did try, didn't I? Thing is, Jess, it'd be no good asking me to try again. I couldn't do it.'

'Don't worry, I won't ask you.'

When he'd gone, she sat down and picked up the evening paper and read each page carefully. No tears blurred her vision, which was good. But then she'd already decided that there would be no more tears. What else there might be in the future, she'd no idea.

As she rose and began to prepare her solitary supper, she knew she'd just have to take each day as it came. Never worked out, did it, to try to make plans?

Fifty-Two

'What you need is cheering up,' Sally told Jess in her office one January day. 'Now we're living in the Ice Age, who doesn't? But I think we should give ourselves a nice day out.' She looked hopefully at Jess's face. 'What do you say?'

Jess thought about it.

'Living in the Ice Age' just about summed up their situation in January 1947, as the whole country bowed in submission to the worst winter since the nineteenth century. Blizzards, snowdrifts, frost that never thawed, iced-up cars, burst pipes – even elderly people could not remember anything quite so severe. To make matters worse, increased demands and difficulties in transportation had brought about a fuel crisis, which was now threatening power cuts. Faced with the worry of perhaps having to close the cinema, how could Jess expect to take a day off?

'Sorry, Sally,' she said at last. 'The way things are, I don't think I'd dare to be away for a whole day.'

'Oh, come on!' Sally flung back her hair, which was now no longer blonde but bright red, and waved a warning finger at Jess. 'That's just a piece of nonsense! When did you last take any

289

time off?'

'I'd like to have a day out, but if we do get these power cuts, you know I'd be needed here.'

'There'll be warnings, they say. Times when to expect them. Anyway, they've no' happened yet. Let's just hop on the train to Glasgow and have a look at the sales, eh?'

'Glasgow?' Jess shook her head. 'I don't think so, Sally.'

'Look, we could plan to go and then if there were any possibilities about power cuts, we'd just stay grounded. I mean, it's no' that far to Glasgow, is it?'

'I suppose we could see if they've anything different in their sales. There's nothing much here.'

'Too right. Nothing but that utility stuff. So, we could look round, have a bit of lunch and get the early train back. My mother can pick up Magnus from school for me, but I'd no' want to be too late home.'

'What day would you suggest we go?'

'Well, you know I don't come in on a Tuesday. So that'd be the best day for me.'

Conscious of Sally's bright eyes on her, Jess hesitated.

'I suppose I could ask Ben to keep an eye on things. And maybe phone in when we get there.'

'Perfect! Shall we say next Tuesday, if you've got nothing in your diary? It will do you good, Jess, I promise you, and you really should look after yourself a bit better, you know. You've been looking so pale lately.'

'Thanks so much for that.' Jess attempted a

smile. 'You haven't changed, have you, since George used to call you a fusspot?'

'And you know what happened to him,' Sally said darkly. 'Do you think Tuesday will be free?'

'I'm sure it is.'

'That's settled, then. Oh, my, I'm really looking forward to a get-together with you, Jess. For a nice long chat, eh?'

Depends on the chat, thought Jess.

The following Tuesday lunchtime, wrapped up in winter coats, hats, scarves, mittens and boots, they made their way to the station, avoiding the unchanging banks of snow at the roadside, gazing up at the great, gaunt city buildings outlined in white.

'Pretty, eh?' Sally asked Jess, as their breath blew in clouds. 'If you hadn't already seen it all for weeks on end.'

'Christmas cards will never be the same again,' Jess said with a smile. 'What would it be like to go abroad for some sun?'

'Can't even imagine it. Here's the station. Careful on the incline, Jess.'

'I'm already walking as though I'm ninety years old,' Jess said cheerfully, realizing that she was beginning to look forward to this snatched day out, was in fact already feeling a guilty pleasure, as though she were playing truant from school.

'Well, you don't look ninety, dear. Your cheeks are quite rosy!'

'That's just with the cold.'

'No, it's because you're escaping,' Sally said

shrewdly. 'When you've finished looking round all the new clothes in Glasgow, you'll be looking quite your old self.'

'I don't even know if I've any clothing coupons left. Haven't thought about clothes for ages.'

'So, you'll have some coupons left. Anyway, we needn't buy anything – can just window-shop if we feel like it.'

As the Glasgow train wasn't in yet, they huddled on to a bench in the waiting room, which was no warmer than the platform but which at least they had to themselves.

'Remember when they used to light fires in the waiting room?' asked Jess. 'Now even the station's got no coal.'

She sat back on the hard wooden bench, pulling up her coat collar and rubbing her arms with her mittened hands, her cheeks still rosy and her face looking prettier, Sally thought, than it had seemed for some time.

'Oh, it's good to see you relaxing, Jess,' she said earnestly. 'You're having a rough time, we all know, but if it's any help, we do understand what you're going through.'

The silence in the waiting room after she'd spoken was as icy as the atmosphere.

'Going through, Sally?' Jess echoed at last. 'Why, what am I supposed to be going through?'

Sally shook her head. 'Look, there's just the two of us. No need to pretend. Might do you good, in fact, to talk about it.'

'Talk about what?'

Sally clicked her tongue. 'Your Rusty, of course.'

'Sally, I am not going to talk about Rusty. Is that why you asked me to come out with you?' Jess's rosy colour was now deepening. 'To talk about him?'

'Oh, Jess, you know nothing was further from my mind! We've been friends for so long, how could you think that? I only wanted to cheer you up, that's all. I never even intended to mention Rusty and I'm sorry now I did.'

Jess lowered her eyes. 'I'm sorry, too, then. It was silly of me to say anything. I suppose I'm just ... over-sensitive at the moment.'

'And who'd blame you? Look, let's say no more, eh? Least said, soonest mended.'

'No, I'd like to know what you mean. When you said everyone understood – what I was going through.'

Sally looked down at her handbag and fiddled with its clasp. 'It's his drinking.'

Jess caught her breath. 'His drinking? You're saying ... everyone knows?'

'Well, dear, it's very difficult to keep secrets in a place like the Princes. We do kind of live in each other's pockets, eh? And Rusty's no' been himself for some time.'

'And nobody's said anything?'

'Well, they wouldn't. But they see the poor lad at lunchtimes, and sometimes in the evenings, you know. Fred told me he'd seen him in the projection box when everybody's gone home, just sitting...'

'Oh, God – drinking alone?'

293

Sally nodded. 'But everybody knows what he went through in the war. They know how hard it is to adjust.'

'I'd no idea anyone knew,' Jess said unhappily. 'No idea at all.'

'Nobody's thinking badly of him, Jess. They'd like to help, only there's nothing they can do. But some of us were wondering if he'd seen a doctor at all? Might be a good idea.'

'Flatly refused. Also walked out of the help group he was going to try.' Jess stood up, shivering. 'In fact, just at the minute, Sally, I can't think of what to do next. But I think that might be our train I can hear – we'd better check.'

'Poor lassie,' Sally murmured, as they hurried out of the waiting room door. 'But things will look up, Jess, they always do. The tide'll turn, you'll see.'

'It is our train,' Jess murmured, determined now to think of something other than her troubles on this day of escape. 'Let's see if we can find a seat.'

'Are you joking?' Sally was turning on a smile. 'War might be over, but it's still standing room only on the trains.'

Surprisingly, though, they did find seats and by the time they arrived at Glasgow Queen Street, were feeling more cheerful and ready to enjoy their little break.

'First stop, coffee,' Sally announced, as they joined the throng moving out from the platform to the main station concourse. Then both she and Jess stopped, as though pulled to a halt by some giant puppet-master's string. For some little way ahead of them was a familiar, graceful figure, now swaying towards a tall man in a dark overcoat who was taking off his hat and calling a name.

'Marguerite! Marguerite! Over here!'

And Marguerite went into his arms.

Fifty-Three

'That was Marguerite,' Jess said dazedly. 'She must have been on our train, and we never knew.'

'Aye, because we were in the waiting room, never saw the folk on the platform.' Sally's face was alight with excitement, as she caught at Jess's arm. 'Come on, let's see where she goes with that fellow, then.'

'No, no.' Jess was holding back. 'I don't want to, I don't want to spy.'

'Think they're going for a taxi, anyway.' Standing tall, Sally was trying to see over the heads of the passengers leaving the station. 'Who can he be, Jess? Ex-RAF, I can tell you that, and an officer. Did you see his handlebar moustache? I can spot those chaps a mile away, though I was army, of course.'

'I don't care who he is,' Jess said wildly. 'I just feel too upset. I mean, what about Ben?'

'What we need is our coffee. Let's get out of here and find somewhere to recover.'

'Recover? I don't think I'm going to recover in a hurry, Sally. After what we've just seen.'

In a small cafe off George Square, they discovered they could get toasted teacakes with butter, and decided to make them an early snack lunch.

'Before we hit the sales,' Sally said cheerfully, but Jess was in no mood to be cheered.

'I don't know that I feel like shopping now,' she said quietly. 'It's really shaken me, seeing Marguerite meeting another man like that.'

'I know, dear, and I'm no' being unfeeling. It's just that I don't want your day spoiled, just when I finally got you to agree to leave work for once.' Sally looked down at the butter deliciously melting on her teacake and finally took a bite, dabbing at her lips with a paper napkin. 'There's nothing we can do, after all. I mean, it's Marguerite's problem, and Ben's – even if he doesn't know it yet.'

'He did tell me he was worried about her,' Jess said after a pause. 'He thought she seemed different. Towards him, he meant.'

'He's been confiding in you?'

'We were sort of confiding in each other.'

'So ... what did you say? About Marguerite?'

'I told him no' to worry.' Jess drank coffee gloomily. 'Said I was sure she hadn't changed, or we'd have heard about it. Now I wish I hadn't said anything.'

'You had to say what you thought.'

'Well, I never in this world dreamed there was another man, Sally. But the way they were on the platform – it's no new thing, is it? I think it's been going on a long time.'

'Can't go on much longer, if you ask me. These things always come to a head sooner or later. And if Ben's already suspicious, he'll probably have it out with Marguerite and then she'll have to make a decision. About what she wants to do.'

'You don't think she'd leave him?' Jess asked fearfully, her heart thumping.

'I think it's quite on the cards.' Sally's tone was matter-of-fact. 'Listen, do you think it'd be greedy to order another teacake? They're really generous with the butter here, eh?'

Fortified by the coffee and food, Jess agreed in the end to go shopping with Sally, though her heart was not in it. Try as she would to take an interest in the sales, she found her thoughts constantly returning to that scene in the station, when she had seen her sister with a man who was not Ben.

But what could she do? Not tell Ben himself, that was for sure. Even to think of seeing him again, meeting his dark gaze, making small talk, sent her heart plummeting. When she knew what she knew.

He had been so sympathetic about Rusty's refusal to seek help. Had tried his best to cheer her up, to find some sort of hope, while his own life, though he didn't know it, was crumbling to pieces around him.

All she could do, Jess decided, was to speak to Marguerite. Surely she couldn't really be contemplating leaving Ben for the man with the handlebar moustache?

While Jess moved unseeingly around the stores, Sally got into conversation with the saleswomen. One older woman, amazingly well made up, considering that cosmetics were so hard to find, seemed determined to get Sally into one of her bargains, while Sally remained just as determined not to buy.

'Thing is, there's no' much here that gets my fancy,' she confided. 'Maybe I'd best wait for these new fashions I've been reading about.'

'What new fashions?' the saleswoman asked frostily. 'What we have is the latest thing, Madam, though much reduced, of course, in price.'

'Well, I did hear that there was something new going to hit us all very soon. All hush-hush, seemingly, but definitely on its way. Some Frenchman's idea, they say.'

'Most fashion ideas come from Paris, Madam, but I can promise you that anything you buy here will be absolutely right. Now, would you perhaps like to try one or two things on?'

'Sorry, we have to be going – our train, you know. Thanks all the same!'

With an apologetic smile, Sally, grasping Jess's arm, moved smoothly towards the lift.

'Hate being pressured,' she whispered. 'Though I suppose these folk have got their job to do.'

'Had you really heard about new fashions?' Jess asked, trying to show interest.

'Sure I had! Looks like we'll all be wearing

skirts to our ankles before the year is out. Suits me, seeing as my legs are as plump as ever. But, listen, Jess, weren't you going to ring Ben, to ask if everything was OK?'

'Oh, I don't think I need, Sally. We'll be back soon.'

'You'll have to speak to him some time, dear.'

Not before I've spoken to Marguerite, thought Jess.

Fifty-Four

At coffee time the following morning, Jess worked on at her desk, waiting for the knock on her door she knew would come. Sure enough, when she had just given another glance at her watch, the light tap sounded.

'Come in!' she called, and rose, as Marguerite put her head round the door.

'Got your note,' she said coolly. 'What's all this about?'

'Take a seat, Marguerite. I just want a word.'

'It had better be quick, my break's nearly over.'

Marguerite, in her waitress's uniform, complete with cap, came slowly forward to take the interview chair. As she sat down, the light from the window fell full on her face, and Jess thought, as she so often did: She's just like Ma, isn't she? Never grows any older. See, hasn't a line on her brow...

'Jess, can you get on with it, whatever it is?' her sister asked irritably. 'I did say I'd to be back soon.'

Jess sat back, her mouth a little dry.

'Thing is, Marguerite, Sally and I went to Glasgow yesterday.'

Only the slightest flicker of her lovely eyes betrayed Marguerite's reaction.

'So?' she asked lightly.

'So, we saw you. On the platform. Meeting someone.'

Marguerite hesitated for a moment, then pulled off her cap and sat with it in her hand.

'All right, you saw me. What do you want me to say?'

'I want you to tell me what's going on, that's all.'

'Is it any of your business?'

'I'm family, aren't I? Apart from that, I'm thinking about Ben.'

'Naturally.'

'What's that supposed to mean?' Jess asked, flushing.

'Just what it sounds like. Naturally, this affects Ben.'

'Well, I'm glad to hear you say so. But who is this fellow you're meeting, Marguerite? How long has it been going on?'

Marguerite looked down at her cap and shrugged. 'I suppose I might as well tell you. His name's Guy Powrie. I met him during the war, when he was a Squadron Leader. Now he's with his father's law firm in Glasgow.'

'You've kept up with him all this time?'

'No, we just met up again about six months ago. In the cafe, when he'd come over for the day on business.' Marguerite gave a little smile. 'Said he couldn't believe his luck.'

'Oh, Marguerite!'

'All right, I feel bad about Ben. I'm no' going to try to make excuses. But these things happen, eh?'

'You and Ben,' Jess said slowly, 'you were so much in love...'

'Too much so.' Marguerite stood up. 'Doesn't last, that sort of love.' She gave Jess a long hard look. 'What are you going to do, then?'

'Me? Nothing. It's you who's got to decide what to do.'

'Are you going to tell Ben?'

'No. I'm hoping he needn't know. I mean, if you break it off with this lawyer fellow.'

'I won't be doing that.'

'You're going to keep on seeing him? Marguerite, you can't. Ben has his suspicions. He told me you seemed different towards him.'

'Did he?' Marguerite smoothed her hair and put on her cap. 'Always the bright one, Ben. Looks like I'd better tell him what's happening.'

'What is happening?' Jess cried desperately. 'Marguerite, what are you going to do?'

Already at the door, her sister looked back.

'Jess, I'm going to ask Ben for a divorce. It's the honest thing to do, eh? Oh, don't look like that! It's no' the end of the world. I'm sure he's just as sick of me as I'm sick of him. We were just honeymoon people, really – never meant to be lifetime partners.'

As soon as she heard the door click on Marguerite, Jess bounded out of her chair and ran after her.

'Marguerite, wait!'

'Oh, what now, Jess?'

'I was just wondering – when are you going to tell Ben, then?'

'Oh, heavens, I don't know. Sometime soon. I want to get things settled.'

'And what about Ma?'

For the first time, Marguerite seemed flustered, her lip trembling, her colour rising.

'I'll tell her – when the time's right, I suppose.'

'She's going to be upset.'

'Yes, but what can I do? It's my life.'

'Folk in her day stayed married, that's the thing.'

'And were miserable. Things are different now.'

'Still difficult, getting a divorce. And expensive.'

Marguerite, recovering her poise, smiled a little.

'I'll have expert help. Guy's father specializes in divorce.'

'Best of luck, then,' Jess said curtly. 'Let me know how things go.'

'You wouldn't come with me, would you? When I tell Ma?'

'No, I wouldn't. This is something you want, Marguerite, you can tell her yourself.'

* * *

302

Back in her office, Jess sat down at her desk, but she couldn't stop thinking of Ben and wondering how he would face Marguerite's news. He would be devastated, she was sure, for it clearly wasn't true that he was as tired of Marguerite as she was tired of him. He still loved her, as had been proved by the way he'd talked of his worries about her. If only Jess hadn't reassured him!

'You think I'm worrying about nothing?' he'd asked, and she'd been quick to tell him it was only a post-war problem that many people were facing. What a mistake! But, to be fair, how could she have told him anything else, when she hadn't then seen Marguerite with the other man? She'd thought Ben and her sister were still lovebirds, just going through a bad patch. Like her and Rusty.

No, not like her and Rusty. For them, the golden days were over, their happiness having melted away, killed, perhaps, by the stress of war. Or maybe would have died anyway. Now, they were facing life alone, for even if they hadn't so far parted, Jess never felt these days that she and Rusty were together. Only Marguerite had the promise of a new love and a new life. At what cost, though? At what cost?

Another tap sounded on her door. Marguerite returned?

But it was only Edie, come to collect the letters for typing.

'Oh, Edie, I'm sorry, I haven't finished them! Just give me a few minutes and I'll bring 'em through.'

'You OK, Jess?' Edie asked kindly.

'Bit of a headache, that's all.'

'Want an aspirin?'

'No – it's going off, thanks.'

'I'll bring you another cup of tea.'

'That'd be grand.'

And as Edie departed, Jess put on her professional hat and got down to the letters she should have finished some time before. Personal life, she thought, that's out. I'm supposed to be at work. But as she later sipped the tea Edie brought her, Ben's sombre gaze still filled her mind and would not fade.

Fifty-Five

Two days passed, during which Jess waited with heavy heart for the inevitable, while Marguerite kept out of her way and Sally's large blue sympathetic eyes kept meeting hers, expressing her wonder at what was going on.

So far, Jess had not told anyone of Marguerite's plans, not even Rusty, though she might have told him if he'd ever come home at a reasonable time when they could have discussed it together. As it was, he only came in to go to bed, where he fell instantly asleep, while Jess lay awake, her thoughts churning, until she had to get up to make tea and sit in the kitchen, wishing she was one who could smoke a cigarette to calm her nerves.

Sometimes she asked herself why she should be so very concerned for Ben. Was it that she was afraid to think of him a free man? Unattached? No, no, she just didn't want him to be hurt, that was all. But underneath her disclaimers, she knew there was that knowledge that he would no longer be her sister's husband. And though that should make no difference, she knew that it might, and shied away from thinking about it.

On the evening of the third day, when Jess had still heard nothing from Ben or her sister, she was astonished to find her mother on her doorstep when she arrived home from work.

'Ma, what are you doing here?' she asked, fumbling with her key, but one look at Addie's reddened eyelids had already told her all she needed to know.

'Ah, don't tell me you don't know!' Addie cried, sweeping into the house. 'Oh, Jess!'

For some moments, they clung together, until Addie pulled herself away to sit in a chair with a handkerchief pressed to her eyes.

'Oh, to think of it, Jess. A divorce in our family and our lovely girl to be the one to want it! I tell you, when she met me out of work this afternoon, I couldn't take in what she was telling me. I couldn't believe it. Marguerite, splitting up with Ben? It just wasn't possible.'

'I know, I know, Ma.' Jess had put on the kettle and was setting out cups and saucers. 'I felt the same, when she told me, but there it is – it's what she's going to do.'

'I always wanted her to make a good marriage, you know, because she's no' like you, Jess – you'd get on anyway, but she'd need a good provider. And she was that attractive, I thought she might meet somebody with family money. A professional man, maybe, who'd give her what she should have.'

'Well, she didn't do too badly with Ben,' Jess remarked. 'He's got a settled job and they've a nice house. They're luckier than a lot of folk, I'd say.'

'Aye, but he was never right for her, Jess! He was never what she was looking for.'

'And what you were looking for, from the sound of it.'

'Never mind me, then.' Addie rattled her teacup. 'Are you no' going to make that tea?'

'Ready now.' Jess filled her cup. 'There, that'll make you feel better.'

'No, it won't.' Addie drank it, anyway. 'It'll take more than a cup of tea to cheer me up, eh? When I know my girl's going to take herself through the divorce courts.'

'You did say Ben was never right for her.'

'So, she made a mistake. But if you take marriage vows, Jess, you keep 'em. Chopping and changing – where would it end?'

Jess studied her mother for a moment or two.

'Ironic, though, that the fellow she's met is just what you'd have wanted for her in the first place. A professional man. Family money in the background. A good provider. Shouldn't mind

306

too much, Ma, if Marguerite gets it right second time?'

Addie's fine blue eyes rested on Jess's face with such unexpected shrewdness, Jess leaped to her feet.

'Don't look like that, Ma. There'll be no second chances for me!'

'There's your doorbell,' Addie said calmly. 'Better see who it is.'

It was Ben.

He was wearing his long black winter overcoat, with a cap over his hair and a scarf muffling his features, but it was still painfully obvious that Marguerite had spoken to him. Everything about him spelled shock and dismay, from his drooped shoulders, to his gloved hands stretched out towards Jess, as though pleading for help.

'Jess, may I come in?' he whispered.

'Oh, Ben!'

Drawing him into the house, she unwound his scarf and gazed sorrowfully into his face.

'My mother's here, Ben, but she'll be going soon.'

'So, Marguerite's told her too?' He gave a desolate smile. 'And we both had to come here to see you?'

'Jess, is it Rusty?' Addie asked, coming into the hallway, but stopping short at the sight of Ben. 'Oh, it's you, Ben.' Her voice wavered. 'How are you, then?'

'All right, thanks, Ma.'

All right? They stared at him, then Addie began the complicated task of dressing for the

307

outside weather, pulling on rubber galoshes over her shoes, buttoning up her coat, tying on a headscarf.

'I'm away, Jess,' she said in a low voice. 'I'll be in touch. Better give this laddie a drink, eh?'

'I have no drink in the house, Ma. He's welcome to a cup of tea or coffee.'

'I don't want any tea, or coffee!' Ben cried. 'Oh, God, I don't want anything!'

But as Jess opened the door for her mother, he put his hand on Addie's arm.

'Shall I walk you to the tram? The pavements are treacherous out there.'

'Och, no, but it's good of you to offer, Ben.' Addie took a sniff of the ice-cold air. 'Maybe too cold for more snow tonight. Don't worry about me – I've been walking on ice like this since before you two were born.'

For a moment, she looked at Ben, then pressed his hand, and throwing her scarf more firmly round her neck and pulling down her hat, set off for her tram.

Fifty-Six

'Think she'll be all right?' Ben asked, as Jess showed him into the kitchen where a one-bar electric fire was burning, for how much longer she didn't know. She was still waiting for cuts.

'Oh, yes. Ma's good on her legs, always has been. You don't mind the kitchen, Ben? There's no coal for the fire next door.'

'Don't mind the kitchen?' He threw his overcoat over a chair. 'Jess, what's there for me to mind, now that Marguerite's going to leave me?'

'I feel so bad, Ben. I feel terrible. Because you asked me about her and I said everything was all right, but it wasn't. I didn't know, though, what was happening.'

'Of course you didn't.' He lit a cigarette. 'Who did? She kept the secret very well.'

'When did she tell you?'

'Today. At twelve thirty precisely. I was getting ready for the matinee when she came into the box, said she wanted to talk to me. I'd seen her at breakfast, of course, when she'd never said a word.'

'She told you at work?' Jess cried. 'Why? Why at work?'

'I suppose she reasoned that I'd behave better

if I thought there were people around. Not so likely to throw a fit and chew the carpet. Isn't that what they said Hitler did, when upset?'

'I can't believe it, Ben. To tell you at work ... Why, that must have been awful! To be told something like that, to be so shocked, and have to keep on...'

'I didn't keep on,' he said quietly, studying his cigarette. 'As I was on my way to work, I'd seen Rusty going into the Lion in Princes Street. As soon as Marguerite had gone, I ran out and brought him in, told him he'd have to do all the performances for me today.'

'And he'd been drinking?'

'No, it was OK, he'd just got there, said he was fine about standing in, hoped I'd feel better soon.'

'But why didn't you come to me, Ben?'

'I couldn't go to you. Not then. All I wanted was to get out of the box and walk, and that's what I did. God knows where I went. All round the West End. Into the Haymarket, I think, then back into town and down into Inverleith Park. Saw folk skating on the pond. Saw a chap fall down. Hurt his arm. Probably had to go to casualty.'

They were silent for a while, until Ben put out his cigarette and raised his eyes to Jess.

'Did you see this fellow Marguerite's found?' he asked roughly. 'This Squadron Leader?'

'I saw him on the station platform in Glasgow.'

'Didn't tell me.'

'How could I, Ben? How could I?'

He shrugged. 'What's he like then?'

'Has handlebar moustaches.'

'Ha! Perfect caricature, eh? Of an RAF officer.'

'You were an officer, Ben.'

'I wasn't a Squadron Leader. I didn't have a father with a law practice to give me a job. I didn't have the sort of money he's got.'

'You think Marguerite's only interested in money?'

'Don't you?'

'She did say ... she did tell me you two had drifted apart. Didn't you say you hadn't been getting on?'

'So, next thing, we're looking at divorce?'

Jess shook her head hopelessly. 'I don't know what to say, Ben. I'm still not believing it's happening.'

'How do you think I feel?' he asked, lowering his voice. 'I'm reeling.'

Suddenly, he stretched out his hand and took Jess's.

'But not for long, Jess. Oh, no, not for long.'

'What do you mean?'

'I mean, I'm going to get over this and quickly, too. If Marguerite can play this game, so can I. She doesn't want me, I don't want her. It's as simple as that.'

Oh, if only it were, Jess thought, as he put on his outdoor clothes and, like Addie, took a look at the outside weather.

'Not too bad. No snow. I'll get home, then, Jess.' He paused. 'No need to worry about meeting Marguerite, that's one good thing.'

311

'Why, where will she be?'

'She's moved herself to your mother's. Didn't Addie say?'

'I'm sure she doesn't know!'

'Nice surprise for her, then, when she gets home.'

His eyes on Jess softened.

'Thanks for listening,' he said hesitantly. 'Never thought, did I, when I offered you my shoulder once that I'd be using yours?' He kissed her cheek. 'Go in, Jess. It may not be snowing, but it's arctic out here.'

'Take care!' she cried, and waited till he was swallowed up in the darkness.

For once, Rusty came home directly he'd left the cinema, disturbing Jess's endless roundabout of thoughts as she went over and over her talk with Ben. It had meant something, that he'd come to her in the end. Come to her for solace, as the only person, perhaps, that he could allow to see into his heart. How much did it all mean? No one could answer that.

'Did you find out what was wrong with Ben?' she asked, as Rusty sat down to a bowl of soup.

'Seemed under the weather.'

'Marguerite is going to leave him.'

Rusty's spoon halted in mid-air. 'She's what?'

'She's met someone else. Told Ben today, just before the matinee.'

'I don't believe it!'

'It's true. She used to know this man in the war, when she was in the WAAFs. Then they met again.'

'And he's got more to offer than Ben?'

'Why do you say that?'

'Lucky guess.'

Jess turned her head, unwilling in spite of it all to hear her sister criticized.

'Come on,' Rusty murmured. 'You know what she's like.'

'I don't want to talk about it.'

'Fair enough. I'm for my bed, anyway.'

Same old story, Jess thought, even though Rusty's eyes were not so glazed as usual. He'd be out like a light, she'd be lying awake, riding her roundabout again, eventually getting up and sitting in the kitchen.

'Might as well get ready, then,' she told Rusty. 'I'll heat the hot water bottle before I do anything else.'

'Very cold tonight,' he agreed, and they went to bed. Saved more talking, thought Jess.

Fifty-Seven

The long hard winter finally gave way to spring and then to summer, and if the rationing was no easier, at least the weather was better. Everyone, including the staff at the Princes, felt more cheerful, with even Ben seeming to cast aside the air of darkness that had held him after his wife's departure, and to be more willing to smile.

All sympathy, of course, had gone to him, rather than Marguerite, whose behaviour most of her colleagues found quite shocking. To leave a good husband like Ben for a great soft fellow like Guy Powrie! Why, it was obvious she'd done it for his money and position, and the fact that she was going to have to wait years for a divorce made it all the more scandalous.

Not that Marguerite was around to know what people thought of her, for almost as soon as she left Ben, she left the cinema cafe, too.

'Oh, yes,' she told Addie and Jess, 'Guy doesn't want me to work as a waitress any more, so I've handed in my notice. He's going to find me a little job in his office, he says.'

'Office work for you, Marguerite?' Addie cried. 'Why, you were never one for paperwork!'

'I'll be more of a receptionist, Ma. Guy thinks I'll be quite good at that.'

'And how long are you planning to stay with me, then? I don't think it's right, Marguerite, I don't, and that's the truth. You're a married woman, you should be with Ben, until things can be made legal.'

Marguerite hesitated, glancing quickly at her mother, and then at Jess, before lowering her eyes.

'Thing is, Ma, I've taken this little flat. They are hard to get, but Guy found it for me. I'm moving in next week.'

'A flat?' Addie cried. 'And you never said? What on earth would you want your own flat for, at this stage?'

'Well, I know you don't want me at home again, so I needed a place to stay until we can get on with the divorce, don't I?'

'Which is going to take years,' Jess put in. 'I told you it wasn't easy getting a divorce.'

'And in the meantime, Guy Powrie comes calling when you're on your own in this flat?' Addie cried. 'Marguerite, that'll be worse than you living here. I'm no' having it, I tell you, I'm no' having you moving into a flat paid for by him and expecting us to believe that there's no hanky-panky going on, as though we were all born yesterday!'

'Guy isn't paying for the flat, I am, out of what I make at the office. And I'm sure I don't know what you mean by hanky-panky. Guy's very correct. Everything will be right and proper.'

'Right and proper?' Her mother laughed. 'Hasn't shown much sign of being right and proper so far, has he?'

Marguerite flushed brightly, but could think of no reply.

'So, how long will this arrangement go on, then? When will you get your divorce?'

'I can't say. Guy's father will do what he can, but seems I'm the guilty party because I left Ben, so they'll have to go for desertion as cause and that takes time.'

'The guilty party?' Addie's lip trembled. 'Oh, Marguerite! What a terrible thing it is, to hear you call yourself that.'

'Well, Scots divorces aren't like English ones, seemingly. There you can just send your man off to a hotel with some woman and there you are, you've got your divorce. Unless they can prove it's a put up job.'

'Why should Ben do that for you?' Jess cried. 'He's the innocent party. Why should he pretend he isn't?'

'He's no' doing anything for me, is he?' Marguerite sighed. 'Look, I'm really sorry if I've hurt him, but there it is – when something's dead, you can't bring it back to life, can you?'

Oh, what terrible words to use to end a marriage, Jess thought, walking slowly back to work. And knew she was not thinking of Marguerite and Ben.

Though Ben appeared to be getting over Marguerite's betrayal remarkably well, Jess was sure that underneath his easy manner, the wound still throbbed. He never admitted it to her, though they sometimes met for a lunchtime snack, or just a walk in the summer air, but she had the feeling he liked to be with her because with her he needn't put on his usual act. They were at ease with each other, and that meant a lot.

Strolling back from the gardens one late August day, they stopped outside a display window of Logie's, one of the city's grandest stores.

'See that?' Ben asked.

'What?'

'That television set.'

Jess studied the large walnut cabinet housing what appeared to be a very small screen, which at that time of day was blank.

'What about it?'

'Not realize you're looking at the future?'

She met his dark eyes. 'I know what you're talking about, but I don't go along with it. Television isn't going to close our cinemas.'

'Not all, no. But maybe in the future quite a lot. They say the number of TV sets sold is going up every year, and the industry's still new. It'll improve – be able to offer more and more.'

'More than a lovely comfortable cinema, with films in colour on a screen you can see? I don't believe it. Look at the titchy little screens the televisions have. They just can't compare.'

'Yes, but folk have to go out to the cinema, don't they? Television, they can see at home. News, sport, drama, even our old films.' Ben shook his head. 'I don't say it's a threat here at the moment, but I think they're already worrying about it in America. You'll have read all the trade articles, I suppose?'

'Of course I have, but I still believe there'll always be an audience for the cinema. What about the young people who don't want to stay at home? They need somewhere to go.'

Ben grinned. 'Better cultivate them. Might be all we'll get.'

Jess shook her head in exasperation. 'Oh, come on, let's go back, this is getting depressing. I bet Mr Syme wouldn't agree with you, anyway. He won't want to be losing his cinemas.'

'If I know him, he'll be moving into the television business at this very moment!'

They walked back, laughing, but in the foyer, Ben's gaze became serious.

317

'Sorry if I sound depressing, Jess. But you know you've no need to worry. Whatever happens, you'll cope, you'll adapt. And anyway, change is a long way off.'

'Well, you'll be all right, too. You can adapt as well as anyone.'

'Yes, but maybe I should be retraining as a television engineer? Rusty, too.'

'Oh, no,' she said quickly. 'No one's going to be retraining. We need you here.'

'Nice to think we're needed.'

'You're no' seriously considering retraining, are you? Maybe moving away?'

'Of course not. I've got my house, I've got my job.' He touched her hand briefly. 'I've got my friends. I'm staying put.'

When he had left her for the projection room, Sally, who was opening up the box office, gave Jess a call.

'He's doing well, eh, Ben? Looking so much better.'

'Yes, he seems OK.'

'Likes to talk to you, dear. A sympathetic ear?'

'We're old friends, Sally.'

'Sure. We're all his friends here. Listen, you know I told you we'd be wearing skirts to our ankles one of these days? Well, I've got one!'

'Oh, let's see!' Forgetting the possible problems lying ahead, Jess was glad to take an interest in the large dress bag Sally was producing from beside her seat. 'Is this the New Look we've all been hearing about?'

'Certainly is. Got it this lunchtime from over

the Bridges.' Sally undid the bag and took out what seemed to Jess an immensely long dark blue skirt which she held against herself, then twirled around. 'Well, what do you think?'

'There seems a huge amount of material in it, Sally. Won't it feel a bit heavy?'

'Och, no. Just different. See these little frills at the top? Fancy, eh? It's supposed to be the answer to wartime austerity.'

'We're still in wartime austerity, if you ask me. I mean, even Princess Elizabeth is going to have to manage on her clothing coupons for her wedding.'

'Is that what they say? I bet folk will send her bagfuls. Now me, I'm spent up – coupons and cash – but I think it's worth it, don't you?'

'Can't help thinking the knee-length skirt's easier to manage.'

Sally made a face. 'Jess, the New Look's fashionable, that's the thing. Who cares if it's easy to manage or not? Now, why don't you go out and buy yourself something new and get Rusty to take you somewhere nice?'

But at the look on Jess's face, Sally flushed a little and began packing away her new skirt.

'Sorry, dear. Speaking out of turn again. Story of my life.'

'Don't worry, Sally,' Jess said quickly. 'It's good advice to go out somewhere. Maybe Rusty and I will try it.'

As she made her way to her office, she knew it was unlikely that they would, and couldn't decide which was gloomier – thinking about Rusty, or that large television set in Logie's window.

All the same, when it came to the evening intermission, she slipped along to the projection
room where she knew Rusty would now have
taken over from Ben, and decided to try him
with Sally's idea. He was out of the box, taking
a break; not smoking, she was relieved to see,
but drinking coffee from a paper cup, while in
the background came the sound of Trevor playing a musical medley on the organ.

When Rusty saw Jess, he raised his eyebrows.

'What's up, then? Cinema on fire, or something?'

'Why talk like that? Can't I look in to see
you?'

He shrugged. 'Usually takes something dra-
matic for you to do that these days.'

Though it was unfair, there was some truth in
it; she didn't often see him during the working
day, but then how much did he want to see her?

'Ben was talking about television today,' she
said brightly. 'Thinks it'll be a threat one day.'

'To cinemas? Goes without saying.'

'You agree with him?'

'Most do.'

'I don't.'

Rusty drained his coffee and crumpled the cup.

'You just don't want anything to happen to the
Princes, but it'll be the second-rate ones that go
under. Folk'll get more choosy about what they
see and where, that's all.'

'I feel a bit more cheerful, hearing all that.'

'Surprise, surprise, I've cheered you up.'

He gave her a long unsmiling look.

'You often talk to Ben these days, don't you?'

'He needs someone to talk to, Rusty. After what's happened.'

'Must have known it would never work out with Marguerite.'

'Why do you say that? They were really in love in the early days.'

'He was never her Mr Right, was he? The one she was always looking for? Soon as she found him, that was it – curtains for Ben.' Rusty glanced at his watch. 'Jess, it's time for me to go. There's the clapping for Trevor.'

'No, wait – I just wanted to say I was talking to Sally, too. Know what she said? I should buy some new clothes and you should take me out somewhere.'

'We need Sally to tell us that?'

'I'd say we did. Seeing as we never do go out, do we?'

'Difficult to arrange, getting time off together. Story of our lives.'

'All right, forget the new clothes – let's just make it Sunday afternoon, the way we used to. You'd like that, wouldn't you?'

'Sure. Let's see what sort of day it is on Sunday, then. Got to go, Jess.'

He's not interested, she thought, watching him return to the projection box. Might just as well have said so. What's the betting that if it's raining on Sunday, he'll be off the hook, anyway, but if it's fine, he'll make some excuse. Why had she bothered asking him? Because she felt a touch of guilt? No, why should she blame herself?

Marguerite's words came back to her, and echoed in her mind as she made her way to her office.

'If something's dead, you can't bring it back to life.'

But as she opened her door, she heard her phone ringing and was glad to let the words go and run to answer it.

'Good, you haven't left yet, Jess,' John Syme's voice said cheerfully. 'Thought I might just catch you. I'm coming over tomorrow morning, about eleven – any chance of your being in?'

'Oh, yes, I'll be here, John. I'll look forward to seeing you.'

But having put down the phone and stared at it for a moment or two, she had to admit she was puzzled. Usually, they met in Glasgow, where she'd been only last week, and John only came over to Edinburgh for a specific reason. So what was the reason this time? He hadn't said.

It was a little disturbing, she didn't know why, except that meeting John Syme could have that effect anyway. What usually happened was that she felt apprehensive until they met, and then relaxed, finding there was nothing to worry about. Probably, tomorrow's experience would be just the same.

Much more worrying was the prospect of higher taxes being imposed on non-British films by the Board of Trade, and that might well be something John wanted to discuss. If it came, Hollywood would be sure to react badly and maybe stop their films coming in altogether, which meant managers having to find more

British films – not easy and not desirable, either. Problems, problems. At least they put personal anxieties on the back burner. For a while.

Fifty-Eight

As the clock in Jess's office neared eleven the following morning, she hastily ran in to check on the coffee with Edie.

'Eveything ready for Mr Syme, Edie? He should be here any minute.'

'Oh, yes, Jess, it's all ready. And I've managed to find some shortbread biscuits – he likes those.'

'Lovely.' Jess gave a quick smile. 'Have to try to please the owner, you know!'

'Always do,' Edie happily replied.

Jess, back in her office, pulled down the jacket of her lightweight navy suit and straightened the skirt, then fiddled with her hair. Why so on edge for this meeting that was, after all, only one of many with John Syme? Impossible to say, but there was no doubt that she felt more nervous even than usual, and would be heartily relieved when the cinema owner finally arrived.

Which he did, as punctually as ever, looking elegant in pale grey with a silk handkerchief in his breast pocket and a dark trilby hat over his well-groomed hair.

'Jess!' He swept off his hat. 'How nice to see you on this fine morning. And is that coffee I smell?'

'You'd like some, John?'

'Yes, please, but let's not linger. I want us to take a stroll in Princes Street.'

'Princes Street?' As Edie served the coffee and handed the shortbread, exchanging smiles with John when he thanked her, Jess raised her eyebrows. 'We're going for a walk?'

'A very short one. As I say, it's a fine morning – it will be good to get the air after my drive.'

But we're not going for the air, Jess thought, as something in John's manner seemed to be increasing her nerves, rather than relaxing them. What are we going for, then? It was crazy, but she couldn't help wondering if it wasn't something to do with television. Hadn't Ben said he was sure their owner would already be interesting himself in the new industry? Maybe he too wanted to show Jess the large television set in Logie's window?

'Let's go, then!' John cried, setting down his cup. 'If you're ready, Jess?'

'I'll just tell Edie I'll be out for a little while.'

'See you in the foyer, then. What film are you showing at the moment?'

'A Danny Kaye. *The Secret Life of Walter Mitty.*'

'Oh, marvellous!' John was already smiling. 'Saw it in Glasgow last week. Remember him as the British air ace? And the surgeon with the watering can? My wife and I were in stitches!'

'It's very popular,' Jess told him. 'Audiences

have been almost as good as 1946 – and they were peak figures, of course.'

'Of course.' Still smiling, John made his way to the foyer, where Jess found him studying the photographs of the stars. Some new ones had, of course, been added: Humphrey Bogart, Robert Mitchum, Danny Kaye himself – but the old favourites were still there.

'Clark Gable, Henry Fonda,' John murmured. 'Still acting, still looking good. Charles Boyer – has he been in much lately? Garbo seems to have become a recluse. Ah, but they're the great ones, eh? No one like them.'

'I agree!' Jess cried, and followed John out into the sunshine.

Princes Street, on an August morning, was filled with visitors pointing out the sights, and local people, mainly women, window-shopping. Nothing new there, but John seemed to want to stand and watch the comings and goings, while Jess, watching him instead, continued to feel a nagging feeling of unease. Suddenly he swung round to look at her.

'What do you see here, Jess? In this part of Princes Street?'

'What do I see? Why, just the usual – the Scott monument, the gardens...'

'No, no, I mean on this side of the street, where we are now.'

'Oh.' She looked around, wondering what on earth he could be wanting her to say. 'Just people, then. And shops.'

'Shops, yes, but what kind?' He shaded his

eyes with his hand and gazed at the smart facades of Jenner's, Logie's and Forsyth's, three of Edinburgh's grandest department stores. 'Smart, wouldn't you say? Shops for the well-to-do?'

'Yes, at this end, they tend to be for that sort of customer.' Jess cleared her throat. 'But there's Woolworth's further to the east, isn't there? And more middle-range stores towards the west. I think we've a pretty good cross-section of shopping in Princes Street, John.'

'But nothing like Keys and Keys,' he said quietly. 'There's the gap, you see.'

'Keys and Keys? They're an English chain, aren't they?'

'A very popular English chain and very keen to come to Scotland. They sell good quality, medium-priced clothes and household furnishings, and also run excellent cafes. Exactly what is needed here, wouldn't you agree?'

'Yes, I suppose so,' she said doubtfully. 'They are interested in Princes Street, then?'

John didn't answer, but turned to look at the clock over the North British Hotel, then checked his watch.

'Twelve o'clock already,' he exclaimed. 'How about a quick drink and a little lunch, Jess?'

'Oh, I don't think...'

'Come on, come on, you can easily be spared, if that's what you're worrying about. You told Edie you'd be out for a while, didn't you, and you can be back soon, if you like. But I need to talk to you, Jess. And in pleasant surroundings.'

Pleasant surroundings. Exactly what the North

British Hotel could offer, but as far as Jess was concerned, she might as well have been in a wartime snack-bar for all the comfort she took in the elegant bar and the handsome dining room. Clearly, John was a regular client here, known to the waiters, certain of what he wanted to order, not only for himself but for Jess, too. Yet what she drank and what she ate were a complete blur, for she knew now that he had brought her here for one reason only, and it was to soften the blow of what he was going to tell her.

And what that might be, she had no idea, except that it was something to do with the English store and with herself, and not, as she had once thought, television. Had John added Keys and Keys to his list of businesses, perhaps? Might he want her to be manager? No, that was ridiculous. She'd done nothing in retail since she worked at Dobson's so long ago. Besides, that wouldn't be any sort of blow, and just the way John kept smiling, then sliding his eyes away from her, she knew whatever was coming her way was something terrible.

'Now I never talk business over a meal,' he was saying, 'but coffee's another matter. Let's have it in the lounge, where there are comfortable chairs.'

'It's very kind of you to give me lunch,' Jess said bravely, when they were settled, with views of Princes Street from their seats in the window and coffee on their little table. 'But I wish you'd tell me whatever it is you want to tell me.'

'It's ... well, I'll admit, Jess, that what I have to say is not so easy to tell.' John stirred his coffee,

327

then studied the spoon. 'Maybe I should have tackled it differently. Just told you straight out from the beginning.'

As she waited, with her eyes fixed on his face, he met her gaze.

'The fact is, Jess, that Keys and Keys want an entry into Princes Street. And they are prepared to pay a very good price for it.'

'But, there is no entry into Princes Street!' she cried. 'There's no space for another department store, is there?'

'Except on the site of the Princes,' he answered softly.

Fifty-Nine

There it was, then, the terrible thing. So terrible, she couldn't take it in. The Princes Street Picture House wasn't a site, it was a cinema. The best, the most beautiful cinema in the city. There was no way a department store could be built on a cinema, was there? So, what was John Syme talking about?

Of course, she knew all the time, but once she'd heard his devastating words, her brain had blocked out their meaning, so that it was only underneath her consciousness that she understood her own question. And could provide an answer. The only way a store could be built on a cinema, was if the cinema were first demolished.

Demolished. But 'demolished' was not a word she could at that moment accept.

'Oh, God, Jess, you've gone so pale,' John muttered. 'Oh, you're not going to faint, are you? It's not as bad as that, not worth fainting over. Waiter, could we have some brandy over here? Quick as you can!'

'I don't want any brandy,' Jess said, putting her hands to her face, as though she could feel her own pallor. 'I'm quite all right.'

'No, no, you're not.' John was twisting in his chair, trying to check the progress of the waiter, who was in fact already running with the brandy.

'Over here, over here, that's right. One for the young lady, and I'll have one, too. Jess, drink that. Go on, it's an order. We have to get you safely back to the Princes, remember. Go on, drink it.'

And she did drink it and felt the feeling flooding back into her, bringing a pain so sharp it was as though someone had plunged a knife into her chest. How was she going to walk around with this knife in her chest? Well, people did. It was a well known fact, people could walk around for ages after being stabbed, before collapsing.

But she was not going to collapse. No, she was going to be strong. And tell John Syme that this terrible thing could not happen.

'I never dreamed you'd take it so badly,' John was murmuring, shaking his head and downing his brandy. 'I knew the Princes meant a lot to you, but not to make you feel there'd been a death or something, if it went.'

A death or something. If the Princes were to be demolished, that's what it would be. A death. No wonder she was feeling so full of grief. Could John really not understand that?

'Tell me what's been happening,' she said as collectedly as possible. 'How did this firm, Keys and Keys, know about the Princes. Did you tell them?'

'Of course not. They did their own researches. Wanted to come to Scotland. Looked in Glasgow, looked in Edinburgh. Found a suitable site in Glasgow, that's all taken care of, but couldn't find anywhere in Princes Street. Nothing available. Then somebody saw the Princes.'

'And you own the Princes.'

'And I own the Princes – well, I and the company. They came to us. Made an offer we couldn't refuse.' John raised his hands apologetically. 'You must see it their way. There are lots of cinemas, but not many on a prime site in Princes Street. All along, seems we've been sitting on a gold mine.'

'You never thought it was too beautiful to pull down? That it would be a great loss?' Jess's eyes were full of angry tears. 'You might say, there are lots of department stores. Why tear down something special to build something that isn't special at all?'

But, of course, she knew why, and the answer was money. They'd been given an offer they couldn't refuse, John Syme and his board, which was why they would not mind destroying the Princes to put up another shop. They were businessmen, and if businessmen received an offer

330

they couldn't refuse, well, they didn't refuse it.

'Isn't special?' John was repeating 'I don't believe Keys and Keys would agree with you there, Jess. They think they are special, and I do, too. They'll be a great asset to Princes Street.'

'And you don't think the Princes is an asset?'

'It is, but the time's coming when we just won't need so many cinemas, Jess. I'm a realist, I'm facing that already. Television won't kill the film industry, but it will bring changes. There'll be fewer cinemas but they'll be bigger, with these wide screens everybody says are coming.' John hesitated. 'You won't want me to say this, but the Princes probably wouldn't have survived anyway – it's too small, too hard to adapt. Why not accept it has to go?'

Jess was silent for some time, too weary to argue any more. Finally, with one last effort, she asked if the Keys and Keys offer had been formally accepted.

'I'm afraid it has.'

'But it's not been finalized yet?'

'Well, that takes time.'

'So, you could still change your minds?'

'No, that's out of the question.'

'I'm sure it could be done. If you wanted to, enough.'

'The point is, Jess, we don't want to at all. I'm sorry, you must face facts. Be strong, because you're in charge. I'll be sending everyone letters, but it will be your job to tell the staff.'

She stared at him, the colour that had only recently returned to her face draining away as, for the first time, she remembered that she was not the only one to grieve over the Princes.

'I'll have to go,' she murmured, snatching up her bag. 'Thank you for the lunch, Mr Syme.'

'Mr Syme? Oh, Jess!'

He lifted his hand and a waiter appeared from nowhere with a folded paper on a silver-plated tray, which John glanced at and covered with notes and coins, nodding as the waiter bowed, then giving his arm to Jess.

'Come on,' he ordered. 'I'll see you back.'

'I'm quite all right, I don't need any help.'

'I'm afraid you've had a shock. My fault. I should have handled this better. Thought I was doing the right thing, preparing you, but it was all wrong, wasn't it?'

'There was no right way,' she said quietly.

Slowly, they left the hotel, Jess allowing John to tuck her arm in his, for she did feel rather strange, and together walked to the Princes and stood looking at it. How elegant it was! How it stood out from all around it, with its pristine walls and its glass doors, shining in the sunlight!

What was going through John's mind, Jess wondered, as he saw again what was to be sacrificed for an offer that could not be refused? Would he be sorry? Would he, after all, change his mind?

'You see, Jess,' he said kindly, as they entered the glass doors, 'it is too small, isn't it? It could never be adapted for the wider screen.'

In the foyer, watched covertly from the box office by Netta, John studied Jess's face.

'We still have a lot to discuss,' he told her, 'but I think you'd better come into Glasgow and we'll go through it all then. For today, I'd go up and have a rest, Jess, if I were you. Try to come to terms with what's been decided.'

'A rest?' She looked away from him, towards the stars' photographs lining the walls. 'I don't see me resting, John.'

'You won't be out of a job yourself, you know. There are plenty of openings for you in Glasgow, or elsewhere, here. Maybe not managerial, but good jobs, all the same.' He patted her shoulder. 'I'll give you details when you come over. We'll hope to place some of the staff, too, so it shouldn't be all gloom and doom when you break the news.'

As he adjusted his trilby and smiled encouragingly, she stared at him incredulously. Had he no idea at all of how folk felt at the Princes? Did he really think they'd be content to be given some job – any job – when the place they loved closed down? He might be a wonderful businessman, but thank heavens he'd never been manager here, for one thing Jess had learned – and he clearly hadn't – was that a manager needed to know what made his staff happy. She'd always done her best to learn that, and if it was all out of her hands now, maybe they'd remember and understand.

'Goodbye, then, Jess,' John called, as he left her. 'Give me a ring to say when you are coming to Glasgow. Make it soon!'

'Jess, are you all right?' Netta asked, as Jess stood without moving. 'You're awful pale.'

'A bit too warm for me today, maybe.' Jess

333

made an effort to smile. 'You just going to open up?'

'In about ten minutes. Think I can see some folk already waiting. Dying to see Danny Kaye!' Netta laughed merrily. 'Did you see that bit where he thought he was the surgeon? Calling for the watering can! Oh, my!'

'Might have a peep in later. Cheer myself up.'

As though anything could, Jess thought, walking with drooping shoulders to her office.

Sixty

Your job to tell the staff, John Syme had told her. And it proved to be the hardest work she'd ever done.

Even getting them all together had been difficult, but somehow she'd managed it. Though most didn't work in the mornings, she'd asked everyone to meet her at ten the following day in the auditorium. And on the stroke of ten, in they filed. Usherettes, cafe staff, cleaning ladies, Edie, Netta, Trevor, Fred and his new assistant, Gus, and the three she'd already told – Ben, Sally and Rusty.

And in the quiet, dusty auditorium, with the curtained screen and silent organ behind her, she broke the news. That the Princes Picture House was to be demolished for its site by a department store, and that everyone, including herself, would lose their jobs. She couldn't be more sorry. Well, they knew that, didn't they?

To begin with, there was stunned silence. People didn't even look at each other, as, like Jess on first hearing it, they couldn't take in the news. With sympathy, she watched, as they struggled to make sense of the words they'd never expected to hear. But who could imagine the Princes cinema's being demolished? It had always been there, hadn't it, a part of Edinburgh's most famous street! At least, nobody could remember when it hadn't been. And how could it possibly be true, that they'd come in that morning, still in work, and now saw their jobs going under the demolition hammer, along with their beautiful workplace? It was too much, so it was. They couldn't be expected to understand.

But, suddenly, the tongues loosened, the eyes flashed, and the words flew. Everyone vied with one another to express disgust, shock and disbelief. It wasn't happening, was it? How could it be? How had Mr Syme sold them out, then? How could he have let the finest cinema in the city go to the owners of a department store who were going to flatten it to the ground?

'What about the beautiful organ?' Trevor cried, almost shedding tears. 'What's going to happen to that?'

'What about all the oak panelling and the lovely pillars?' Sally demanded. 'And our pictures of the stars? That's an archive, that is! That shouldn't be destroyed.'

'None of it should be destroyed,' Ben said grimly. 'But, that's business for you. Everything

335

bows to money.'

'I suppose you canna blame Keys and Keys for wanting in to Princes Street,' Joan Baxter said cautiously. 'They'd know nothing about our cinema.'

'Well, John Syme does,' Ben retorted. 'He's the one I blame, not the store. He didn't have to accept their offer, did he?'

'An offer he couldn't refuse,' Jess said, blinking away tears.

She looked at Rusty, who was lighting a cigarette and saying nothing, but then she'd already given him the news the previous evening.

'So, what television might never have done, Keys and Keys have managed,' he said softly. 'I'm sorry, Jess. There'll never be another cinema like the Princes.'

She was so touched by his sympathy, she could think of no more to say, and was almost made uneasy by the way he could still surprise her.

Now, trying to show strength before the dismay of those around her, she remembered that she should be passing on John Syme's message of hope to the staff.

'I just want to tell you all,' she announced, 'that Mr Syme said there would probably be jobs going in Glasgow, or even in Edinburgh, if you wanted to apply. So, don't be too downhearted about finding other work.'

'We don't want other work,' Pam from the cafe cried, her face twisting. 'We like it here!'

'And I'd got the cafe just the way I wanted it,' sighed Joan Baxter. 'Now I'll have to start all over again.'

'Aye, same as Vera and me,' Mrs Watts, the senior cleaner put in. 'And this place is classy, eh? Such marble and woodwork! Where else would you see that, then?'

'Soon as you get keen on something, away it goes,' Vera said dolefully. 'But I never thought a whole picture house would go.'

'Jobs in Edinburgh?' Renie burst out. 'Have you seen some of Mr Syme's other cinemas? They're nothing like the Princes, I can tell you!'

'They are not,' Faith agreed. 'And I for one will never work in Glasgow. Who wants to travel in every day – pay out rail fare and get home God knows when! I'll find ma own job, and no thanks to Mr Syme, eh?'

'Me too,' Edna chimed, and Edie and Fred nodded their heads.

'It's me for retirement,' Fred declared. 'Mebbe do odd jobs when I feel like it, eh?'

'And I've worked in a nice place too long,' Edie whispered, wiping her eyes. 'There are no picture houses like this one, I might retire, too.'

'How about you, Jess?' Joan asked Jess. 'You got anything in mind?'

'Nothing at all,' Jess answered flatly. 'I can't even think about it.'

'You'll find something good!' someone shouted, and other voices agreed.

'Somebody'll snap you up, Jess!'

'Who would that be?' She laughed briefly. 'Edie, shall we serve the tea now? There's tea and coffee in the staffroom, everyone, if you'd like to make your way there.'

'And coconut biscuits!' Edie cried, brightening. 'Used my own points to get them.'

'Never find anyone else like you, Edie,' Jess told her. 'And isn't it time those biscuits came off the ration?

'Thanks very much for coming, everyone. And I wish you all good luck for the future.'

'Too late to wish the Princes good luck,' Ben said, drinking his coffee. 'Ah, what a world we live in, don't we? Everything good seems to go to the wall.'

'Aye, and all those folk in the future buying their undies at Keys and Keys will never know what they're missing,' Renie said with a crooked little grin. 'But what are you going to do now, Ben? Look for something here?'

'Dunno,' he answered, his brown-black eyes fixed on Jess, who was advancing with the tea-pot. 'I wouldn't mind Glasgow, to tell you the truth. I'm footloose and fancy free now, you know. Or will be, one day.'

'Shame we're not, eh, Jess?' Renie laughed. 'Only joking, of course.'

'Of course,' Ben said, still looking at Jess, but her thoughts were far away.

Sixty-One

'It's a disgrace!' Addie cried, when given the news of what was going to happen to the Princes. 'It's a scandal! To pull down that lovely place just for another shop. Whatever were the owners thinking of?'

'The money, Ma,' Marguerite told her. 'What else?'

She turned her eyes to Jess, who had thought by now, a couple of days later, that she'd be feeling better, but was in fact feeling worse. Only now was the reality of the situation beginning to sink in. The Princes to go, her job to go, perhaps her marriage, too, in spite of Rusty's occasional sympathetic moments.

At least people who knew the Princes felt as she did. Poor George Hawthorne, of course. He'd been so upset over the news, Daisy said it had almost set him back. As though they needed another department store! Mind you, Keys and Keys, she'd heard, did have some very nice things, but to say that they were replacing the Princes, well, George would never get over it.

'You will find something else?' he'd asked Jess anxiously. 'Mustn't let your talents go to waste, you know. There's that nice art deco place in Leith – you could try there. Not quite the same as the Princes, but might suit?'

'Nothing is the same as the Princes,' she had declared. 'I'm no' sure yet what I want to do.'

'What about Ben?' Marguerite was asking quietly. 'What's he going to do?'

'He'll have to hope someone wants a projectionist. He did once mention retraining as a television engineer, but I don't think he was serious.'

'And Rusty?' asked Addie. 'Is he going to stick with projection work?'

'I don't know about Rusty,' Jess answered, after a pause. 'We haven't discussed the future.'

Her mother and sister studied her for a moment, saying nothing, but thinking a lot, Jess knew. She picked up her jacket and bag, and said she'd better get back to the cinema – had only looked in to give her mother the bad news.

'And I'd better get back to my flat,' Marguerite said, rising. 'I've got Guy coming round with his sister for a little supper.'

'You should've said,' her mother exclaimed. 'I could've rustled up something nice.'

Marguerite shook her head. 'Got to show what I can do, Ma, thanks all the same. Especially as Rowena's coming. She's an expert on everything.'

'Lucky you to be moving into that family,' Addie said acidly. 'That's if you ever do.'

'Oh, I'll move in, all right,' Marguerite retorted. 'I'll get my divorce one of these days.'

Addie, shaking her head dolefully, put her hand on Jess's arm.

'You tell that fellow in Glasgow you want a good job out of him, it's the least he can do. Did you say you were going over tomorrow?'

'Yes, tomorrow, but I don't want a job out of Mr Syme.' Jess kissed her mother's cheek. 'Don't know what I want yet. Look, I'll let you know how things go.'

'Aye, keep in touch. Both of you, eh?'

She'd no need to worry about that, the sisters told her, as they gave her a last hug, and left the flat for the tram stop.

'When you see Ben, tell him I'm sorry,' Marguerite murmured to Jess. 'About his job.'

'You think he'd want to hear that from you?'

'Of course. I still care about what happens to him, you know. In fact, I feel pretty bad about this latest blow. I mean, losing his job as well as me.'

'I think he'll survive, Marguerite.'

'Well, I just wish there was something I could do.'

'I'm afraid there's nothing you can do.'

As her tram came thundering up and halted, Jess climbed aboard.

'For any of us!' she shouted. And was borne away.

Sixty-Two

The meeting with John Syme was exactly the ordeal Jess had feared. He was very pleasant, very assiduous in seeing that she was comfortable in his office, had coffee, everything she wanted, but had no idea at all of how painful she was finding the details of the demise of the Princes.

Of course, he didn't tell her how much the department store would be paying for the cinema, only that the deal would be finalized by the autumn and that work would probably begin on the demolition by early next year. When the building of the new store would begin was not yet clear, as the owners were considering various plans, but it would certainly incorporate all the latest designs and be, as John said again, with a smile, a wonderful asset to Princes Street.

'And what about us?' Jess asked coldly. 'The staff? When do we get our cards?'

'Oh, not before Christmas, Jess. No need to worry about that. We hope that everyone will stay in post until then.'

'To make it easier for you, you mean?' Jess drew her brows together. 'I really don't think you can expect people to stay on if they see some job they want to try for.'

'Perhaps not, but as I explained, there will be a good chance of placing them elsewhere in our organization.' John's smile was still pleasant, but his eyes were steely. 'It would therefore be in their interest to stay on, I think you'll agree.'

Jess looked down at the notebook on her knee, deciding she needn't explain that several members of his staff had already decided not to work for him again. As for herself, she hoped he wouldn't offer her anything, but he was already passing her details of an assistant manager's job at the Citadel, a cinema on the outskirts of Glasgow, which might become vacant later in the year.

'You should really consider this,' he urged. 'Even as an interim thing. It's bigger than the Princes, there'd be plenty for you to do – maybe better experience.'

'It's kind of you, John, to tell me about it, but I'm no' interested in travelling to Glasgow.'

'Jess, you may not have the choice.'

'Who knows what my choices will be?' she asked, rising. 'I've no plans to move before the Princes closes, though, if that's any consolation to you.'

'I'd be very grateful,' he said hastily, walking with her to the door. 'Now, can I offer you tea before your train?'

'No, thanks, I'd like to be on my way.'

The stood, exchanging glances, then John put out his hand, which after a moment she shook.

'I'm truly sorry about the way things have worked out,' he murmured. 'But you do understand why we had to make our decision, don't

343

you?'

'Oh, yes, I understand.'

'Change is a part of life, you know. Nothing stays the same.'

'I know that's true.'

'We'll need to meet again, of course, but I'll be in touch. Thanks for coming in today.'

'Thanks for all your information. Goodbye, John.'

'Goodbye for now, Jess.'

After doing a little window-shopping, to take her mind off her troubles, Jess arrived at the station to find the Edinburgh train already at the platform and already full. She should have remembered, it was the first of the commuter trains; should have dispensed with the shopping and taken something earlier. Oh, well! It was all on a par with her dismal day, wasn't it? At least there was a corridor with a rail where she could stand.

'Jess!' called a tall, dark-haired man already leaning there.

'Ben!' she cried. And immediately felt her spirits lift. What a bit of luck, to find Ben on the train! Company all the way home, even if they had to stand, and from the smile on his face, he was as pleased to see her as she to see him. But, then, he seemed happy, anyway.

'What have you been doing in Glasgow?' she asked, as the train started and they stood swaying together, hanging on to the brass window rail. 'And looking so smart!'

'Wearing this jacket?' He laughed. 'Happens to be pre-war, like most of my clothes. But that's

344

good, if you think I look smart. I've been to an interview.'

'Ben, you never said! Where?'

'I told Rusty, had to ask him to do my shifts. Should have checked with you this morning if it was OK, but you'd disappeared.'

'To see John Syme.' Her face darkened a little. 'Oh, it was so awful, Ben, so sad. But you know you needn't get my OK to swap shifts with Rusty. He never told me, anyway. So, where was this interview?'

'At the New Emperor. Head Projectionist is the job, and it's a big concern, Jess. I'm really keen.'

'The New Emperor? Is that anywhere near the Citadel?'

'Hell, no, that's way out in the sticks. No, the New Emperor's bang in the middle of town. Very big, very up to date, and willing to spend a bomb on doing what it takes to make it very, very different from television.'

As she met his shining eyes, Jess was surprised by his enthusiasm, for he was the downbeat man, not one to show too much feeling. Except, of course, when he'd been in love with Marguerite.

'I can see you were impressed,' she said slowly. 'But what exactly do they want to do?'

'Well, you know there's talk of wider screens coming one day? They'll not be here for some time, but eventually they'll show the sort of spectacle TV just won't be able to match. What the Emperor is doing is salting away funds to be able to adapt the cinema as soon as the new

345

screens come. And in the meantime, spending money on better equipment, better seats, better facilities, everything to make the cinema more attractive. I just wish you could have seen the projection room, Jess. Was I impressed? I'll say!'

He grasped her hand. 'I tell you, this is the future we're looking at and I want in! Don't you?'

'You know what I want,' she said shortly.

'Yes, and I understand, of course I do. I mean, I love the Princes as much as anyone. But if I have to move on, well, the Emperor's where I want to go.'

'Have you been offered the job, then?'

He gave a rueful grin. 'Not so far. There were several candidates – well, there would be, of course, for a job like that. And the money's good – more than I'm getting.'

'So, they'll be letting you know?'

'Yes.' He released her hand and shrugged. 'In the lap of the gods, as they say. Oh, I don't suppose I have a snowball's chance in hell, but at least I've seen what I want and know what to look for.'

'If you got it, I was going to say we'd miss you,' she said in a low voice. 'But, of course, we'll all of us soon be gone ourselves, won't we?'

'How long have we got? Did Symes say?'

'Till Christmas. Demolition will probably start in the New Year.'

Quietly, he drew her towards him and held her for a moment. 'Ah, Jess, I'm sorry. It's such a

346

bolt from the blue, eh? None of us could ever have expected it.'

'I suppose I'll get used to it, eventually.'

'Listen...' As she left his arms, he caught at her hand again. 'How about you and me having something to eat when we arrive? I'm getting a wee bit tired of my culinary efforts.'

'I was thinking of going back to the Princes.'

'No need to do that. They can manage without you, and they won't know what time you got back from Glasgow, anyway. Come on, cheer me up.'

'You're cheered up, already,' she said with a smile. 'I'm the one who needs cheering up.'

'And I'm the man to do it. I know a place where they might just have something good on the menu.'

'You weren't thinking of the cinema cafe?'

His eyes sharpened. 'Why, are you?'

'Just thought it'd be handy.'

'You really want folk to see us together?'

Her eyes widened. 'You're thinking about Rusty? He won't mind if we have a meal. You are my brother-in-law.'

'For now.' He pressed her hand. 'Ah, come on, Jess, let's push the boat out! In case I don't have anything to celebrate, eh?'

She laughed and for a moment lost the saddened look that had clung to her of late. 'All right, Ben, let's go to this place you've found. It's a long time since I've been out anywhere, to be honest.'

Sixty-Three

Ben's restaurant was as good as he'd promised, even offering steaks with sauces Jess hadn't seen in years, and Scottish desserts with cream.

'Is this meal really in the price limit we used to have?' Jess whispered. 'Or have they scrapped that five bob rule?'

'I just pay what's on the bill,' Ben answered with a grin. 'No questions asked, eh? Only thing they haven't got is much of a choice of wine. But I feel I'm intoxicated enough as it is.'

'Thinking about your new job?'

'Thinking about you.'

At the intensity of his gaze, she blushed and looked down at her plate. Had he really said that? She was beginning to feel rather intoxicated herself, though she had drunk very little, and knew it was the effect of this man sitting across the table from her. This man she had known for so long, who had married her sister, who was part of her family – and suddenly seemed a stranger.

'I'll get the bill,' Ben said softly. 'And then I'll take you home.'

'There's no need, Ben. It's out of your way. I can get the tram.'

'You want to spoil my evening? I've been

looking forward to taking you home as soon as I saw you on the train.'

'Ben, that's ridiculous!'

'OK, maybe I'm exaggerating, but it did cross my mind that we might have a meal, and then we'd be on our own.'

She was still blushing, but managed to say, 'I think you're forgetting who we are, Ben.'

'No,' he said firmly. 'No one knows better, who we are.'

Dusk was slowly descending over the city as they made their way to Jess's flat, walking arm in arm, not speaking, each very conscious of the other in a way that was quite new. Or, for Jess, maybe not. She could remember, if she would let herself remember, feeling the power of Ben's presence before. But that was a long time ago, when he'd been Henry Fonda, or any one of a number of Hollywood stars who'd held her in thrall, and she hadn't thought of him like that in years. Certainly, not since he'd married her sister.

And he was still married to her sister. She'd better not forget that. Or that on her own finger was a wedding ring.

At her door, she took out her key with fingers that were trembling, and turned to Ben.

'It's been a lovely evening, Ben. Thank you very much.'

'Aren't you going to invite me in?'

She looked around, as though a neighbour might be looking at them, but the street was empty, and Ben gave a quick grin.

'Can't see anyone with binoculars trained on us, if that's what you're worried about. I believe I have been to this house before, as a matter of fact.'

Tonight's different, she wanted to cry. Tonight's dangerous!

But she only turned back to her door and fiddled with her key, which would not turn, until Ben took it from her and smartly opened the door.

'How about some coffee?' he asked, as they walked in.

'We've had coffee.'

'Just thought it'd give you something to do.'

'I need something to do?'

'Oh, Jess, darling, you're the same as me.' He pulled her into his arms, his eyes in the gloom of the unlit sitting room, fixed on her face. 'You're as nervous as a kitten, and so am I. Because you know things have changed for us, haven't they?'

'Ben, we shouldn't be doing this, it's no' right...'

For answer, he pressed his mouth to hers and as the long moments passed, she felt the starlight that had so completely left her returning and shining and sending her up, up, into the stratosphere. Where she would have stayed, except that sooner or later, she and Ben had to take breath and stand back, looking at each other and laughing dazedly, finally sinking to Jess's settee and clinging to each other.

'Ah, Jess, you don't know how long I've been waiting to do that,' Ben was gasping. 'How long I've been watching and hoping – has it been the

350

same for you?'

'No, I never thought of you – of us – this way. How could I – the way things are?'

'You did think of me once though, didn't you?' He gently ran his hand down her face. 'I always knew, you know, what you thought.'

'You did?' She pulled a little away. 'I wish you hadn't told me, then.'

'Why?' He brought her back to lean against him. 'It was sweet. I was flattered, to tell you the truth, that someone like you should be attracted to me.'

'You never said anything at the time.'

'Only because I thought you were too young.'

'I wasn't that young, Ben.'

The room was darkening further still and it was hard now for her to make out his features. Again, she pulled herself away.

'And then you met Marguerite, didn't you? No hesitation there.'

'Jess, she was older, she seemed right for me.' He sat up. 'Seemed is the word. And I suppose I was swept off my feet, couldn't see straight. Couldn't see that I was marrying the wrong sister. Ah, Jess, come here!'

They kissed again, fiercely clinging and caressing, until Jess leaped up and said she must put on the lamp – see the time – Rusty would be home.

'And you must go, Ben. Forget this ever happened. It's crazy, there's no future in it. Let's no' get involved again.'

'Jess, what do you mean? No future? Of course we have a future! I may be still married,

351

but I'm on the way to freedom, and so could you be. You know Rusty's never been the one for you. Be honest, that's true, isn't it? And things are worse now between you because of his drinking. You've every right to be released.' He kissed her gently. 'Released to me, Jess. Because it's been in my mind a long time that we should be together. One day, marry. Why not?'

'You're going too fast, Ben. Things aren't so easy for us.'

'If we care enough, we can make them easy. Steer round the rocks. Just takes the will.'

Shaking her head, she switched on a table lamp, seeing his face, so serious, come into light, then glanced at the clock and caught her breath.

'Oh, God, Ben, it's late. Please go now, and we'll see each other tomorrow.'

'There's no harm in my being here,' he murmured, as she made him move to the door. 'I mean, Rusty needn't think that there is.'

'He'd only need to look at our faces,' she said quietly, 'to know where the harm was.'

'He doesn't even love you!' Ben cried.

But in the end they parted, and she watched him go, turning often to look back at her, until he had rounded the corner and was out of sight. Then she closed the door and came back into the living room, where she sat for some time, trying to define her churning feelings, only remembering the ecstasy of Ben's kisses and the magic feeling of walking in starlight once again.

When Rusty finally came home, it was late, and

she knew he had taken his own way to pleasure via his favourite pub.

'How'd the meeting go?' he remembered to ask.

'We've got till Christmas. Then the demolition starts.'

'Could be worse, I suppose.'

'I met Ben on the train coming back,' she said casually. 'He'd had a good interview.'

'Did he get the job?'

'Doesn't know yet. We ... had a meal together, then he looked in here for a minute.'

'A meal?' Rusty's eyes were strangely clear. 'What was that in aid of, then?'

'Think we needed cheering up. Or I did.'

'He could always cheer you up.'

Jess was silent. She felt the glow of her earlier feelings leaving her, and a sharp little stab of guilt pierce her, as Rusty lay back in his chair and closed his eyes. Was it true, he didn't love her? It was a long time since he'd shown any signs of love, that was for sure. Why should she feel guilty for accepting love from elsewhere, then, if he didn't offer any of his own?

He looked weary, as he lay there, and she remembered he'd had a long day in the projection box. Maybe she should make him something to eat?

As she moved to ask him, his eyes flew open and rested on her, still with the long clear gaze she used to know. Then he looked away and pulled himself to his feet.

'Think I'll away to bed. No, I don't want anything to eat, I'm pretty whacked. Just want

353

some sleep.'

'Me, too,' Jess murmured.

She knew it was unlikely she would sleep.

Sixty-Four

'I can't make you out,' Sally said, sitting one morning in the interview chair in Jess's office, and drinking the coffee Edie had kindly provided. It was Sally's turn to open up the box office at one o'clock, but she'd come in early, just 'to have a word', she said, and now was studying Jess's face with round interested eyes.

'Suppose I'll have to ask why,' Jess said with a resigned smile. 'As though you're no' going to tell me.'

'Well, one minute you're down, looking as though the roof's fallen in, and I think, oh, she's depressed about the Princes. The next, you're on top of the world, smiling and blushing, like somebody seventeen, and I don't know what to think.' Sally finished her coffee. 'Or maybe I do. Is it something to do with Ben, dear?'

'Ben?' Whether or not Jess was like somebody seventeen, she was certainly blushing. 'How d'you mean?'

'Well, he seems to be hanging around you more than he used to. Is there something going on?'

'Sally, I don't know if I can talk about it,' Jess

began, then shook her head. 'Oh, why don't I just admit it? It's all wrong, I know, but it's happened. Somehow or other, we seem to be in love.'

Sally stared, then gave a little whistle.

'Oh dear,' she whispered. 'Oh dear, Jess. What a situation, eh? He's no' divorced yet, you've still got Rusty. What are you hoping to do?'

'I don't know.'

'What about Rusty, then? Is it all over with him? I'd be sorry. He's a dear, sweet lad.'

'He has his problems,' Jess said stiffly.

'I know, dear, I know. And I always used to think you were keen on Ben.'

'That was a long time ago. We're both different people now.'

'I'm sure,' Sally murmured.

'And the thing is, Ben might be moving to Glasgow, if he gets this job he's in for. I don't know if that would make the situation any easier.'

'Don't think so.' Sally was shaking her head. 'Seeing as you can't marry him anyway.'

Jess looked at her sharply. 'He's going to be free when the divorce comes through. I suppose I could be free, too. In time.'

'Wouldn't do any good, dear. His wife's still alive and you're her sister. According to law, that'd be a forbidden marriage.'

'What?' Jess had gone quite white. 'A forbidden marriage? What are you talking about?'

'Well, you know you can't just marry anybody, Jess. There are lists of folk that are out of bounds. Always have been. People underage or too closely related, that sort of thing. Sisters and brothers of married people are included.'

'Are you sure, Sally? I mean, we're no' blood relations.'

'Counted as part of the family. Oh, poor girl – did you never hear of this? Now you're looking like a ghost.' Sally jumped up and went to put her arm round Jess. 'I only know about it myself because of a family friend. She wanted to marry her brother-in-law after her sister had got divorced, but she was told it wasn't permitted.'

'What did she do?'

Sally shrugged. 'What Arnold and I did, if you remember. Naughty, naughty, eh? Of course, we got married in the end, but this girl lived with the guy for years. Some folk looked down their noses, but what could she do?'

Jess dabbed at her lips with a handkerchief, but said nothing.

'I don't suppose Ben knows anything about the law, either,' Sally remarked. 'He'd never be expecting you to do what that girl did.'

'No,' Jess said in a low voice. 'He knows nothing about that law. Who would?'

'Except me?' Sally put her hand on Jess's arm. 'Hey, don't shoot the messenger, eh?'

'I'm just glad you told me, Sally. Ben and me – we'd have to know.'

'Aye, well don't forget that the law might be changed one of these days. I think I did hear that the English are talking of it, but of course, our laws are different. Look, thanks for the coffee – I'd better go and open up.' Sally gave a long sigh. 'No' that I've the heart for it. Wish we

356

could move out now, to be honest.'

'I don't wish that,' Jess said, rising. 'I don't want to see the Princes flattened.'

'We none of us want that, dear.'

When Sally had gone, Jess sat very still, trying to come to terms with what she'd been told. She seemed to be remembering now, that she'd heard of this sort of ban on certain marriages before, probably at the kirk. Had never taken much notice of it. Had never for a moment thought it could apply to her.

But, she was Marguerite's sister, and Marguerite had been Ben's wife, so Ben, even if they both became free, could never be hers. Unless...

Unless she was prepared to do what Sally's friend, and Sally herself, had once done. Live with a man without marrying him. Jess recalled now how surprised she'd been when Sally had laughingly told her that she and Arnold wouldn't be needing a honeymoon. Surprised, not shocked. No, what was shocking about it? If you loved somebody enough, you might be willing to do it. She'd wondered at the time if she would be willing herself, but it had all seemed so remote. Not something she need think about.

But, oh God – her fingers tightened on the pencil she was holding and heard it snap – she was thinking about it now.

It was almost one o'clock when Ben looked in, grinning so widely he seemed for once to have lost all connection with the dark, tragic heroes he usually resembled. He was still handsome,

357

though.

'Don't tell me, you got the job!' Jess cried, leaping up from her desk.

'How d'you guess? Yes, I got the job.'

He closed the door and came to her, taking her into his arms and kissing her.

'Oh, Jess, I can't tell you how glad I was to get that call! I thought they'd write, but they phoned, said they'd be putting the offer in writing later, but they wanted to make sure of me. Such a relief ... I'd really set my heart on it.'

'I'm so glad for you,' she said softly. 'It's wonderful news. When will you have to start?'

'October. Think Rusty can hold the fort till we close?'

'We certainly won't be taking on anyone else.'

She moved from his arms, her mind on his success, but still glancing at the clock, which made him laugh and shake his head.

'Same old Jess, still caring about the matinee being on time, even though we're winding down to oblivion? OK, OK, I'm on my way. But, first, when are we going to celebrate?'

'When can we both get away?'

'Tonight. I'll ask Rusty to do my evening shift.'

'No, Ben, I don't think so. I wouldn't be happy about that.'

'No. No, that was insensitive of me. Make it tomorrow, then.' He caught at her hands. 'Come to my place, Jess. I'll do my party piece – ham omelettes. Or for my second trick – mushrooms instead of ham.' He grew serious. 'Will you come, Jess?'

'I'll come. If you go now and start showing that James Mason film before there's a riot.'

'Consider me gone.' He blew her a kiss from the door, and left her to her thoughts and her sandwiches. These days, she didn't always feel like seeing people in the cafe.

Sixty-Five

It was some time since Jess had been to Ben's house, and when she stepped through the door, drawn by his hand, she felt ill at ease, for this had been her sister's house, too. He caught her mood and sighed.

'Ah, you're feeling guilty, aren't you? There's no need. You won't find any traces of Marguerite – she took everything with her when she went, and I've put all Mother's stuff back. As you can see.'

They stood looking round at the late Mrs Daniel's ornaments, artificial flower arrangements and embroidered cushions, and Ben gave a shrug.

'It was all in the attic, so I thought I might as well have it around again, seeing as there was only me to please.'

'I think it's lovely, Ben. Part of your home. Though I understand why Marguerite wanted to make changes.' Jess hesitated. 'I mean, it was her home, too.'

'No longer.' Ben took her arm. 'Come into the kitchen. Everything's ready.'

'No omelettes?' Jess asked, staring at two large chops on a plate.

'No eggs. Had to go cap in hand to the butcher, and he let me have these gigot chops.' Ben grinned. 'I haven't let on that Marguerite's gone, though he must be wondering by now what's happened to her. She could always dazzle him into letting her have more than the ration.'

'Like Ma.'

'Exactly. Now, what do I do? Just put these under the grill? Better do some veg first, I suppose.'

'Oh, come on, I'll do it!' Jess cried, pushing him to one side. 'It'll be better than watching you!'

'What a relief! Thanks, Jess. And for your reward, I can give you – guess what – a glass of wine. I've been saving the bottle for weeks.'

It was very pleasant for the two of them, cooking and eating the meal, the atmosphere light-hearted, the feeling of shared love deepening. Except that, at the back of her mind, Jess knew she was going to have to ask Ben about that law Sally had sprung on her as a bombshell. Nothing could have such a devastating effect on their plans, unless they could somehow get round it, but the only way she could think of their getting round it was to do something she hadn't yet truly faced.

When they'd washed the dishes – something Jess insisted on – they moved to the living room, where they sat together on the sofa, moving aside some of Mrs Daniel's cushions, and looking into each other's eyes.

'Jess,' Ben murmured, reaching to take her into his arms. 'Oh, Jess!'

But she knew she had to be very strong here and hold back long enough to speak to him. For if she once responded to his love-making, she would be so lost in her own feelings, she would find it too difficult to speak at all.

'Ben, I have to ask you something,' she told him, lightly pushing him away. 'It's very important.'

'Sounds ominous.' His fine eyes were suddenly a little wary. 'But ask away.'

'Well, I saw Sally yesterday and she told me about some marriage law.' Jess's voice faltered. 'To be honest, it was pretty shattering.'

Keeping his eyes on her face, he said nothing.

'Because it means we can't get married. Seemingly, it's not allowed, because I'm your wife's sister. They count us as part of the family, even though your wife has left you.'

As he still said nothing, she snatched at his hand.

'But you didn't know about it, did you? You'd have said, wouldn't you?'

Finally, he lowered his eyes, though he left his hand in hers.

'I did sort of know about it,' he answered.

'Sort of know? You mean, you did know? And you never told me?' Jess pulled her hand away. 'What was the idea? Were you going to pretend it didn't exist?'

'Of course not. I was going to discuss it with you, but ... well ... it's early days with us, isn't it? And I didn't want to put you off, telling you we could never get married.'

'I had to know, Ben! You know I had to be told!'

'Yes, but I was going to make some enquiries first. I mean, this is a law that's bound to be changed, and a lawyer chap I know says they're already thinking of it in England.'

'England?'

'Yes, there are plans to sweep away some of these old prohibitions in a new marriage act. Might become law in only a year or two. So, you see, we'd be all right, because Scotland will probably follow suit. What I'm saying is, we needn't just give up. That's why I didn't talk about it at first – because I wanted to bring some hope.'

As she gazed at him without speaking, he took back her hand.

'You see how it was, Jess? I wasn't trying to keep anything from you. That would have been impossible, anyway. All I wanted was to find something positive for us.'

'So, what do we do? What can we do?'

He smoothed back her hair and looked at her tenderly.

'Couldn't we both go to Glasgow? Maybe you could find a job. Weren't you asking about the Citadel Cinema? Is there something going there?'

'Assistant manager's job coming up later this year. Mr Syme wanted me to take it, but I told him I didn't want it.'

'But you might want it now? Look, you could have your place, I could have mine.' He sat back, folding his arms. 'I'd never ask you to live with me. I know it'd be wrong to expect that.'

He paused, waiting for her to speak, but when she stayed silent went on:

'But if we were both in Glasgow, we could see each other and have our own relationship, until we find out what's going to happen. With the divorces, I mean, and that damned law. Would you consider it?'

'I've no' even spoken to Rusty, yet. I don't know what my situation would be.'

'But you could speak to him. Tell him what's happened between us.' Ben hesitated. 'I think he already has a pretty good idea, anyway.'

'He might have.'

'Well, then, you could speak to him.'

'All right, I will.'

'You'd feel happier to have things out in the open anyway, wouldn't you?'

'I suppose I would. I don't like deceiving him.'

'And I'm not happy about it, either. If we care about each other, and we do, let's clear the air. Why not, Jess?'

'It's a big step, Ben.' Her gaze on him was troubled.

'It is,' he said steadily. 'You'd have to be sure.'

'And it's all happened so quickly.'

'Not for me. I've been thinking about it for a very long time. And loving me – that's not something new for you, is it?'

'A lot's happened since the early days.'

Yet it was true, the starlight of the long ago still touched him. Allowed him to make her come alive. Feel passionate, wanted, as she hadn't felt in such a long, long, weary time. It was as though they were both being offered a second chance.

Yet, the rocks were still there, weren't they? The rocks Ben had said he'd steer round? They would have to see what they could do.

'I'll try to speak to Rusty,' she said in a low voice. 'And maybe I'd better go home now, anyway. He might already be back.'

'We've hardly had any time together!'

'Ben, we had to talk.'

'Why do women always find the need to talk?' he asked fondly, but Jess didn't smile. She was glad they'd talked, glad they'd considered their situation. Only still wished that Ben had told her of that vital law before she'd asked him about it.

For a last moment, though, they lay together on the sofa, exchanging deep kisses, revelling in their closeness, until Jess finally pulled herself up and said she must run for her tram.

'I'll come with you,' Ben said at once.

'Better not. Just in case Rusty's back.'

'Oh, God, how I wish we needn't worry like this!'

'Goes with the kisses,' she said quietly.

On reaching home, she found her fears justified. Rusty was already there.

'You didn't go to the pub tonight?' she asked, trying to sound her natural self.

'I don't always go to the pub,' he answered

364

mildly.

'Usually you do.' She hung up her jacket, fussed with her hair. 'I was just out for a breath of air, myself.'

'Bit late, wasn't it?'

'It wasn't dark. Would you like something to eat?'

'No thanks. I had a good meal at the cafe before the evening shift.'

They exchanged long level glances, and she knew that this would be as good a time as any to tell him about herself and Ben. But then she looked away, deciding to leave it to some other time. It was late, they were tired. She didn't feel like it.

'Bed, then,' Rusty said. 'Same old routine.'

She looked at him, surprised. He felt the same, then?

'It's what most people have, isn't it? Routine?'

'I don't mind it, as a matter of fact.'

'Can be comforting.'

'Yes.'

And with that, they went to bed, and, surprisingly for Jess, slept long and deeply. In the morning, however, she didn't really feel refreshed.

Sixty-Six

In mid-September, Jess was asked to attend another meeting with John Syme in Glasgow, where he told her, as pleasantly as possible, that Keys and Keys would take over ownership of the Princes on the first of December.

'I'm afraid it means notices going out earlier than Christmas, Jess. Sorry about that.'

'Going out when?'

'Third week in November.' John gave a regretful smile. 'So people will be finishing at the end of the month.'

Jess tightened her lips. 'That's a nice Christmas present, John.'

'I know, I know. But we could hardly expect Keys and Keys to pay out wages when they're just waiting for the demolition men.'

'And they're coming when?' Jess asked, wincing a little. 'Earlier than the New Year now?'

'No, I think they'll wait till after Hogmanay. But the whole cinema and the cafe will have to be cleared in December. All photographs and equipment, furnishings, seats, the Wurlitzer organ, the lot. In fact, we already have a buyer for the organ, and several cinemas are interested in the photographs and furnishings. I don't think we'll have any difficulty getting buyers, materials still being so hard to get.'

'When ... when will we have to show our last picture, then?'

John looked thoughtful. 'I should say that last week, when the notices go out. You'll have to find something good, Jess. So that we can go out with a flourish.'

'With a funeral march, I'd say.'

'Ah, now, Jess, we've been through this before. Change has to come. We agreed on that.' John rose to refill their coffee cups from the Cona machine in the corner of his office. 'And if the board were to find enough to make small bonuses to those leaving, would that sweeten the pill?'

'It would! It would make all the difference, John!'

'All right, I'll see what I can do. Don't say anything for the moment, though.' As they drank their coffee, he studied her. 'You're looking a little under the weather, Jess. Are things getting you down?'

'You could say that.'

'Have you given any more thought to that job at the Citadel? Don't fancy following Ben Daniel, for example? I must say, I wasn't too pleased to hear he'd jumped the gun and got himself a job in Glasgow. Now your husband will have to try to cope on his own in the pro-jection box until we close.'

'Yes, well, I might look at the details,' Jess said hoarsely. 'Though I'm no' sure what I want to do at the moment.'

And that's no lie, she thought sombrely.

* * *

Back in her office, she read through the particulars of the job at the Citadel. The salary was good, but the picture of the cinema was dreary. Just a large, characterless building dating from the late 1930s, but not even art deco in style. Not in any style at all, unless you could say functional. Some of the Glasgow cinemas were very attractive, if not, of course, as attractive as the Princes, but this was not one of them.

And then there was the drawback of being only assistant manager, instead of manager, with the manager being an unknown quantity. Might be nice, might be awful. Did she want to work for someone else, anyway, when she'd been used to making her own decisions, running the cinema her way?

Of course, even if she applied for the job, she might not get it, and when her heart lifted at the idea of not getting it, she put the particulars away. She would not be applying to work at the Citadel, and that was final.

Glancing at her clock, she saw that it was time for the intermission and Ben's tea break, which meant he would be looking in – something he'd lately taken to doing, disregarding Edie's stares. Sure enough, his tap came on the door, and he slid in, closing the door behind him and coming to take her in his arms.

'Well, how did it go with old Syme?' he asked, releasing her. 'You're not looking too happy, so I guess there was no good news?'

Relieved that he had not asked her again about speaking to Rusty, Jess filled him in on what would be happening to the Princes, carefully omitting any mention of possible bonuses.

'H'm, that's a let-down, eh? Bringing the closing date forward from Christmas? Just what I'd expected, though. How about the demolition men? Are they coming any earlier?'

In spite of her efforts, tears filled her eyes and spilled down her cheeks.

'After Hogmanay,' she said thickly. 'And before that, everything will be sold, even the organ. Poor Trevor, he'll be crying, like me.'

'Oh, Jess!' Ben held her tightly. 'I won't rest till you're out of here and all this nightmare's over. Come to Glasgow, sweetheart, come to Glasgow with me. Did you find out any more about the Citadel job?'

'I don't want it, Ben, I really don't want it. Look, I got the details. Here's a photo. It's no' me, is it? I could never work in a place like that.'

Ben studied the picture. 'Well, I don't know, Jess, it's not too bad. Good size and modern. It would probably adapt well to the new screens.'

'Is that all that matters? I couldn't consider it.'

'Even as a temporary measure? Until something more attractive turned up?

'I might have to wait for ages. I couldn't risk it.'

'OK, though you might want to have another think about it when you feel better.' Ben quickly kissed her wet cheeks. 'I mean, does it matter where you work, as long as we can see each other?'

'It matters to me!'

'Yes, of course. Sorry. I'm just wanting to

369

make sure you join me. Look, I'll have to go. We'll meet tomorrow, shall we, and talk?'

'All right.' She watched him go, then wiped her eyes and threw the details of the Citadel job into her waste-paper basket, just as Edie came in with a cup of tea.

'Why, Jess, what's wrong? Has something upset you?'

'No more than usual. It's just a cold, Edie. Nothing to worry about.'

'If you say, so,' Edie murmured, backing out, while Jess drank her tea and attempted to recover herself.

Sixty-Seven

Jess left work at seven that evening, deciding that she'd done enough. Ben was on late shift, Rusty probably in one of his haunts; she was free to sit on a bench in the evening sunshine, looking across to the Princes. Where she could think.

Something heavy was weighing round her heart, and it was not just to do with the demise of that dear cinema over there. For a while she didn't want to face what it might be, but slowly, slowly, she let herself admit it. The burden was to do with herself and Ben.

At first, their relationship that had so suddenly taken off, bursting across her sky like some amazing shooting star, had seemed wonderful. Thrilling. Carrying her from her old life to something new, something she'd really wanted. But it had come to her, only that day, with fearful truth, that she didn't want it any more. Didn't want to take the job at the Citadel. Didn't want to have her own flat and risk sharing Ben's. Didn't at all want to go to Glasgow.

How terrible, how fickle! But she knew the fault wasn't only hers. Ben claimed to love her, wanting her to go to Glasgow, come what may. Even not minding that if she took the Citadel job, she would hate it. Even concealing at first that until a prohibiting law was changed, they couldn't hope to get married.

Why was he doing this? She had the strongest feeling now that he was doing it because of Marguerite. Perhaps trying to prove to her that he could be just as happy with her sister as he'd ever been with her. How much she must have hurt him! There was no way he could have got over her and felt so strongly for Jess, she'd been foolish to think so. It was true, she did care for him, special man of the past that he was, but, sitting on the bench in Princes Street, looking into her own mind, she knew now that the feeling she had for him was not enough. Not enough to go with him where he wanted to go. Not enough to leave Rusty.

Heavens, where had that come from? Was it true? Could it be? Leaping up, she began to hurry towards the Bridges to catch her tram, her thoughts in fresh turmoil.

After all that had gone wrong between them,

371

after he'd become so different from the Rusty she'd married, was it possible he was still the one for her? It seemed hard to believe, yet the fact remained, she hadn't been able to tell him about herself and Ben. She hadn't even been able to hint that she might be thinking of leaving him. And that could only be because, in her heart, she'd known all along that she didn't want to.

Gradually, as she waited at the tram stop, all the problems connected with taking on Ben and going to Glasgow began to melt away, and she was filled with a wonderfully intense relief. She was free. Free of an intolerable burden she'd placed on her own back. So free, she left the stop and began to walk with amazing energy all the way to Newington. Over the Bridges, into Nicolson Street, into Clerk Street, moving fast as though on wings.

She would have to tell Ben, of course, that she'd changed her mind, and whatever his motives in wanting her, she was going to feel bad about it. First, Marguerite, now Marguerite's sister, had let him down. How he would hate them both! But there was nothing to be done. She'd made a mistake and had only just avoided making another, even more serious than the first. If there'd been a church handy, maybe she'd have gone in and sent up a prayer of gratitude.

There was a church, but she didn't go in, for her eye had been caught by a small building off Clerk Street that seemed vaguely familiar. There was a notice on its door that read 'Dependency

Helpline – all welcome', and then of course she remembered. This was where Rusty had come once to please her, but had not stayed.

What made her push open the door and go in, she didn't know, but when a friendly, middle-aged woman in the vestibule gave her an enquiring smile, she heard herself say, 'I thought I might just look in for a moment, if that's all right?'

'Of course, my dear, this is an open meeting. Visitors are welcome.'

'Shall I just go in?'

'If it's your first time, perhaps you'd like me to take you? We have a speaker on his feet at present, but I think he's nearly finished. We've already had a prayer and gone through the steps to be taken to achieve freedom from addiction. Another time, we could go through those with you.'

'Oh, but I'm no' addicted!' Jess cried, and the woman's smile was kindly.

'I think I hear our second speaker taking the floor. Shall we go in together?'

'Yes, please!' Jess said, trembling, for she too had heard the new voice and knew it well. It was Rusty's.

He was standing in front of a circle of people sitting on wooden chairs. He looked pale, but composed, and even from her distance away, she could tell that his remarkable eyes were as bright as when she'd first known him.

'My name is Russell,' she had already heard him say. Now he was continuing, 'And I think ... I hope ... that I am recovering from my addiction. When I spoke to you before, I believe I told you that I'd begun to have a problem when I was in the RAF, but I wouldn't admit it. When the war was over, I still had a problem, because I could only face the world after a drink. There was someone who cared for me, who tried to make me get help, and I came here, but I couldn't stay. It was only when I knew I had to try again or lose everything, that I came back and found the way to peace with myself. That's all I can say at present. I hope to speak to you again soon.'

'Thank you, Russell,' someone said, and someone else stood up and said there would be a topic put forward for discussion, but by then Rusty's eyes were wide on Jess and he was running towards her, hands outstretched.

'Jess?' he whispered. 'You're here? You've found me?'

It all seemed a little unreal after that, with Rusty making his goodbyes to a tall, grey-haired man he said was his mentor and the friendly woman at the door he called June, and then he and Jess were in the street and Jess was shedding tears. Which were real enough.

'Oh, Rusty, I'm so sorry, I never knew you'd been trying to give up drinking. I never knew you'd been coming here.'

'Been coming for some time. Knew I had to.' His voice was low. 'If I'd any chance ... of keeping you.'

'Oh, Rusty, why didn't you tell me? It would have meant so much...'

'I wanted to wait until I was sure it was going to work.'

'I could have helped.' Jess put her hankie to her eyes. 'But I didn't realize, and I've been ... well, I've been ... so foolish ... I can't tell you...'

'Ssh.' He put his hand over her lips, as they walked together towards home. 'You don't have to tell me anything.'

'You know?'

'All I know is you don't have to tell me anything. If we've both done things we regret, the slate's clean now. We start again. Agreed?'

She knew she didn't need to speak.

As soon as they reached home, it was as though they were on honeymoon. They went at once to bed, slipping out of their clothes and making love as they'd never made it before, afterwards lying together, not talking, just being content. After moving so far apart, to be again as one was like living some amazing dream that was still continuing after waking.

Eventually, of course, they felt hungry and cooked the bacon ration and the last two eggs, drank tea, and seemed as blissfully content still, until Rusty said quietly, 'Think we can make it work this time, Jess? I know it will depend on me.'

'There are two of us, Rusty. It won't just depend on you.'

'I've given you a rough time.'

'I should have been more understanding.' She lowered her eyes. 'And I've a lot to be sorry for.'

'We said the slate was clean, didn't we?

375

'Oh, Rusty, we did!'

After a long relieved embrace, they moved to easier matters. The time had come, Rusty said, to spend his father's house money on a place of their own in Edinburgh, if they could find one. And maybe think about a family?

'Is the time right for that too, Jess?'

'Think it might be. But you'll need a job.'

'I'm considering television.'

'Television!'

'If you can't beat 'em, join 'em. There are courses I could do, for television engineers. And maybe you might think of one?'

'As an engineer?' She laughed.

'As a producer, or something in that line. I've heard there are courses for that sort of thing too, and you'd be good.'

'After I've had my family, of course?' She laughed again, and flung her arms around him. 'Oh, Rusty, whatever we do, we'll be together, that's what matters. It's taken us a long time to learn that lesson, eh?'

'It's in my head now,' he said seriously. 'But thank God you found me tonight.'

'Rusty, I'd have found you anyway. It was all I wanted to do.'

Later, her thoughts turned to Ben, for her conscience still pricked her. She hoped he wouldn't be too upset, and somehow was sure he wouldn't be. He'd been hurt, but not by her, and time was the only thing for healing. Perhaps she owed him something, anyway, for he had pointed her on the way back to real happiness. And glancing at

376

Rusty, washing up and whistling, she dearly wanted Ben, hero of her youth, to find it too.

Sixty-Eight

It was a Sunday in January, the day before the demolition men were due. Huddled together at the glass entrance doors of the Princes cinema, chilled figures waited for the Keys and Keys representative to arrive to let them in. For a last look round, they'd said. By which they meant, a last goodbye.

'He's late,' Jess said, standing with her arm in Rusty's, next to her mother and Derry. 'Wouldn't he be?'

'Sunday morning,' Addie answered, rubbing her cold nose. 'He'll have wanted his lie-in.'

'At least he's letting us look round,' George Hawthorne murmured. 'Couldn't bear not seeing the old place for the last time.'

'As long as you don't catch pneumonia!' Daisy cried, tucking his scarf closer into his coat collar.

'I think this is him coming now,' Trevor whispered, as a tall young man in a long overcoat and trilby hat came strolling towards them.

'Morning everybody, sorry I'm late,' the young man said cheerfully. 'I'm Fergus Henderson from Keys and Keys, all set to let you in. Everybody ready?'

'We're ready,' Jess said with cold lips, and

watched with the others as he opened the entrance door and stood back. 'How long have we got?'

'Reckon an hour should do it, don't you? It'll be cold in there.' He grinned. 'And there's no coffee.'

'That's where he's wrong,' Sally murmured and patted her carrier bag. 'I've got a couple of flasks in here.'

'And so have I,' Addie said.

'Addie's always prepared,' Derry murmured fondly. 'Must have been a Girl Guide.'

Jess said nothing, as she watched everyone filing in. Edie, Fred and Gus; Renie, Edna and Faith; Joan, Pam, Kate and Ruthie from the cafe; Mrs Watts and Vera, the cleaners; Sally and Arnold, with young Magnus jumping ahead; and Netta, sneezing already. No Marguerite, who'd just said it wasn't for her, and no Ben, of course, though he'd sent a card saying he'd be thinking of everyone on that last morning. He and Jess had parted on better terms than she'd hoped for, perhaps because he'd realised, as she had, that what they'd had was never real. It had been a great relief to her that he was willing to keep in touch, and was doing well in his new post.

'You coming?' cried Addie, looking back, and Jess, with Rusty, stepped through the glass doors.

How it hit her like a blow! The coldness of it all, the emptiness. No photographs lining the walls, no carpets, no flowers. And in the auditorium, no organ, no curtains, only rows and rows of empty

378

seats and the vacant screen. Everything hushed, covered in dust, like a tomb somebody had opened after many, many years.

Yet it wasn't long since there'd been a film on that screen – *Miracle on 34th Street* – which Jess had once thought of screening at Christmas, it being a sweet, sentimental Christmas story, but it had turned out to be instead their very last showing. All the patrons, sitting on those now empty seats, had loved it. They'd said so. Said it had been a terrible shame, that the Princes was going under. But they knew there was nothing anyone could do.

'How are you feeling?' Rusty asked gently.

'Stunned.'

'Poor Jess. I'm going along to see the projection room. Somebody's already bought the equipment.'

'And the organ,' Trevor sighed. 'I've got another job in Portobello, but I'm going to miss my Wurlitzer. How long will I last?'

'I'll stay here,' Jess told Rusty.

She didn't add that she would be listening to the voices. But voices there were, all around her.

'Good morning, ladies, and welcome to the Princes ... I'm Sally Dollar ... what's your name, dear? Jessica Raeburn ... Any chance of a coffee? I'm Russell MacVail, always known as Rusty ... Miss Raeburn, please ... If you want the job, it's yours...'

Tears pricked her eyes, but she willed them not to fall. There could be no point in tears now.

'Remember when I told you to nip into the

circle?' Sally was asking. 'You looked so scared, as though you'd no right! Now what was that film you saw?'

'It was *Jezebel*,' Edna told her, grinning. 'Funny how you remember these things, eh?'

'Strange,' Jess agreed, though it seemed to her only natural to remember everything about the Princes, and she knew she always would.

'Like to go and see the office?' George was asking, but when she shook her head, he said no, he didn't want to see it either.

'Come and have some coffee!' cried Daisy, who was another to have brought a Thermos, and then Addie and Sally, and Joan Baxter, too, produced theirs, graciously offering Mr Henderson a cup, and everyone stood in the foyer, trying to warm themselves up, knowing it was time to go.

'Seen enough?' asked Mr Henderson, swinging his keys, as Edie burst into tears, and Renie sniffed and Netta sneezed.

'We've seen enough,' Jess agreed. 'Thanks for letting us in, we appreciate it.'

'Sad for you, we know. Don't think we don't understand at Keys and Keys. It's just the way things work out, eh?' He hesitated a moment. 'You've all got new jobs, I take it?'

Yes, apart from Fred and Edie who had decided to retire, most had new jobs, either in cinemas or cafes, although Rusty's was only a fill-in until he began his television course at one of the technical colleges in September. Only Sally and Jess herself had nothing planned, and if Sally said she was going to enjoy herself doing nothing, Jess had her suspicions that she might in fact be fully occupied. Not for ever, even if she turned out to be right and she'd be bringing up Ma's first grandchild, for she'd certainly be looking round one day, wanting to run something, as Addie herself would say. But that was in the future. Now there was only the present, and their sad, sad goodbyes.

Once again, they were outside the glass doors, and Mr Henderson was locking them.

'That it?' he asked, with his cheerful smile.

'That's it,' Jess said.

'Goodbye, then, and the best of luck!'

Away he went with his keys, and those left looked at one another and then, for the last time, at the fine, white, still-standing building. They would not be coming to see the demolition, or even the terrible hole it would leave. Oh, no, no! Some time, of course, they'd have to see the new store, rising on the site, but for the moment, they put that out of their minds and thought of their future.

'After all, tomorrow is another day,' Scarlett O'Hara had said in *Gone With the Wind*, the Princes' most popular film ever, and it was true. There might never be another film like that, thought Jess. There would certainly never be another Princes. But with any luck, a little of its starlight would go with her and Rusty and the others into their new lives. Life went on, whatever happened.

'It'll be a bit late, but are you two coming back

with Derry and me for your dinner?' Addie said to Jess and Rusty.

'Fancy needing to ask!' they exclaimed.

And, as people began to walk slowly away from the Princes, Jess and Rusty, holding hands, followed Addie and Derry across the street to the station, and did not look back.